NORTH HILL

William Zink

Sugar Loaf Press

ISBN: 978-0-578-28707-2

Sugar Loaf Press

This is a work of fiction. People and events have been manufactured
in the author's mind, and any resemblance to those in the real
world is entirely coincidental.

Cover design by Dave Skittles

Printed in U.S.A.

For brothers everywhere.

Main Characters:

Mike Beck (Dad), *Catarina's husband*
Catarina Beck (Mom), *Mike's wife*
Gram, *Catarina's mom, first generation Italian American*
Anthony, *son, 22*
Britt, *daughter, 21*
Sissy, *daughter, 20*
Frankie, *son, 19*
Tommy, *son, 18*
Nick, *son, 17*
Puck, *son 16*
Squirt, *son, 6*
Sally, *infant daughter*
Aunt Sarah, *Catarina's aunt, Gram's sister-in-law*
Uncle Ben, *Catarina's uncle, Gram's brother-in-law*
Aunt Franny, *Catarina's aunt, Gram's sister-in-law*
Aunt Myrtle, *Catarina's sister, Bonnie's sister-in-law*
Bonnie Bonnell, *Aunt Myrtle's sister-in-law*
Sir Henry, *Mike's right-hand man*
Sandy (Buzzy), *girl next door*
Teresa Del Rosa, *girl next door*
Ollie, *Frankie's friend*
Hoss, *Frankie's friend*
Jack, *gas station attendant*
Lennie, *neighborhood bully*
Lennie's dad, *ex-con*
Father Nigh, *priest*
Father Mann, *priest*
Father MacGregor, *pastor*
Mr. Capp, *neighbor*
Mrs. Shiner, *neighbor*

Breakfast, a Key

I wake to the smell of burnt oatmeal. Normally, such an acrid pungency would prompt someone of my tender age to burrow back beneath the covers, waiting until the bitter air is replaced with something more agreeable like frying sausage or scrambled eggs or perhaps even a dozen Krispy Kremes just procured by one of my loving and adoring big sisters. But youth has no patience and hunger little pride.

I sit on the side of the mattress, knees like dull knives to either side of my face, and rub my big toe. I stubbed it yesterday while running from those junior mobsters trying to steal the money Mom gave me for a few groceries. Off I was to fetch the usual basics—a box of powdered milk, three loaves of Wonder bread, a canister of Quaker Oats oatmeal, and a carton of Benson & Hedges cigarettes—when they jumped out from behind the bushes. Lucky for me I have this uncanny knack for spotting budding criminals hiding behind the old arborvitae. Plus, I'm fairly fleet of foot when the situation, such as familial sustenance, requires it. I can dodge and weave with the best of them.

I push on my knees, stand up, and survey Shangri-La. I live on the third floor, the *attic*, of this old house, along with four of my five brothers. Yeah, you heard me. I have five brothers. And three sisters, though Sally, being less than a year old, hardly counts. The girls are down on the second floor in an actual room to themselves. More about them later. Nick, just a year older than me, is wound like a pretzel around one of Brigitte's legs, a *Mad* magazine over his face, his BB gun lying over his left ankle. The rickety floor fan's right in front of his single bed. He gets a bed while me and Squirt only have mattresses plopped on the floor like soggy bread. In fact, everybody has beds except us two. Tommy's over on the right side of the window near the only potential bit of fresh air to reach us, himself clutching Brigitte's chest, a smile as big as the ocean on his sleeping mug. Squirt, on this even thinner mattress than mine, is sort of squashed into the far corner by Anthony's bed. He, meaning Squirt, is half-awake and I can see some movement underneath his sheet. He's been getting to know his six-year-old bod lately, so the rest of us try and leave him alone as much as possible. Anthony, the platoon leader of this here rag-tag outfit and genuine military man (he's taking ROTC at Akron U, though he's also considering entering the priesthood after college), looks blissfully oblivious to the mayhem and mess that is the third floor. A crooked black and white of General George S. Patton, framed, looks down with grim confidence from the slanted wall above his studio bed. Frankie, in his first year of art school at Akron, sleeps out in his Volkswagen bus now that summer's here. Some guys have all the luck.

I tidy up a bit before the old bulldog rouses—no need to have unnecessary punishment before the sun's barely above the rooftops, is there. Magazines and comic books go on the small shelf against the wall; plates, bowls, glasses, and various utensils are gathered onto a single plate crusted with day-old spaghetti sauce and placed at the foot of the stairs; shoes, shirts, underwear, and socks are lumped in a pile outside the overflowing plastic laundry basket; Brigitte, her parts scattered to the four corners of the room, is collected and slid behind the small door leading to the crawl space where Mom wouldn't think to look. I move Nick's weight bench in front of the door and put the bar laden with a full fifty pounds on the rack, just for insurance. I find an odd pack of matches on the floor and shove it beneath Tommy's mattress—

2

the usual hiding place for such potentially explosive contraband. Then, like the good soldier Anthony taught me to be, I make my bed so there's not a ripple, not a crease, not a single defect in its cottony white contours. You know what Anthony does? He checks our beds and if there's so much as the slightest imperfection in it, he'll mess it up and have us make it all over again. He's Dad's long arm of the law up here where Dad can't go.

Following the malodor, I pick up the dirty dishes and half lean, half slide against the banister on my way to the landing, turn, and flutter on down to the second floor. All's quiet. Mom and Dad's door immediately to my left is open, the room glistening in sunlight, unoccupied. Mom's dark rosary hangs prominently around the porcelain statue of the Virgin Mary on their dresser. The girls' room is predictably closed to the world, as is the door to the right, their lounge. Yeah, I said *lounge*. Britt and Sissy brought Sally into their room so they could turn the other one into a lounge, a pad, a place of gossipy leisure where Dad was somehow convinced into installing a separate phone line. Sure, Britt pays for it out of money she earns from working part-time at the office, but it hardly seems fair that the two of them get one phone and the rest of the household has to share another. The closed doors don't mean a thing, since they keep them closed day and night, occupado or empty. The glossy photo of the Fab Four taped to the lounge door makes mockery of me. So cheery and clean and successful. I wince, sneer, and turn my head with contempt. I'd stop at the bathroom, but with my hands full of the precariously perched pile of used dishes, I defer and continue the descent. Down to the second landing, turn, and I'm spilled into the hall connecting the living room, dining room, and kitchen, my ultimate destination.

"Here," I say, handing Britt the dirty dishes.

"What?" she says, pretending she doesn't know what's going on. I remove my hands of the mess just as she realizes the whole thing's about to crash. Her bleach-blonde, short-clipped mod haircut jumps like a spooked poodle.

"Where's Mom?" I do inquire. A pertinent question, since Mom would never burn the oatmeal.

3

"You guys shouldn't leave these up there so long," she says. "You'll draw rats."

Wow, she's styling it today with the miniskirt and go-go boots and long fake eyelashes. And Dad puts up with it.

"That's why I brought them down," I tell her. "So, you're going to chastise instead of praise, eh?" I slide past Dad, sitting at the head of the kitchen table with his back toward me, and give Gram a kiss on the head. "Morning, Gram." Gram sits on the church pew along the wall, staring right into Dad's jolly profile, whether the table is packed or not.

"The day nearly over, and you now just getting up?" She gives a big whole-body sigh that nobody responds to. A big sigher, she is.

"Aw," I say. "Come on now. I'm the first private in the platoon vertical and of sound mind, and that includes Anthony, the drill sergeant himself."

"It's time they get up," Dad grumble-mumbles.

"When I was a girl in Sorrento," Gram goes on, "my mama have me up to feed the goats and go to the market." Her finger comes off her lap and takes aim at the ceiling.

"Who are you pointing to?" I say, my eyes glancing skyward.

"You know who," she says. "You know who and you should be careful. You good boy, Puck, but sometimes. You jokey all the time. I like a joke, sure, but you can't joke all the time."

Dad, raising the left corner of the newspaper to block out Gram's sourpuss mug, gives me a surreptitious lift of the old eyes. He normally ignores me, so I appreciate the facial gesture of empathy.

"We don't have any goats, Gram," I say all cheery-like. "Perhaps you haven't noticed, but we live in an urban area. A *city*, Gram. No goats for miles and miles."

"Don't get smart," says Britt, bopping me on the head with a fly swatter.

"I'm not being smart," I tell her. "I'm just reassuring her that if we had goats, I'd be up at the crack of dawn milking away and tossing them scraps. Well, if we had any." I bend down and give Gram a kiss on the cheek. She squirms and giggles like a little

4

kid.

I sit on the bench on the other side of the table, to Dad's right. It's always strange sitting at the table with elbow room. And it *is* unusual, us getting up so late. More than unusual—it's downright insubordinate. But then we were up into the wee hours rearranging Brigitte's body parts into various creative and fascinating ways, with Anthony himself as impromptu instructor. He might be our bulldog sarge, but he's bursting with hormones like the rest of us.

"Something smells yummy," I say facetiously.

"Stop," says Britt. "You try making it sometime."

"So, where's Mom?" I ask again. I sure do hate repeating myself.

"She can't find her key," says Britt, nodding out the kitchen window.

"Who, Mom?"

"Buzzy." Buzzy's the reclusive girl next door.

"What key?" I say, dumbfounded.

"The house key. Mom's over there helping her look for it."

"That explains the burnt oatmeal. Ever think of reading the two-sentence instructions on the cylindrical canister?"

Britt gives me another bop of the fly swatter. And to think, Squirt mouths that thing on a daily basis.

"We had four goats," Gram utters, adrift in her own la-la land. "I love them all. They like my own brothers and sisters. I wonder where they are now."

Dad turns his head just a hair in Gram's direction and tries not to sneer. "Why don't you go help your mother look for the key," he says, turning back to sanity and my mug. It's not really a question, you understand.

"Right now?"

"Son."

"Yes, sir."

"A brown one . . . and a black one . . . and a white one . . ."

"Here," says Britt, putting a day-old doughnut in my hand. I sneak on out of there before Dad notices I've absconded with one of his stale delectables.

5

I cut through the hedges along the driveway and pop out into Buzzy's front yard, dispensing of the doughnut in three bites. I find Mom and Buzzy standing by the rusted old drum, a pile of black ash beside it. The drum is smoldering. It's where they burn most of their trash.

Mom's all somber and sad-looking, and Buzzy's in even worse shape, with genuine tears bleeding down both cheeks. I never got this close to her before, never got a good look at her. She doesn't come off her porch for more than a minute or two, and that's to toss more garbage into the smoldering drum. Her mom, whose name none of us knows, she'll sit in her yard in a chair watching the traffic of Tallmadge Avenue go by. She sits there like a Sherman tank waiting to be refueled, legs out wide, hands on thighs. Just sits there and stares. I look at Buzzy. She's sort of pretty, actually, even with that short haircut. I try and picture her with long hair and lipstick and maybe wearing one of Britt's or Sissy's tops instead of that white T-shirt with the rolled-up sleeves.

"Dad said you needed help," I say to Mom.

"Puck, you know Sandy," she says.

"Hey." I force a smile.

Buzzy doesn't flinch; those tears keep coming.

"She lost her house key," says Mom. "She's looked in the ashes, but she can't find it. I've looked too, but it doesn't seem to be here."

I keep the old mandible clamped shut. The elephant in the yard—why she's looking in the ash pile for a house key—ain't going to come out of *these* lips.

I get on my knees and start sifting through the ashes.

"Use this," and Mom hands me a spatula, presumably from Buzzy's house, since I don't recognize it.

"What kind is it?" This time I address Buzzy. She lifts her pointed chin. Her big brown eyes look like shot moons.

"It's just a key," she says.

"But is it shiny? Big? Small? A skeleton key?"

"It's not a *skeleton key,*" says Buzzy with sarcasm so thick I realize I offended her.

6

"I'm just saying, it helps if I know what I'm looking for."

"She's upset," says Mom.

"It's a regular key," says Buzzy. "Kind of shiny, I guess. I never paid much attention to it. It's gone. I know it's gone."

I keep on looking, but there's not much recognizable in the ash pile. The end of a charred piece of wood. A couple paper clips. A corner of a cereal box. But there's no key.

"How about in the drum?" I ask her.

"I don't know," says Buzzy.

"You want me to look?"

"It's burning."

"I can dump it out if you want me to," I tell her.

Buzzy looks more pained than ever. She turns her head to the house in a way like maybe it hurts her to do it. I'm standing straight up now not bothering to wipe my sooty hands yet, waiting.

She tells me to go ahead and so I feel the rim of the drum to see if it's hot and, since it's barely warm, dump it on its side and jiggle the smoldering trash and black and gray ashes out. Buzzy gets down with me and takes the spatula from my hand and picks through it.

"Puck . . ." says Mom, nodding. She means to have me do it for Buzzy, but I know that Buzzy wants to do it herself. I do what I can, flicking at things with a stick.

"It's not here," says Buzzy. "What am I going to do? I've lost it. The key's not here. What will I tell her?"

The spatula drops from her blackened palm into the soot.

"I'm . . . sure your mom will understand," says Mom. "I can talk to her. Would you like that? Sandy, I'm sure it will be all right."

Buzzy looks like a house on fire.

"You don't understand! Leave my mother alone! Stay away from here!" She shoves Mom on the shoulders, then does the same thing to me.

She starts running toward her house and then, like there's some invisible barbed-wire fence ten feet away from the porch, she stops. She jumps in place flapping those thin, white arms, and

7

then starts running around the yard. Just running and running like it's some kind of cinder track.

I scoop up most of the ashes with the drum sideways, then turn it upright. I try and make things just like they were, not better and not worse, but exactly the same. I let Mom go through the hedges first. Buzzy starts throwing rocks at us and saying all kinds of cuss words. I want to protect Mom and protect Buzzy at the same time, but it's pretty tough to do either.

When we get back in the house everybody's packed around the table like you might see in a submarine. You know, bodies just crammed side by side with no room, hunched over, looking somewhat miserable. They're all shoveling in the burnt oatmeal. Nick's got a *Mad* magazine to his face, while Anthony's reading some military pamphlet. Sissy's standing off to the side ironing her hair on the ironing board. She likes it straight as a rail, just like old Joan Baez. Mom pops her head over Tommy's shoulder to take a look in his bowl, then makes a face.

"I tried, Mom," says Britt, "I really did."

Mom starts making toast and tosses the pieces on a plate as soon as they come out. Our toaster is industrial-sized and can do six slices at a time. She brings out some cut celery sticks, an unusual item on the breakfast menu to be sure, but nobody complains and we snatch them up.

Dad sets down the Sports page and I grab it before Nick can. Lucky for me the *Mad* magazine has him distracted. I smile at him big and wide. He ignores me.

"Well?" says Dad from behind the Lifestyle section, his least-favorite part of the paper.

"What's that, Dad?" I say.

He looks at Mom. "What was that all about?" He means over at Buzzy's.

"Oh," says Mom, "nothing really."

Dad's not one to dig for more info than is absolutely necessary. But he couldn't help seeing me wash the soot from my hands, and I'm sure he heard Buzzy yelling.

"You sure about that?" he says.

Mom comes over and rubs his shoulders and kisses the top of

his head.

"Would you like me to fry up some eggs?" Mom's a whiz at keeping Dad on an even keel. She's a real study in diversionary dialogue.

"I'm fine," says Dad, patting her hand.

"I don't mind. You can't go till lunch on that."

"It's all right. You have enough to do."

"Are you sure?"

"I'm sure."

"Hey, Mom," says Squirt. "I'd like some eggs!"

"She didn't ask you," I tell him.

"But I want some!"

"Eat your oatmeal."

"But it's burnt."

"What's your point, kid?" I ask him, hands clasped above the table, giving him the droopy eyes.

He makes a frown, crosses his arms, and pouts. Wow. And he thinks that's going to work *here*? The kid's got gumption, he's got spunk. But a heck of a lot to learn.

"Something's burning," says Tommy.

I raise my eyes all full of sarcasm. "Oatmeal? Remember?"

"No, I mean really burning."

I look over and see the tip of Sissy's hair caught on the pointed part of the iron as she slides it across the ironing board. It's sizzling like melting plastic.

I jump up and flick it away. She slugs me.

"Don't," she says.

"I was trying to save your head from going up in flames," I tell her. I wag the end of her singed hair in her surly mug.

"Oh," she says. "I'm sorry, Puck." She touches my arm in sisterly affection.

Sally, over in the high chair, dissatisfied with leftover mashed lima beans, tosses them on the floor. Britt moves to calm the kid down, slips on the lima beans, and goes flying. Hits the old linoleum with a thud, but before she does the wooden burnt-oatmeal spoon in her hand whips around, sending the sticky stuff all over the kitchen.

9

Mom just keeps on rubbing Dad's shoulders. He lifts the paper higher so he can't see anything else.

"Look," he says, "there's a plant sale at Bob's Greenhouse."

"Oh, really?"

"That's what it says. What do you think about that?"

"I wonder if they have marigolds. You know how I love marigolds."

"Sure, why not?"

"Maybe I'll take a drive over there today," says Mom.

"Yes," he says, patting her hand, "why don't you."

Mom helps Britt clean up the lima bean mess and then they calm Sally down. Dad wheels back from the table, turns around, and heads toward the stairs leading to the side door. Anthony and Tommy get up to go help him down.

"Have a nice day at work," Mom says to him.

"You too," he says.

After breakfast, me and Nick and Frankie scrub the kitchen floor. It's only been two weeks since we did it last, but the oatmeal moved it up on the to-do list. Since we're at it, Mom has us do the kitchen walls, and then the dining room walls. After lunch we hit the front yard. Seems Dad spotted a few weeds mixed in with the lush fescue greenery. Frankie and Nick have real weed diggers, but I have to use a table knife. We don't wander around the yard haphazardly looking for the old dandelion, no sir. Dad showed us long ago how to do it methodically, systematically, so every square inch of the yard is scoured. We get on our hands and knees, side by side, and move forward like a phalanx, each of us uprooting the ones that fall within our path. I do feel sort of bad yanking them out. Especially the odd time I get one with the whole root like a carrot. I hate being the hands of death, even if it is to some dumb old weeds. Weeds are just plants that nobody wants. I understand their predicament. No, I do. But listen to this. I've got this patch on the shady side of the house where the others don't go much where I replant some of them. There's good dirt over there. I coil the long carrot roots in holes I dig with the hand trowel, cover them up, and water them. Sometimes they don't make it, but sometimes they do. When they form the white

10

balls of seeds, I'll take them to the front and blow on them so they disperse throughout the yard. It's a form of treachery, I suppose, and I'd really be in for it if Dad caught me. But somebody's got to stand up for the weeds.

Sign From Above

A couple days later Anthony's in the drive straddling his black Honda 50 like it's Brigitte come to life, just in the shade of the garage. He revs the engine about a hundred times, making Squirt go bonkers. The engine sounds like a VW with that quick and friendly *chuck-a-chuck-a-chuck-a-chuck-a* sound.

"Do it! Do it!" hollers Squirt.

Always with a soft spot for little ones, Anthony moves his wrist and revs it a few more times. Squirt takes off running around the pool like a dog just let out of the pound.

Tommy's going with him, and comes out of the house and gets on his own Honda. They have twin bikes, see. They think they're the James Dean and Marlon Brando of North Hill, and maybe they are. I know I envy the hell out of them. Actually, Tommy's more like Steve McQueen with that wavy blond hair, the languid way he walks, and his optimistic blue eyes. He doesn't look like the rest of us, which is maybe why Britt has a fondness for him. Those two are like boyfriend and girlfriend, it's weird. I say this as Britt bursts out of the house and hops on the back of Tommy's bike. She wraps her arms around his waist and gives me a wave, her big false eyelashes blinking with delight. Tommy slips on his helmet, which is just like Anthony's, and fastens the chin strap to the other side.

"Where are you going?" I ask them.

Anthony turns his head. "Huh?"

"Where are you going?" I say louder.

He shakes his head and says he can't hear. They turn their bikes around, ease down the suicide hill of our drive, and head onto the Indy 500 of Tallmadge Avenue to who knows where.

From out of the Volkswagen bus steps Frankie and Nick. Sometimes Nick sleeps with Frankie to get some fresh air and escape the general lunacy of the third floor, and last night was one of those nights. When Nick sleeps with Frankie, I take Nick's bed and Squirt takes my mattress. See how things work around here? The bus is only about ten years old, but it doesn't run. It's one of those camper models where the roof pops up and has benches that fold down into a bed. Frankie's trying to get it to run, but he doesn't know much about engines, plus he's sort of short in the cash department. Dad brought it in from the garage. By garage I mean his automotive garage, not our garage. He bought it off some guy who didn't want to deal with it anymore, and he says Sir Henry's going to work on it pretty soon. If Sir Henry touches it, that means it'll be humming like a top in no time.

"Dad says we have to do Mr. Capp's," I tell them.

"It's been a week already?" says Frankie. He stretches big and wide and strums his chest with his fingers like a bear, though he's about as skinny as a weasel. Where Tommy might not look like the rest of us, Frankie is different in that he's an artist, a musician, a poet, and overall subscriber to the Jack Kerouac philosophy of life. Tommy's so hip and cares so little about Dad's George S. Patton routine that Dad respects him for it. Frankie doesn't get that mulligan, however, since Dad views artsy types with more than a heap of skepticism, and even contempt.

"He said right now."

"There's your answer," says Nick.

"Oatmeal?" says Frankie.

"What do you think?" I tell him.

"Oh boy," he says smacking his lips together. "Yum-yum."

Inside, we sit down at the table and have a couple bowls each of the sticky stuff. Gram's down in the family room snoozing on the couch. The family room's her room now since she moved in with us last year, which sort of sucks. She doesn't have a bed, she doesn't *want* a bed, but sleeps on the couch the way old people like to do. Still, she has her dresser and personal items scattered around. We built the addition two years ago, and when I say we, I mean Anthony, Tommy, Frankie, Nick, and me, with dear old Dad micromanaging every nail and two-by-four. Measure twice, cut once, that's his motto. It was sweet and we could pretty much stay out of Mom and Dad's hair, since they usually sit in the living room. That is, until Gram took it over. Don't get me wrong, I love her and all, even if she still worships her fascist hero, Mussolini, but I sure do miss the family room.

Squirt's going round in circles with his tongue on the floor. At first I think he's somehow got it glued there, but when I realize he's just good at keeping his tongue in the same place, I give a nod of appreciation.

"Like a plucked grasshopper leg that won't shut off," says Nick.

"The poor kid," says Frankie. "He'll either make millions or it's prison for him."

Squirt gets up and runs through the dining room, through the living room, then back into the kitchen. He keeps it up and we all know he's going to break something and get in some serious trouble. He makes these noises, Squirt does. Not like a person. Not like an animal. Not like anything in nature or in the city. He's like this spinning top that never winds down. Whenever he's doing his routine and Dad's around, I keep my eye on the gun cabinet, you know, just in case I have to interject. I don't really think Dad would go that far, but try being around after the boys at the garage have had a couple tough engines and he comes home to find the candy dish broken in pieces because the kid's been running all through the house, which is against the rules to begin with. And then watch as he takes one of the BB guns and aims it at Dad's nose, all the while making those crazy herky-jerky sounds. Yeah, then tell me I've got nothing to worry about.

"We better take him with us," says Nick. "If he breaks some-

14

thing, we're all in for it."

"Got some rope?" says Frankie.

"Come on," I say.

"I mean to tie him up—not to hang him."

The three of us seem more like a work crew sometimes. Anthony and Tommy work too, sure, but they've got most favored nation status with the old man. We get all the flunky work, like mowing Mr. Capp's lawn every week.

We rinse off the oatmeal bowls and leave them in the sink, then corral Squirt and head two doors down to Mr. Capp's.

Frankie, being the oldest, knocks on the door. The Capps' dog, Queenie, starts barking and runs to the door. She's a big German shepherd and looks and sounds dangerous, but she only hates cats and strangers. Mrs. Capp comes to the door, and we answer the questions she always asks. She's in her nightgown half the time and never seems to step out of the shadows of their house. She has a heart condition and has a pacemaker, and so we try and be as nice and friendly to her as we can.

Mr. Capp comes along and steps outside, holding back Queenie by the chain. His curled-up arthritic fingers hurt to look at. He always takes us around to his garage to show us the mower, this Stone Age rotary model, even though we know where it is. He's a nice old guy, I guess. He drinks a lot and his face has that veiny redness going on, and we'd rather just get on with it, if you know what I mean.

"You boys ever seen pictures of a Spitfire?" he says, tapping this old oily poster of said plane on the wall of his garage. Mr. Capp is English, sort of. His history's fuzzy. By all accounts he's been in America since before the war, and might have even fought in the US military, not the British. So, why he's always feeding us his English superiority stuff, I'm not sure. It's a head scratcher.

"Did you pilot one, Mr. Capp?" Nick asks, and I want to kick him.

"Me? Oh, if I were to be so lucky, boys. But the Spitfire—she was the prettiest, most well-designed, most ferocious fighter of the war. She single-handedly kept the Germans at bay until

America finally decided to join in." He starts wagging his curled-up finger. "Those Krauts didn't know what hit them the first time we sent them up to fight off the Messerschmitts. They were a good aircraft too. The Germans are precise engineers. But you see, we were fighting for our *lives*. We weren't fighting for land or conquest—but for our houses and farms—our churches and cities. That's a whole different thing altogether. The Krauts underestimated the resolve of the British people. A classic mistake made by conquerors greater than Adolf Hitler, let me tell you! But then, you're German, aren't you? There's no shame in that, boys. It's not your fault your leader was a brutal mass murderer. We English had Henry the Eighth. Not exactly in the same league as your Hitler, but a tyrant nonetheless. Isn't it strange how history keeps repeating itself? I wonder why that is. You'd think with all the knowledge we have now filling the libraries of the world, people would be too smart to let someone hoodwink them into going along with such abominable schemes. Eh? Don't you think, boys?"

"I don't know, Mr. Capp," I say. "We're not German, really. We're actually part German, part Italian, and part Irish."

"Of course," he says. "You're American. *We're* American, aren't we?"

"Yes, sir."

"That's the great thing about America—you can forget your past and become someone entirely new. America is the country of newness, which has its flaws, of course. A culture has to remember its roots, otherwise there's no tie to the past."

I'm half following his circular diatribe, but mostly I'm trying to control my breathing so I won't pass out.

"We better start mowing," Frankie says. "I hear it's supposed to rain today."

"Rain? I don't think so." Mr. Capp makes a grimace of worry.

"Well, you never know, now, do you," says Frankie. "Make hay while the sun shines and all."

Mr. Capp pats us on the shoulder, and I mean all of us, like we're Queenie's new canine chums over for a visit. The mowing's a real relief compared to listening to him go on. Wow. I

16

mean, is that where I'm headed some day?

The yard's not big, but the back's twice as long as the front, just like ours. There are piles of dogshit everywhere, and bones, and the odd stick lying randomly in the grass. We collect all that in a paper bag first. Nick makes me shovel the dogshit while he holds the bag.

"What's he feed that dog?" I say, trying not to barf as I nudge the giant-sized piles onto the end of the shovel.

I mow the front, but Nick takes over in back, being the biggest, strongest, and fastest. Me and Frankie keep an eye on Squirt, making sure he doesn't run off somewhere.

Frankie takes out a small sketchpad from his back pocket.

"Hey, Squirt," he says. "Hold still. I want to sketch you."

Squirt sits on this rock as still as he can. There's a row of rocks making a border for Mr. Capp's roses. Me and Frankie are on a rock too. Nick takes off his shirt and tosses it to me. I ball it up and put it on a rock so it's not in the grass or in the dirt.

Frankie sketches people whenever he can. When he sketches me, I feel like I'm somebody. I don't know if Squirt feels that way. I wonder what he *does* think. He rocks forward and back, clutching his fingers together, then mashing them into his mouth. I'm afraid for him. I've heard things. He doesn't know it, but there's been talk of sending him somewhere. Mom wouldn't stand for it, but Dad's patience has its limits. Gram said he'd be sent off over her dead body. But he does things, besides the crazy noises and running around all the time. He puts forks in the sockets. He plays with matches more than the rest of us. He's careless with them and lights things in the house. He burned some leaves in the family room once. And there's the peeing on the missals. He sleepwalks and comes downstairs and pulls out the drawer of Mom's desk where she keeps the old missals, and pees on them. Everybody but Dad thinks it's the funniest thing—even Mom— and she's the one who saves them. I wish there was a way to settle him down. To let him know he's moved into dangerous territory. I surely don't know what Mom would do without him. In some ways he's the source of a lot of her anxiety, but then I think he's got to be her favorite the way he makes her laugh. He's like a release valve in this pressure cooker family. I just don't know what she'd do if Dad had him sent away.

"Squirt, you're moving," Frankie says chuckling to himself. "Hold still. You don't want blurry eyes, do you?"

Squirt makes his eyes go cross-eyed.

"Keep doing that and they'll stay that way," I tell him.

"Liar, liar, pants on fire," he shouts back.

"Easy, boy," Frankie tells him. "I'm working on your face. Keep it between the lines."

Frankie turns the page in his sketchpad and starts on me. He doesn't tell Squirt he's done or he'll hop up and start racing around the yard. As I'm holding still, I look through Miss Jane's yard and see ours. It's strange seeing it from here. It seems like any other backyard, except ours is the only one with a pool in it. Still, it has the same worn-out garage, the same chain-link fence around it. The same sadness in the way the hot sun's melting the foliage of the trees, the way it's been doing for a million years. Yet, when we're there it seems like the only place in the universe. Like it's the only place there is.

Nick finishes mowing. We take the hand clippers and trim around the rocks and out front by the sidewalk and curb, then rake the grass into a pile in the back corner of the yard, where Mr. Capp wants it. He uses the clippings for mulch. I'll say one thing about him: he sure has nice roses, that Mr. Capp. He wears a straw hat and works in the evenings mostly when it's cool, like it is in England. His roses smell as nice as they look. They all smell good, no matter what color they are. Mrs. Capp never comes out in their yard. The only time I've seen her outside the house is getting in or out of their car. I wonder if he cuts roses for her. He has Queenie and his roses. I wonder what she has. I hope he does take her some of those roses. It'd probably cheer her up if he did. They'd make the whole house smell good.

When we get back I sit in the grass and bet Squirt he can't run around the pool a hundred times.

"Want to see me?" he says with his fists on his hips.

"You bet I do," I tell him.

And away he goes, tearing around and around it like a Tasmanian devil.

Frankie, who went inside for a drink, sits down beside me.

"Now you're thinking," he says. "How many has he done?"

"Beats me," I say.

"The kid makes me tired just watching him." He's eating a banana and offers me a piece. We finish it off and then he holds up the peel like he's going to toss it in Squirt's path. "For comic relief," he says. I shake my head, laughing a little, and he drops it off to the side.

Squirt slows down, even walks, but never stops.

"How many have I gone?" he asks, gasping, barely able to speak.

"Twelve," I tell him.

"That's all?"

"You're doing great. Keep it up!"

"There's got to be a way to make money on that energy," says Frankie.

"He just goes and goes," I say.

"Yes, he does."

"I don't know," I say.

"You don't know what?"

"There's something about the guy."

"Like what?"

"Well," I say, "I'm not sure. He reminds me of somebody."

"Him?"

"Doesn't he remind you of somebody?"

Frankie watches Squirt make two more passes.

"I'm drawing a blank, man," he says.

"Nobody?"

"He's a singular gift," says Frankie.

"Why do you think he bugs him so much?"

"Why does who bug who?"

"He bug Dad."

Frankie thinks it over. Squirt passes by again, sweating, looking like he's going to drop, but he doesn't. He keeps going. He's not going to stop for anything.

"I don't know, man. You got me."

19

"He's just like him," I say. "That's Dad about forty years ago."

"You might have something there, Puck," says Frankie. "You just might have something there."

We watch Squirt run and run. He keeps asking how many laps he's gone, and I keep telling him. When I tell him he's done a hundred he stops, leans against the side of the pool catching his breath, and points right at me.

"I told you," he says. "I told you I could do it."

Frankie claps, slowly, impressed.

Squirt wipes his face with his shirt.

"Go tell Sissy to give you a Popsicle," I say.

He walks by, stiff, wincing.

"I deserve two," he says. "I'm going to tell her I deserve *two*."

"Yeah, you do that," I say. "Why not?"

After some time, Anthony and Tommy and Britt pull up the drive. We stay where we are and Anthony and Tommy head inside, but Britt comes over and sits down at the picnic table to our left. She's fussing with her hair after removing her helmet. Her cheeks are pink from the sun and wind.

"How was the ride?" I ask her.

"Oh, it was so much fun!" she says.

"Maybe Dad will get you a motorcycle for Christmas."

She laughs, not big, just a chuckle. "What are you guys doing?"

"Staring at the pool," I say.

"Have you seen Dad?"

"Why would Dad be here?"

"No, I know he's at work," she says with an odd, startled look. "All right, I just wondered."

Me and Frankie look at each other like she's gone daft. Dad doesn't come home early from work, ever, for anything. Well, okay, he did bring Mom those flowers once on her birthday, and he stopped at the hospital for an hour or so when Mom was having trouble when she was carrying Squirt. But that's pretty much it.

"The kid's inside," Frankie says to her. "He should be docile for a while. We tried our best."

"We saw a blimp," she says.

"Is that right?" says Frankie.

"We followed it all over Akron. It was so much fun."

"Yeah, you said that," Frankie says.

"We followed it for over an hour. We almost lost it—we had to stop and get gas. Did you see it?"

We shake our heads. I look up without moving my head, just my eyes.

"We were mowing," I say. "That's probably why we didn't see it."

"Every time I see a blimp, something happens," says Frankie.

"Something happens?" I say.

"That's right."

"Something good or something bad?"

"Either, or," he says. "But it's strange, every time I see one, the road up ahead takes a dogleg one way or another."

Britt gets up to go in, and Frankie goes in with her. I sit there and after some time lean back on my elbows, eyes closed to the blinding sun. I wait and wait, but don't hear the big-fan whir of the blimp. You always hear that low, soothing whir before seeing it ease out from behind the trees like some silvery beast. I want so bad for it to show, but it doesn't. It's disappointing, and, succumbing to my midday fatigue, I fall asleep.

But then I jolt awake. Squirt's kicking my foot. Kicking it with crazy enthusiasm, even for him.

"Look!" he shouts, pointing straight up to the sky.

There, so close it looks like you can reach up and hold it, floats the Goodyear blimp. Big and shiny and the pride of Akron. It comes out from the trees, passes in front of some clouds, and disappears beyond the treetops on the other side. We wave the whole time and Squirt, even though he just ran a marathon, jumps up and down like a lunatic.

I hear something to my left. Frankie squats down beside me and drapes his arm around my shoulder.

"Well, brother," he says. "Let the fun begin."

21

Voices in the Night

"Hey," says Nick. He's stabbing at me with a wooden yardstick from his bed to my mattress. It's some crazy hour of the night. The third floor's stifling with killer heat and humidity.

"What is it?" I say, waving the yardstick away, then snatching it from him.

"I heard something downstairs."

"Like what?"

"I don't know, I just heard something."

"Squirt's probably sleepwalking," I say.

"He's right there," he says.

He gives me an eyeful and we both listen.

"Let's go check it out," he says.

"What for?"

"We have to."

"Britt watches TV late sometimes," I say.

"Puck, I know I heard something."

"Could just be the TV."

"We better find out."

"I don't know," I tell him. "What if, you know, it's a burglar?"

"Then we sure as hell better find out."

We listen some more. I mouth the softening end of the yard-

22

stick, thinking it over.

"Come here," he says, and he leads me to the BB guns leaned into the corner. He takes one, puts it across his lap, and starts filling it with BBs.

"What are you doing?"

"Shhhhh," he says. "You're going to wake up the rest of them."

"I don't know, Nick," I say. "I think we should get Dad, or at least wake up Anthony or Tommy."

"There's no time," he says. "If we wake them up, they'll just tell us to go back to sleep. If there is a burglar down there and he sneaks into Mom and Dad's room, he'll probably kill them both. What's Dad going to do? We have to get down there before he comes upstairs."

"But if we yell right now, Dad'll wake up. He'll know what to do."

Nick shakes his head.

"He can't do anything, you know that. You and me—we can get him before he knows what hit him. We're ready for anything."

"I wouldn't say *anything.*"

"Here," he says, handing me the gun. "It's loaded."

He starts putting BBs into the other gun, his meaty thumb pushing them one at a time into the hole. When he's got it loaded he lifts the gun to his eye, takes aim at the top of the banister, swings it around to Tommy, then Anthony, then Squirt, then back again to the rattly old floor fan. I've seen him hit rocks and birds and a squirrel once, but shooting a full-grown man's a whole different thing. And I'm not so sure a few BBs are going to slow down some raging murderer.

We sneak over to the top of the stairs. Nick reaches down to the pile of clothes and miscellaneous junk along the wall and brings up an old coonskin cap and puts it on. My eyes go wide. I fumble around for another one, but I think Mom made earmuffs out of the others a couple winters ago. We make our way down to the landing, then to the second floor. All the doors are closed, except for the bathroom. The Fab Four on the lounge door add levi-

23

ty to this looming night of terror.

Nick's hunched over like he's on the scent of some big game animal, the dull tip of the BB gun leading the way as we go down the stairs to the second landing. I make sure to give him a cushion of a few feet so I don't get in his way.

He curls his face around the corner to get a look at the hall and, since the coast is clear, we creep down those final few steps. He turns back and gives me a funny look. Nods his head in the general direction of the living room. We stand flat against the wall and listen.

"It was *you* who walk up to them, not *me*. I was too shy. I never approach a boy in my life. You were the one. They standing by the rocks, trying to act manly in their swimsuits."

"That's Gram," I whisper to him. He puts a finger to his lips to keep me quiet.

"No, we not even dressed for swimming—we think we take the short cut across the beach to see Papa at his boat. Mama forgot to give him his lunch. He let us play on the boat. He remove the hooks and poles and nets, and then we play without getting hurt. It was our boat—a boat to sail the oceans in. Oh, how handsome he was. He treat us like royalty. I thought he was royalty himself. He seem like it to me. He was so handsome and sure of himself. Everybody come to our boat, his boat, because he somebody they all want to be like or be around. Even dogs—they come around too . . . Those boys thought they were something else in their new swimsuits. You walk right up to them. I don't remember what you say. Something crazy, I sure. You not fear nothing. I feared a lot of things, Rosina, but not you. You fear nothing."

"Who's she talking to?" I whisper to Nick.

"I don't know," he says. "I never heard her talk that way. She looks loopy. Look at her eyes."

"The only time she talks to herself is when she's talking to the picture of Mussolini on her wall."

"She probably got into Mom's Old Crow. That stuff will do it to you, all right."

"I never heard Mom talk like that after the Old Crow."

24

"Well," says Nick, "maybe it's because she has so many of us to talk to and doesn't need to talk to herself."

Nick makes a motion for me to lay down the gun, and so I do. He puts his beside it, and then we crouch down and watch so we can understand better what she's saying.

"After that day he write me letters, and finally I meet him in the olive trees on hill between the stream and field. We go there after sunset. I make you lock our bedroom door in case Mama want to come in. I sneak out the window and down the tree. I afraid of many things, but not of climbing trees, not climbing one to see my boy in the olive grove. His letters wear me down. He just like Papa in the way he make me melt and feel sluggish like a tired dog. It was good kind of feeling. I never have before, but it was the very best kind of feeling. I rush to see him. It was our first time together in the olives. They not ripe yet; just little buds of hope. He bring me a carnation and I hold it the whole time. It was so wonderful. I wish things could have been different. God not want Carmelo and me to be together. Oh, we could have had a wonderful life together, Rosina. We could have, really and truly." Gram shrugs sad and pitiful, staring into the blank TV. "Oh, well. I here, and you there in Sorrento, and he is there somewhere in the hills. I hope he is happy. After my family, here, I then hope he is the happiest he can be. He like Papa, like a bright star in the sky, a light for others to look at and find joy."

I don't want to leave Gram there. Something about her makes me sad and hopeful at the same time. Maybe it's the Old Crow, but she doesn't seem drunk. She never gets drunk, not really. Sitting there in her tight, pointed shoes and that same dress she wears every day, and her thick glasses, and the way she went on about the olive grove and the man, Carmelo, and her papa, and Rosina, and the boat; it makes me want to cry for her. It's the same way I felt when me and Mom were running from Buzzy's rocks, and then I turned around to see her mad and desperate with those bug eyes and mute screams coming out of her thin lips. I'm just glad Nick is with me. Nick always makes me feel good, like nothing too bad is going to happen.

"You hear it?" he says then. We have the BB guns in our

hands and are about to go back upstairs.

I shake my head.

"The noise—I hear it again. Don't you hear it?"

"I thought Gram was the noise," I say.

We listen, our ears turned toward the kitchen, and this time I do hear it. It seems to be coming from outside.

"Let's go," he says.

We walk all quiet and stealthy-like to the kitchen and go to the sink and let our heads rise slow and easy until we can look out the square window. I think it's coming from the garage, which is open, but it's hard to tell and so I move my eyes to the side a little the way you do when you want to see something at night. I wait and wait, my neck getting stiff from holding it in the same position for so long, and finally I do see something. And not just something, but somebody.

"It's Frankie," I say. "What's he doing up?"

"I don't know," says Nick, as mystified as me. "Let's go see."

Well, we get out to the garage, which like I said is open, but all darkish and spooky in the middle of the night. Frankie's sitting in the beat-up old leather chair the neighbor cats sleep on. You'd think seeing us coming out for a late night pow-pow would have surprised him, but he just gives us a nod and Nick sits in a folding chair and I sit on the cold cement floor, like we do this sort of thing every night.

He's smoking. His chair is far enough in the garage so you can't see much of him or the glow of the cigarette from the house. Smart guy, that Frankie. But my eyes wander around for the gas can that might be nearby, which would make him not so smart.

"What are you guys doing up at this hour?" he says. He's not wearing his glasses, and the depressions on the sides of his nose are easy to see, even in the dark. He gives a nod to Nick's gun. "You thought I was a burglar?"

"I heard some noises," says Nick.

"I thought I was quiet."

"You just getting home?" I ask him.

Frankie winces as he takes a drag from the cig, then hands it

26

to Nick who holds it like you would a metal pipe, if you had to hold a pipe with the ends of your fingers.

"Not too long ago, yeah."

"I didn't hear a car," says Nick.

"I hoofed it from the highway."

Nick doesn't bother offering me a hit, which I'm glad for, and gives it back to Frankie. Nick finally coughs after trying not to. His eyes get watery.

"What's the matter, Frankie," I say to him. "Can't you sleep?"

"Well, yeah, sort of," he says. "Not really."

There's a pause, long enough to take a nap in, and I get the feeling something's up.

"He's all right," Nick says, meaning me.

"I know he's all right."

"I'd say something in front of him before I would about any-body. He's all right."

Frankie nods a little. He's smoking like a fiend and tapping his bare foot against the cement of the garage floor.

"Something the matter, Frankie?" I ask him.

"You can tell him," says Nick.

"Sure, sure I can," he says. "We're all brothers here. That's what we are." He takes a long hit from the cig, then blows out the smoke real slow. "The thing is, Puck, I had this vehicular en-counter with another stationary vehicle."

"He bumped Aunt Myrtle's car into somebody," says Nick.

"Shit, Frankie," I say.

"Yeah, shit is right."

"I mean, *fuck*."

Nick looks down at me. "Hey. Watch it."

"What happened?"

"I knew I shouldn't have taken it," says Frankie, shaking his head.

"Does Dad know?"

"Why do you think I'm sitting here worrying about it? Naw, he doesn't know. Yet."

"I won't tell him," I say.

27

"Of course you won't."

"It's not too bad," says Nick. "It's in the back. She won't notice. I'd keep it away from here, though."

"That's what I'm trying to figure out. How can I get it fixed before somebody sees it."

"Anthony might know somebody," says Nick.

"Are you serious, man?" says Frankie. Even I have to laugh at that one.

"Yeah, maybe not." Nick thinks some more. "Sir Henry's pretty cool. He could bang it out in no time. It's only a small dent."

"I don't know," I say, intercepting the cig from Frankie on its way to Nick. "He's Dad's right arm. He's more like his first son than Anthony. I don't think I'd risk it."

"I know she'll let me borrow it again," says Frankie. "I just have to line something up."

"Hell, we can do it," says Nick.

"You ever pound out a dent?" Frankie says, just as I start coughing. I try and stifle it with my arm.

"I've seen Sir Henry do it," comes back Nick. "It can't be that hard." He shrugs. "Why don't you just let her find it? She'll think somebody did it in a parking lot."

Frankie thinks it over. He really gives it the old once around.

"I couldn't do that, man," he says. "Not to Aunt Myrtle. I'd rather just tell her what happened."

"Dad'll kill you," I do intone.

Nick gives me a look and snatches the cigarette nub away just before I start hacking again.

"Keep it down," he says.

"Yeah," says Frankie. "I'm pretty sure Dad will blow a gasket or two over it."

"I bet if you told Aunt Myrtle, she wouldn't tell Dad," I say. "She's a liberal. She wouldn't want to see you get killed."

"He could be right," says Nick. "I bet she'd keep it under wraps."

"I thought about that," says Frankie. "Thing is, I banged her car up six months ago, worse than this, and I *did* tell her. She

28

kept it between us. I just finished paying her back last month. I don't think I could go back to her again. She'd probably still do it, but how would she look at me from then on?"

"Yeah, she'd probably think you were a real loser," I say.

Nick looks down at me again.

"I don't know, man," he says to Frankie. "You might want to think about it. You don't want to face Dad, do you?"

"He'll kill you, Frankie, he'll just kill you," I blurt out. "Especially if he finds out you wrecked her car before."

This time Nick gives me the old bony elbow, right in the cheek.

"I know somebody," says Frankie, "We might be able to work something out. I'll have to think about it."

"It'll be all right, Frankie," I tell him. "It's just a dent."

"It sort of is just a dent, and it sort of isn't," he says.

"What do you mean?"

"I mean sure, it *is* just a dent. That's a fact. It's not that big and wouldn't be too hard to fix, if you knew how to do it. But in terms of what it represents about *me*, it's a whole lot more. There's symbolism in that dent. You dig what I'm saying?"

I think it over. The garage smells good. I like the smell of garages, especially ours. The twin Hondas are in the back barely visible in the shadows, but it's nice knowing they're there. The tools hanging on the pegboard along the wall behind Frankie make me feel good too. So does the vise at the edge of the workbench, and the push broom leaned against the wall.

I notice Frankie's harmonica in the pocket of his shirt.

"Play something," I tell him.

"Man, he'll wake up Dad," says Nick.

"It's cool," says Frankie. He gets up to pull down the garage door and me and Nick help him. We do it real slow, as slow as we've ever done it, and it barely makes any sound.

He tells us to hold on and he goes out the side door and comes back with his acoustic guitar.

Frankie sits down and tunes the guitar some, and even while he's tuning it it sounds good and I wish the three of us could sit together until the sun comes up. He plays and sings low in his husky, gravelly voice, mostly Beatles songs, but some other stuff too. He plays *The Times They Are a-Changin'*, and some Stones, and then a few folkie songs I don't know. Nick takes Frankie's harmonica and fumbles around with it. I wish I had something to do. I wish I could sing, but I can't. Frankie's always trying to get me to sing, and I've tried it now and then, but I'm no good at it. Frankie never cares. He says it's not the pitch that comes out, but the soul that you put into it. He's the opposite of Dad. Dad's about results. Frankie's about the effort, the enthusiasm, and the journey. I feel good when I'm with Frankie and Nick. When Frankie's playing and we're away from Dad, and nobody has anywhere else to be, it's beautiful. I see fireballs of hope and joy. In the garage, now, I see them on the pegboard on top of all the tools. I see them in Frankie's smile and in Nick's broad shoulders. I see them in our feet tapping on the garage floor, the rhythm of newness and optimism. The world's in flux, you can feel it the minute you step onto the sidewalk. It's in the air. It's in the newspapers, on TV, at the kitchen table. It's in the music, in the clothes, and most of all in the faces of everybody I know. It's in my head day and night—it won't stop throbbing bright and full of color.

Squirt in Trouble

Me and Sissy are across the street at Romano's, which isn't
where Mom does her normal shopping, but where she sends us
almost every day to get bread, eggs, milk—when she decides we
deserve a break from powdered milk for a day—or anything else
she so happens to need. Sometimes I wonder if she sends us over
hoping one of us won't make it across the racetrack of Tallmadge
Avenue, you know, whittling this gargantuan family down a
notch or two. But that would be a pitiful thought, now, wouldn't
it.

We're on the bench around the corner from Romano's next to
the dirt parking lot. Sissy's got a bag of potato chips in her hands,
squeezing it like she always does. For some reason she likes to
squeeze the bag until all the chips are crushed. Sissy's got on her
jeans with flower patches she embroidered on the fronts. I have
rectangular patches on the knees of my jeans. Mom sewed them
there to cover up the holes, not for decoration. I can really talk to
Sissy. I can talk to Britt too, but Sissy has a way of listening, sort
of like Frankie. Wherever she is, it's like there's nowhere else to
be. She's not looking ahead, she's not looking behind. She has
her eyes on exactly where she is at the time. Yet, there's a melancholy about her. Not a sadness, just melancholy. Like she
knows more than the world will let her. She watches Squirt and

Sally when Mom's busy. Britt works at the office, and so Sissy has to do the babysitting. She helps Dad at the garage doing paperwork, and she works a couple days a week at the counter taking phone calls and dealing with customers, but she has a fair amount of free time. Since she graduated a couple years ago, she's been deciding what she wants to do. It must be a painful thing, not knowing. I have a couple years left before I have to know, but I'm already starting to think about it. Sissy says she wants to do social work, but she hasn't applied at college for it. It's like she's floating along without anything tying her down to the ground.

I bought a Hershey's bar and offer her a piece. She sets the bag of potato chips aside and takes it. The men who walk by or get in and out of their cars in the parking lot look at Sissy. Some smile with plain friendliness, but others have something else in mind. It makes me uncomfortable and mad. Sissy keeps her head lowered some, or off to the side, whereas I can look anywhere I want.

She tells me she wants to join this march. The march is going down Tallmadge Avenue right past our house.

"Really?" I say. "Have you told Sergeant Carter yet?"

"Not yet," she says.

"And you say it's a women's march?"

"Yeah."

"Well," I say, taking a deep breath to think, then letting it out again, "you can either prep him ahead of time and maybe he'll get used to the idea, or you can shock him right before it so he won't have time to think about it."

"Or I can not tell him at all," she says.

"Yeah, yeah—you could do that. But I don't know if that's such a hot idea. He'd rather be pissed at you than know you weren't up-front with him. You have to think long-term on this one."

"Why don't you march with me?" she says.

"Me?" I laugh.

"Why not?"

"Me?"

32

"Sure. Don't you believe in equal rights for women?"

"I believe in equal rights for my behind," I say to her. "It's one thing if you march. You *are* a woman. I don't have to tell you what Dad would think of me, what he'd do to me, if I skipped along with you."

"Good way to meet girls," she says.

"True," I say. "You do have a point there."

"Think about it."

"Sure, I'll think about it. But if I decide not to, just remember—I'll be with you in spirit."

She gives me the old elbow to the ribs. "You goof."

I give her another piece of the Hershey's bar and we're about to leave when Mom of all people comes up to us. She's got Sally in her arms, bouncing her like a yo-yo on her hip trying to quell the kid's bawling eyes.

"Squirt's been put down the sewer," she shouts big and loud right in our shocked mugs. "Not just that, but Lennie—*he's* the one who did it—he pounded a nail into Squirt's skull. Help him, Puck—there's nobody else at home!"

Sissy drops the bag of chips, which Mom does duly retrieve from the concrete, expertly holding onto little Sally as the kid turns upside down, and the four of us make the dangerous trek back across the street. We head straight for Crestwood, which is the brick side street around the corner by Ernie's Barber Shop. It's the typical place where bad things happen. Well, one of them anyway, and we trot around the corner and sure enough there's a group of kids about halfway down toward Spellman. The waters don't exactly part, but there's a general backing up when they see Mom. We head straight for the center of the mass where Lennie stands there, feet splayed and bruised-up arms and legs—white as Elmer's glue—giving me the creeps. He doesn't move back or have any fear in his eyes. He just stands with splayed feet on top of the manhole cover.

Sissy walks up to him.

"Did you put our brother in the sewer?" she says to him.

Lennie doesn't give any reaction.

"Who are you?" he says. His voice is like cold mud.

33

"I'm his sister."

"So?"

"So, is he down there?"

I look at the manhole cover and think of poor Squirt down there with the rats and dirty water, hoping he doesn't try and eat anything. It must be pitch black.

"Why?"

"Look," I tell him, "get him out. Get him out now."

Lennie, who's nearly grown-up and is big for his age, a lot bigger than me, doesn't move.

"I don't have to do anything." He folds his arms over his blubbery chest.

"Get him out of there this instant," says Mom.

"Sorry," he says. "He's a mouthy little fucker. He shouldn't have been mouthing off."

"Squirt," I say to the manhole cover. "Are you all right?" I don't hear anything. "Quiet," I tell them. "Shut up so I can hear."

"I'm calling Dad," says Sissy, and she runs off toward the house.

"Squirt," I say. "Squirt—can you hear me? Are you down there?"

There's no answer, but I can hear him crying. Finally, he says something, real faint.

"What? I didn't hear you?" I say, turning my head.

"I want Mom," he says all weak-like and afraid.

"I'm right here, honey," says Mom, bobbing Sally on her hip trying to keep her calm. "I'm here—I'm not going anywhere. We're going to get you out. It'll be all right, honey—Daddy's coming."

"Mom?" he says, and then he starts bawling, way louder than before.

"I'm here, baby—Mommy's here. And Puck. And Sally. Daddy's on his way. He'll get you out—don't worry."

"I want to go home," he cries. "I want to go home."

"We'll get you out, Squirt," I tell him. "Dad's coming."

Well, it seems like an hour, though it's probably only a few minutes, and along comes Nick with Sissy. Nick's bigger than anybody there, except Lennie.

"Let him out," says Nick.

"Make me."

"Do it."

"Yeah, sure I will," says Lennie.

Nick, who I just notice has his slingshot with him, raises it, pulls back the thick rubber band about as far as I've ever seen it, and lets go. Lennie lets out a horrible scream, clutching his white arm. The kids back up as Nick puts another penny in the small leather pouch and pulls back on the rubber band again. He aims it straight at Lennie's head, the back of his head, because Lennie's already slithering off toward his house, wherever that is.

Some kids scramble, but most stay where they are. Nick gets down and tries lifting up the manhole cover, but there's nowhere to get a good grip and it's heavy as all hell.

"Help me," he says to me, and I get down with him and we both try to get the thing up, but there's just nothing to hold onto. I'm about to run to the house for Dad's crowbar, when there comes a rumble and the kids really part this time.

It's a big, bald-headed man who we all figure is Lennie's dad. Whoever he is he has a crowbar in his right fist.

Me and Nick jump up and start peddling backward, getting ready to run, but the man doesn't come for us. He drops to his knees, sticks that crowbar in one of the holes of the manhole cover, and pries it up some. When he's got it up about a foot, he drops the crowbar and lifts the cover away and tosses it on the bricks. It rolls around on itself all thick and dangerous, and I can't believe any human being could lift, let alone toss, a thing that heavy.

He bends down and when he comes back up, Squirt's in his arms. He swings him around and sets him down on the street, and Squirt runs to Mom.

"That your boy?" he says to her.

"Yes—if that was your son, he—"

"I already beat him for it," he says. Then, turning to Nick with the darkest, meanest face you ever saw, says, "Hit my boy with that slingshot again and it'll be the last thing you ever do."

He picks up the crowbar, turns around, and goes back the way he came.

Back home, Mom has Squirt up on the counter by the kitchen sink. She's wiping him off—he's a dirty mess—and she's looking at his head. Seems Lennie actually did put a nail to him. Maybe to scare him, maybe more. But there's a small hole in his scalp after Mom wipes away the blood.

"What'd you say to make him so mad?" I ask him. I'm straddling one of the benches at the table, eating a piece of bread and butter. Gram's come out of her hovel and is sitting along the wall on her church pew.

"I don't know," says Squirt. "Nothing."

"You had to say something."

"He's just a bully," says Sissy.

"I'm not saying he started it, but he must have said something."

"He's nothing but a bully, and so is his father."

"But, Squirt," I keep digging, "you *must* have, you *had* to have said *something*."

"You'll probably need a tetanus shot," says Mom, still examining Squirt's head.

"That nasty man," says Gram, wagging her finger. "He ought to be in jail. He nothing but a bully. His son is bully because he's a bully."

"Can't argue with you there, Gram," I say. "But," back to Squirt one final time, "you mean you didn't say anything, you didn't do anything? He just walked up to you with a nail and a hammer and decided to try it out on your head, and then he puts you down the sewer just because, heck, I don't know, he felt like it? I mean, that doesn't make any sense. It doesn't make any sense at all."

Squirt, who's sucking on a Popsicle, gets this funny look, like I just solved some big mystery.

"Yeah," he says. "That's what he said. That's what he told the kids. He wanted to see what it felt like."

"What, Squirt? What *what* felt like?"

"He said he wanted to see what it felt like to put a nail in somebody's head. He said he ain't never done that before. He said his daddy put him in a sewer once and it was time somebody else was put down one too."

"Oh," says Gram, who makes the sign of the cross. "Lord help us."

Delish New Dish

It's Friday, which means a big dinner and a big night. Mom's had a roast cooking for hours. Everybody's around the table. You have to put your arms in front of you on your lap when you're not using your hands—there's not enough room to have them at your sides. Britt and Sissy have been up helping her put things out, and Gram too, but now that it's time to eat we're all at the table and Gram is on her pew, staring into the side of Dad's head.

Speaking of Dad—he never made it home to see if Squirt was dead or alive. I don't know if he was busy or if he wanted us to sort things out on our own. He's like that. A big believer in self-reliance and, even when it comes to his own progeny, natural selection. I'm not saying he wouldn't have been awful upset if he had driven up and found Squirt under that manhole cover. He's got a temper, all right, and would have had some choice words for Lennie. But most of his anger would've been from having to be pulled away from work and us not having the wherewithal to settle matters on our own. Fight your own battles, that's what he says. Once when I told him, you mean like England and France and Poland and Czechoslovakia in WWII, he gave me this real pained look like he gives Squirt all the time. Remember—he's mostly German and those Germans pretty much forgot to get in line when they were handing out sense of humor cards.

Dinners at our house are pragmatic affairs. Not that there's no talking allowed. But our stomachs are so hollow, the main focus is on whatever sustenance happens to be floating down from the heaven of Mom's loving arms.

She sets down the industrial-sized pot on the table—after I swiftly place a nearby rag on the spot for her so the pot won't burn the surface—and we all start drooling like hyenas in front of a dead elephant.

The chant begins, *"We want the food. We want the food. We want the food."* All of us with a fork in one hand and knife in the other, banging on the table like prisoners. Dad makes a frown and raises his hand like the Pope. All chanting stops.

Mom takes hold of the handle of the lid with both hands and lugs it away. To our surprise there's not a roast in the pot but a, well, none of us really knows what it is.

Squirt gives voice to the synchronized thoughts in our brains.

"What's *that*?"

Probably because he's still got the big red blotch on his head, Dad doesn't react too bad.

"You mean those," says Sissy, and sure enough she's right. There are two of them, whatever they are.

Surely, they are the strangest-looking objects I think I've ever set eyes on. They smell just like a pot roast, they do, making them all the more mystifying. But instead of being a nice roasted dark-brown color, they're gray.

"It's tongue," says Anthony.

"What do you mean?" says Squirt.

"I mean, it's cow's tongue."

"I don't get it." Squirt looks lost.

"Close your mouth at the table," says Britt. "It's rude."

"But what does he mean?" Squirt's all panicky. His cheeks turn red to match the nail wound. "What does that *mean*—it's cow's tongue? I don't know what that means?"

Tommy starts chuckling. He tries to suppress it, he really does, but he can't help it and has to duck his head into his shirt collar.

"We used to have this on the Farm," says Mom. "And," she

hesitates, "other times. Your Dad loves it."

"Oh my God," says Sissy, her fork dropping from her hand.

"But there's two of them," says Squirt. "How can there be two of them?"

"We're a big family," smiles Mom.

"They're from two cows, dummy," I chime in.

"That's enough." Dad gives me the pointed finger.

"Oh, just eat it," Britt tells him. "Mom spent all day on it. Don't be so ungrateful."

Gram, who never eats much at dinner, says, "When I was a girl in Sorrento, we always had fish for dinner. Papa was fisherman and we never had to eat organs of animals. He always made sure we had fish—fresh fish—for dinner. Only poor people ate animal organs. We *were* poor, I guess, but we never had to eat a tongue. What kind of food is that—cow's tongue?"

"I thought tongues were muscles," I say.

"No, I think they're organs," says Nick.

"Really?"

"I read about it once, maybe in science class," he says.

"I don't know why you make it," Gram says, speaking to Mom. "Your papa not like it. I not like it. I hate it at the Farm. Why you bring it up from the dead?"

"Dad likes it," Mom tells her, meaning *our* dad. "That's why. It's good." She's speaking to us now. "Try it—it's good."

Dad starts cutting into it. Frankie, who's just come in, squeezes in between me and Sissy, which makes Squirt fall on the floor.

"Hey," he whines and gets up. Everybody on our bench scoots together to give the kid a few inches.

"You're late," says Dad.

"What are those round things?" Squirt, who's up on his elbows watching Dad slice up the tongue, asks.

"Those are taste buds," says Anthony.

"Sorry," says Frankie to Dad.

Squirt's eyes go up with surprise, then drop with confusion.

Gram continues with her soliloquy to the side of Dad's head. "Octopus, squid—yes, of course. They delicacies—a step above

40

regular fish. Clams, oysters, mussels—we steam them and have them with spaghet. But I never heard of no one eating a cow's tongue before I married your father, Catarina." She gives a single laugh making her body lurch. "Why not eat an ear, or a tail?"

"They ate those, too," says Mom, shoveling spinach on our plates. "You have a bad memory. I remember you eating it at the Farm."

Gram tosses her hand in the air like she's pushing the thought away. "If I eat it, I don't remember. Some things you are better off forgetting." She emphasizes that last statement by leaning in closer to Dad, who only moves his eyes some.

Everybody, no matter what we think of tongue, starts eating. All except Frankie.

"I've decided to become a vegetarian," he says.

"Just now?" Britt says with a slight smirk.

Mom, with Sally on her hip, bouncing away, huffs, "Well, that's just great. What are you going to eat?"

"I'm fine, Mom," he says. "It's not the tongue. I've been a vegetarian for a while."

"You had fish sticks last week," says Squirt.

"I eat fish, just not red meat."

"Fish is good for you," declares Gram. "Everyone should eat more fish—not the tongues of animals."

"You'll eat what's put on the table," says Dad with no expression whatsoever, sticking his fork into a sizable piece of tongue loaded with taste buds. "This isn't a cafeteria."

"He'll wither away," says Mom. "Look at him already. Nothing but skin and bones."

"I'll cook you a nice pasta dinner, Frankie," Gram says. She starts to get up.

"Sit down, Mom," says Mom. She gets two hard-boiled eggs leftover from breakfast and hands them to Frankie.

"Thanks," he says.

"Don't count on eggs every evening," says Dad. "You'll eat what we eat."

Frankie nods all sheepish-like, but starts in on the eggs.

We devour one and a half of the two tongues. The rest, Mom

41

says, is for Dad, who presumably likes tongue sandwiches. For dessert we each get half a canned peach in a bowl. It takes me two bites to down mine. We help clear the table and then sit back down on the benches because Mom wants to say the rosary. We usually do it only during Lent or on some other religious occasion, but I think Squirt getting the nail in the head has made her particularly fearful.

I get out the basket for her, which is crammed under the sink next to the plunger, and put it in the middle of the table. She sets a blanket and then Sally in it. That's the way we do it. Whoever's the baby at the time gets put in the basket in the middle of the table, and then we say the rosary while it's screaming or puking or whatever else babies do. Mom sits down for it. The kitchen's hot as Hades with the heat from the oven roasting the two tongues all day, and it's pretty apparent not everybody put on the old deodorant this morning. Mom starts with the Apostles' Creed, rolls into the Our Father, but by the Hail Marys Dad takes lead and the pace picks up considerably. I don't think there's a Catholic on the planet who can zip through the rosary like Dad on a Friday night, a baby with a full diaper bawling its head off two feet from his ears, and the kitchen like Death Valley packed to the gills with sweating bodies. Before you know it, Mom's collecting all the rosaries and dropping them back in the drawer, and we head outside for some fresh air. All except Sissy and Anthony, who are on KP duty this week.

There's a car in the drive, about a ten-year-old Chevy Bel Air, red, with its hood up and Sir Henry underneath it. Frankie, Tommy, Nick, and me crowd around.

"What's wrong with it?" Nick asks him.

"Not sure yet," says Sir Henry without turning around.

"Sure is a nice one," I do say. And a beauty, she is. Hardly any rust, no dents, pretty new paint job. Like Brigitte on wheels.

Somebody must have brought it over from the garage before dinner. Sir Henry can't drive since he's legally blind. The only thing he can see is what's a couple inches from his nose. He has these special thick glasses, plus a loop he has attached to the right side that he swings down to magnify things. He's Dad's best mechanic because he doesn't make mistakes. He's slow, it takes him twice as long to fix a car as the other guys, but there aren't any redos with Sir Henry. Dad's been having cars brought over from the garage after hours lately so Sir Henry can work on them in the drive. Dad directs and Sir Henry does the work—that's the way it is with him, and that's the way it is with the rest of us.

"Need anything?" I ask him.

"Not yet," he says. "Still trying to figure out the problem."

"Is she running?"

"Yeah, she's running. But she'll stall at a light."

"Could be the carburetor," says Tommy.

"Could be. That's what I'm looking at. Or the gas line leading to it."

Sir Henry turns his head away from the engine. He's feeling the gas line. He's facing Nick, but to him Nick's but a blurry spot. He's seeing with his hands. That's what Dad says. Sir Henry is a reliable mechanic because he sees with his hands, and hands don't get distracted or see what they want to see, they see what's there and that's it. He lives on the west side of North Hill, on the other side of Main, in the basement of this house. He lives alone. All he does is work. He doesn't have a girl, or get drunk, or blow his money on stuff. He works. He doesn't wear expensive clothes, or have much furniture in his place. He works. He never declines when Dad says there's another car to look at. He and Dad are like a single thing. It's weird, kind of neat, but kind of unsettling. Dad has a certain way of talking to Sir Henry that's different from the way he talks to us. Not like a partner exactly, not like a son; both, sort of. He's never had a bad thing to say about him. I've never heard him reprimand Sir Henry, the few times he's made a mistake. It's like the way he treats Mom, though without the hugs or kisses.

"Here it is," Sir Henry says.

"You got it?" I say to him.

Sir Henry swings his arm toward us, offering his fingers. We give them a smell.

"Gas," says Tommy.

"Is there a hole in the line?" I ask him.

43

Sir Henry nods his head.

"Can you fix it?" I say.

Nick gives me the look and I feel dumb for asking.

"It'll need a new line. Your dad doesn't have any here."

"Bet there's plenty at the garage," I say. "You going to get her fixed tonight?"

Sir Henry comes out from beneath the hood, wiping his hands on a rag. He doesn't say anything. He's wearing a regular white T-shirt instead of his normal B&G Automotive shirt with his name on it, which means he probably went home after work and had dinner already.

Anthony brings Dad out from the side door of the house and sets him by the car. He looks up from his wheelchair with worry on his face; of course, he can't see into the engine.

"Sir Henry found the problem," I say, giving him the good news.

"I see," he says.

Sir Henry's still wiping his hands on the rag, but then steps over and puts his fingers down under Dad's nose so he can smell the gas.

"Isn't that great, Dad?"

"Sure," he says, still with his usual frown.

"It's the gas line," I say. "Sir Henry found it in no time. Put another line in and she's as good as new. She sure is a beauty, too."

It's like he doesn't hear me. He's looking at the car, but it's like he's thinking too hard to hear.

"You boys better get cleaned up if you're going out tonight," he says. "Sir Henry and I need to talk about the car."

"Yes, sir," says Tommy, who doesn't waste any time and heads right in.

"You want any help, Dad?" I say. "I can help Sir Henry put in a new line. I'll ride to the garage with you to get another one. I don't have anything going on tonight."

"No," he says, "you go on in. Sir Henry and I will take care of it. You boys get cleaned up. Anthony, we may need you to drive it back to the garage."

44

"Yes, sir," says Anthony.

I feel something on my arm and realize it's Nick. He pulls me away.

"Hey," I whisper to him. "What're you doing?"

"Come on," he says.

"Damn, Nick," I say to him. "That hurts."

"Can't you tell when Dad wants us to make ourselves scarce? He's got business with Sir Henry—business, and that's none of *our* business. Things are fine. He's in a good mood. It's Friday night. Don't screw it up."

He guides me through the side door and up the few stairs to the kitchen. Mom and Britt and Sissy and Gram are in the kitchen not doing anything, just sitting at the table. Dinner hasn't been cleaned up yet. I head their way.

"Hey, can I have another half a peach, Mom? Mine was kind of scrawny. I think I got the smallest one in the can and, well, I sure would enjoy another half." I get but two steps and there's Nick's hand again, pulling me back.

He pushes me to the stairs and halfway up starts punching my ass cheeks one at a time, you know, playful like. We get up to the third floor and I fall onto my mattress and he starts punching me playful, like he did up the stairs, and then we start wrestling around, but since he's a lot bigger he gets on top of me in no time and has me pinned on my back, his thighs on either side of my chest. He holds my arms to the cold wood floor by the wrists. He holds me there and it's not fun after a while, and I tell him to get off, only he won't. Nick's never been a teaser, not to me, and I don't get it. I struggle but he won't get up. I'm getting mad, but it doesn't matter, he sits there like a bag of cement.

"Let me up," I tell him. "Let me up."

"Are you blind?" he says. "What's the matter with you?"

"What are you talking about?"

"Don't you know what's going on? Mr. Gordon took all the money from the bank account. He cleaned out the garage—he took everything. The tools. The machines. All the cars they were working on. Everything, and then he skipped town. The bank might take the garage. Puck, Dad's broke."

45

Friday Night Euchre

It's about an hour later and I'm taking a brief look at Brigitte, using a magnifying glass for closer scrutiny, when I hear some noise at the side door. I pile all her parts into the crawl space, then scurry downstairs—sliding like a pro backward down the banister and past the girl's lounge which is booming and bopping to *Sgt. Pepper's*.

It's about 7:00 post meridiem, the usual time when Frankie's bandmates come over. Sure enough, he and Ollie are in the kitchen shooting the shit at the table, messing around with the modeling clay Squirt's playing with. Squirt's making little soldiers. They're making girls and guitars. Pretty soon Britt and Sissy come down, and then the four of them take to the dining room.

We aren't allowed in the dining room much—it's for special occasions like Christmas and Thanksgiving and when company comes over—but Friday nights we're allowed to sit at the table and play euchre before heading out. Ollie's Frankie's best friend and the drummer of his band. Ollie has it in for Sissy. He likes to be her partner and makes sure to compliment her on her moves, and if she makes a bad move or reneges he doesn't care at all and says he messed up the hand even when he didn't. Tommy comes down and sits next to Britt, while me and Nick stand hovered over the table. It's Ollie and Sissy against Frankie and Britt on

46

this one. Nick and Tommy have the winners.

Mom and Dad are on the living room couch against the front window facing us through the open French doors, and Gram is in the rocker with the afghan over her knees. Old Frank Sinatra's singing low and chocolatey smooth on the console stereo. We have the portable radio on the buffet between the Hummels and the antique water pitcher thumping out The Stones, Buffalo Springfield, The 5th Dimension, The Youngbloods, and The Temptations. Mom and Dad are side by side like a couple of kids on a date. Mom's got her hand on Dad's leg and they're talking way too low to hear with all the music going. They're in their world over there and we're in ours in the dining room.

Anthony comes down and after a while we can smell the popcorn from the kitchen, and he walks in with a big bowl of it and puts it on the card table beside the dining room table we're playing on. He doesn't want to play, but stands watching and tells Nick and Tommy, who are now playing Ollie and Sissy, what they're doing wrong. Hoss is supposed to be here. He's Frankie's bass player. I tried playing bass, and you'd think it would be easier than a guitar, but I couldn't do it. I tried the drums, and I can't do that either. I've been practicing on Frankie's old acoustic guitar and he says I can play in the band if they ever decide to go with two guitars, but for now they're a trio.

Dad's still in his B&G Automotive shirt, but his face is cleaned up and he shaved after dinner; I can smell his aftershave all the way in the dining room. Sissy and Britt have on miniskirts, which Dad isn't too keen on, but Mom says they're what the girls are wearing now. She tells Dad they can't judge them too harshly because in their day girls wore skirts to their knees and that was scandalous. And before that, it was the old rumble seat that was causing tectonic plates to grind. Great-Aunt Ida, she rode in a rumble seat once or twice and for that single reason had a reputation worse than Mata Hari. Gram likes to grumble about the miniskirts too, and bikinis, and just about any other thing she catches sight of with her nearly broken-down eyes, but that seems sort of odd since she also likes to talk about skinny-dipping in the grottoes with her family around the island of Capri.

"I saw you over on campus the other day," Ollie says to Sissy. He's sitting up straight with his mouth in this goofy, wide smile so his teeth are peeking from the crack of his lips.

"On campus? I don't think so."

"No? I thought for sure it was you."

"No," says Sissy. "Why would I be on campus?"

"Aren't you taking classes now?"

"Who told you that?"

"I don't know," says Ollie. "Somebody. I don't know who. Maybe you did, Frankie."

"Me? Not me. But hey—it's an honest mistake. A pretty girl like Sissy here's bound to grab anybody's attention."

"Well, whoever it was sure looked like you," says Ollie to Sissy.

"Maybe so, but it wasn't."

"No, I guess not. And all this time, I thought it was." He makes a goofy smile, but Sissy's not paying attention.

Frankie tilts his head down to look over his glasses at Nick, and then at me, and we can hardly keep from busting out laughing.

Frankie lifts his head and pushes up his glasses. "Hey, Ollie, you think your dad will let us use his station wagon next weekend?"

"Oh, I don't know, Frankie," he says. "I'm not allowed to drive it too often."

"I thought you said he'd let you use it."

"I said I thought he might," says Ollie. "I can ask him."

"Go ahead and ask him," says Frankie. He turns his head toward Sissy. "Didn't you say you were going to our next show, Sissy?"

"I might," she says, not paying much attention. She's licking her lips deciding what card to play.

"I thought you said you were," says Frankie. "Ollie's got a solo lined up in a couple songs. The guy's amazing."

"Really, Frankie?" says Ollie, surprised as all get-out.

"Sure, man," he says. "We talked about it."

Ollie shakes his head. "I don't remember."

"Sure," says Frankie. "We got to get you more solos, man. You're like the backbone of the band. Sissy—you've seen the guy play. He gets better every time he even looks at his drumsticks. You better come see us play before you have to pay to see us. And I mean pay a lot."

I see Frankie wink at Nick. Nobody sees him but me.

"Frankie," says Nick, "was that Ginger Baker you were playing out in the bus the other night?"

"What night was that?"

"I don't know," says Nick. "It sounded like Ginger Baker though."

"That was Ollie," he says.

"What do you mean?"

"I was playing back a tape we made. That wasn't Ginger Baker—that was Ollie. This guy right here."

Nick looks impressed. "Jesus," he says.

"Yeah, no kidding. I told you. This kid's got the chops. He's going places. Sissy," he says, turning toward her again, "you have to see the boy play. You need to bring all your friends. You too, Britt."

Nick misplays and he and Tommy get euchred. Tommy tosses his hands in the air, like what the hell? Of course, Nick did it on purpose.

"Yeah, see what you can do about getting the station wagon," says Frankie. "Maybe we can fit your brother's big amp in. That would improve our sound about a thousand percent."

"I should be able to use it," says Ollie.

"Your old man's a good guy," says Frankie. "Yeah, see if your brother would let us use that amp for the gig. It sure would improve our chances of getting a manager."

"You guys are getting a manager?" Tommy says to him.

Frankie and Nick both give him the look.

"We're trying," says Frankie. He's got his eyes narrowed at him. "We're pretty close."

"And I thought you were just doing church basements and free concerts at Patterson Park," Tommy says.

"We're close," says Frankie. "That's how you get manage-

49

ment. You have a big sound by having a big amp, and you need a big car to transport it. That's how you get a manager. That's how it's done."

"Don't you have to practice to get good? I never hear you guys practice."

Nick clears his throat. "Your deal, man," he says, handing the cards to Tommy.

"Yeah, your deal, Tommy," says Frankie. "Deal those cards."

Mom gets up and starts dancing by herself. I like to watch her dance. Watching Mom dance is about the only time Dad seems like a real person, and nobody's afraid and we don't have to worry about what we say to him. Gram watches her and smiles in her thick glasses, that green afghan on her knees. Watching Mom dance brightens Gram up like nothing else, except maybe Squirt when he goes into one of his crazy routines. It's like she has Dad right there with her, and not like she's alone at all. It's easy to think of them in high school before the war, dancing, and it's easy to picture them before Dad got polio when they danced in that very spot. She'll make her way over to Dad, reach down so he can touch her fingers for a while, and then she'll shimmy away. Her eyes close and open, but mostly stay closed. They open only so she doesn't hit the wall or trip. Dad's got it bad for Mom like nobody I've seen. She's got it bad for him too. They had it for each other on first sight, that's a fact. Lightning struck. God took His mighty hand, reached it down through the clouds, and waved it over those two. You might think he's the way he is because he needs her now, because without her he'd be lost, and that's true. But that's not what it is. He was that way at sixteen. All through the war. And after the war, when they started popping out babies together. I see him and I want what he's got. I want to look at somebody the way he looks at Mom. I want somebody like Mom who'd walk through fire for me.

"Hey, look," Nick says with an elbow to Frankie when he sees them touching hands, and I know why.

"Uh-oh," says Frankie. "Jesus. Please, God, no."

The last thing this family needs is another mouth to feed. Hell, there's no room at the table.

Anthony tells us he's going to make some fudge. We head into the kitchen, and a short while later Hoss comes in wearing some new Beatle boots. Frankie and Nick notice right off, and Frankie gives a whistle.

"Well, blow me down," he says. "Ollie, we're going to have to up our game. Looks like the man's rounding third and heading for home."

Hoss, who's tall and slim and quiet, along the lines of John Entwistle, sits down at the table with the rest of us, except for me and Anthony, who are standing. Squirt wanders out from the living room, and we take turns looking at his head.

"I say we take a drill to Lennie's nose," says Ollie. "You let me know the next time Lennie bothers you," he tells Squirt.

"Come here," says Frankie. "I never got a look at the proverbial hole in the head."

Squirt leans his head toward Frankie, who whistles something fierce. "Holy tamole, kid," he says. "Next time, tie his shoelaces together and run for the hills."

"I ran," says Squirt, "but somebody tripped me."

Frankie pushes his head back up and Squirt stands there all mighty and proud, like he just won some kind of contest.

"Okay," says Frankie, "go back to *Batman*. We have adult conversations to get on with."

"*Batman*'s not on," says Squirt.

"Here, you can sit by me," says Sissy, who makes room for him on the bench.

While Anthony's at the stove making fudge, we fiddle around with the clay some, and Frankie lays out his current plan for the band.

"So, I've been thinking about the name again," he says to Ollie. Frankie told me and Nick all this yesterday, so I'm anxious to hear how he crafts it for Ollie's delicate ears.

"Oh yeah?" says Ollie, perking up some.

"Yeah," says Frankie. "The thing is, I'm not so sure Wet Paint communicates the kind of direction we've been heading in lately." He's tapping a hunk of clay onto the tabletop, looking uncomfortable.

"You don't like it?" says Ollie. Ollie was the one who conjured the name last Friday night.

"It's not bad," says Frankie. "It's a, you know, good point of departure."

"I thought you guys liked it," he says, looking to Frankie and Hoss all panicky-like.

"It kind of sucks," says Hoss. "If you really want to know."

Ollie looks brokenhearted. "I thought you liked it."

"Not really," says Hoss. "No offense, Ollie."

The conversation dries up for a while, and then they start tossing out new names like, The North Hillers, Rolling Rubbish, The Renaissance Men, Sons of Silence, and, my particular favorite, Bluesy Blues.

"Yeah," chimes in Sissy. "I like that one too."

"All right," says Frankie, who's been molding a gavel from several hunks of clay, "It's Bluesy Blues, then." He hits the clay gavel on the table with a thud. "Come on. Let's go get some ice cream."

Britt checks herself in the side of the toaster on the counter since there's no mirror within ten feet. Frankie, Tommy, Nick, Hoss, Ollie, and the girls head on out in Hoss's 1964 Ford Fairlane and Britt's VW Bug, which is parked in its usual spot in the dirt space across the street next to Romano's.

Me and Squirt stay with Anthony.

We watch him make the fudge, and after he's done cooking it and pouring it onto the cookie sheet, he pushes the empty bowl toward us. I let Squirt have most of it and pretty soon he's a fudgy mess. I clean him up after he's done, and we head into the living room, where we sit at the dining room table playing war. A while later they all come back with a couple half gallons of ice cream and sit back down at the kitchen table. The fudge isn't quite set, which makes it perfect to cut a square and pile a couple heaping scoops of the old vanilla on top of it.

"You sure make good fudge," says Hoss to Anthony.

I help Squirt get cleaned up again and he tears off to the living room to plant himself in front of the TV.

Anthony gets his guitar from upstairs and he and Frankie play and sing folk songs while the girls stand, Britt leaned against the doorway and Sissy on her own a few feet from Ollie. Ollie joins in singing, but Hoss doesn't and I don't and Nick doesn't. Tommy does.

They sing Bob Dylan and Joan Baez, and Anthony, because he's older, sings a couple Everly Brothers songs. I like it all. Frankie thinks Anthony is square and the Everly Brothers are square, but I like it all. He thinks Glenn Miller is a dinosaur and Frank Sinatra is old and behind the times, but I like it all. I like the slow dancing Mom does, and I like the tambourine jive girls do on TV. I like Squirt and the way he doesn't care about anything, and I like Dad and all his rules and order. I like everything that's happening. It's frightening and powerful, and I like it all. I don't want Tommy to go to Vietnam, and I like how he wants to go. I like women's lib and the marches and the signs, and I like men like Dad and women like Mom. It all makes sense if you don't choose sides. I like it all, but I can't straddle it all; I can't be it all; I can't consume it all. It's too much too strong too big. It's too big for one person or one generation to be. I want to be a priest like Anthony might be, and I want to be a soldier like Tommy's going to be, and I want to be a hippie like Frankie and Sissy are becoming, and I want to be good-looking and smooth and strong like Nick, and I want to be a car whiz like Sir Henry. I want to be a thousand different people. It's the time we live in. It's what it's all about.

Good Neighbors

It's good ol' Saturday. Every Saturday morning at the crack of dawn, while all the sane people of this fine country are still asleep in their beds, we're roused from our own bliss by Dad. He calls up the stairwell at us as he's walking on his crutches to the steps, singing, *It's good ol' Saaaaaaturdaaaaaay* like he's the happiest guy in the world, like it's Christmas or something. The guy's a real sadist. Good ol' Saturday means projects. You know, like rotating the tires on the cars, fixing the washing machine, scrubbing the floors, washing all the windows on the house inside and out, trimming the bushes, or, as is the case today, painting the garage.

The five of us older boys sit down at the kitchen table for some Corn Flakes, but nobody made milk last night. Anthony gets out the box of powdered milk, adds some to a jug of water, and stirs it up. What comes out is this lumpy, warm, watery stuff that ensures we never have friends over for breakfast.

"Jesus," I say.

"Eat it," says Anthony, smiling like Dad would, chomping a mouthful with real pleasure.

"But it's warm. And lumpy."

"Eat it," he repeats after a swallow.

"Couldn't you have at least run the water until it got cold?"

"Are you asking me to waste water?"

"This shit basically is water," I tell him. "But cold water beats warm water on cereal. Ask anybody in prison."

"People are starving in China," he says. "Don't you know?"

One time there were red ants in the cereal. Anthony ate it anyway, just to prove how manly he was. Said it added protein to his meal. That's the kind of surrogate dad we're dealing with.

"No, I don't know," I say. "How would I know? I've never been to China and neither have you."

"They've got kids starving all over the place. We live like kings compared to them."

I raise my eyebrows. I'm the only one. Frankie, Tommy, Nick—they all take whatever Anthony dishes out because he's the oldest and the eyes and ears of Dad. But not me. I'm low man on the totem pole—what have I got to lose? I send it right back at him. I think he enjoys it.

"Kings, huh?"

"That's right. You, Puck, live in the greatest country, in one of the greatest states, in one of the best cities in the world. *You.* Don't you feel lucky?"

Okay, now the guy's being facetious. That's a word Mom uses all the time—*facetious*.

"I feel hungry, horny. Not so much lucky."

"Give the boy some oysters," says Tommy. "That's what he needs."

"Why, so he can do a number on Brigitte?" says Anthony.

"The poor, poor lass," says Frankie.

"Look," I do declare, "you're talking as the A-Number-One Firstborn. Dad's body double. You know, somebody who *is* lucky."

"So are you," Anthony says, all smarmy but definitely *not* facetious-like.

"If you haven't noticed, I'm son number five," I say. "I have a pretty clear idea what *unlucky* looks like."

"I don't get it," says Anthony. "Speak English."

"How about this," I say. "You have privilege *I'll* never know, merely because your sperm got there four places ahead of me."

"You're blaming me for that?"

"No, I'm not blaming you. But it's a fact. Your reality and mine are light-years apart in this here asylum."

"You're the hammer, he's the nail, Anthony," says Tommy.

"Hey," says Frankie, "that's a good title to a song."

I shovel a spoonful of soggy Corn Flakes into my mouth and give him a grin. "I'm just saying."

It's broiling outside with the flaky whiteness of the garage bouncing back at us. The boards are rotted top and bottom, but the middle parts are okay. We each have a scraper. Well, I don't. I have a putty knife. We only have four real scrapers. Me and Nick and Tommy are on the side, and Frankie's around back with Anthony against the chain-link fence next to the Del Rosas. Mr. Del Rosa's in his backyard hosing down his tomatoes. He stands there in his flip-flops and tight shorts, a white T-shirt clung over his hairy abdomen. I say *abdomen* and not *stomach*, like he's a toad or something, which is sort of what he looks like. His head's like his abdomen, kind of hairy, kind of puffy; glistening with sweat like a basted turkey. There I go with the animal similes again. His tomatoes—they'll climb all the way up to the second story, where he can reach them by stepping out his bedroom window onto the flat part of the roof. He has the tallest plants and he produces the most tomatoes of anybody around, and that says a lot.

"How you doing, boys?" he calls over in his baritone voice, tossing his deep-set dark eyes at us.

"Fine, Mr. Del Rosa," says Anthony. We always let Anthony handle the adult conversations whenever possible, and he's glad to do it.

"Sorry to hear about your dad," he says. "He'll bounce back. Your dad's a winner."

"Thanks, Mr. Del Rosa," says Anthony.

"You boys let me know if there's anything I can do. I know your dad would never ask for help from anybody, that's why I'm telling you. Anything. Anything at all—just come over and let me know."

"We will," says Anthony. "And thanks."

56

I can't see Anthony or Frankie, but I can hear them. None of us stops working while Anthony's talking to Mr. Del Rosa. The scraping marches on just like Sherman to the sea. Never know when Dad might wheel out with his magnifying glass.

"You're good kids," I hear him say. "Not like my punk son. You boys are good, don't let anybody tell you anything else. Don't listen to anybody. You're good kids."

Mr. Del Rosa's a bricklayer, a builder. He's got brick layer hands. They're like gorilla hands. He's squat like a gorilla. His head is pointed at the top like a gorilla. Pretty soon we smell the grill. He always grills Saturdays. Seems like that thing is going all day long. It's torture. He does up steaks and hamburgers and Italian sausages. For some reason the wind always brings the smoke right toward us, right in our faces, killing us.

"Damn," Nick says.

"I bet Dad put us out here on purpose, knowing he was going to grill," I say as a cloud of heavenly smoke blows by.

"Aw, Puck," says Tommy, facetious as hell. "That's an awful thing to say."

"I may be dumb, but I ain't stupid," I say, borrowing one of Dad's favorite expressions.

"Didn't get enough watery milk and Corn Flakes?"

"I think I'm going to pass out," I say. "Seriously. There's nothing in the tank. The sun's killing me. I ain't going to make it, fellas."

Sometimes when we're bored, we stand in front of Anthony's full-length mirror that's leaned against the sloped ceiling of the third floor and see who can make the biggest hole in their stomachs. We suck in air to blow up our chest, then pull in our stomachs. I can usually make mine as deep as a football is wide. When our stomachs are resting we all have these lines on them between the individual muscles, not because we're muscular, but because we don't have any fat on us. Gram once said that if she boiled down my body fat for lamp oil, I wouldn't make enough to burn two minutes.

We scrape for a few hours, getting all the big, obvious chunks of paint off, then we start hitting it with the sandpaper. We start with 100-grit, but we'll finish with 220. We're all around the back now, next to the Del Rosa's. The sun's hammering away on our necks and backs with our shirts off. We take turns trotting inside for water breaks, but none of us takes too long for fear of Dad's invisible hand reaching out and cracking the whip.

Britt and Sissy come out with a basket of laundry and hang it on the line. Mostly sheets and whites. The line runs from the back of the house to the chain-link fence. Mom does it sometimes, and Gram will help her, but the girls do it on Saturdays. There's always somebody with laundry hanging out to dry in their backyard unless it's raining. Britt and Sissy go back inside and the laundry starts baking under the sun just like us.

I'm sanding and sanding, coughing as the dust gets in my parched lungs, when I hear something behind us.

"Here," says Mrs. Del Rosa.

We all turn around and she's standing there with her head barely above the top of the chain-link fence holding a plate, and on the plate are Italian sausages in buns with grilled onions smothered all over them. She holds the plate over the fence and we grab as fast as we can and start eating. I give Frankie a look, the recent vegetarian, and he holds up his sausage like he's making a toast.

"You're good boys. You're starving. Look at you—why, you have no meat on your bones. Your mama's a good lady. She works hard all day long. I'm not saying she's not a good lady, but you need more meat on your bones. Why, you're going to starve."

We don't say anything, not even thanks, we just keep eating. A few minutes later and miracle of miracles the Del Rosa's daughter, Teresa, comes over carrying a plate of hamburgers. I don't know what looks better—the hamburgers or her. She's the hottest thing in the neighborhood, in Nick's grade, and he's about the only guy in school who has the nerve to say a word to her because he's as big a deal as she is. While she's holding up the plate our eyes are glued to her, but hers are on Nick. Mrs. Del Rosa waddles off to sit with Mr. Del Rosa in their folding chairs, and she puts her feet in this kiddie pool right beside his. They sit there Saturdays with their feet in the kiddie pool reading the paper, eating all day long.

"You boys sure look hot," says Teresa Del Rosa. She's up on her toes for no reason I can gather, but it makes her taller and brings her closer, and her thigh muscles come on and off like beacons at sea.

"We sure are," I say.

"You make these?" says Tommy. Tommy's got it bad for Teresa, and he tries using his blue eyes to reel her in, but she's only looking at Nick.

"Me? I didn't make them," she says. "Papa did."

Nick's enjoying it, I can tell. The one guy in the whole world *she's* got it bad for, and he's playing it cool.

"They sure are good," I say. Teresa's one of the more developed girls you'll ever see, and since she's staring at Nick ignoring the rest of us, it's easy to appreciate that development without the worry of offending her.

"Are you going to swim later?" she says. She means in our pool, of course.

"Maybe," I tell her. "Why don't you come over?"

"She's not talking to you," Anthony says, all wise-guy-like.

"I'd probably come over if somebody asked me," she says. She's waiting for Nick, but he's not taking the bait.

"You can swim in our pool any time you want," I say. "You don't need to ask. Hell, you can swim in it right now while we're slaving away here. Won't bother us any. We'll be here another thirty hours—you might as well take advantage of the peace and calm while you can, before Squirt takes to it."

Nick finishes up his hamburger. The first sign he's the least bit flustered by the roller coaster ride before our eyes is the big hard swallow he takes on the last bite. Gets stuck in his throat and his eyes go red. I go to pat him on the back, you know, so he doesn't choke to death, and he shrugs me off.

"I might go later," he tells her in this wheezy, high-pitched voice. It goes great with the red, watery eyes.

Teresa Del Rosa doesn't bat an eye.

"Okay," she says, giving us serfs a nod and a smile. "Great."

She turns around and heads back inside, all of us following her with our eyes. We see the Del Rosas sweating in their chairs with their feet in the kiddie pool waving at us, and we wave back. Boy, they sure are good neighbors.

A couple more hours go by. Like sand through the hourglass, dear reader, like sand through the hourglass.

At some point—I've lost track of space and time—Sissy calls from the door of the family room for us to come in for lunch. Lunch? I figure it's dinner time by now. We drop the sandpaper and trudge inside. Tommy tries to trip Frankie from behind but Frankie catches himself and goes after him and they race around the pool. Anthony tells them to knock it off.

We sit down on the benches; there are five bowls on the table waiting for us. In the wink of an eye Sissy fills them with steaming-hot oatmeal. You might think she's being kind and considerate, having such sustenance ready to plop in our laps the second we come in, and I guess maybe she is. But she's what you might call part of the support network of this here work detail. It's her job to get us in and out of the house as fast as possible. Nobody had to tell her—it's not like Dad had to make a point of it. She understands her role just like we understand ours. We're a well-oiled human labor machine, yes we are, and damn proud of it.

We each get a hunk of bread on the side, along with a pickle wedge. You wouldn't think we'd be hungry since we just had the burgers and sausages not too long ago, but in our house when a meal presents itself you don't refuse. Even oatmeal and bread. Like lions on the old Serengeti, you never know when the next prolonged period of unexpected fasting might come along. The oatmeal isn't too bad this time, especially with the now-cooled powdered milk and three spoons of sugar on it. And the bread—Mom bakes the best on North Hill.

"Where's Mom?" Tommy asks, quite coincidently.

"At the store," says Sissy.

"With Squirt and Sally?"

She nods. "Britt went with them."

Jesus. The poor woman.

"How about Dad?" I inquire most casually.

"He went out with Sir Henry. I'm not sure where they went."

"Don't know when he'll be back?"

"He didn't say."

Well, of course he didn't *say*. But that doesn't mean she couldn't infer by the clothes he was wearing, what he and Sir Henry were talking about, how fast he scarfed down breakfast, whether Sir Henry put the wheelchair in the back of the station wagon or left it here, etc., etc. Sometimes I think she and Britt are living in another dimension. Makes me want to bang my head against the nearest telephone pole.

"How's Tony?" Tommy grins. We all grin. Well, not Anthony. He's staring straight ahead chewing the cud, having another mental sword fight between priest and soldier, I presume.

"Yeah," I chime in, "how's *Tony*? *Tony*."

Sissy shakes her head and rolls her eyes like Mom, like we're dumber than shit.

"Come on, guys," says Anthony. "Leave her alone."

"Tony. Tony."

"Tony's fine," she says all even-like. She's scrubbing the oatmeal pan at the sink, her back conveniently to us.

"How was the date?" Tommy asks.

"Fine."

"Just fine?"

"Fine."

"Oh," says Tommy, "I bet he's fine. I bet he's real fine."

"Did you see a movie, Sissy?" I ask.

"Not really," she says.

"What do you mean, *not really*?" says Tommy. "How do you *not really* see a movie?"

"We watched TV at his house," she says to me, not to the rapt audience in general. "But we didn't go to the movies."

"Tony better step it up," says Nick.

"That's right," Tommy tells him. "Our Sissy ain't going to put up with TV at the parents' house. You tell him that, Sissy? You tell him next time it better be a steak dinner *and* a movie at the movie theater?"

I see Anthony go psychedelic in the eyes staring out the window. We all see it and take a look ourselves. Wouldn't you know it, but Teresa Del Rosa's taken us up on the offer and is lying on the deck of the pool, *our* pool, in nothing but her teeny-weeny white bikini. And to think, sometimes I've doubted the existence of God.

On our way out the door we all give Sissy a kiss on the cheek. It makes her laugh, and that's a good thing.

We're back at the garage, using the 220-grit sandpaper so it'll pass Dad's eagle-eye inspection. The thing is, Dad knows exactly how long it takes to scrape, sand, wipe, and paint the garage. He probably calculated the time in his head last night in bed, you know, the way some guys think about where to take the kids on vacation. So, right there lies Teresa Del Rosa, the prettiest, ripest, most desirable peach for miles and miles, barely a stitch on, lying on *our* pool deck. But if we head over to even chat with her for a while, let alone change into our bathing suits and join her for a dip, Dad'll sniff it out like a French pig on the truffle trail.

Tommy takes us to the front of the garage, where neither she nor the Del Rosas can see us.

"Listen," he says. "Anthony, I know you're the oldest. I know you're Dad when Dad's not here. But, are you with us?"

"Am I with you doing what?" comes back Anthony, his glasses steamed up from his sweating head.

"Look, as long as we get the garage done, and done right, Dad should have no complaints. *You* should have no complaints; am I right?"

Anthony mulls it over, checking for loopholes in Tommy's succinct and thus far fairly accurate proposal. "Sure."

"All right, then. Here's what we do. We're not exactly working at a fast pace. We're not dogging it, but we can move faster and still maintain Dad's level of quality control. I say we go over in shifts, two at a time, so three are always working. All we have is some touch-up sanding, wiping down, and then painting to do. The three that work will work faster, but carefully, doing a good job. No messing around, no bullshitting. Just working our asses off. The other two will get fifteen minutes at a time. When the fifteen minutes is up, one person of the duo leaves and one person working replaces him. Fifteen minutes later, the next person leaves and another worker takes their place. We'll each get the same amount of time with her, thirty minutes, and we'll each work the same amount."

"Sounds reasonable," says Frankie. "We should start oldest to youngest, like we always do."

"Hey," I say, "That's not fair."

"Don't worry, slick, you'll have plenty of time with her," says Nick.

"But she might leave."

"She won't leave," he grins. "At least not before I get my time with her, and you'll be there for half of it."

Good point. We head back, and Anthony and Frankie, with smiles a mile wide, peel off this chain gang and climb up the ladder of the deck to chat up Teresa. The three of us get right to work. We finish the sanding, then start wiping down the whole thing with damp rags. As I'm dipping my rag into the bucket of muddy water, I see Teresa up on her elbows, Anthony and Frankie not an arm's reach from her loveliness. I don't think I've ever seen anything so sweet and spectacular in my life.

"Nick," I say. "You've been with girls."

"I've been with some," he says.

"What's it like?"

"What's what like?"

"You know," I say. "When you're with them. When you're, you know, with them."

Tommy chuckles. He chuckles even with a cigarette dangling from his mouth.

Nick, who's been with plenty of girls, thinks about it. "I don't know," he says. "It's pretty nice."

"Can't you describe it?"

"Not really," he says.

"How come?"

"You're slowing down," says Tommy. "We have to keep moving."

"I guess because it's not like anything else," says Nick. "How can I describe something that's not like anything else?"

"It's like jerking off," says Tommy. I can hear him sucking on his cig. The Del Rosas can see him smoking, but they'd never squeal on us. Not the poor sons of a cripple.

"No, it's not," says Nick.

"It's like jerking off, only softer," says Tommy. "Like you have a wet warm rag around you."

Nick makes a face. "It's not anything like that," he says.

Tommy, though he's older than Nick, hasn't had near the experience with girls that Nick has. Plus, Nick's a romantic. Which makes the next exchange between us sort of mystifying.

"Remember the night when we had tongue?"

"I remember," I say.

"Wasn't that the craziest, wildest thing you ever had?"

"It sure was."

"What if you had to describe it to somebody who's never had it before; how would you do it?"

"That'd be pretty tough," I tell him.

"Yeah," he says, "and why's that?"

"Because I don't know *what* it was like."

"There you go."

"What do you mean?"

"That's what it's like being with a girl."

"Tongue? You're saying being with a girl is like tongue?"

"I'm saying being with a girl is so crazy, so different, there's no way I can describe it to you. All I can tell you is that it *is* so crazy and different. And fucking great," he adds.

Somehow Nick's description, contrasted with the beautiful vision of Teresa Del Rosa up on the deck, doesn't make sense. I can't get the thought of those taste buds on the end of my fork out of my mind as I climb up the ladder to sit with Nick a while later, but when I see her bright, and fresh, and soft-looking, I understand what Dad might have felt the first time he saw Mom up close. I can see how a guy would do just about anything for a girl he had the hots for, and it strikes me how that could be a miracle or a curse, depending on a lot of things.

Nick's on the other side of Teresa. There's nowhere else for me to sit, except beside her. I leave some space between us, but her bare legs are only inches away from mine. She smiles at me. They're talking, but she turns and smiles, then turns back to Nick. She's got perfume on, and has these small dangly earrings hanging from her ears. Her dark hair is long and wavy, falling halfway down her back, which is tanned like the rest of her. I was the one talking to her before, but now I can't. She has suntan lotion on, and it mixes with her perfume and the natural sweat smell of her body into something spicy and exotic. I don't know what they're saying. They were talking about school, but now they're talking about something else, I don't know what, it's just muffled noise because my head's swimming. No, it really is, I mean it.

She turns to me, pointing, and I'm staring into her big brown eyes.

"So, you're a year apart?"

"Who, me?" I say.

She nods and when she does some hair falls into her face and she brushes it back, curling some around her ear. When she breathes the top of her bathing suit fills up, but it doesn't hold everything, and it's too much. I mean, it's really too much.

"Yeah," I hear Nick say.

"And you're the last boy?" she says to me.

"Second to last," Nick says. "Squirt's the last boy."

"That's right," she says. "I forgot about Squirt. He's cute. I like to watch him run around your yard."

"He's a regular riot," says Nick.

"There are so many of you. It's hard to keep all of you straight."

"Well, you know," I say, giving her a wink.

Nick raises his eyes in surprise. "Come again, slick?"

"He-he-he," I chuckle. "Our mom and dad are good Catholics."

She laughs some. "Very good Catholics."

"Me, not so much," I say.

Nick brings back his head, in greater surprise than before. Since Teresa's looking at me, she doesn't see.

"Is that right?"

"I mean, hey—I follow most of the main rules," I say. "Who wants to end up in eternal damnation, right? But I think there are a dozen or so that could be trimmed off and everybody'd be happier for it."

Nick leans forward so he's breathing on Teresa's shoulder. "Like what?"

"Like, I don't know, maybe not eating meat on Friday during Lent."

"How's that a problem?" says Nick. "We barely have meat once or twice a week as it is."

"But only because we can't afford any more. What if we were like your dad," I say to Teresa. When I look into her eyes I feel my throat get tight. "With all the steak and hamburgers and sausage he grills, I bet he'd love to have something other than fish sticks on a Friday night during Lent."

"He likes fish," she says. "Mom bakes salmon or we get an Emidio's pizza on Fridays during Lent."

"Sure, sure," I say, "but let's say he forgot what day it was and he was dying for a big juicy hamburger. You think God would care?"

She smiles, pleasantly, and looks down. "Oh, I don't know. We don't mind. I don't think those little rules are any big deal. They give you something to follow. Without them, I don't think most of us would know what in the world to do most of the time, especially when life gets hard." She looks up then, at me. "But I understand what you're trying to say, Puck, I do," she says, and touches her hand to my arm.

From the corner of my eye I see Nick. He's still leaning into Teresa like he wants to bust out laughing.

She asks if she can get in the pool and we tell her sure, swim to your heart's content. She turns around and goes down the ladder right beside me. She keeps her head above water for a while but then dives under, doing these slow dolphin-like moves where she comes up for a breath, then rolls gracefully back down with her feet together. Jesus, I think to myself, she's part mermaid.

"You should come in," she tells us as she hangs on the far

66

edge of the pool.

I give Nick a look. The temptation is severe, dear reader, oh it is. But there's no way we can do it. She looks so beautiful with the sunshine making the water sparkle all around her. She lets her legs float in front of her and starts kicking, slowly, just enough to make her whole body move side to side and up and down. Her breasts look they're going to roll right out of her top. I'm pretty much in a state of numbness sitting there watching her. She and Nick start talking again, but all I hear is this background noise, this buzz in my ears. I see birds in the sky flying way up there, circling the crescent moon, and then I hear voices all around me, like I'm at a baseball game and the crowd suddenly roars after a big play. I start coughing, choking on something I can't get out. Jesus, I think to myself, what's everybody looking at me for?

"Hey," I say like I'm coming out of a dream, "what are you guys doing?"

Nick's leaned over me, water dripping from his nose. He's all wet. He's all wet with his clothes still on.

"Puck," he says, worried-looking, but like he wants to laugh. "You fell in. You stood up and fell right in the pool."

The rest of them are there too, along with Teresa Del Rosa. She dips her hand in the pool and drips water on my face. She does that a few times. Everybody thinks it's funny as hell that I got up, passed out, and fell in the pool, except Teresa Del Rosa, who says she's glad I didn't drown.

Jesus and Me

Church is always a blast. We don't go to St. Martha's, which is only a block away; we go to St. Christopher's, where Mom went as a kid. It's halfway between our house and the Falls. We'd walk, but that would be a good distance to push Dad, especially over the uneven sidewalks. Plus, they have a special parking lot for him right beside the stairs. The ride is always a lot of fun with Mom chain-smoking up front, and however many of us are crammed in the back two seats. Sometimes the older ones like Anthony and Frankie and Britt go Saturday nights, or another service Sunday morning, and sometimes Squirt and Sally don't go and stay home with whoever's lucky enough to watch them. I'm not being *facetious*, you'll note. I'm a middle kid, which means I'm always there, holding my breath the whole way so I don't die of asphyxiation. There's nearly always some bickering between two of us, usually having to do with the lack of room and the infringement of someone's personal space, and by the time we get there Dad's mad as hell but has to switch gears real fast and file away his anger for later. We are at church, you know.

Nick gets out Dad's wheelchair, which is mashing me and Squirt in the very back. The wheelchair sort of sits on top of us the brief way there, but there's never any harm done unless Dad makes a sudden stop, and then you might get some metal to the temple. Sometimes we take him up in his wheelchair and sometimes one of the older boys carries him up, it just depends on who's there and what Dad wants to do. Today, it's the wheelchair. Dad slides aboard and then Nick wheels him to the bottom of the stairs leading up to church. I take hold of the footrests for support. Usually, one of the older boys would do it, but I was bumped up to footrest apprentice a few months ago. The way you take somebody in a wheelchair up a flight of steps is, the guy holding the grips goes up backward, while the guy holding the footrests steadies the chair. The important thing is that the footrest guy never *lifts* on the footrests. Lifting them only causes more weight and strain on the guy holding the grips, making it a lot harder. Other men offer to help sometimes, but none of us, including Dad, allows them to, unless there's only one of us Beck boys around. We could haul Dad up the Lincoln Memorial steps if we had to because we know what the hell we're doing.

We get him up and inside. All the cripples and various other people with sundry afflictions used to sit in the first couple pews, you know, like putting all the lepers in one place. I hated that, seeing Dad with all those people. It was pitiful and embarrassing and, let's be frank, humiliating for him. They changed things up, as they tend to do in the church every few hundred years, and now all the cripples and mental cases are peppered throughout the pews. We sit in the first pew, however, as a special place of honor and pity. From left to right, facing the altar, it's Dad, Sissy, Tommy, Nick, me, Mom, Squirt, and Anthony. Think about that order. Think about it long and hard, dear reader.

Today it's Father Nigh taking lead, with Father MacGregor, the pastor, as his sidekick. I'm glad it's Father Nigh, who I like. He's youngish, tall, balding, and loud. I don't mean loud in a bad way. There's good loud and bad loud. Father Nigh has a voice that projects; a deep, confident, and joyful voice. A voice that makes you listen and believe what he says. He likes kids, he likes a lot of what's happening in our generation, and he likes *me*, personally. Father MacGregor doesn't like squat, and because of it the two get along like oil and water, even though Father Nigh has the patience of a saint.

I'm sitting up straight, like we're all forced to, and I'm half listening to Father Nigh and half thinking, trying to stave off a coughing fit from the incense. Funny how I can feel people's eyes on the back of my head. I don't know whose they are at any given moment, but I know they're there. Could be the eyes of strangers, could be girls from school. Or adults Mom and Dad know but who're completely unknown to me. Their eyes aren't on us because we happen to be in the first pew, but because of Dad and our sorrowful situation. By now most of the congregation's heard about the garage. Add that cherry on top to the banana split of pity they already have for us and, well, it's a little hard to swallow. I want to slide down onto the floor and never get up. I mean, you don't know what it's like—the eyes of pity—constantly on you. And I don't just mean in the back of the head. It's way worse when they're right on you, face-to-face, usually adults, of course, because kids don't have much pity for anything. Well, except maybe some girls do. But the adults. After mass, there they'll be, coming up to Dad, leaning over, shaking hands, glancing down the line at us like we're a row of kittens waiting to be euthanized. Look, I get it. They're just trying to be nice, they have sympathy for us, which I guess is a good thing. But the last thing I need is pity or sympathy in the form of those sad, sorrowful mugs.

Father Nigh is talking, and I'm looking at the big crucifix up on the wall behind him. It's larger than life. Jesus must be twenty feet tall—a real giant image of pain, misery, and guilt. You're really going to hate me for saying this, but I don't see what the fuss is all about. They talk about how much Jesus suffered, how we need to feel guilty about it, like they know anything about real suffering. Christ—I'm living with a guy who lives in perpetual pain. Jesus had what—a day, an afternoon? Not decades. I don't mean any disrespect, I really don't, but come on. You have no idea. Come to our house when it's time to carry Dad upstairs, how about that? Or listen to him wail when you accidently bang into one of shins, you know, where those third-degree burns he got in the gasoline fire after the war never heal. Watch him struggle when none of the older boys are around to carry him up, as he inches his way upstairs on his own. How about the time he slipped on the ice walking from the car and broke his leg? Or the time he went flying down the stairs in his wheelchair and laid there until somebody found him a half hour later? His knee was on fire from infection, but he wouldn't go see a doctor. He couldn't afford it. The guy can't even sleep without hurting. He can't move. He has to lie on one side all night long. I could go on, but I'm sure you're bored. Maybe as bored as I am hearing about how Jesus suffered. People who swallow all that pain and guilt stuff don't know what real, perpetual agony looks like. What it *feels* like. I don't need Jesus. I've got Dad. I don't mean I don't love Jesus, I do. I think He's the shining light we all should aspire to be. But the guilt for His suffering, that's what I'm talking about. Why would I look to Jesus, who lived two thousand years ago, when I've got Dad as a constant reminder of how lucky I am? That's all the guilt I need and, honestly, all I can take.

Now, here's the thing that's really going to blow you away. I'd be sent to the nuthouse if anybody else knew what I'm about to tell you. Most nights as I'm lying in bed, looking up at the darkness of the ceiling to those cracks, barely visible at night, but they're there, like stars in the sky . . . I talk to Him. Jesus, I mean. I do, really, only I don't do it aloud, I do it in my mind. I have these dialogues with Him and Dad. The three of us are sitting in lawn chairs at this beautiful lake. The sun is shining, the temperature is perfect—not too hot to make Dad's shins hurt. Jesus hasn't been crucified yet. He doesn't know anything about it. We're under a willow tree. This grand giant of a willow shading us real nice. We have a small table with a pitcher of ice-cold lemonade on it, or sometimes iced tea. We talk about anything we want, anything that comes to mind. Nothing's off topic. Nothing's taboo. Around us, with BB guns in their hands, are the twelve apostles. They're facing outward like sentinels, making sure nobody and nothing interferes with us. Dad's more like he is with Mom, not the way he normally is with me. Jesus is like our brother and like our father. Sometimes I walk to the lake with

Dad, and other times I walk with Jesus. Whereas the church is all about judgement, He doesn't judge anything I say. He doesn't condemn me for anything I've done. All that's made up by men. He's not about any of that. He's someone you can reason with, and He only concerns Himself with the truth. When I'm with Him, I get a boost. He makes me want to be better and work harder and, well, just overall be who I know I should be. His acceptance frees me. The wall between me and Dad isn't there. It's Dad, Jesus, and me—a new triumvirate, a tangible trinity. The father, son, and Holy One. I walk with Jesus every night. Without it, I think I'd explode.

Of the Farm

Little did we know that painting the garage was a setup, mere practice, for the following week. Dad drives Frankie, Nick, Tommy, and me down to the Farm so we can help Uncle Ben paint his house. The evening before we go, me and Nick meet Teresa Del Rosa at the chain-link fence, on the far side of the garage where even her parents can't see us, on account of this sawed-off stubby tree. Evidently, the day at our pool hooked her and hooked her good. They do a little kissing, and whispering, and nuzzling some. You might wonder why I'm with them, but apparently Teresa requested my presence. I guess I'm some kind of chaperone. It sure is torture watching the two of them, though. I'd do anything to be in Nick's shoes.

Tommy's riding up front with Dad, while Frankie, Nick, Squirt, and me are behind them. Squirt's not staying with us at the Farm. Dad brought him along to get him out of Mom's hair for a few hours.

Dad's dinking with the hand break.

"Damn it, anyway," he says.

Squirt puts his chin up over the front seat.

"What's the matter, Dad, is it loose?"

"I don't know," he says to him. He keeps dinking with it, barely putting it on, then letting up, as we're cruising by the greenery beyond Akron.

"You'll have to have Sir Henry take a look at it."

"Yes," he says. "I will."

"It still works, doesn't it? We're not going to get in a wreck, are we?"

"No, son," he says. "It's just a little sloppy."

"Hell—I mean heck—sloppy's okay. Sloppy never hurt anything—did it, Dad?"

"Why don't you sit back, son," he says.

"Okay," says Squirt. "Hey—you're going over the speed limit, by the way."

"Thank you, son."

"Don't mention it, Dad. I don't want you getting a ticket."

"Why don't you sit back now."

"Yes, sir. I am. See?"

Squirt sits back and Nick gives him a look.

Sir Henry rigs up a hand break on whatever car Dad has at the time. It's this lever that sits right under the steering wheel and you push on it and it pushes down the normal break with a rod that connects all the way down. Sir Henry also puts a gas pedal on the left side, since Dad's right leg and foot are way worse than his left. It's attached with a bar to the accelerator. Sometimes Frankie or Nick use the hand break when they drive, just for kicks. I can't wait to get my license—that's the first thing I'm going to do when Dad's not around—try out the old hand break.

The Farm's over an hour away, past New Philadelphia but before Urichsville. There's not much out that way but fields of corn and some rolling hills. We get pretty close and Dad starts revving the engine of the station wagon. I can see that grin, as slight as it is, and he turns his head to Tommy and winks. We know what's coming. There's a series of hills and when you go over them fast, your stomach shoots through your chest and comes back down, and it's just like being on a roller coaster.

"Do it, Dad, do it!" Squirt tells him, about crawling onto the front seat.

"Get back, son," Dad barks at him, and he sits back.

He's got his foot to the floor and we're really flying. Up and over the first hill we go, and the car comes off the road maybe just an inch—but hey, we're airborne—and we come back down and the car bounces, jostling us around. He doesn't back down. He's gripping the steering wheel with that long, sharp nose almost to the horn; he doesn't let up one bit and we gather speed down to the bottom and back up—over the next hill. This time we come off nearly a foot and bang back down, rattling us inside the car like a bunch of caged monkeys. Dad's laughing, just laughing his ass off—he *never* laughs like this! Not even when Uncle Dale's telling his Korean War jokes. He's laughing and bobbing his head anticipating the next hill—the last one—like some cowboy riding the biggest, baddest bull on the ranch. We're whooping and hollering and waiting for the big one—a little tense, I admit, because Dad never goes this fast—and then zoom—away we go like some insane bunch of astronauts over the wide blue horizon—when suddenly Dad slams his hand on that hand break, does a shimmy-shimmy-shake right and then left nearly losing control along the gravelly opposite side of the road, and comes this close to plowing into an Amish buggy. We roar on by, and then I look back to see the horse rearing up kicking the air and those straw hats flying out the windows, and I imagine they're as surprised as we are. Dad looks like his eyes might pop out of his head and we laugh this nervous titter like a room full of old ladies.

"Don't tell your mother," he says a couple miles later.

The Farm sits all alone along this old road. It's white and plain looking. About the only sign of humanity, other than the Farm itself, is this black oil pump moving like a sloth up and down off to the right. That oil pump never moves too fast, but never stops either, just like time itself. Dad pulls the car up the gravel-and-grass drive and stops as it curves toward the barn, near the old wheel-shaped sharpening stone.

We climb out, get Dad in his wheelchair, and push him toward the house. You have to be real careful pushing him over grass or he'll go flying out of his chair.

Nobody gets up to greet us, but there they are, the three of them sitting in chairs under the maple tree just outside the back.

Uncle Ben, Aunt Sarah, and Aunt Franny. We say hello to them. Aunt Sarah, who has a humped back and is bent over real bad from arthritis, smiles her wide smile and looks up at us and seems about to cry from happiness, and Aunt Franny nods and smiles, but not nearly as much as Aunt Sarah. Uncle Ben does get up so he can bend down to shake hands with Dad, but then he sits back down in his chair. He's got one shoe with a four-inch heel on it to compensate for the shorter leg. He's the only man I know who uses crutches like Dad. They're wooden, not aluminum, and Uncle Ben can hobble around without them over short distances. There aren't any other chairs, so we stand there while Dad and the three of them make idle conversation.

After some time we go inside through the mud porch, where we'd normally take off our boots and hang up work clothes, but since nobody's dirty we pass on through to the kitchen. There's a sink to the right with a window overlooking the garden. The sink doesn't have a faucet because there's no running water in the house. They have electricity, but no water. You have to get water from the pump outside, near where we just were. They have a table set in the sitting room and we wheel dad to one end and then sit down. We say grace with our heads bowed and then start eating. We have fried chicken, sliced tomatoes, beans, homemade bread with butter and honey, and in the middle of the table sits a fresh-baked elderberry pie—my very favorite. We dig in and scarf down the meal like hungry wolves, barely listening to the adults chatting away.

We clear the table and then help Aunt Franny do the dishes. Tommy hauls in water with a metal bucket from the pump outside, careful not to spill any. The pump's the only source of drinking water at the Farm, so you don't play with the pump and you don't spill any water.

The adults sit in back under the maple tree and talk. There's a light breeze that makes all the trees come alive and pushes the long grass in waves like wheat fields. We head down to the creek, which is below the house some. It's not a big creek, but if it rains it'll widen pretty quick. Right now it's barely trickling. Some of that long-stranded algae trails with the current like green witch's hair. We look for crayfish under rocks and find some. Aunt Franny fries up the tails in butter when we catch enough, but we just let them go for now and decide we can always catch them again.

Squirt wanders downstream, too far for our comfort.

"Hey," Nick calls to him. "Stay where we can see you."

Tommy and Frankie pull out some cigarettes and start smoking, along with Nick.

"Look at him," says Frankie. "He's getting his shoes wet. Dad'll be happy about that."

"Hey!" calls Nick. "Take your shoes off or get out of the creek!"

Tommy's leaned back into the bank, surrounded by weeds. "This is the life," he says. "Yeah, this is the life, all right."

"Soak it in, man," says Frankie. "Take a mental picture of this for when you need a boost over in the jungle."

Tommy seems quieter than normal, like he's thinking about something but not sure about it. His blue eyes look past us to the hill and the tops of the old apple trees of the orchard.

"You afraid?" I ask him.

"Sure, he's afraid," says Nick.

"Are you, Tommy?"

"I don't really think about it," he says. He takes a drag from his cig, wincing as he sucks in the smoke, then blows it out the side of his mouth. "I guess I'm scared of the whole thing. Leaving home. Leaving you guys and going to boot camp."

"At least Dad prepared you for *that*," says Nick.

"Yeah, he sure did," says Tommy.

"Those Viet Cong are another story," Frankie says. "Dad's training might not do the trick for those guys. Keep your head low, and don't volunteer to lead the pack when you go out for a midnight stroll."

"You going to be able to write when you get there, Tommy?" says Nick.

"I guess I will," he says. "Sure, why not?"

"I'll write you, man. I'll send you whatever you want."

"Send me a lock from Brigitte's hair," Tommy jokes.

"From her head?" Frankie says.

"Surprise me."

"I'll write you too," I tell Tommy. "You're going to be okay. You're the best shot in the family. You're going to be all right, Tommy."

He takes a drag, winces, and nods at me.

"Hey, Tommy, can I ride your bike while you're gone?" Nick asks him.

"Have at it," Tommy says, swinging his arm out wide. "Ride it. Take it. It's yours. All you guys can ride it."

Nick takes the cigarette from him. "Thanks, man."

"Hey," I say to Tommy. "Where do you and Anthony go when you ride your bikes? You never say."

"We just ride, man," he says. "We don't have anywhere in mind."

"You go all over Akron?"

"We go wherever we want, wherever our turn signals want to go." Tommy's talking the way Frankie talks now, which seems strange coming out of his mouth.

"Do you go to Fairlawn and the Falls?"

"We go everywhere, Puck. The bikes take us everywhere."

"Out to Mogadore and Portage Lakes?"

"We've been everywhere on them," he says.

"Yeah," I say to him. "Think about that, Tommy, when you're over there. Think about riding your Honda when you come home again. You can go anywhere you want, even out of Ohio."

"Sure he will," says Frankie. "He's going to take an epic trip to the Wild West and beyond. After Vietnam, there'll be nothing holding this guy back."

Frankie pulls out a harmonica from his pocket. He fiddles around some, then starts playing *Git Along Little Dogies*. Tommy, who's got the best voice in the family, sings along. The thing is, pretty soon Frankie starts changing the lyrics and it turns into *Eat Some Tongue if You're Hungry*, with one of the lines going, *You know that those tastebuds will make us all groan.* Me and Nick just listen, we're all cracking up, and as I'm listening I try

78

and imagine what it's going to be like for Tommy over in Vietnam. I think of all the images I've seen on TV and in the paper. I know how Frankie and Sissy feel about it, and most kids our age. But I'm not thinking of that—I'm thinking of the danger. I watch Tommy singing and making up lyrics. He's the smoothest, most carefree guy around. What's Vietnam going to do to somebody like him?

We hear the old cowbell ringing and head up. Squirt's not staying with us, but then we find out Tommy's not staying either. We unload the painting gear, then help Dad into the car and load the wheelchair in back. Squirt gets the whole second seat to himself and lies down with his hands behind his head and writhes around like he got zapped with a cattle prod. Jesus, what a little freak. We say so long to Tommy and wave as the station wagon backs onto the road, then pulls forward and heads off. Dad gives the honk—four dits, then two more—which is Morse code for *hi*. We stand and wave until they disappear over the rolling hills.

It's not all the way light when Uncle Ben calls for us. We're in the barn on some hay in sleeping bags. The cows are on one side of the barn, we're on the other. We go inside and breakfast is ready at the kitchen table. Breakfast isn't like at our house. Our plates are stacked with sausage, eggs, bacon, fried potatoes, with bread and jam on the side.

Aunt Sarah has her eyes on us the whole time. She looks at us with that smile and long gray hair pulled back in a bun, her body bent to the right side. She's so small and shrunk down, her head barely comes above the table. There's something about her. Seems like light could come from her any second. You know how there are people who don't have to say anything, who have light in their souls so plain and obvious it seems to shoot right out their bodies? Well, that's how it is with Aunt Sarah.

After breakfast we walk around the house a couple times and decide to start in back first. It doesn't look like it needs as much scraping, and we figure we can get away with going straight to the 220-grit sandpaper when it's time to sand. Uncle Ben comes out on his wooden crutches. He wears a white long-sleeved shirt with the sleeves rolled up his forearms and old-looking trousers.

"You boys look like you know what you're doing. Got it all figured out?"

"I think we know what to do," says Frankie.

"You need anything, let me know. Lunch is at twelve o'clock. Just go on in."

He heads to the outhouse, about thirty yards from the house beyond the garden, with a small roll of newspapers tucked under his arm. That's what you use in the outhouse, newspapers. You sure as hell don't *read* the paper. It smells so bad in there, you get in and get out as fast as you can.

Frankie says we should prep one side at a time, top to bottom. I'm not too keen on heights, plus I'm the youngest and have the least amount of experience, so Frankie does most of the high ladder stuff. He's up on the extension ladder, Nick's on the old rickety wooden ladder doing the middle stuff, and I'm down in the underworld doing the low work. We scrape, sand, and wipe down the back, then move to the north side. It's shady there, which is good because it's heating up. We're about halfway done with the north side when we head in for lunch. I'm starved. On the kitchen table are ham-and-cheese sandwiches, potato salad, bread and butter, and lemonade.

Uncle Ben, Aunt Sarah, and Aunt Franny sit with us. There's only the sound of a fly buzzing against the screen and a car passing by every few minutes. We're so hungry, we don't think to talk. When we're finished we start cleaning up, but Aunt Franny says she can do it, and we head back outside.

We finish the north side, then move to the west, the side facing the road. It gets more weather and the siding is a lot worse off. There's a lot more scraping and sanding to do. We're not nearly done when Uncle Ben tells us dinner's ready. We have pot roast, potatoes, green beans, and bread and butter. Uncle Ben has a single bottle of beer.

"You boys drink beer?" he asks.

I'm afraid to even move.

"No, sir," says Nick.

"You want to try it?"

The three of us look at one another. Hell yeah, we say without saying.

Aunt Franny goes to the icebox and gets three bottles of beer and opens them with a bottle opener by the sink, then sets them in front of our plates. Uncle Ben doesn't say anything or act like it's a big event. We drink the beer. It's the worst-tasting stuff I've ever had. It's worse than liver and onions. It's even worse than tongue.

"You boys like baseball?" Uncle Ben asks us.

"I do," says Nick.

"Me too," I say.

"I like baseball. I don't follow football so much, but I listen to baseball games now and then."

He takes a sip of beer and sets the bottle on the table, leaving his hand around it. Aunt Sarah sits to his left, small and shy, holding up her head with her arthritic hand, looking at us, smiling.

"God bless you," she says quietly. I don't know if she's talking to herself or to us.

We walk over the hill into the old orchard and sit down, each of us leaning against a different apple tree. The breeze is nice and sweet-smelling. It's hot still, but the breeze takes it away some. The apple trees are broken and withered. Their trunks are rotted. There are some small apples on the limbs, some time from being ready to pick, but I don't think Uncle Ben sprays them anymore; they'll be full of worms. It's a sad place, but it feels good. I think of how Mom used to sit here, when it was tended and a bright place. And Gram, before her, not long after arriving from Italy, sat here too with Grandpa when they were courting. We sit and let the breeze blow over us, and then later we go back to the house and they want to play euchre, and we do. Since we play it all the time we have to ease up and lose on purpose, but it's nice to be where we came from, and we go to bed before dark, watching the swallows come and go through the big open barn door.

The next day we're sanding when these walkers come along. Two guys and two girls. They're hippies. They have backpacks

81

over their shoulders, long hair, and clothes that look like they haven't been washed in weeks. They smell too. They're wearing beads around their necks and strange-looking floppy hats. Their faces are burnt, with deep-set, hungry eyes.

They ask if we have any water, and so we take them around back and pump water into the tin cup, careful not to spill any, and they drink it like they haven't had any all day. They're traveling from New Hampshire, mostly thumbing rides, but walking when they have to.

"We'd sure appreciate anything you could offer," says Matt, the shorter of the two guys.

"You look starved," says Frankie. "Let me ask my uncle. I bet we can give you something."

It's close enough to quitting time, so we help Aunt Sarah and Aunt Franny fix dinner. Uncle Ben wakes up from his rocking chair to the smell and noise and walks over on his wooden crutches, sits down, and doesn't seem surprised at the strangers at the table. He smokes his pipe, which smells like apples, and listens, upright and rigid, only moving his head.

"Pennsylvania was rough," says Matt. "We couldn't get rides through much of it. We had to walk a lot more than we thought we would. Ohio's been good so far. It's been hot, though. This is the best meal we've had in a week," he says. "I can't tell you how wonderful it tastes. It's like we've come to the Promised Land already. Bless you, brothers and sisters." He looks to each of us, and so do his friends. "Bless you all for your kindness and spirit of generosity."

"Where are you headed?" asks Frankie.

"California, man," says the other guy, whose name is Paul. He's taller, thinner, with cheekbones that jut out like elbows from his face.

"That's a long way to be thumbing," says Frankie.

"We'll get there soon enough," he says. "Lord willing, we'll meet folks like you just when we need it. It's all planned out. *We* don't know the plan, but He does."

"What's going on out there, in California?" I say.

The girl beside me, Karen, who seems about my age, says,

"What's out there? What's out there are people like us. California is where souls fly free as birds, you know? The true land of milk and honey. Where nobody gets uptight and nobody tries to put you in a straitjacket."

"Where freedom's really freedom," says Matt. "Where dreams aren't dreams anymore, but reality. Can you dig that? It's like here, in this wonderful, glorious house, without the thumb of governmental power. It's beautiful there. It's really beautiful."

We were going to get baths tonight, but it's obvious they need them more than the three of us. Aunt Franny has us take the big metal tub into the grass, between the house and the garden. We have two buckets, and me and Nick, we're pumping water into them and dumping the water into the tub, and when it gets about half full Karen undresses and sits down in it. The three of us go to leave, when she tells us there's no reason, that that's what they mean about real freedom, and so we get more water and dump it into the tub between her crossed legs.

"Sorry, but it would take hours to heat up enough water for all of you," Aunt Franny says, surprisingly casual about the naked girl. It's cold enough to make Karen laugh and shout some, and then the other girl, Linda, starts undressing and Aunt Franny says we should go inside and give them privacy.

"You don't have to do that," says Matt, "but we appreciate your concern. Thank you."

We're helping with the dishes, but I'm still in shock. I've seen some pictures Anthony has, and we have Brigitte, but I've never come close to seeing an actual naked girl before. It's like I don't know how to process it in my brain. Karen was just a plain girl in ratty clothes until she took them off, and then it was like bringing a birthday cake out of a box.

Aunt Franny says they can sleep in the barn with us for the night, and tomorrow she'll drive them into town, where they'll have a better chance of getting a ride. We get settled in, but nobody wants to go to sleep. We gave them some of our clothes to wear overnight, even the two girls, who are wearing our shorts and shirts, so Aunt Franny can wash theirs. She's going to wash the clothes in their backpacks too.

"Tell me more about California," Frankie says to them. "Have you been there?"

Matt nods. He looks younger with wet hair and his face clean and beard combed, wearing my T-shirt and jeans. "I've been there before," he says. "It's beautiful, man. Winters are mild and summers are just right. Mellow and vibrating with cosmic truths. The people are out of this world. They seem like they might be from another planet; they might as well be. No squares allowed. You'd really dig it."

"You going to San Francisco?" Frankie says.

"Where else?"

"Wow," he says. "Far out."

"You should come with us, man," says Matt.

"Yeah," says Linda, who's wearing Nick's football jersey. "Come along. I think you need to."

Frankie rubs his chin, grinning. "Wouldn't that be something. But I don't know how I'd swing a thing like that."

"Put one foot in front of the other," says Matt. "That's all there is to it. Don't think, just do. Don't think, just be, just love, just create and let go. San Fran's waiting, man."

Karen takes hold of my hand, leans into my ear, and says, "Come on."

We go up these wooden steps nailed to the side of the barn to the upper level.

"You guys be careful," calls Frankie.

"It's cool, man," I hear Paul say. "They'll be all right."

We sit in the hay together and don't say much. It's vast, like church, but the shadows are dark and deep and full of more mystery than church. It smells of wood and animals and hay. It's like we've ascended to some mythical place. We look around, amazed, afraid in some way. At least I am.

Then Karen leans into me and nuzzles around a little, waiting, moving her lips near mine until I finally kiss her, and she kisses back slow but determined, like Teresa Del Rosa did with Nick behind the garage. I've kissed girls, but just pecks, and not with our bodies pressed so close. I'm embarrassed she'll feel how excited I am. Whenever she tries really pressing her full body

84

against me I keep her away, or stop altogether.

"What's the matter?" she says.

"Nothing," I tell her.

"Don't you want to?"

"Sure," I say, "but aren't you with one of them?"

"Not the way you think about it," she says. She puts her hand to my face. "Hey, relax. Everything's cool. It's really okay. It's just you and me here. There's nobody else. This is our time under the stars. It's not about anybody else. Just you, and me, and now. Let yourself go."

I don't understand. Her answer excites me, but makes me feel sad too.

She starts kissing me. She moves her leg over mine, then swings herself on top of me. I hear her make this small gasp. I'm too embarrassed.

"I can't," I tell her.

"But why?" She's kissing me and moving against me.

"I have a girlfriend," I say.

"You do?"

"Yeah."

"But she's not here," she says.

"I know, but I can't," I say. "I wouldn't feel right."

"But don't you see—it *is* all right. She's not here. But I am."

"But it isn't right."

"Don't tell me you're a square."

"No," I bristle. "I'm not a square."

"Then I don't see what the big deal is. You like me. I like you. It's a beautiful summer night. It's perfect."

Her fingers stroke the side of my temple as she waits. Her smile hasn't left. It's like everything, no matter what happens, is wonderful.

"I'm sorry," I tell her.

"Don't be sorry," she says. "Don't ever be sorry, about any-thing." She looks at me with her big hopeful eyes.

She keeps trying, but it's no use. I don't respond to her kisses, and she finally rolls off. We lie back in the hay. I watch her body, peripherally, as it moves up and down to her breathing. I reconsider, I'm half inclined to roll on top of her, but I resist. She takes my hand and a while later I fall asleep.

We get up early the next morning and start sanding. They don't get up until around 10:00. They head in wearing our clothes, and then come out an hour later after having breakfast wearing theirs. Nick and Frankie come down from the ladders to say goodbye, but I keep on working. They're all together hugging and shaking hands, but I stay where I am. Frankie calls me over and I tell him I'm good, we need to catch up, and I keep moving the block of sandpaper against the siding as I'm getting poked by the big lilac bush. I see Karen from the corner of my eye looking my way, but she doesn't come over. She gets in the car with the other three, and Aunt Franny backs the car onto the road, and then drives off.

"Hey," Nick says after they're gone. He hits me on the arm with his glove. "What gives?"

I can't tell them. I can't tell them how good she felt. I can't tell them how free she was and what she wanted from me. I can't tell them how much I wanted to, but how I couldn't, how I moved her hand away time and again until she finally gave up. I can't tell them because they wouldn't understand. All I could think about was Dad. I couldn't do it because I swore to Jesus that I wouldn't. I swore I wouldn't until Dad's legs got better. I was talking to Him not long ago about why Dad's legs hadn't been healed, even though all of us pray for it every night. Jesus was unusually quiet, and didn't respond. It made me think harder. It occurred to me that He wanted me to figure it out for myself. I thought of Abraham and what he was willing to sacrifice. I didn't have anything like that to offer in return for a miracle. The only thing I had was the thing I think about all the time. The thing I wonder about. The thing that frightens me. The biggest mystery known to man. So I promised I wouldn't allow myself the pleasures of being with a girl in exchange for Dad's legs getting better. If I keep my promise, Dad's legs might heal. No, I'm sure of it. It's nothing like what Abraham had to forfeit. If I can't do it, then what kind of a son am I? I couldn't tell Karen that. She'd have thought I was crazy. No one talks to Jesus. How could I, in a matter of a few minutes, convince her that I do? And Frankie and Nick—they'd really think I lost it. They'd just laugh. I hope Jesus will forgive my lie about having a girlfriend. It was the only way I could keep my promise, the only way Dad will ever walk again.

It takes two more days to finish the house. Dad and Anthony come to pick us up in the evening. They stay for dinner, we have fried chicken, and then head home. Uncle Ben, and Aunt Sarah, and Aunt Franny, they live in another world. I wish I could live in their world, but I know I'd miss North Hill. I wonder what'll happen to Karen and her friends when they get to California. I think about it all the way home.

A Bummer Night

We're eating corn on the cob. We each get one ear, though Dad gets more if he wants it, and so does Tommy. Along with the corn we're having vermicelli. Between the pot of hot water for the corn, the pot of hot water for the vermicelli, and the pot of sauce that's been cooking all day long, the kitchen's a Swedish sauna, just plain miserable. Nobody wants to rub against anybody else, but that's impossible, and there's some bickering going on, putting the old scowl on Dad's mug.

I try to liven things up a bit.

"I caught two green snakes behind Jennings School," I say.

"Oh, God," says Sissy. "You didn't bring them in *here*, did you?"

"Sure, I did," I tell her. "You don't want to see them?"

"Dad," she about shouts, looking his way for help.

"He didn't bring them in the house," Dad says.

"Can I see?" Squirt starts to get up, but then Dad gives him the look.

"They're in a box out in the garage," I tell him. "I'll show you after we eat."

Nick sucks in big air, then burps. The man's got guts.

"Dad," Sissy says.

"Sorry," Nick says, putting his fist to his mouth to stifle a

88

laugh.

"We are half German," says Tommy. "Burping's a way to pay a compliment in Germany."

"How about if the other half uses proper manners," says Mom, giving her sarcastic wince.

"Anybody see my other riding glove?" says Anthony.

"Where'd you leave it?" I ask him.

"Well, if I knew that I wouldn't be asking, would I."

"Is it black?" asks Sissy.

"Yeah."

"I saw something black floating in the pool."

"Did you get it out?" Anthony knows he can't get up from the table to check. He's all panicky.

"I thought a squirrel fell in," she says.

"So you left a poor drowning squirrel in the pool?" says Tommy.

"I wasn't going to touch that thing."

"Could've been a rat," I say. "I saw one last week by the trash cans."

"It wasn't a rat," says Dad. "Tommy and I shot them all. There were only two."

"Good job, Tommy," I tell him.

"Great vermicelli, Mom," says Frankie. "Delish."

"I'm glad you like it," she says.

"Best pasta on North Hill," says Gram, wagging her fat finger.

Mom reaches out her hand for Frankie's plate. His pithy compliment was code for more vermicelli.

Britt walks in all office-looking with her skirt and bag and bright clothes. She kisses Mom, then leans down to kiss Dad. Everybody on the bench nearest to Gram scoots down to make room. Britt sits down sideways, legs crossed, and Mom gives her a piping-hot plate of vermicelli and an ear of steaming corn.

Britt clears her throat. She looks like she could cry any second.

"Mom, your car just rolled down the drive," she says, digging her teeth into the corn. It's a diversionary tactic; well played, sis.

"Oh, that's not my car, honey," says Mom, who's lit up a cig to add to the general lack of breathable air in the place.

"I think it is." Britt doesn't lift her mouth when she says it, and her eyes stay down like a dog who's just peed on the rug.

"Honey, my car is in the driveway." Mom blows smoke out the side of her mouth, casual, unconcerned. I hold my breath until the cloud passes.

"I think it is," Britt says weakly.

By now Dad's stopped eating. He thinks for a second, then looks to Britt sitting beside him.

"Sorry," she says, then bursts into tears.

"Don't blame her," says Gram with some resolve and authority. "It not her fault. She been working all day. You no get mad at her!"

Anthony gets up and looks out the window.

"Fuck," he says, and he runs out the door. Some of us get up to follow him.

"Sit down," says Dad, his anger not quite up to speed with his shock. "Tommy, Frankie, go out and help Anthony."

Mom, who'd turned for the briefest of seconds to see her 1965 Chevy Impala no longer in the drive, swings back around, eyes squinting as she sucks on that cigarette for all it's worth. I can see her starting to tear up.

"It nobody's fault," says Gram with her stubby finger in the air. She seems to be talking to Dad. "It was accident. That's life. I hope to Jesus no one was hurt, except maybe that Lennie. If the car roll down the driveway and kill him, ah, the world is better off."

Dad keeps chewing the corn. He's got a kernel on his lower lip and I want to flick it off for him, I really do, but I'm afraid to put my hand near him.

The boys come in.

"It hit a tree in the lot across the street," says Anthony.

"Anybody hurt?" says Dad, who turns back because he can't quite see him.

"No, sir."

"Did it hit another car?" He's still got that piece of corn on

90

his lip.

Anthony shakes his head. "No."

"Praise the Lord," says Mom, who, though quite the follower of Catholic doctrine, isn't one to use such expressions in normal conversation.

"See?" says Gram. "See—what's the big deal? It just a car. You have Henry bang it out. No big deal. Nothing to worry about."

Dad rubs his face and the kernel falls off. Since it doesn't look like Anthony's going to sit back down, Squirt asks the obvious.

"You want your piece of corn, Anthony?"

"What the hell?" say Nick.

"Watch your mouth," says Dad.

"I know," says Nick, "but he's got his own piece. Anthony's not finished."

"It's all right," says Anthony. "Go ahead, Squirt. You can have it."

Squirt grabs the cob off Anthony's plate. Gram folds her arms over her chest like she's enjoying a show. She starts laughing, but puts her hand to her mouth. She darts her head around the table like a bird.

"Look," she says. "He's starved. The car roll down the driveway—ha!—what does he care? They starved. Your kids are starved, Catarina."

I look back at Mom. She's flicking her front teeth with her thumb. Seems like she's a million miles away.

"I quit," she says.

She takes her cigarette, grinds it into the counter next to the sink, then drops it into the paper bag on the floor with all the corn husks in it.

"What do you mean, Mom?" says Squirt.

"I mean I quit," she repeats. "I'm done. I've had it."

"What are you quitting, Mom?" he says. "You mean smoking—are you going to quit smoking?"

She wipes away these tears made black by her mascara. "No," she says real weak-like.

"I wish you would quit, Mom," says Squirt. "Sure would be a lot easier to breathe in here."

She wipes her hands on a rag and then, with most of us looking while chewing on corn, she goes out the side door. Gram's still darting her head around, but now she seems confused. I know how she feels. I know Mom's upset about her car rolling down the drive, but I don't quite follow what she means. I'm not sure what exactly she's quitting.

Mom's car is mangled in back, but nothing Sir Henry can't fix. The bumper's pushed in, the back windshield's smashed, and there's some scratches all over from the tree branches. I feel real bad for Mom. The car's the one thing that seems to make her feel like she's not a mom and maybe some actress in a movie. She goes out sometimes just to drive it on the freeway up to the Falls, where she grew up. She told me how she rides by her old house and cruises through the old neighborhood, just thinking of how things used to be for her. The car's about the only thing, other than maybe her clothes and jewelry, that's hers and nobody else's.

Dad has all us boys come out into the drive. He doesn't say much, but he's got the big scowl. He has Anthony put a chair in front of him, and he's got the electric clippers that Britt brought out. He doesn't give us lickings anymore, we're too big for that, except for Squirt. He switched to buzz jobs a couple years ago. It doesn't hurt as much as a licking, but the effects last a whole lot longer. The humiliation is there for everybody to see instead of being hidden on your butt or the back of your legs.

He starts with Anthony, and it's no big deal for him because he likes it short anyway. Tommy goes to sit down, but Dad says he's not getting one. We all drop our jaws in shock. Frankie's next. Well, things get interesting. Frankie doesn't sit down directly.

"Come on, Dad," he says a few feet away from the chair. "How about if we talk it over."

"Sit down," he says.

"But I'm not twelve, man," he says. "I'm in college, for Christ's sake."

"What did you say?"

"Look, why're you doing this? What'd we do? Mom was the one who didn't put the break on—not us. Why do you want to make us look like freaks?"

"I said sit down," Dad says, about as mad as I've seen him in a while.

"No," says Frankie, not looking him in the eye, but nearly so.

"Get your butt over here," Dad says.

"I'm sorry, man, but this is bullshit. This is—this is some crazy bullshit. I know you're upset. Mom's upset. Everybody's upset. I'm sorry about the car, but none of us did it. *Mom* did it. We all know that. It's called an accident, an *accident*, Dad. Everybody makes mistakes, it happens to everybody. I mean, do you hate us? Why would you want to do this unless you hated us?"

Dad, like he didn't hear a thing Frankie said, nods to Anthony, who comes on over. Anthony calls for Tommy. Tommy comes over and they chase Frankie around Mom's car. They finally get hold of him and bring him to the chair. By now everybody's out from the kitchen—Sissy, Britt, and Squirt. Mr. and Mrs. Del Rosa are at the chain-link fence holding it with their fingers, along with Teresa. Even Buzzy's standing in the gap in the hedges with her mom, who rarely lifts herself out of her chair for anything. They're all looking, and so are me and Nick, standing right there.

"Set him down," Dad tells Anthony and Tommy.

Frankie struggles hard, they can't handle him, and Dad tells Nick to help.

I look up at him. I'm pleading inside for him not to do it. I don't want him to disobey Dad, because that'll put *him* in more hot water than Frankie, but he just can't hold Frankie down. He can't. Not Frankie.

Nick walks with his head down to stand in front of him, then slowly lifts it to look Frankie in the eyes. Frankie's not struggling anymore, but waiting to see what Nick will do.

Nick puts his hands on Frankie's shoulders. You can see him fighting with himself, you can see he doesn't want to. He's gentle and has the saddest eyes for Frankie.

"I'm sorry, man," he says.

"Nick," I say. "Don't."

Dad gives me a harsh look. I know I'm in for it, but I don't care. I don't understand. I don't understand why Dad's forcing them to do it.

Frankie goes limp. Tommy and Anthony do most of the holding, but they know Frankie's given up and they look past him at each other sort of snickering, like it's all some big joke. Dad shears Frankie extra rough, extra short. He had this personality in front to compensate for the short sides and back, and he looked cool, just like all the other kids his age. Now it's all gone. He's a freak. I make sure I watch it all. I have to see it.

Dad motions for me next and tells Anthony and Tommy to hold me down. I sit without being forced and try and shake off their hands, but they keep their grip on my arms.

"You guys are real tough," I say. "Wow."

"You tell them!" I hear Buzzy call from the hedges. "Fascists!"

"What's next—pinning old men to the ground for spitting on the sidewalk?"

Just like with Frankie, Dad seems to do it rough on purpose. I get nicked a couple times but I don't let on. I hear Sissy gasp and I know I'm bleeding.

When Dad's finished I stand up, wrenching my arms from the two thugs in my own family. I turn around, glaring at them.

"You enjoy that, boys? Well, that's the last time you ever lay a hand on me. Next time either of you do, you're going to wake up with a baseball bat to the head. Got it?"

They start coming toward me but I don't wait. I don't want anyone, especially them, to see me lose it and I run inside and up to the third floor.

Looking for Mom

I wake up the next morning and feel the back of my head. It has this constant breeze on it now. Nick's awake, but Anthony and Tommy aren't there. Squirt's sleeping with his chin over the side of the bed, getting wayward gusts from the fan.

"Mom's not back yet," says Nick. He looks different now with his sheared head, like some kind of big insect.

I don't answer right off because I'm still ticked at him, but then I do. "Where is she?"

"I don't know. Nobody knows. Anthony and Dad and Tommy are out looking for her."

"But I don't get it," I say. "Why isn't she back?"

"Things are bad," says Nick. "Dad's selling the boat. Did you know that?"

"But why?"

"Don't you know how bad things are?"

I shrug. "I don't know. I guess."

"He's trying to keep things going at the garage, but he can't pay anybody—so they all left. Sir Henry's the only one that stuck around. It's just Sir Henry and Dad, and Dad can't do much. Sissy's helping them."

"Fixing cars?"

"She calls people. She's trying to get business. Plus, they

need more help and she's trying to find mechanics. Hey," he says.

"What?"

"There was nothing I could do. What did you expect me to do?"

I don't say anything. He looks just as bad as me and Frankie.

"Where's Frankie?"

"Out in the bus."

"Did you talk to him?" My eyes dart up to his head.

"He's all right, Puck. It's just hair. It grows back."

"If it's just hair, then why did Dad have to cut it off?"

Nick looks more than miffed. "You take things too personally."

I shake my head to myself. I don't get him sometimes. "You think Mom will come back today?"

"Who knows?"

"Did they call anybody? Maybe she went to visit Aunt Myrtle."

"Britt and Sissy called around. Nobody knows where she went. Nobody knows where she is."

"I want to go look for her," I say. "Come on."

"Britt wants us to stay here."

"Did Dad say that?"

"Well, Britt did, so Dad'll back her up."

"Aw, I don't care," I tell him. "What else can Dad do to me? I'm too old for the belt."

"You want to bet?"

"Frankie will help find Mom. Let's go see him."

We go out and I knock on the door to the VW bus. It takes him a while, but Frankie opens the door.

"What are you doing?" I ask him.

"Drawing," he says.

"What are you drawing?"

"I'm drawing a self-portrait," he says, and he shows me a couple pages from his sketchbook. The drawings aren't like the other sketches he does. The lines are thick, like he bore down on the pencil. His head looks like an egg with dots on it where his

96

stubble is. "Pretty fucking nice, isn't it," he says with that sarcasm of his.

"Yeah," I tell him.

"You want to help look for Mom?" says Nick.

"I don't think I want to talk to you," Frankie says. "Come back in a year or two."

"I didn't have a choice," says Nick.

"You always have a choice," he says.

"You could have told Dad no," I say to Nick. "You stood up to Lennie."

"Lennie's not my dad. Lennie's not about to lose his house."

Frankie, intentionally turning away from Nick, says to me, "Any idea where she went? Out of the country, if she's smart."

I tell him what I know and he grabs a pack of cigarettes and his wallet, locks the door to the bus, and we head out. Only thing is, we don't know where to look. Everybody's been called already. Sure, she could be at one of those places anyway, you know, laying low, but Mom wouldn't tell somebody to lie and say she wasn't there when she was. Most likely she went somewhere on her own. We're heading west on Tallmadge, then stop by the filling station to think about it. We ask Jack, the guy who runs it, if he's seen her. He's rubbing an oily rag against his hand, thinking.

"Not lately, boys," he says. "She came in a few days ago and got gas. But I haven't seen her today." He grins looking at our heads. "What'd you guys do this time?"

We act like we don't hear him and start walking again.

"Where could she go that's open all night?" says Nick.

"A coffee shop, maybe," says Frankie.

"Mom doesn't go to coffee shops," I say.

"A bar, but they close at one or two."

"A *bar*," I say to him. "Mom?"

"Yeah, a *bar*," he says.

"Why would she go to some bar?"

"Same reason anybody goes to a bar," says Frankie.

"Mom's not some drunk," I say, all snide-like.

"Come on, man," says Nick. "Let's go downtown. That's

where she goes in her car sometimes. She likes to go to the Loew's Theatre with Aunt Myrtle."

"Yeah, I don't see Mom spending all night at the movies," says Frankie.

"Well, it beats standing here. We can search North Hill and the Falls, but that's a lot of territory. I say she went downtown. Shopping makes her feel good. Maybe that's what she's doing."

We cross the street and start walking backward, trying to thumb a ride. We turn on Main, and not long after some young guy in a pickup stops. We jump in the back and he heads over the viaduct that connects North Hill with downtown over the Little Cuyahoga River, and once we're across we pile out.

"Thanks, man," says Frankie, and he gives him the peace sign, then me and Nick do too.

Downtown's bustling pretty good and it's exciting to be there. People stare at us, and it takes me a second to realize it's our bald heads. I'd rather be naked than walking the streets with this buzz job. We cup our hands to windowpanes of shops on our way to the Loew's, but when we get there we aren't allowed in to look for her. Nick tries chatting up the girl at the ticket booth, but she sneers at him like he's some creep. Mom's probably not in there anyway.

While we're standing under the marquee of the Loew's, Frankie hits Nick in the shoulder soft and playful, like he wants to really pound on him and like he really doesn't, and Nick opens his arms to the clouds like he's saying *Take me, man, I deserve it.* Nick says he has a few dollars, so we stop in Harry's Diner, which is this old railroad car turned into a restaurant. We slide into a booth and hand the waitress the pile of dirty dishes left there from the people before us, and we only get Cokes, but Nick buys Frankie a doughnut to partially make up for helping Dad skin his head. The place is dirty and clean at the same time and it reminds me of the third floor. There's a jukebox at the far end, but we don't have the money and just flip through the songs at our table. There's only one small AC in the corner by the cook and his grill, and it's pretty bubbly, all right, now that it's late morning. If you lean back real far you can look out our window and see the big revolving BJ sign up on the Beacon Journal building showing the time and the temperature nonstop. That old gray sign's been going round for a million years.

"You guys want to go to this gig out in Kent?" Frankie asks us. I've never seen him with hair this short. I didn't know he had a mole on the left side of his head.

"When is it?" says Nick.

"Saturday night. I think I can get you guys in. I got a buddy in Kent. I'm going to take Aunt Myrtle's car over and he's going to fix it for me."

Nick looks up at his head. "You sure you're up for singing in public, man?"

"Don't worry, I'm going to wear a hat. I'm going to set a trend."

"You think so?" says Nick with some skepticism.

"I'll go," I tell him. "If Dad lets me."

"He'll be all right," says Frankie. "He'll want you out of his hair; I mean, wouldn't you?"

"Sure," I say. "But he's still pretty mad at me."

"Aw, he's got so much on his mind, being mad at you is like number twenty-five on his list," says Frankie.

"Where is it?" says Nick.

"At this bowling alley. My buddy's brother runs it. We're going to play the gig, and he's going to fix the car. It's just our second gig. It's nothing big, but it'll get you out of the house."

"Is Ollie bringing his brother's big amp?" I ask him.

"He better, or it's adios for Ollie."

Nick buys himself a doughnut, then, and asks Frankie if he wants another one, but he says he doesn't.

"I don't know," says Frankie, looking around the diner. "This is kind of like the old needle in the haystack."

"What do you want to do?" says Nick.

"I think Mom just had one of those burst pipes, you know? She's probably all right now."

"Let's get her something," I say.

"Get her something?" says Frankie. "Like what?"

"I don't know. A new coat. A necklace or something."

"A *car*," says Nick, laughing.

"We're downtown," I say. "This is where she'd buy something. That might make her want to stay."

"We're a little short in the cash department," says Nick.

"We could, you know, take something," I say.

"You mean steal something," says Nick. "Bad idea."

"I know," I say, feeling rotten for even suggesting it. "It was just an idea."

"Hey, no, it's not a bad idea, not completely," says Frankie. "You know, take from the rich, give to the mother of nine. But if we got caught, well. . ." He chuckles all uneasy-like.

"We could at least look," I say.

"Might as well," says Frankie. "This place is starting to make me nauseous."

We head over to O'Neil's on Main Street. O'Neil's is one of two big department stores in downtown, the other being Polsky's, which is right across the street. We look around the first floor among the handbags, jewelry, wigs, and various accessories women seem to like. Frankie pulls down a blonde wig from a rack and puts it on my head.

"She'll love it," he says.

We wander through the shoe area, but none of us has the faintest idea what shoes Mom would want, and we end up in the lingerie section. Nick holds up a bra hefty enough for two cantaloupes.

"Jesus," I say. "Don't scare me like that."

Two old ladies, bent, carrying handbags on their forearms like Easter baskets, pad on by and give us the narrow eyes.

"A gift for Mom," Frankie says to them. "Quite the breeder."

We take the escalator to the second floor and flip through some fabrics and patterns, since Mom's a big-time sewer, but it's like looking at the shoes and we're completely lost. We wander through the cameras, and I make a point to stop and have the middle-aged gentleman in the turtle neck and double-breasted jacket show me several models. Mr. Turtleneck is unimpressed as I *click-click-click* at Nick and Frankie, and says something under his breath about the cameras not being toys and if we don't have the money to purchase one, we might be better off in the record section. Truer words, dear reader, truer words were never spoken. I hand him back the camera, pretending to nearly drop it just to see his face of horror.

We browse through the records and since it's not too busy we each take a listening booth. Frankie has trouble closing the small door to his booth and we crack up as the miniskirted girl helps him out. I listen to Buffalo Springfield, Nick's got Steppenwolf, and Frankie has some jazz record. It sure sounds good with the headphones on. I'm about half asleep sometime later when Nick raps on my glass door. We put the records back and wait as Nick chats with the girl and ends up getting her phone number.

"Hey, I thought you were seeing Teresa?" I say to him as we hop on the escalator going down.

"I'm not married yet," he says, leaned all casual-like against the moving handrail.

We don't know what to do, so we head back over the viaduct on the way to the gorge. I start kicking a beer can as we go, you know, just to pass the time. I kick it a few blocks until I slice it off into the gutter where it'll probably stay for a few months. Nobody picks us up and by the time we're almost to Tallmadge, we decide to stick closer to home. We go to Patterson Park and sit in one of the concrete tunnels and smoke a few cigs. I'm getting used to smoking and don't cough as much. Across the park some kids are on the swings, and some moms are with their babies in strollers. Two kids try and slide down the big hill on cardboard, but don't get too far. In winter we go sled riding down the hill. Last year I got a bloody nose when I plowed into some people walking up. I was on a saucer going round and round and had no control whatsoever. Those damn things.

"We should probably be looking for Mom," I say.

"Yeah," says Frankie. "But she could be anywhere."

"I hate to think of her out there alone. What if she's in trouble?"

Frankie gives a big sigh. "The thought has occurred to me."

"What if?"

"I'm trying not to think about it," he says.

101

"Dad's out looking for her," says Nick.

"I hate thinking that she was sad enough to leave," I say. "She got so sad, she left."

"She's happy most of the time," says Nick. "At least I think she is."

"Well, it's not anything specific," says Frankie.

"What do you mean?" I ask him.

"Don't take it personally, if that's what you're getting at."

"I don't know how else to take it," I tell him.

"It's just the numbers," he says. "There's too many of us."

"True," says Nick.

"I know," I say. "But there's nothing we can do about that."

"Not unless somebody wants to take Squirt off our hands," says Nick all facetious-like.

When we get home there's a truck in the driveway, backed in, and they're hitching up *Sunshine Sammy* to it. Some dirty-looking guy with a fat, greasy face is doing it, acting like it's a real pain for him, and Anthony and Tommy are helping him. Dad's sitting near the pool off to the side so he won't get in the way. He nods at us, which is reassuring, because it means he can't be too mad. Squirt is running circles around the pool. Mom's sitting at the picnic table by Dad eating some ice cream. I want to jump up and down and run over and give her a kiss, but I play it cool, considering the demise of Dad's favorite toy. Britt's standing behind Dad rubbing his shoulders. He looks content. Not happy, but content. The boat will give us some cushion for a few weeks. It sure was a nice boat. They had some good times riding that thing. Yes, sir. It was a mighty fine ski boat, that *Sunshine Sammy*.

A few minutes later, Squirt runs into the side of the garage and gets up with a bloody nose screaming like a cat being nailed to the wall. Mom and Britt run over, and I run over too. His nose is a bloody mess. Mom and Britt take him inside and I stand there with my right hand dripping blood looking down at Dad. He's got the scowl now, because of Squirt, and probably the boat. The boat to Dad was like the Impala is to Mom. It was where he got the most pleasure in life, I'd say. He liked nothing better than to

102

go fishing or take Anthony and Tommy skiing in it. That was his way to freedom, like the Impala is Mom's. I'm looking for my own vehicle of freedom. When I find it, I hope nothing wrecks it or nobody has to buy it from me because I'm broke.

Meatballs

I hear this scream from over the hedges. I'm helping Nick change tires in the garage. Dad's been getting some dummy work, changing tires, and passing it on to me and Nick. It's not much, but every bit helps, like he says. It's hot as shit in the garage, but Dad bought two cases of Coke and we're allowed to have as many as we want. I'm bloated on my second one. So, we hear the scream and run through the hedges. Standing in her yard is Buzzy, and a few feet away from her is a dog I've never seen before. It's average size, smaller than Queenie, but it's hunched over, aimed right at Buzzy. She's afraid to move. Behind Buzzy, some distance away, is her mom sitting in that chair next to the smoldering drum. She's got this umbrella stuck on a pole, which keeps her skin as white as tripe. She's turned in her chair away from Tallmadge Avenue after hearing the scream.

"Don't move," Nick tells Buzzy. He's in a football stance, hands out, face forward.

He shuffles his feet a little, nervous-like, and then he takes off toward the dog, making all kinds of crazy shouts, waving his fists at it, and generally looking like a guy on drugs gone berserk. The dog backs up, showing its teeth, and it seems like it's going to run off, but then it swings around and comes at Nick, taking a flying leap. Nick turns and the dog misses him, landing hard on the ground. It gets up and goes after Nick again, but he's ready. He kicks the thing, not a perfect kick, but he gets it on the upper neck and on the lower part of the chin. It falls, makes a whimper, and looks up at Nick. Nick doesn't wait. He kicks it solid in the mouth and this time the dog staggers sideways. The stagger turns into a trot, and then it starts galloping away to the edge of the yard and out into the street. It's hard to follow through the bushes and traffic, but it disappears without any sound of being hit.

Buzzy's mom, still turned, yells at Nick.

"What the hell did you do that for? I ought to call the cops on you. Get out of my yard—both of you. Go on."

Turns out Nick didn't come out completely unscathed. He's got a scratch on his arm, pretty deep. Buzzy, standing where her mom can't see her, looks frozen. She seems about to say something, then looks back at her mom, who's still glaring at me and Nick, waiting for us to leave. Buzzy shakes her head. She clasps her hands together, shaking them, and tears up. She runs into the house.

I can't be sure, but it looked like she was trying to tell Nick thanks.

Mom's frying up meatballs, which is unusual, but I figure she's doing it extra special for leaving us a few days ago. Gram is right beside her, a foot shorter, using the wooden spoon to move them around on the pan so they don't burn. Gram cuts off a piece of one with a fork and feeds it to me. It's unbelievably good and I kiss Gram on the head.

"Oh, you," she says, waving that sauced-up spoon at me.

"What was that noise?" Mom asks.

"Just some dog."

"It sounded like it was fighting."

"It left," I say. "I never saw it before."

I get a drink of water to wash away the Coke sugariness in my mouth, then go back out and keep changing tires for a few more hours until it's almost dinnertime. Me and Nick, we use the bar soap at the spigot at the back of the house to get the grease and rubber marks off our hands. Sissy and Squirt are in the pool splashing around and it sure is strange hearing all that fun so close to my miserable weariness. Tommy rides up on his Honda, parks it in the garage next to our pile of tires, then comes over to the pool. He's got some fish in a fish trap and a couple catfish on a stringer. The fish in the trap are dead, they're bluegill, but the catfish are still kicking. Squirt swims up wearing Anthony's goggles and snorkel from the time Dad took Tommy and him to Florida. He sees the catfish writhing on the stringer and Tommy holds them up so he can get a better look.

"What do you think of those, Squirt?" I ask him. I've been going out of my way to be extra nice to him since the nail in the head. I figure he needs it.

"Why don't you put them in the pool?" he says, his tanned arms hanging over the side.

Nick looks up at Tommy and cocks his head and makes that clowny look. It means he thinks it's not such a bad idea. Tommy, with a cig hanging from his lower lip like it's glued there, removes the cats one by one and drops them into the pool. By now Sissy's up on the deck, staying as far away from those fish as she can. The catfish swim along the blue bottom like sharks, swishing from side to side instead of in a straight line. Squirt dives down with the flippers and follows them. He's a natural swimmer and with the flippers on he has no trouble keeping up, only rising to the surface to breathe. Nick, still in the shorts he wore all day working, climbs up the ladder to the deck, gets a running start, and does a cannonball into the pool. He swims beside Squirt underwater, going from one catfish to another. Tommy takes his fishing pole, which was still on the back of his Honda, and tells Nick to bring one of the catfish over. I toss Nick the hand net so he can scoop it up. Tommy hooks the catfish and tosses him back in the pool, letting out a fair amount of line. He plays with the catfish and then gives me the pole so I can give it a try. I'm surprised at how much fight is left in him. I have the drag set halfway and he still pulls line until I tighten it down some. It's a tough old cat and fights like a tiger.

It's about then I see Teresa Del Rosa coming through the gate of the chain-link fence. She's wearing her bikini and looks like a movie star. She climbs up the ladder and, pointing her hands above her head, her feet at the edge of the deck, dives right in. We're not allowed to dive in the pool—somebody might hit their head and kill themselves—but nobody's going to tell Teresa Del Rosa. She bobs up and I don't think Nick notices her yet; he's still with Squirt watching me yank on the hooked catfish. Either Nick still doesn't see her or he's ignoring her, I can't tell which, but she puts her back to the side of the pool and drapes her arms over the side so she's above water some. Her bikini top's floating up around her neck. Her boobs bounce all white and free like a couple water balloons, only a lot better-looking. Me and Anthony stand with our mouths open, and when Nick comes up he sees us not her, then looks back to see what we see. He glides over to her and tells her, and she's about as embarrassed as can be and covers herself, dancing on her toes, and we look away as much as we hate to while she gets herself together. When I turn back around she's already up on the deck and before you know it she's racing through the gate and into her house.

It's time for dinner anyway, so Nick unhooks the catfish and we head in.

Another steam bath at the Beck's place. It's so hot Gram has her shirt untucked and unbuttoned halfway up her stomach, not necessarily a good look for her. Dad's tired-looking, waiting until Mom puts the plate of spaghetti under his nose. She pauses to see his eyes light up at the meatballs. She puts two big ones on his plate and when she does he takes her hand and squeezes it real nice.

"Hope you like them," she says to him.

We each get one meatball, except for Tommy, who gets two. There's more, plenty more for a change, but Mom always starts us off with one of whatever we're having. Waste not, want not, you know?

I dig right into my meatball, ignoring the spaghetti. I can't believe we're actually having them for a change. I want to eat it as slow as possible, but I can't help myself and pretty much inhale it in a few bites. I start twirling the spaghetti around my fork, leaning down low to the plate, which prompts a frown from Dad, though when my eyes dart up at Mom she gives me the old happy

107

smirk.

"May I please have another meatball?" Anthony asks, lifting his plate. Mom puts another on top of his mess of spaghetti.

"Can I have another one?" asks Nick, who's still a tad wet and without a shirt on. He gets one too.

The rest of us are still on our first, but those two cut into their second like they're on a mission. As it turns out, tonight they're sitting right across from one another and, without making an official proclamation about it, they seem to be having a contest.

Anthony lifts his plate, and then Nick does right after.

Mom puts one on Anthony's but holds up a finger making him wait until she's got another on Nick's.

"Okay," she says. "Go."

They lean down close to their plates and go at it. Anthony cuts his with the side of his fork, but Nick spears his and lifts the whole thing up, taking a giant bite. Nick is a lot bigger than Anthony, but Anthony has the advantage of age, intimidation, and the fact that Nick's still recovering from the Cokes. Gram stands up, strumming her bare belly, and hits Dad in the arm with the back of her hand.

"Look!" she says. "Maybe they could make money doing that."

Dad, who's barely into his second meatball, winces. He'd wince more, but Mom's enjoying it. And not just Mom—everybody's watching. Without waiting, she sets another meatball on each plate. Nick's eyes are droopy, like he's tired, but Anthony's chewing away fast. It's Nick's big bites against Anthony's smaller but faster ones. Nick stabs his fourth meatball, but Anthony's still got a ways to go on his third. We're up on our feet. Just as Anthony finishes his third and starts on his fourth, Nick perks up and starts chewing a lot faster and before you know it he's got the fourth one down and he's on to the fifth.

"You ready to give up?" says Anthony, smiling, making those small chews.

"You're a meatball behind, slick," comes back Nick.

"You might be ahead, but I can do this all night. Haven't you read *The Tortoise and the Hare*?"

Nick polishes off the fifth in no time, while Anthony is barely into his fourth. Nick takes his paper towel and dabs the corner of his mouth to show Anthony how easy it's going for him. The thing is, Anthony doesn't like to lose. I'm glad as hell it's looking like Nick's going to beat him and get back at him for holding me and Frankie down, but if he's not careful the kitchen's going to be covered in spaghetti sauce. Anthony stabs what's left of his meatball, which is most of it, and lifts it up to his face. He turns it, like he's deciding what to do. Nick's not slowing up a bit. He takes number six between his fingers and holds it up to his face.

"I think my hare just blew by your turtle," he says, and shoves the whole thing into his mouth. Anthony's eyes look like somebody turned out the lights in them. All of us cheer.

Sweet redemption, I think to myself. That'll teach him to hold down me and Frankie.

Then Anthony looks real bad. His hand shoots to his mouth and he makes this gurgling sound like a cat about ready to hurl up a fur ball. He jumps up and runs to the small bathroom just around the corner and we hear him bringing all those meatballs back up.

"Oh, that's nice," says Sissy, setting her fork down. "I think I'm done."

"What's a matter—he no like?" Gram says in jest. She punches Dad in the arm. "Hey, you. Don't you think that's funny? Wake up, you."

Dad rubs his temple with his hand. He cuts into his meatball and lifts it to his mouth. "Couldn't he shut the door?" he says. "Couldn't he at least shut the door?"

Later on I'm lying upstairs—good God it's hot. Anthony's on his side with the fan blowing directly on him; none of the air's getting on us at all. Nick's on his back on his bed looking like a seal on a rock. He's not moving, but he's satisfied, you can tell. I have Brigitte out on my bed. She's there sideways and her arms keep falling off. I feel I just have to look at her after seeing Teresa Del Rosa lose her top. Plus, I keep thinking about Karen sitting in the tub, and then later up in the hay. As I'm looking at Brigitte, the intensity of my longings is something I can barely control, it's powerful all right, and she seems like more than a mannequin. She turns into flesh and blood right before my eyes, complete with that soft skin and dreamy eyes and sweet smell girls have, and her mysterious body parts are right there. She's like this alien from another planet because, let's face it, that's pretty much how girls appear, to me anyway. I sure want to reach out and touch her, I don't know why. She's like this dinner Mom cooked that looks and smells really good that I can't wait to dig into.

I roll onto my back and stare at the ceiling with its dark cracks, and I'm up there with Jesus and Dad at the lake. We're not in a circle the way we normally are, we're in the lawn chairs facing the lake, looking at the hazy day, watching two small sailboats in the distance glide across the water. Dad's not in his wheelchair, not this time. He's younger, but Jesus is the same age. He's always the same. Dad's watching those boats and I'm watching him. One's following the other. Whatever the one in the lead does, whichever way it turns, the one behind does the same thing, not crowding it, leaving enough space so there's no edginess between them. Their movements are graceful and it's soothing to follow their slow progress. Dad gets up and goes to the edge of the lake and puts his hands above his eyes because of the glare from the setting sun. It's strange seeing him on his feet without crutches. You might think I don't think about that, but I do, a lot. I wonder what he'd really be like walking. Everybody's got a certain way they walk. I wonder how he'd be. He turns back to me and points at the sailboats, which are nearly gone now, and I smile at him to let him know I see them and I appreciate them, but I haven't looked at the boats since he got up. My eyes are on him the whole time.

I turn to Jesus and ask Him if that's really how it would be, if Dad will really be able to walk if I keep my promise to Him and keep my hands off girls. Jesus doesn't answer right off, and that has me worried. But then He reassures me that yes, a deal is a deal, and Dad will be returning to us soon in his real image, and it'll all be wonderful and whatever worries we have, they'll be small because we'll have him whole again. Then, I can hardly believe it's coming out of my mouth, I say what if I just kissed a girl? Would kissing break the deal? It's not touching. It's not doing anything Mom or Dad would disapprove of. I tell Him how I can't stop thinking about Teresa Del Rosa, especially now that I've seen her breasts, and I'm still thinking of Karen in the tub, and her hand and body pressing me in the hay. I tell Him I might be heading into dangerous waters if Dad doesn't stand up soon. I don't necessarily *want* to touch a girl, but it's like some maniac has been dumped in my brain and he's at the steering wheel—my normal thoughts aren't the ones in control.

Jesus doesn't answer. I'm afraid to ask Him again—I think I may have pushed my luck too far by asking the question, and so I let it lie. I sit and watch Dad standing at the water, the dimming sun over the horizon now. The ache is powerful. It's the ache of so many things.

A Day at the Lake

Frankie's gig in Kent got cancelled. Turns out his friend didn't know squat about banging out dents. He wanted Frankie and the band to play at the bowling alley anyway, but Frankie told him to take a hike. Aunt Myrtle's still driving around without being the wiser, though Frankie's afraid time is running out and somebody's going to notice. He says the guilt is killing him. Good thing is, Aunt Myrtle walks most places, including to our house, because she has a mild heart condition and walking is supposed to help her, so her car isn't over too much.

Aunt Myrtle lives with her sister-in-law, Bonnie Bonnell. Well, since Uncle Don died some years ago, I don't know if you'd still consider them sister-in-laws. Bonnie's older than Aunt Myrtle, and she doesn't walk anywhere. She hardly drives anymore either, on account of her eyes are bad with cataracts. Aunt Myrtle and Bonnie Bonnell come over once a week, maybe every two weeks in the Corvair, and today is one of those days. Bonnie always brings a box of chocolates. You know, the kind of chocolates in the little dark paper cups like miniature cupcake holders. You have to mash some of the chocolates down a little when you don't know what's inside; you sure as hell don't want one of those pink creamy ones or the kind with nuts in them. Aunt Myrtle and Bonnie always wear dresses. I've never seen either of them in pants or jeans. I think *I'd* have a heart attack if that happened. Aunt Myrtle's into pill-box hats. Whenever she has one on, Frankie goes into Bob Dylan's *Leopard-Skin Pill-Box Hat*. Never in front of her, of course, but after we head outside to do something constructive.

Me and Frankie, we're in the garage taking inventory of the tires. Dad has this notebook where we log the models of tires, the date we changed them, how long they took, etc., etc. It about exhausts me just writing all that stuff down—more than actually changing the tires. But he says we have to do it, we're running a real business here. We're double-checking the tires that are finished against the ones we still have to do. We made some hay this week, really busted our butts, so Dad is letting us take Aunt Myrtle's Corvair to the lake for a few hours. Frankie was going to use the opportunity to get the dent fixed, but there's not enough time. Plus, it'd look awful fishy if we came back with dry hair and not smelling of algae water and gasoline from the lake. Plus, plus, you'll never guess who's coming along? I mean, you'll *never* guess. Teresa Del Rosa *and* Buzzy—I mean Sandy—from next door. It was Mom's idea to ask Sandy and after she said it I thought to myself how nice and right that would be. She hardly ever gets out of that house and could use the sunshine.

We're about finished up with inventory when Nick comes out dressed like he's going on a date. It makes me envious thinking of him and Teresa Del Rosa. Me and Frankie go in and wash our hands, then get our towels and suits that Mom has on the bench for us. I make sure I kiss Mom before I leave, and since I kiss her I don't want Aunt Myrtle and Bonnie feeling bad and so I kiss them too. Their cheeks are super soft and they both smell like powder.

"Thanks for the candy," I tell Bonnie. "And thanks for letting us use your car, Aunt Myrtle."

Frankie, now obligated, gives the three of them a kiss and we're out the door.

Standing beside Nick next to the Corvair are Teresa Del Rosa, holding a rather large picnic basket, and Sandy. Teresa's looking scrumptious as always. Sandy's got on a pair of jeans cut off around mid-thigh and a nice shirt, and around her neck is a camera hanging by a leather strap. She's clutching her towel to her chest and has her chin on it, like she's sad or she's thinking. The five of us get in and we head out.

Frankie picks up a girl, Maria, who's dad owns some kind of meat company or slaughterhouse, I'm not really sure, it's all a bit vague, but she seems nice enough and sits next to Frankie in the crack between the two seats, with me on the other side. In the back are Nick, Teresa Del Rosa, and Sandy.

"Sandy," I say, turning around to look back, "did that dog ever come back?"

"It better not," she says.

"That was some mean dog."

She's taking pictures with her camera. Of me when I turn around, of the back of Frankie's head, and of Nick and Teresa sitting beside her.

"What kind of camera you have there?" says Frankie, looking in the rear-view mirror.

"What do you mean?" she says.

"What kind is it?"

"Well, it's just the same model that Henri Cartier-Bresson used," she says. She says it like Frankie asked her something offensive.

"Is that so?" says Frankie.

"Why wouldn't it be? I said it, didn't I."

"Is that a Leica?"

Sandy shows real surprise. She has the camera up to her eye, but drops it when Frankie says that.

"Yeah," she says.

"My dad had a Leica. It was a good camera. I like rangefinders better than SLRs. How about you? You must be a rangefinder fan."

Sandy seems at a loss for words. We're all looking at her. We don't mean to be, we're just trying to keep her in the conversation.

"I like your shoes," says Teresa Del Rosa. "I have some like

114

those, but mine are brown."

"I like your mouth," says Sandy. "You have a perfect mouth." She clicks the camera a few times inches away from Teresa Del Rosa's mouth. She's right—it is a first-rate mouth.

I don't say much else until we get to Cutter Lake. Me and Nick and Maria hide in the trunk, which is in front under the hood, before we pay, and then we pile out once Frankie parks the Corvair under a tree.

For the first time, and I mean for the very first time ever, I see the slightest smirk on the corner of Sandy's mouth as I'm brushing myself off.

"And here I thought you were the squeakiest-clean kid on the planet," she says, clicking another pic of me.

We get a spot behind most of the other people where it rises uphill some, out in this open wasteland of grass. Teresa Del Rosa has a blanket big enough for everyone, so we don't bother lying on our small towels. Me and Frankie have to go change into our suits, but Nick and the girls have theirs on underneath their clothes. We come back and Teresa's not in her usual white bikini, she's in a purple one, while Sandy's in a black bathing suit not as skimpy, more like something her mom might wear. Well, her mom back in the day, if you know what I mean. I'm stunned because I never thought of her as a girl before, let alone a good-looking girl—not with that short butch haircut and the unusual clothes she wears. But she looks pretty good, I'll have to admit, and I know I'm sort of staring, more out of shock than anything else. She lifts up her camera and fires a few off at me. We head down to the water and get in.

It's warm and we move along with our heads above water walking on the muddy bottom until we're away from the crowd. Frankie's real good at squirting water between his teeth. He can shoot it about five feet, and Maria seems to get a laugh from it. We swim slow almost to the line of buoys. The water gets cold out there. We swim along the buoys as they curve back toward the shore, but stop when we can stand again. The trees on the far shore are blowing some, and they look nice and inviting and I wonder what it would be like over there. I'm always doing that,

115

wondering what things are like in places I'm not.

"What happened to your guys' hair?" says Maria. "Frankie, I've never seen it like this." She runs her fingers over his stubble.

"Pretty sexy, ain't it?"

"But what happened? You used to have such nice hair."

"What are you talking about?" says Frankie. "I've always been like this."

Maria splashes him playfully and Frankie splashes her back, though not hard.

Teresa Del Rosa's got her arms over Nick's shoulders and they're drifting away just as Frankie and Maria get into a real splash fight. Frankie gets her good, dunks her head under, then takes off running in slow-mo in waist-deep water. Me and Sandy are hunched down by the buoys and don't say anything. I keep looking back to watch Maria chase Frankie through the mass of kids.

"They're funny," I say.

"Yeah," she says.

With just her head above water she looks like me with that short hair.

"My mom does it all the time," she says.

"She does what?"

"Shaves my head. I get it. Parents are evil."

"Well, yeah, they sure do odd things sometimes."

"I saw you," she says. "I saw how you wanted to take a sledgehammer to your dad."

I give her a weak nod and turn back again. "Where'd they go? I hope Maria gets him good."

"What kind of sadist makes brothers fight brothers? He seemed to be enjoying it. I watched the whole thing. I saw it all. I got pictures too."

"Yeah," I say, sort of uncomfortable.

"I bet you wanted to poke Anthony's eyes out. You should have."

I don't say anything and start wading into the shallower water. "I think I'm going to go to the blanket for a while," I say.

"You do you," she says.

116

Frankie and Maria are at the blanket, but Nick and Teresa Del Rosa are still in the water. I towel off and lie on my back feeling the heavy sun all over me. I can feel my skin tighten as I dry.

"Where'd she go?" Frankie asks.

"Still in the water."

"You didn't abandon her?"

I shake my head on the blanket and reply in monotone, "She wanted to swim some more."

Nick and Teresa Del Rosa come back and Nick shakes his head like a dog over the blanket. He means it as a joke, but the cold water feels good. They dry off and lean up on their elbows, and then she asks if he wants her to rub lotion on him. Of course he does, and so she goes at it. Teresa gets on her knees and bends over Nick's body and starts rubbing lotion on him, and I have to look away. Frankie and Maria are on their sides and Frankie's flitting this long piece of grass along her shoulder and hip. Nick flips over and Teresa does his back, and then she lies on her back and he spreads lotion all over her. I look part of the time, but it's too much and I have to roll onto my stomach and turn my head the other way.

I'm just about asleep when I hear a voice.

"You're going to burn," says Teresa Del Rosa, and I feel her hand on my back. She's rubbing lotion on me, squirting the hot stuff straight from the bottle. I picture her hand as she moves it across my skin. My body's tired. It's dead tired from changing tires all week. My fingers hurt from prying the tires off the rims, and my back hurts from moving them. Teresa's hand is like something from heaven and I can't believe it's her, Teresa Del Rosa, rubbing that lotion on me. She tells me to turn over and she rubs it on my front, then tosses the bottle next to me. "You're all set, kid," she says, and goes back to Nick. The four of them decide to go for a walk on the trail up in the woods, but I tell them I'll stay and watch our things.

I take Frankie's harmonica and start messing around with it, working out a few songs. This guy some blankets over has a guitar and he's doing like me, just fiddling around playing some folkie riffs, and so I listen and try and play along with him.

When Sandy comes back she sits down and dries off, but stays upright, watching people. She picks up her camera and takes a few shots. Her white skin is shocking. Her mannerisms, the way she sits, her expressions, even her husky voice, seem more like a guy's. But she's got the body of a girl, all right. It's certainly interesting.

"How much film you got in there?" I ask her.

"It's my second roll," she says. "Didn't you see me change rolls?"

"No."

"In the car. I'm fast."

"You must have a lot of pictures," I say.

"I don't print everything," she says. "I only print the ones I like, which are a select few."

"You have a darkroom?"

"Sure. Where else do you think I print them?"

She has her towel draped over her shoulders with her head ducked down, like some dogs you see chained outside.

"You want some lotion?" I ask her, holding the bottle up. She shakes her head, her mouth sucking on the wet towel.

"What happened to your dad?" she asks. "Why is he in a wheelchair?"

"He got polio. Right before I was born."

She nods, still with her mouth on the towel. It's like she's trying to work out something in her mind.

"That's heavy stuff," she says.

I shrug. I never like talking about it. It's not that it hurts to talk about or anything like that; but people always ask the same questions, and then here comes the pity party. It's all intolerable.

"Tell me," she says, lifting her head, looking me right in the eyes. "Tell me the exact moment when you found out. When *he* found out. I want to know what that felt like. I bet it just crushed the family to bits."

Now, *that's* different, I think to myself. She asks like a kid would, without thinking the question over in her mind whether it might be too sensitive or offend me. She just blurts it out. It's a dose of fresh air, especially with all the subterfuge going on in

118

our house. I don't mind telling her one bit.

"Like I said, I wasn't born yet," I say. "My mom was pregnant with me. This was in 1952. I *think* I have the story right; it's funny how something like that, something so important, is fuzzy in my mind."

"It doesn't matter if it's exactly right," she says. "Tell me what you know."

"My dad was working a couple jobs. Both mechanical type stuff. He was working some long hours. He'd come home, eat with the family, then go out for a few more hours and work some more. One night after dinner, he didn't go to his second job because he said he was too tired. The washer was broke, so he thought he'd go down and fix it. He wasn't feeling good. He thought he had the flu, maybe. He went down to the basement and fixed the washer, but when he went to go back upstairs he couldn't. He had to slide up."

"You mean on his butt?"

"That's right. That's when they called the ambulance."

"Jesus," she says.

Sandy's eyes are boring right through me, digging into my soul. Her mouth's hung open, and her breathing is big and loud.

"The very last time he walked on his own was when he went down to fix that washer," she says. "He never walked again?"

I shake my head.

"But he didn't die," she says. "He didn't *die*."

"No," I say. "He was in the hospital for six months. In an iron lung for a while. They thought he *was* going to die. Mom was in at the same time at some point, having me. He used to work on all parts of a car, but in the hospital his boss gave him menial type things to work on so he could keep making money. You know, like fixing carburetors. That's what he did once he was out of the iron lung but still in the hospital. A friend stopped by the house and gave Mom a blank check. He said write it for whatever you want. I don't know how much she wrote it for, or if she did at all, but that's how we got by. Dad has some good friends."

"But what did you all feel?" she says. "What did a mom with all those mouths to feed feel when she got the news?"

119

"I'm not sure," I tell her. "They were pretty small and didn't understand what was going on. That same year Mom told them there was no Santa Claus because they couldn't afford presents."

She turns her head, fast, like she wants to blurt something out, then says, "See—I mean—that's worth the film to put it on. I wish I was there. I wish I could have taken a picture. But you can't always do that, can you. God damn, that's not fair. I want to document crucial moments like that. It's not right that they come and go and evaporate into thin air. I don't want to document *my* life—it's too painful, I live it every second, so why on earth would I want to constantly relive *it*. But your story, Puck, is the stuff of Shakespearean tragedies. So are most people's—they just don't see it. When you're in the thick of it, you don't see it, you just don't see it. You don't see the good, and you don't see the bad—it's just life, the only life you know. But to everybody else, your small drama isn't small at all—it's epic. And anybody that doesn't see the importance of every teeny-tiny story out there, well, those are the real zombies of the world and somebody ought to just take a nuclear bomb to their brain."

I can't respond right off, it's like something's in my throat. Her eyes are big and glossy. Her lower lip hangs down all fat and red, and I can't stand it anymore, I just can't take another second, and I lean in and kiss her. She doesn't rear back like you might think, but takes my head with both hands and kisses me back. She's even more aggressive than Karen was in the hay, and she leans into me without thinking we're out in broad daylight in front of about a million people. I tell her no, just like I told Karen, but I don't mean no for good, just no not here and now. I want to take her up into the woods, but we can't leave our things.

We sit staring at each other, then after a while we lean back and relax some. Seems like both of us are stuck and can't think of much to say. I ask her if she wants some lotion now and she rolls onto her stomach and unties the back of her top. Her back is incredibly smooth and soft, but her shoulders have muscles on them. I ask if she wants the back of her legs done and she says she does. Her legs aren't shaved like most girls, but the hair's not thick and her legs feel even better than her back. When I get

120

close to her bathing suit bottoms I bring my hand back down, but she tells me to get everywhere or she'll burn. I do it, kind of fast, and then lie down on my stomach with my head facing her, and I watch her closed eyes and lips and cheeks. She has the same effect on me that Karen did in the hay and Teresa Del Rosa did when she rubbed lotion on me, and I can't roll over for a while. I don't mean for it to happen and I'm embarrassed and try and think of other things, but I think Sandy knows. She looks at me and brushes my face with her hand and smirks. She just smirks and Jesus, I think to myself, this world sure is full of surprises.

I want to take her into the woods when Frankie and Nick get back, but when they do it's almost two hours later and Frankie says we better be heading home. They don't know, and I don't think Sandy wants them to, so we keep things under wraps. Everybody's tired and in the car Maria leans into Frankie and closes her eyes, and Teresa Del Rosa leans into Nick, and both of them have their eyes closed. I'm not sure if Sandy does or not, but then I hear the click of her Leica and I know she's awake. All I can think about is what she felt like when I was kissing her, and what we might have done in the woods.

Two Surprises

The party for Tommy is coming up soon. Things are tight and we've been having oatmeal more often, sometimes a couple times a week for dinner alone. I'm sure Mom and Dad are saving every dime they can to pay for the party, even though our parties aren't ever fancy affairs and shouldn't cost too much. The tire-changing job is humming along. Dad had us rearrange some things so our workspace takes up almost the whole garage. It seems like a real business. Nick decided not to play football this fall. He says he would rather work and make money than play some stupid game. Nick was the best tight end they had. His coach stopped over and talked to Dad, but when he left he had this scowl just like Dad's and I knew Nick wasn't going back. Mom's been particularly bubbly these days, and so is Dad around her, but not so much any other time.

There's a reason for the effervescence bursting from Mom. Turns out she's going to have another baby. She got the word not two days ago. You can't tell yet. Whenever Mom's pregnant she gets happy. She's happy the whole nine months. Not that she's like Dad all the other time, but she told me once she loved being pregnant. The first thing I thought about was where we'd put it. I guess Britt and Sissy could bring another baby in with them, but that might be kind of a tough squeeze. They could give up their

122

lounge and Mom could turn it back into a proper bedroom, but that'd kill them, especially Sissy, who's on their private line with Tony all the time. I think of the possibility of the new kid being up with us on the third floor. There's a chance, since the girls have Dad pretty much in their back pocket, but it would mean Mom and the girls having to trot up and down all the time, and that might be a deal-breaker for them.

I'm on my bed staring at the ceiling, wondering about it all. The other thing I'm thinking of, the thing I can't shake out of my mind, is Sandy. Isn't that a kicker? Yeah, I know. I think about Teresa Del Rosa too, and Karen up in the hay, but Sandy's stuck in my head and won't leave. I've been tormented trying to decide if I've broken the deal. I think kissing is a common occurrence, but I'm pretty sure if we would've gone up into the woods I would've shattered the deal completely. Sandy's skin was softer than anything I've ever felt. I didn't know something could be so soft. And I don't know why the softness is so appealing.

Nick's on his bed with the fan blowing on him, tossing the football into the air.

"Hey," I say to him. "Does Teresa have soft skin?"

"What?" He heard me, but I think he's unprepared for the question.

"Teresa Del Rosa. What's her skin like when you touch it?"

"Is it *soft*?"

"Yeah."

"It's real soft," he says.

"You know Sandy?"

"Who?"

"Buzzy."

"Yeah, what about her?"

"When you guys were on your hike, we were laying there and she needed some suntan lotion on her. You know how white she is. She asked me to put some on her. I couldn't say no. I couldn't let her burn. So, when I rubbed it on her, I noticed it was pretty soft. Is Teresa's skin like that? Real soft?"

"Yeah, it's pretty fucking soft," he says.

"You like it?"

"Why wouldn't I? That's how girls are." He turns his head toward me, holding onto the football. "You like Sandy?"

"Sandy?"

"Sure," he says. "You like her?"

"She's a year ahead of me," I say.

"So what. Do you like her?"

"You mean when we went to the lake? Sure, she was all right. Kind of weird, you know, but she's not too bad."

"It's okay, man," he says. "You don't need to defend yourself."

"You don't think I *like* her like her?"

"Puck," he says, "relax. She's not bad-looking."

"No," I say, turning over my lip, thinking about it, "she's not bad-looking."

"You think we went for a hike all that time?" he says.

"I don't know. You guys were gone for a while."

"He went on the trail, but that didn't take too long."

"Yeah," I say.

"Frankie and Maria went one way and we went the other way. We didn't do much. If that's what you think."

"Oh."

"Turns out . . ."

"Yeah?"

He shifts to his side to look at me, hugging the football like a pillow. I turn on my side to face him. "Puck, you can't tell anybody."

"Tell them what?"

"I mean it, man—not even Frankie. Frankie wouldn't squeal, but I don't want anybody knowing."

"I won't squeal," I tell him. He knows it, but I tell him anyway.

"We were sitting there, just talking I swear, when she says she's thought about killing herself."

"What?"

"Yeah. That's what she said."

"But, why?"

"It's weird, man. She's not sure herself. She said sometimes

124

she wants to end everything. She says it's too much to take."

"*Her?* Every guy in school's got the hots for her."

"I know," he says.

"That's crazy."

"She's been . . . taking pills."

"What kind of pills?"

"I don't know. When we were in the woods, she said she had some in her purse if I wanted to go back to the blanket and get one. I don't know what kind they were. She said she took one before she came over that day. She takes one or two most days."

I can't believe it. Teresa Del Rosa, the hottest girl on North Hill, thinking of killing herself. It doesn't make any sense.

"Nick, don't do it," I tell him. "Nobody's worth it, not even her."

"I'm not," he says. "I don't do that shit. But, isn't that wild?"

"Man," I say. "Do you think her parents know?"

He shakes his head. "I don't think so. You know Mr. Del Rosa. She'd be grounded for a long time if he knew she was popping pills."

"She always seems happy to me," I say.

Nick cocks his head the way he does when he says something ironic. "Maybe that's why."

"But, Nick."

"Yeah?"

"If Teresa Del Rosa's that bad off, with everything she's got going for her . . ."

"Yeah?"

"What kind of chance do we have?"

Nick thinks about it. "I guess she might not be as happy as she seems," he says. "Who knows what's going on at her house, or inside her head? You know that kid, Eggy?"

"Yeah—the kid who takes that turtle everywhere."

"He's pretty bad off, man. Way worse off than Squirt."

"That guy's a riot," I say.

"Yeah, and he's my age," says Nick.

I can't help it and start laughing to myself, then so does Nick. I shake my head just thinking about him.

"But the thing is," he says, "he's as happy as can be."

"True," I say, still laughing a little.

"I mean, we might think he has no reason in the world to be happy with that short leg and the way his arm is, pulling that turtle all over North Hill in his wagon. He gets bullied all the time, man, all the *time*."

"I know," I say. "The poor guy."

"Sure, the poor guy," says Nick. "But maybe not, *the poor guy*. Why should we feel sorry for him if he's happy?"

"I guess so."

"And maybe Teresa's the opposite. Maybe to us, she has it all. Great looks. Brainy. A mom and dad who treat her like a princess. The superstar of high school. But all that doesn't mean squat if inside there's shit going on we don't know about."

"Like what?"

"Hell, I don't know," he says. "Could be anything."

"Or, maybe she just likes popping pills. You know?"

"Maybe," he says.

"Yeah, maybe that's it," I say. "Maybe she's experimenting. That's not too smart, but better than doing them because she's depressed."

"Either way, I don't know," he says.

"You don't know what?"

"I don't know if I want to deal with something like that. You said it. She might be Teresa Del Rosa, but maybe Teresa Del Rosa isn't who everybody thinks she is."

Father Mann and the Cherry Tree

Frankie's helping Nick with the tires today, so I'm doing Mr. Capp's yard by myself. It's hot. The cicadas are thumping away up in the trees and those wispy clouds don't seem to move at all across the sky, making time stand still.

"Are you playing baseball this summer?" Mr. Capp says to me. We're in the back. Queenie's out with us, sniffing the garage for something to kill. I try not to look at his veiny face, but I find myself staring at him. I can smell his booze breath a mile away.

"No, Mr. Capp," I say.

"A boy like you—you should be playing baseball. I played cricket when I was your age. I played cricket and football, what you call soccer over here. I don't know why you're not playing. I thought it was the American pastime."

"I don't have a whole lot of spare time," I say to him. God. Help me, please.

"Every boy should have a sport they can play. It's the way to build character."

"I'll tell Ironside that," I say under my breath.

"What was that?"

"I said, I'll see what I can do. Yeah, you're probably right."

"You have your whole life to work, son," he says. "Doesn't your dad know that?"

"Guess not."

"Things may be tough with him losing his job, but that doesn't mean he should ruin *your* life as well. My father was relocated once, and he didn't take that out on us. You have to keep things separate. That's how it works. People who don't understand that are bound to alienate their own children. Do you understand what I'm trying to tell you, son?"

Good God. Mr. Capp's looking down at me with those bulging eyes and veiny cheeks. How about laying off the bottle, Mr. Capp, I think to myself—ever think about that? Ever consider how your drinking might be putting a dent or two in your own family fun house? I've got a ton of shit to do today, and you're not paying me a dime, so will you please, for the love of God, go back inside and take your wolf with you?

I realize what that mental meltdown might cost my soul, but sometimes, dear reader, I can't help myself. A body can only take so much horseshit.

I cut Mr. Capp's grass, then get out of there before he comes back out to feed me more of his barley-induced philosophy. When I get home, Nick and Frankie are waiting with two buckets.

"What now?" I say.

"We have to pick Mrs. Shiner's cherries," says Frankie. "And you thought today wasn't your lucky day."

"At least she's sober," I say to him.

Frankie grins at me and gives a friendly punch to my arm. "Let's hit it," he says.

Me and Nick carry the ladder while Frankie carries the buckets down Tallmadge Avenue almost to St. Martha's. Mrs. Shiner's cherry tree is out front. She's waiting for us and before anything else hands Frankie a folded-up twenty-dollar bill.

"Mrs. Shiner," say Frankie. "You don't need to pay us."

"Oh, why, yes I do. If you didn't pick these cherries, they'd fall on the ground and create a terrible mess. You should see the driveway when they aren't picked. Also, the birds come to eat the cherries and then they do their business on the car. It's awful getting the car cleaned. You boys are doing me a favor, and I hardly think twenty dollars is enough but, well, it's what I can afford to pay you."

Frankie reluctantly takes the money and slips it into his pocket.

"You don't mind if we smoke, do you Mrs. Shiner?" he asks her.

"No," she says, "I don't mind. If you'll pick up your discarded cigarettes, though, I would appreciate it."

Mrs. Shiner is a nice old lady. She gives us vegetables from her garden. I especially like the rhubarb. Her husband died some years ago; I vaguely remember the funeral. Mr. Shiner worked at one of the tire factories, I can't remember which one. He was a foreman. He was a good old guy and used to say hi to us on our way to school.

I hold the ladder while Nick starts picking the high branches. Frankie works on the lower ones. I don't think Mrs. Shiner has the tree sprayed anymore. You can see the scars of worm holes on most of the cherries. I guess it doesn't matter much once they're pitted and put into a pie. Frankie gives me a hit of the cigarette. It's one of those new cigarettes he's been smoking and it tastes bitter. I give it back to him.

Nick drops a couple cherries on my head.

"Waste not, want not," I say, looking up at him.

"Hold the bucket. I want to see if I can hit it."

"I'd hope you could. It's big enough. And close enough."

He drops one and I catch it with the bucket. He drops another, and I catch that too. He goes to drop a third and he leans back too far and the ladder, which I'm not holding at the moment, starts falling back with him. Just before it bangs into another branch he grabs onto a limb and holds on. There he is, feet dangling, and me and Frankie are too stunned to say or do anything, though Frankie does chuckle a little. Nick wouldn't get killed if he fell, just bruised up.

"Help," he sort of wheezes.

I push the ladder toward him until it bangs against the branch it was on before, and he curls his legs over and onto it, and then grabs it with his hands. He comes down the ladder with some

129

consternation.

"What the hell," he says to me. "What the hell are you do-ing?"

"Now, Nick," says Frankie, sitting in the shade of the cherry tree, taking a puff of his cig, "you told him to hold the bucket. How can he hold the bucket and hold the ladder at the same time?"

"Yeah," I nod at him, "that's right. How could I?"

"Fuck, man," he says. "Why don't you go up there?"

"I'll go up," I say. "I don't care."

"Go ahead, slick," he says. "Be my guest."

I make like one of the Three Stooges, you know, giving him the wise-guy bit, and start climbing. Hell, it's only seven rungs up. Even I can handle that. Nick sits down with Frankie under the tree as I drop cherries in the general vicinity of the bucket.

"That's *pot*," I hear Nick say, and I don't know what he means. I figure he's talking about the bucket.

I like it up in the tree. Last year we found a bird's nest, but we left it alone. I was picking with Anthony and he said it wouldn't be right to take it. The bird's nest isn't here this year. I wonder where it went and where the birds who lived in it are. It's hard to think about birds in winter. Those skinny little feet must get pret-ty cold. I mean, why doesn't the blood freeze in them—

"You gave Puck a hit?" I hear Nick say, loud, but like he's trying not to be loud.

"Hey," I call down. "What about Puck?"

It's weird seeing them sitting there looking up at me. Frankie's chuckling, but Nick's not smiling. He's got Dad's wor-ried scowl.

"Come down," he says to me and I, being a good, obedient grunt, obey.

I figure since they're sitting down I'll sit down too.

"You all right?" Nick says.

"Yeah," I tell him. "Why wouldn't I be?"

"You're not feeling strange or anything?"

Frankie looks like his bones went Jell-O on him; his arms are like noodles along his open thighs, and his eyes are real skinny.

"You don't like these?" Frankie says, holding up the cig, which now is just a nub.

"Not really," I make a wince. "They're too bitter."

"The Beatles like them," says Frankie. "Dylan likes them," he chuckles. "Most of your virtuosos in the jazz realm have a particular fondness for them."

"It's pot," says Nick. "Frankie, you're nuts for doing it out here."

"Pot?" I say. "What do you mean?"

Frankie gurgles up a laugh, then starts coughing. He hands the little nub to me so he doesn't drop it.

"Hello, boys," we hear somebody say. That somebody turns out to be Father Mann, the youngest priest of St. Christopher's triumvirate. He's hip, he's cool. He's so young it's hard to believe he's a priest and not a bag boy at Acme.

"Hi, Father," I say. Nick and Frankie sit there like mute pigeons.

"Helping Mrs. Shiner, are you? You Beck boys are real workers."

"We try," says Frankie then, pretty loud. "It helps keep the belt on Dad's pants."

I don't think Father Mann gets the reference. He just nods and grins.

"Want some cherries, Father?" I ask, holding up the bucket.

"No, no," he says, waving me off. "I just ate. They look pretty tasty, though. No, I'm just out for a walk. Beautiful day, isn't it? I just wanted to say hello."

"It *is* a beautiful day," says Frankie. "Somebody up there likes us."

Me and Nick don't turn our heads, but move our eyes to look at one another.

"Want a smoke?" Frankie says. Not such an odd question, considering we all know Father Mann smokes and does so openly and regularly.

"Thanks," Father says, patting the front of his white shirt. "I left mine back at the rectory."

Frankie's holding up the stub, then realizes it would be rude

131

to give him the nearly expired cig. "Here," he says, digging into his shirt pocket, "take it." He hands Father Mann a fresh one, the same new kind without filters that look more like small white cigars than cigarettes.

Surprisingly, Father Mann sits down on the ground with us. Frankie lights a match and raises it to Father's cigarette. Father sucks on it in short, deep drags to get it going. He blows out the smoke and I smell the bitterness. His eyes about double in size.

"You like that, Father?" says Frankie.

Frankie hands me the nub of his and I figure I'll give it another try. I take a long drag and let out the smoke. It's not too bad actually. I hold it out for Nick, but he sits stone-faced, looking like he wants to attack something.

"Yeah," Father sort of wheezes. "It's real nice."

"A man's got to have his vices, even if he's a priest—eh, Father?" says Frankie.

Father nods, then takes another puff.

We sit there smoking, and then start in on the cherries. They're the freshest, plumpest, sweetest cherries you ever did taste. We all wave at pedestrians going past, mostly people we know. They give us the strangest looks.

"Our brother Anthony is thinking about becoming a priest," says Frankie, which Father Mann already knows. "Got any advice for the old ballbuster?"

Father holds the cigarette in front of him, sort of close. "Did you roll these yourself?" he says.

"Why, sure, Father. It's the only way."

"These are very good cigarettes," he says.

Frankie pulls out another one and lights it up. We smoke some more and eat more cherries. I sure do love my brothers, I think to myself. Yeah, they're pretty great guys. And Father Mann is a swell guy, too. It's just a wonderful day with the cars whizzing along Tallmadge Avenue and the friendly faces floating by.

"*Rect*ory," Frankie suddenly says, sort of loud. "Why do they call it a *rect*ory?"

"Hmm?" says Father.

132

"*Rec*tory . . . *Rec*tory . . . Don't you think that's a strange thing to call it? *Rec*tory . . . I mean, the obvious implication stares you right in the kisser, don't you think?"

"You'll have to teach me how to roll one," says Father. "I need to show Father Nigh."

We smoke a little more. It's quite pleasurable under the cherry tree. I give Father a light elbow to the side. "Don't you hate it when the white wafer gets stuck to the roof of your mouth? And you can't touch it!"

"I always chew, on the *side*," Father says. "Try it next time." His eyes are big and his smile is hilarious. I feel like laughing my head off.

"*Rec*tory . . . *Rec*tory . . . *Rec*tory . . . Yup, Anthony's on his way to becoming one of the robed. *That'll* last about two days."

Nick keeps shaking his head at me, but all I can do is laugh at him. I laugh so hard I roll onto my side. Father Mann laughs with me.

"Father, why don't you climb up that ladder and see if you can hit us with the cherries?" says Frankie.

Father Mann goes to get up, but falls over to his right. He tries again, with the help of Frankie and me pushing him up, but Nick rushes between him and the ladder.

"Father," he says, "I think Mrs. Feroni is waiting for you at church."

"Mrs. who?"

"Mrs. Feroni." For some reason Father's having a tough time standing on his own. Nick gives him some assistance. "That's right. Something about confession, communion maybe."

"Or concubine!" says Frankie, sticking his pointed finger into the air.

"You better get back there. She's waiting."

"At *church*?"

"She sure is. I think you're late." Nick sort of scoots him along the yard and onto the sidewalk. "It was nice talking to you, Father. You might not want to mention that you stopped here. See you later."

Father heads down the sidewalk, giggling as he goes. Me and

Frankie wave bye-bye.

"Nice going," says Nick. He sure does seem mad.

"What's the matter with you, you old party pooper," says Frankie. He starts tossing cherries at him.

Nick goes on to tell me that when he said pot, he meant *pot, marijuana*, and that Frankie just handed Father Mann a joint. Handed him a joint and got him high.

I'm lying back staring up at Nick. I'm laughing, but then I think it over.

"Well shit," I say. "We're all going straight to hell. No doubt about it."

The Weight

The evening before Tommy's party, Dad goes fishing with Tommy and Anthony. We still have a small fishing boat with a Mercury 6.6 hp engine on it. Nothing like *Sunshine Sammy*, but it gets Dad in and out of the lagoons and coves of Mogadore, which is where he catches most of his fish. They're hoping to catch enough for the fish fry. He has some in the freezer downstairs from earlier this summer, and Uncle Dobbs is going to bring some walleye from his fishing trip to Canada. It's going to take a lot of bluegill with all the people coming.

Me and Nick are supposed to clean out the garage while they're gone. We have to make room in case it rains. That means hauling most everything out, then putting it back in more organized than it was. We're supposed to put the tires around the back and side so people don't see them. Mom has three card tables and chairs we're going to put up inside. Not much we can do about the gasoline and oily smell, but most people are used to it in garages. Even if it doesn't rain, it'll be a good place to sit out from under the sun. It's supposed to be ninety degrees tomorrow.

Frankie is scooping out the pool with the long-handled net, mostly dead bees, Japanese beetles, and the odd leaf. He'd normally just dump the net on the ground, but since the whole idea is to make things nice and neat for the party, he's dumping it in one of the metal trash cans. Sissy's got Tony over. They're sitting on the picnic table cutting out placemats. They're sitting on the same side of the picnic table and it seems like they're having more of a picnic than working. I mean, how hard can it be to cut out placemats? Gram's at the chain-link fence sitting in a chair, chatting it up with Mrs. Del Rosa, who's in her own chair facing her. Gram's somebody the older Italian ladies of North Hill like talking to, since she came over on the boat instead of being born here.

I'm rolling a tire out to the far side of the garage, when I see Sandy. She's standing there close to the sawed-off stubby tree.

"Hey," she says.

"Hey," I say back.

"What are you doing?" she says.

"Cleaning out the garage."

"You guys do that a lot."

"My dad ascribes to the idle-hands thing."

"Good to know you can change a tire," she says, "in case we're out and about and one blows on us."

"I'm your man," I say.

She's just showered, you can tell by her wet hair and shoulders. She has on a man's shirt, short-sleeved, and baggy pants, but no shoes.

"Here," and she pushes some rolled up papers through one of the holes in the chain-link fence.

"What's this?"

"Look at them later," she says. "Not now."

"All right," I say.

"I can't stay. I'm going with Mom downtown."

"Shopping?"

"Something like that," she says. "I'm the diversion while she puts things in her big purse."

"Oh yeah?"

"Sure. You think we could afford a Leica?"

"I did kind of wonder about that," I say.

"Leicas are some of the best cameras out there. That's why I stole one instead of some cheap Japanese model."

"Yeah, well, you're talking to somebody who knows diddly about cameras," I say."

"You're cute. Come here," she says.

She takes hold of the top of the chain-link fence and rises up on her toes, and we kiss over it. Her tongue darts around like a hooked minnow, and it's hard to keep up with it.

"Don't get caught," I tell her.

"I'll try not to," she says.

I stick the roll in my back pocket until I get to the garage, then hide it in Dad's tall cabinet before Nick sees me.

We move out all the tires, bring in the tables and chairs, and put the plastic tablecloths on the tables and set rocks on the corners so they won't blow away. There's a nice breeze in the garage with the back door open.

As Nick heads inside I tell him I'm going across the street to Romano's to buy a case of Coke for Mom. I take the roll from the cabinet, then go across Tallmadge Avenue and sit around the side of the building. The roll of papers is a series of photographs. They're from the day at Cutter Lake, in the car and at the beach, plus a few she must have taken from behind the hedges of me moving tires, and some from a few days ago when I dug out a bush for Mom. They're good, really good. I'm not saying I'm an expert on photography, but they look like they could be in a newspaper or a magazine. They're not just pictures of me smiling at the camera. In fact, there aren't any of those phony things. They're all candids. Like she was invisible when she took them. The ones of me changing tires are dirty and sweaty and miserable-looking, and the ones of me walking from the car toward the beach have me with my head down, maybe thinking, maybe looking at a bee, maybe humming a song to myself, it's hard to tell. The pictures let your own mind fill in the gaps. They're stories, little compressed stories, and they speak to you. I shuffle through them a couple times and then set them on the bench.

I lean back, deflated and defeated, dear reader, a balloon with no air. I feel small and unimportant, more than usual. What did I do today? I moved tires out of a garage and put up some tables, something any idiot could do. Sandy printed *these*, evidence of a truly inspired and talented soul. And here I was not long ago feeling sorry for *her*. Christ. She has her mom, and I have Dad. She squeezes insight and art from her pain; I squeeze pimples in the mirror at night. She's going somewhere, that's pretty easy to see. Meanwhile, I'm learning how to become a janitor. That's what I get out of this. That's the fruit of my labors. How to become a fucking janitor.

I cross back over to the house. Sissy and Tony are on the front porch swing.

"How's it going, Puck?" Sissy says.

I don't answer. It's too pitiful. I trudge past them to the side door and go up into the kitchen, where Mom and Gram and Britt and Squirt are huddled around the table making cookies. Christ. Cookies. They're making cookies.

"Did you get the Coke, honey?" Mom asks me.

"I forgot."

She looks at me with a weak wince. "What were you doing over there?"

"Figuring out how to blow my brains out," I say.

"What?"

"I'm being facetious, Mom," I say.

"How's the garage look?"

"Spectacular."

"Look, Puck," says Squirt, holding up a sugar cookie. It's in the shape of a fish.

"That's nice, kid," I tell him.

"Do you want to make some?" he asks.

"Maybe later," I say. "What's for dinner?" I lift my eyes, hopeful, though I don't smell anything.

"Today's self-serve," says Mom. "Make a sandwich, or look in the icebox. There should be something in there."

There's nothing. Part of a watermelon. A half-eaten piece of fried chicken, uncovered and dehydrated. Some celery, some carrots. A half pitcher of powdered milk. Pickles. Mustard. Ketchup. Some onions. Good God. I close the door.

"I can make you some oatmeal real quick," says Mom.

"He look sick," says Gram. "He look like he going to throw

up."

"Take off your shoes," says Britt. "We just mopped in here. And don't leave them on the steps," she calls as I leave the kitchen, "Dad might trip on them!"

I lie in bed. My friend, the cracked ceiling, greets me. Nick's on his bed with the fan blowing on him, tossing the football in the air. I'm hot. I'm dying. I get up and move the fan so it's in front of me. Nick gets up, shoves me onto my bed, and puts it back where it was. I roll onto my side, away from him. I close my eyes. I want everything to go away. I want it all to change. I want to go to sleep, wake up, and be somewhere else, like I've been living in some bad dream my whole life.

Thankfully, I drift away, into a pleasant half sleep. In it, Sandy comes up to the third floor and sits down on my bed. I turn to look at her, she strokes my head, pushing back my sweaty hair. She keeps stroking my hair, and she's humming something soft and soothing. I let my hand fall onto her leg. I squeeze it. It's soft, but muscular. There's no subterfuge, no rubbing of lotion. My hand touches her leg because I want to, and she wants me to. She bends down and kisses me on the lips the way she did at the lake. I feel powerful. It's a pleasant, calm feeling of power. The muscles on the top of her thigh are rigid; they extend from her knee to where her leg joins her body. It's not far, there, and I know I could reach it easily, I know she would welcome it and is perhaps waiting for it. I don't, not because I fear I'm breaking the covenant with Jesus, but because I'm happy just holding her leg and kissing her.

"Hey," I hear Frankie say. He's nudging me. "Hey, Dad wants you."

It's nearly dark. Nick is asleep on his side, the fan beside him, a *Mad* magazine by his nose. I sit up.

"Now," says Frankie. "He wants you now."

It's not that late, but the house is quiet. Mom is on the couch in the living room, watching TV as she stitches something on a shirt. Gram is on the couch down in the family room. The lights are out, except for the light over the kitchen sink.

"Down here, son," I hear him say from the small stairwell

leading to the side door.

"Yes?" I say from the few steps above him.

"I'd like you to carry me up."

"Now?" I say.

"Yes," he says. "You've seen the other boys do it. I don't think it will be hard for you. With Tommy leaving soon, and maybe Frankie too, you need to learn."

I walk down to where he's standing. He can stand on his own by leaning against the door jamb and holding onto the opposite side, and he can walk up the stairs on his own using the leg with the metal brace as a fulcrum, then swinging the other leg up, one step at a time. But when he's tired, like tonight, he likes to be carried up. He smells like the lake and fish. They must have cleaned the fish when they got home. He's probably mad that I didn't help them.

I'm not sure what I'm doing. I've seen them do it hundreds of times, but it's different now that I'm doing it. I squat down facing the same way he is. He turns, slowly, then lets his weight fall on-to me. He's heavy. I'm surprised at his bulk. He wraps his arms around my neck and holds on tight.

"Now just stand up?" I ask him.

It's difficult for him to speak. "Yes," he ekes out. "Hold onto the railing."

I uncoil myself from the squat, but remain bent over. You have to stay bent over the whole time, that much I know, in order to keep him from sliding off. He's heavy, but now that I've got my legs under me it's not too bad. His limp legs dangle and bump into the backs of my legs. His belt buckle digs into my lower back. His forearms cut off the air to my lungs.

I go up the first few steps, holding the railing as he said. I see Frankie standing by the sink, legs crossed, casually sipping a glass of milk and eating a sugar cookie. I feel to my left where the railing ends and there's the short stretch of wall before the steps leading upstairs. I shuffle my way there, touching the wall as a guide, until I feel the handrail to the longer steps up to the second floor. I grip it fast and hard. He moans. His moans can mean pain or they can mean a release from pain. Carrying him up

140

hurts, but it stretches his back, and is therapeutic. But having him moan mere inches from my ear, feeling his limp body on my own, is something I am unprepared for. I feel his pain jolt right through me. His frustration. His torture. I start ascending the stairs and see Mom on the couch, legs curled beneath herself, watching TV, sewing, oblivious to what I instinctively know will be a moment knifed into my memory. A thousand daggers of guilt slice my fragile mind. I picture his shin burns clanging my calves. I see the resentment that he often harbors when gazing at me. The dark eyes of the others loom from above, condemning me for causing him further pain, for being born, for existing. I feel myself fail. My legs burn. I'm too young, I'm not mature enough to handle this weight. I mouth for help, silently, but know there will be none coming. I wonder, I pray, what have I done to deserve this? Was I a villain in another life? Is this proof of karma? What else could explain the agony heaped upon him, and now me?

There comes a light. I see it as my eyelids flutter. The light twinkles white, in the vague shape of the cross. It spins, it throbs, remaining as bright as the sun. I reach out, stretching my arm, extending my fingers; if I could only touch it. He moans. I wail in mirrored, harmonious torment. The flashing light blinds me, turns away, then is reduced to miniature. It solidifies, becomes concrete, and I see that it's a crucifix on a necklace, and the necklace is worn by none other than Sandy, beautiful oddball Sandy, reaching down to grasp my hand, to help me up, to lift me from sure tragedy and, at the very least, give me another day to try and work through the chaos and lunacy in my mind.

I get to the top of the stairs and then have to travel the naked steps to their bedroom without a railing or wall. I take short, sure steps. To my right, the Fab Four gaze at me from the door of the girls' lounge, so smart, so certain, and so wise, but did they ever have to bear something like this? How many Lennons or McCartneys emerge from such wells of human carnage?

I carry him to his bed where I crouch, my back nearly broken. He puts his hands on the bed and I slip from beneath him; he pivots and sits down, then releases his brace from its straightened

141

position so he can move his legs around. He's withered, worn. He isn't Dad now, but a symbol of my predetermined destiny. A destiny whose precise details may not be known, but whose main avenues have been mapped and paved. I yearn to embrace him. I ache to have one moment where he concedes and I am confirmed, where I exist, where I matter as much to him as the older ones. Where he feels how his pain is transferable, as any other commodity, and has accumulated in my burgeoning heart.

The moment passes as I leave the room and go up to the third floor. I may become a janitor someday, but I'll be one versed in universal sorrow, a silent trumpeter of the damned.

Tommy's Party

Coming downstairs, I smell bacon. Anthony and Frankie and Tommy are making breakfast. Anthony has an apron on, and Tommy has on Dad's cowboy hat.

"Sit down, friend," says Tommy, and when I do he puts a clean plate in front of me, Anthony slops some eggs on it, and Frankie gives me two slices of bacon along with a piece of buttered toast.

"What's this?" I ask them.

"What does it look like?" says Frankie. "You have ten minutes. If you finish quick, I'll slip you another slice of bacon."

I've rarely had two slices of bacon at one sitting, let alone three.

"When's everybody coming?" I say.

"Soon," says Tommy. "So eat up."

"How's your back?" says Frankie.

"It's all right," I say.

"You carry Dad up last night?" says Tommy.

"Yeah."

"Welcome to the club." His eyes look brighter and bluer than ever.

"Think about it," says Anthony, "all that experience carrying Dad upstairs; hauling your pack around Vietnam will be a piece

143

of cake."

"And who says the Beck boys aren't being prepared for life," says Frankie.

"*I* never said that," says Anthony.

"No, you never did."

I eat fast and do get a third slice of bacon, just as I was promised, along with another smaller piece of toast. I down it with a few swigs of warm powdered milk.

Me and Nick pull the small red wagon across the street to Romano's to get some ice. We pile on six bags, and Nick carries two more, one on each shoulder. We dump the ice in a couple plastic tubs and stuff bottles and cans of pop and beer in, and then start setting up a small platform for Frankie's band. He wanted to play in the garage, but since we set up the tables there the band has to play back to the right of the pool by the gate to the Del Rosa's. Frankie moves the VW bus off the driveway and to the left of the pool so it's out of the way. Dad comes out and we set up the fryer for him. The girls are out, lugging more chairs and setting up more flimsy tables for food. Mom has Squirt play in the pool to stay out of everybody's way. We all glance over now and then to make sure he hasn't drowned.

They start arriving around noon and an hour later the place is packed inside and out with close to a hundred people. I'm with Frankie, Nick, Teresa Del Rosa, Ollie and Hoss, and our cousin, Mick, on the far side of the bus next to the chain-link fence. Mick's a drummer same as Ollie. Frankie's invited Mick to sit in on a few songs, which doesn't go over too well with Ollie. Mick's hair covers his ears and falls long in back. We look like something out of the 50s next to him. Teresa Del Rosa's looking nice and delectable in her dress. She has her hair pulled back in a ponytail, making her cheekbones pop out. She's between Ollie and Mick, not beside Nick.

"We'll do a set with you," Frankie says to Ollie, then Mick's going to come on for a few, and then you'll come back on."

"Yeah, I mean, okay," says Ollie, not exactly thrilled with the idea. "It's just that, I mean, I didn't know I was going to be sharing time with another drummer."

"Mick's my cousin," says Frankie. "What do you want me to do? They came all the way from Pittsburgh to see Tommy off. He's a drummer too. He's my cousin. He has to play with us."

"Hey, man," says Mick, "it's cool. I don't need to play if it's going cause a stink. It's cool."

"Naw, man," says Frankie. "Ollie's cool. You're cool, aren't you, man? He gets it. It'll be great. Ollie, you'll be on for *Help*, *Norwegian Wood*, *Eve of Destruction*, *Sympathy for the Devil*, *Satisfaction*, *Subterranean Homesick Blues*, and *My Back Pages*. Then, Mick will come on and we'll do *My Generation*, *Hey Joe*, *I Can See For Miles*, *Street Fighting Man*, and *The Kids Are Alright*. Ollie, you'll come back and we'll finish with *The Weight*, *Rocky Raccoon*, *Back in the U.S.S.R.*, *Sunshine of Your Love*, *Money*, *Don't Let Me Down*, and *Gimme Some Lovin'*. The encore is going to be *Like a Rolling Stone*. The second encore is *Sgt. Pepper's*. And the third encore is *Hey Jude*. For that one, we'll have Mick come back up and sing with us. Anybody else can come up and sing. Teresa, you want to sing?"

"Aw," she says, shier than normal with all our eyes glued to her, "I don't really sing."

"Everybody can sing," says Mick.

"Hey," says Ollie, "that sounds like I'll be out for more than a few songs, Frankie. I mean, it's more than a few."

Frankie looks at him like he just ripped one. He's pissed at Ollie for not coming through on his dad's station wagon and the big amp. What was supposed to be this big-deal gig in the garage has fizzled into some low-brow affair behind the pool.

He turns back to Teresa. "Yeah, so as Mick was so astutely trying to say, you'll be fine. It'll be great. You should. You'll be the star of the show."

Mom calls me over. As I'm leaving, I hear Ollie still going on. That Ollie.

"Can you help your dad, honey," she says. She hands me a plate with a paper towel on it.

Dad's frying the fish. The girls have them dipped in flour already. There's a full plate beside him, and I'm holding the plate where the done ones go. I'm not quite following why I'm required, since there's plenty of room on the small table for the plate I'm holding. After frying them on one side, he flips them over and fries them on the other side. About six or seven bluegill can fit in the skillet at a time. I do the math. There are at least two hundred bluegill between what they caught last night and what Mom thawed from the freezer. I'll be standing here when the crickets start chirping.

"They sure look good," I say.

"Hold the plate closer," says Dad. He starts lifting them with the curled spatula onto the plate. "Closer."

He takes the salt shaker and taps it with his forefinger, sprinkling them with salt. They look damn good, and I'm hungry as hell, even though I had three slices of bacon with breakfast.

"Go take those inside the garage," he says. "Tell them more is on the way."

"Jawohl, Herr Kommandant," I say, turn and click my heels together, and I'm off. The garage is full of those waiting for fish, those already eating hamburgers and hotdogs and potato salad etc. etc., and *everyone* drinking beer, Blatz and Schlitz being the preferred brew.

"Puck," says my Aunt Josephine, who's a short woman with always-perfect, just-right hair, and who's always glad to see me. "My gosh, it's been over a year. Look at you." She opens her arms and, since I'm holding the goods, all I can do is lean in for the perfumed kiss.

"Fish from Herr Hitler," I say, clicking my heels. I move mechanically, like a robot, like a tool, and place the plate of sizzling bluegill in their midst.

"Did you say *Hitler*?" Uncle Kenny, her husband, sharp as a whip, grins, his eyes darting up to my head, then back down. The twinkle in his eye says it all, says it all, dear reader.

I click my heels, do a swift about face, and march back to my post, arms and legs in Gestapo goose step. When I reach my station I continue, picking up the new plate with the new clean paper towel on it, and stare straight ahead.

"Private Pissant, reporting for duty, mein Fuhrer," I say. I'm howling inside. Balls of insanity bounce inside my head. I have nothing to lose. "Thank you for allowing me the opportunity to remain estranged from cousins who I haven't seen in months, aunts and uncles who are dying to say hello and maybe even slip me a fiver, and Frankie's band possibly headlined by the hottest vixen this side of Richard Nixon. Thank you for recognizing that I'd much rather stand like a statue, seen but not heard, your ever-faithful hands and feet, now and forever, amen."

Dad's too preoccupied and we're too much in the public eye for him to go off the rails. He gives me that look, and a few minutes later slides more crispy fish onto the waiting plate.

"Now," he says, "take that plate to the garage and if you're still a Nazi when you get back, I'm going to tan your butt in front of your cousins, and aunts, and uncles, and Teresa Del Rosa. Do I make myself clear?"

"Yes, sir," I answer, all sarcasm gone, back to my usual downtrodden self.

Dad, in foolish despair, replaces me with Squirt. I'm off the hook. Quickly, before they're all gone, I grab two hot dogs, squeeze on the old mustard and ketchup, lift an ice-cold Mountain Dew from the bone-numbing depths of the plastic tub, and search for a place where the jackals of servitude won't think to look.

To the front porch I do trot, only to find it swarming with a writhing sea of young, vaguely identifiable cousins compressed onto the swing, leaning against the railing, or sitting so close on the steps I have to tiptoe through them like I'm traversing a field of land mines.

"Off, one of you," I say, and a blood relative with reddish hair and droopy eyes jumps down from the swing. "You too," I say, looking to who seems to be his brother. "I'm bigger than you. Elbow room, you know." Down he hops.

"What happened to your hair?" the second hopper asks. He's a cute kid with a wide head.

"Shorn like a sheep," I do declare.

"Wha-a-a-t?" he laughs like a machine gun.

"What do *you* think happened to it?" I ask him, semi-serious now.

"I don't know," he says.

"Good."

"Do you want my pie?" says another kid, the one beside me.

"That's not pie, that's quiche. No, I don't go in for quiche, thanks."

"It's gross."

"Ever have tongue?" I ask him. The kid sticks out his tongue. "You know what's really gross, is that fish you got there."

"You want it?" he says. "It smells."

"That's right," I tell him. "It smells, it's gross, and moms want you to eat it more than spinach or peas." He rattles his head around. "I guess I'll take it. Here, put it on my plate. I don't want to eat it, but I don't want you getting sick. Anybody else doesn't want their fish? Come on now, better save room for the ice cream."

About half of them come over and dump their untouched bluegill onto my plate. I dig into one, cutting a line along the dorsal fin then peeling back that half to keep the bones away.

"Hey, who wants an extra scoop of ice cream?" All hands go up and I pick this light-haired kid with a nose like a doorknob. "Okay, you run and grab a saltshaker from one of the tables. If anybody asks, tell them Aunt Beck needs it and you'll bring it right back." Off goes the little minion. Back he comes, quick as a flash, with Nick walking close behind. Nick steps up to the swing, picks three pieces of fish from my plate, and puts them on his.

"You shouldn't steal fish from little kids," he says, waving the final unknown relative from the swing, and sits down.

"They didn't like it," I tell him. "I didn't want to see it go to waste."

Nick takes the saltshaker from my plate and sprinkles some over his fish, then sets the shaker on his plate.

"Frankie's going to start in a few minutes," he says.

"How's Ollie?"

Nick shrugs. "He'll get over it. Plus, Mick's a better drummer."

"Yeah, but it's Ollie's drum set," I say. "He could decide to take his drum set and go home."

"Not likely," says Nick. "Not in front of all these people. He'd be out of the band. Frankie'd never speak to him again."

"He may be out already since he didn't bring the amp."

"Could be," he says.

"What's up with you and Teresa?"

"What do you mean?"

"You guys didn't seem so chummy before," I say.

"She's all right," he says.

"Is she—" but then I pause, remembering all the eyes and ears on us. "How's the problem she's been having?"

"About the same. She doesn't say much about it. But I can tell. You know."

"Is she today?"

"I'm not sure. I don't think so yet."

"And her parents? In the know?"

He shakes his head. "If they knew, she'd be locked in the house. They don't know."

"I still don't get it," I say. "If somebody like that's not happy, what chance do I have?"

Nick looks up from his plate for the first time and smirks at me. He takes another piece of fish from my plate.

"When do we get ice cream?" the first cousin I bumped asks.

"Not for a little while," I say. "They're still churning it down at the store."

"No they're not," says one of the wiser ones.

"It's going to be weird," I say to Nick. "Tommy being gone."

"No, they're not churning nothing at no store," goes on the budding Huckleberry. I ignore him.

"I don't know," Nick says.

"You don't know what?"

"Vietnam. I hope he's ready."

"He grew up on North Hill," I say. "He should be ready."

"Don't you watch the news?" he says. "North Hill's nothing compared to Vietnam. Nothing in America's like Vietnam. I don't care how tough a place is, or how badass you are, it's a whole different world over there. I don't think he knows what

149

he's getting into, but Mom does. She reads the paper. She watches the news. You know when she left? You know where she went? She ended up in a cemetery, at this guy's grave. The cops found her and called Dad. She was lying by his grave. She read about him in the paper. He went over to Vietnam and two months later he's in a body bag. As young as Tommy. One day he's at a family fish fry like this, enjoying himself, and the next day he's over getting shot at, and then he does get shot and killed. Puck," he says about as down and sad as I've seen him, "there's a real good chance he won't be coming home. You know that. You have to know that. Mom didn't stay away because of her car. She was broke down because of Tommy leaving for Vietnam." Nick, not prone to overdramatize things, shakes his head. I see the kids looking at him. "And now she's pregnant again. She's got to wonder—what's the point? She carries a kid for nine months, then takes care of it, feeds it, protects it, raises it . . . so it can go off to Vietnam and get killed? It tears me up and I'm just his brother, not his mom."

I get up and start walking up the drive, but then stop. Dad's at the fryer, sweating, putting fish onto the plate on the table beside him. Uncle Dobbs is with him. He probably liked me being there. Sure, he doesn't say much, but that's him, he's a reticent guy. I'm a real fuck, I am. And there's Mom, with my aunts who are rubbing her belly over her dress. Just as happy and proud as can be. She loves being pregnant. She said it's better than anything. She said she loves being pregnant, and she loves doing laundry, and folding clothes, and ironing. Women aren't supposed to like those things now. Not the younger ones. They spit on women who do. Like somebody's holding a gun to their heads, forcing them to do it. Why don't they leave them alone? Like they have any idea what being a mom is really like. Like they know what Dad does to support the family, the things he goes through. Who made them God to decide what moms or dads or anybody should do? It's probably going to be her last one. We didn't even look that hard for her. She was at a cemetery crying over some stranger's grave, and we sat in a diner like nothing was wrong. Bob Dylan would probably say it's cool, don't sweat it. But it's not cool. It's selfish and unappreciative. It's being a real punk. There's no value in being cool. What's it mean, anyway? Sir Henry's cool. Dad's cool. Mom's cool. Sandy's cool. Bonnie Bonnell's cool. Father Mann and Father Nigh are cool. Bob Dylan's just a punk. Fuck Dylan. Elvis is cool. He did what his country asked of him. He got his hair buzzed. He put in his time like anybody else, like Tommy's going to do. That's a cool dude. Not some punk who strings words together hyped up on speed. But I love him, Dylan. He's right, without knowing exactly why he's right. Elvis can be right, and Dylan can be right. Maybe that's God's gift, making somebody magical without them knowing why. Maybe that's who Jesus was, a Dylan two thousand years ago.

Frankie's band is in the middle of the first set. I walk past Dad where he can't see me and go stand by the pool where I can watch. The pool is filled with splashing kids. Some of my aunts are in the pool and on the deck, swinging their legs out and in, skimming the water. The band is good. Not real tight, but what can you expect, they only practice once every week or two. I gaze back at Dad. Uncle Al's with him now. I'm glad. He and Uncle Al are like brothers. If Uncle Al's with him then it means he's not lonely, in fact he's sure to be happy. I turn back around to watch the band. Frankie's got a good, gravelly voice and can really play the guitar. He's got a presence. The girls see it. It's like he's not my brother when he's playing, like he's put on some new skin and is a different person. I don't know what I'll do when Tommy leaves for Vietnam, and Frankie, if he does go, leaves for California. Teresa Del Rosa's up there, off to the side near the chain-link fence. She's moving her head as the band plays. She has a flower over her ear. I wonder if she put it there or if Nick did. I feel a tug on my arm. It's some of the cousins from the porch.

"Hey, is it time for ice cream now?" one of them asks.

"Sure," I say. "I'll get you some ice cream."

I go across the street to Romano's and buy a gallon of Neapolitan, chocolate, and vanilla each, and bring it all back and set it up inside the garage. I start dishing it out, but then hand them the scooper and tell them they can get whatever they want.

I put on my swim suit and slide in the pool and stay where I can still watch the band. The water's warm but it still cools me off. I drape my arms over the edge and close my eyes and listen to the band. I listen until they finish the first set, and then when Mick plays the middle set, and then when Ollie comes back banging harder than before as the third set begins. I have my eyes closed the entire time. It's like I'm invisible. If I can't see them, maybe nobody will see me.

When I do open my eyes everything is contrasty from having them shut so long. I hear some of the uncles behind me in the garage playing poker. I imagine Dad's wheeled up to the table, but he's not playing. He doesn't have time for poker. But he enjoys watching as much as playing. He enjoys just being with my uncles. Not as many are watching the band now, and then Teresa Del Rosa gets in there with them. She steps up to the mike, and then they play *As Tears Go By*. She sounds better than Marianne Faithful and I'm blown away, I just can't believe it. She's tentative and her voice breaks some, especially on the high parts, but she's got the pitch and she's got the look; she seems like she's been in a band longer than the rest of the band, except maybe for Frankie, and you can see them all look at her, stunned just as I am.

I get out and change, and when I come back out Father Nigh's talking to Tommy with Mom and Dad and Anthony. I can't hear them, but Father's got his hand on Tommy's shoulder and it looks like he's saying a lot of good things about him, probably wishing him luck, and then Father closes his eyes tight, you can see his thick fingers tense on Tommy's shoulder, and he says a prayer. I see Mom wipe her eyes and I know she's crying. Tommy's still got his hair, but Dad's going to buzz him for the army in a couple days. He still looks like some beach bum with his tan and that blowing hair.

I don't see Nick or Frankie. I find them on the other side of the bus with some of the others.

"What'd you tink?" asks Mick. He says *tink* instead of *think*.

"You guys were really good," I tell him. "Really good."

152

"This girl's got the pipes," says Frankie to Teresa, who's sitting on the ground cross-legged. She smiles, but doesn't say anything.

"I heard. You guys all sounded good."

They pass a can of Coke around. From the secretive way they're acting I guess there's beer in the can. There's so much beer at family parties, you could walk off with a case and nobody'd miss it. When it comes around to Nick, who's sitting next to Teresa, he declines, but she takes a swig. Everybody seems happy when she does.

"We offered her a job," says Frankie. "If she wants it."

"I don't know yet," Teresa says, embarrassed by it and probably by the way we're staring at her.

"Here, cuz," says Mick, lifting the can, "have a sip of *Coke*."

"I take it and, without making eye contact with Nick, tilt back my head. It tastes bitter, like liquid radishes. But it's not as bad as the stuff I had at the Farm.

"There's more where that came from," says Mick.

I make a surprised face. "Yeah?" I still can't look at Nick.

"We got ourselves a supply that'll last us all night."

"He's too young," says Nick.

"Aw," says Mick. "Him? Why, I was pouring beer on my Corn Flakes at his age."

Nick chuckles, but it's not his normal chuckle. My eyes slowly raise up but he's staring into the ground, playing with a stick. Teresa's got her head dropped against him, holding onto his arm with both hands like it's a lamppost and she's waiting for a ride.

"Well, now," says Frankie. "Shall we retire to the bus and play some euchre?"

I think about going in with them, but decide I better not. I suddenly feel like I don't belong, like the things that might go on in the bus are beyond where I can stretch myself. When Nick files past me he nods like I'm doing the right thing. I don't know if I am or not.

The adults are in the garage playing cards. Some of the kids are in the pool, some are inside messing around, maybe watching TV. I wish it was tomorrow and I was back changing tires. When

I'm changing tires, as long as I'm working, Dad doesn't mess with me. He'll keep people away so they don't interfere with my productivity. The girls can't boss me around either. As long as I'm working, I have value, I can daydream and escape.

I stick my hand in one of the plastic tubs and bring up a Sprite. I take it and go around the back and then to the side of the garage and sit on some of the tires we stacked. I can hear the howling and laughing in the garage. It's comforting hearing the happiness just on the other side of the wall. The tires seem like they have personality, like they're alive with thoughts. It's not true, and it's a strange thought but, well, that's how it is.

"Hey," I hear somebody whisper. I look around but don't see anybody.

"Where are you?" I say.

"Here," the voice says louder, still in a throaty whisper.

I keep looking, and then I see this fluttering over to my left. It's Sandy inside her house waving from a downstairs window. She's gray and hazy because of the screen. I sit up, glad to see her.

"What are you doing?" I say. "Why didn't you come over?"

She's sitting in a chair sideways, nose nearly pressing the screen.

"You didn't ask me," she says. "Nice pals you got there," her eyes shooting around to the tires. "I should have brought my camera."

"Come over now. You can sit with me."

"I can't," she says.

"How come?"

"You never said if you liked the pictures," she says. "What did you think?"

"I liked them," I tell her.

"Did you, really?"

"Yeah, I did," I say. "They were pretty amazing."

"Aw, what do you know about photography," she says. "It's like me telling Paul McCartney, *hey, nice song.*"

I don't say anything. I take a sip of Sprite.

"I heard the band," she says. "Not bad."

154

"Did you hear Teresa?"

"I don't think so."

"She was something else."

"I was up and down, back and forth, if you know what I mean."

"Not really," I say.

"I mean, look, you've seen my mom. You've got to have some idea of what it might be like to live here. It's all I can do to keep from getting the boot. Speaking of which, guess what?"

I shake my head. "I don't know."

"I got caught," she says.

"Caught? Caught doing what?"

"You know, when we went shopping. *I* didn't get caught actually; she did. But she had me take the rap for it because I'm a minor. I won't get near the sentence she would."

"I don't understand," I say.

"We got caught, Puck," she says like she's talking to some idiot. "*Mom* got caught, sort of, and said *I* was the one who put the necklace in her purse. She claimed she had no idea how it got in there so I, knowing the routine, said I did it. I admitted it on the spot. You should have seen me—I don't think I've ever done a better acting job in all my life."

"So, what does that mean?" I ask her.

"Man," she says, "you really are a square. It means, since it's my third offense in under two years, and I was on probation already for stealing some shoes, that I'll have to serve some time."

"Time, like jail?"

"Sure, what do you expect? But it won't be bad—it's for underage kids. I mean, how bad can it be?"

"That's awful," I say. "I'm really sorry." I'm leaned forward now, pressing my nose to the chain-link fence.

"It's no big deal," she says. "Couldn't be much worse than living here. Maybe the house will burn down before I get out. Wouldn't that be some good luck for a change."

"You don't mean that," I say. "Come on."

"Are you serious?" She has her arms crossed. "You don't know. You don't know anything about me or this house."

155

"But jail, Sandy," I say. "You're talking about *jail*."

"Maybe I won't go," she shrugs. "Who knows? I thought about skipping out before they get the chance to take me away."

"You mean run away?"

She laughs. "You make it sound like I'm a little kid. It's called escape, Puck. And you—you should come with me."

"Oh," I shake my head.

"You got it just as bad. You know you do. Let's do it together." Her eyes, coming forward now in the dim light, seem to glow white.

"I couldn't leave," I say. "I don't *want* to leave. And you shouldn't either."

"Puck," she says. "You're so trapped, you don't even know there's a cage around you. It's been there all your life. They've got you so conditioned, so dependent on them, yeah, you can't imagine not being here. But you're not like them. Just like I'm not like her. There's a whole world out there without tires, and getting beat up on the way to school, and the stink of oatmeal every morning—God, I smell that shit *every morning*—and *polio*. You didn't ask for that."

"Neither did my dad," I tell her.

"No, but you can't worry about him. You need to worry about yourself. You're a person too."

"But I do worry about him," I say.

"Puck, don't you see—you don't have to. You have brothers and sisters. They don't have your mind. They don't have the dreams you have. Let them take care of your dad."

"You talk like you know more about me than you do," I say, somewhat skeptical.

"I know that you ache every day changing those damn tires. I know you wanted to go into the woods with me, and if we had you might trust me now and understand that I care about you. I have feelings for you, Puck. I'm not sure what they are exactly, but I do, I can't deny it. And you do too, I can feel it. *That's* what life is. You're special, Puck."

"Me?" I shake my head. "You're the one with the talent. I saw your pictures. You're going somewhere. I've got nothing

156

like that."

"I don't know," she says. "I think I have some talent. Thanks—it *does* mean a lot to me for you to say that. But, Puck, if I didn't think you were a budding artist, I wouldn't waste two ticks on you."

"I'm no artist," I tell her, a little offended that she said so. "I'm a simpleton."

"Hey—listen—I have to go." She turns her head back into the dark depths of her house. "To be continued, Puck. So, don't go with me. Don't believe anything I've said except this one thing: You're somebody. You're anything but simple. *That's* what prison does to you. It makes you believe you're worthless because in prison you have no worth. But there's an Oz just waiting for you, Puck." She gets up, hurriedly, and bends to the screen. "I'll go to jail if I have to because it's better than this. But I'd rather escape. I want you, I need you to go with me."

I sit awhile as the gray of twilight turns bleak. The party in the garage is going strong. I can see the light inside Frankie's bus, but the bus is quiet. I think about going out there, but it's too late. I go inside; Gram is asleep on the living room couch, and Sissy is watching TV with the volume down low. A bunch of kids are in the family room, including Squirt, glued to the small red TV that's been set up on Gram's dresser. The kitchen isn't completely cleaned up and there are some eaten bluegill on a couple plates. I take a salt shaker and eat the tails, which are like fishy potato chips, sprinkling salt on each one.

The third floor is empty, except for Anthony, who's at his desk, fingers to his forehead, reading something. I lie on my mattress looking at the ceiling.

"Anthony?" I say.

"Yeah, Puck?"

I thought I knew what I wanted to say, but I rethink it. "Have you decided if you're going to be a priest or a soldier yet?"

I'm not looking at him, but then I do; he's moving his head some, massaging his fingers into his temple like he's got a headache. "No," he says.

"Did you talk to Father today?"

"Yeah," he says. "But I still don't know."

I've got the football in my hands now, but I don't toss it up like Nick does. I squeeze it and feel the laces, but that's all.

"It's a hard thing to do, I bet."

He doesn't answer, and that's just as well. I'm not the only one, then. It's comforting to know I'm not the only one.

Off to Vietnam, Pallbearers for Hire

The day we drop Tommy off at the Cleveland airport it's raining, but then the sun comes out just as we're about there and that makes the drabness go away some. It's just Dad, Nick, and me along with Tommy. Mom couldn't come. What I mean is, she was too broken up to come. She intended to, she got dressed for it, but when it came time for her to get in the station wagon she broke down so much that Anthony, who was going to go as well, had to stay and tend to her.

The sun on the wet pavement of the huge parking lot is like a mirror, and it brightens things up. I'm wheeling Dad, making sure I go around the puddles and not through them. It takes us a while to find the elevators, but we eventually do. We come out of the elevator and check Tommy in at the airline, then pass through security. We go down to the gate and sit down. The floor is like a school cafeteria with the white, shiny but scuffed linoleum. My eyes wander out the enormous windows to the planes landing and taking off looking like giant stiff buzzards. Tommy's hair is short now. Dad cut his hair last night in the kitchen with most of us watching. It was a happy haircut and we groaned good-naturedly when his bangs were cut off, like when a batter strikes out with the bases loaded.

Dad and Tommy talk about the time they went to Florida with

Anthony scuba diving.

"Those were some good lobsters," says Dad. "God, they were good."

"There were a lot of them," says Tommy. "They were easy to catch."

"I was worried. You were down a long time."

"Yeah, but not that far. You should have seen it down there. It was so clear. Remember the blue crabs that old guy kept in the tank outside the bait shop? I couldn't believe how big they were. Nick, the guy's hands were all cut up. He rented us the boat, and his hands were cut up like you wouldn't believe. He had these giant blue crabs as big as lobsters in a tank. I wonder what he was doing with them."

"Probably selling them to the restaurants," says Dad.

"Yeah, probably."

"God, it was hot."

"The water sure felt good," says Tommy. "Nick, you should come with us next time. You need to take some lessons."

"Where'd you take them—at the Y?" says Nick.

"Yeah. Take lessons while I'm gone and then when I get back we'll go."

They announce a flight change and we listen, but it's not Tommy's flight. Dad's facing Tommy, who's in the closest plastic chair beside him, and then there's Nick, and then me. Dad's fingers are dark with grease. He was working on a carburetor just before we left.

"Puck," says Dad, "you should have seen the crabs."

"Yeah, I bet," I say.

He holds up his hands and shows me the spread. "Like this. Unbelievable."

"Did you eat the fish?" I ask him.

"I don't remember," Dad says to Tommy. "Did we eat them?"

"I don't think so," he says.

"We had some of the lobster, but I don't remember eating the fish. I don't know what kind they were—do you?"

Tommy shakes his head. "Didn't you say they were blues?"

"I don't remember," says Dad. "They fought like the devil,

though, when you came up with them."

"That's because they were speared, not hooked," says Tommy. "Maybe we didn't eat them because we didn't know what they were."

"But we must have eaten them," says Dad. "We wouldn't waste fish."

"No, we wouldn't."

"Ocean fish fight more than lake fish, pound for pound."

"Sure seems like they do."

"Those walleye Uncle Dobbs brought to the party," says Dad shaking his head. "Did you have any?"

"No," says Tommy, "just the bluegill. Good?"

"God, were they good. The bluegill were good, don't get me wrong. But oh, man, those walleye. That was awful nice of him to bring them. He only has so many. You can only bring so many across the border."

Tommy listens and nods. He seems more mature suddenly, like he's an old army buddy of Dad's. Dad doesn't seem to be talking down to him, but across to him. He's half wanting to get on with it, to see Tommy off, and half looking like he took a wrong turn somewhere and is afraid to ask for directions.

"I've never been on a plane," says Tommy. "It's a good way to go on your first plane ride, going to serve your country."

Dad doesn't say anything.

They announce that it's time for boarding, and Tommy stands up with his duffel bag right away. He shakes Dad's hand first, then Nick's, then mine. Then he bends down and kisses Dad, and Dad grabs him behind the neck and holds his face to his. I've never seen Dad cry, but his eyes are teary now. Tommy doesn't wait, but gets in line. There's a short woman in front of him and another short woman behind him, with a toddler. He stands out with his hair down to nothing, and the duffel bag, and his tan, and his youth. He gets to just before the tunnel where they're checking tickets, and then he walks into the tunnel without looking back. My ears are ringing. It's like everyone else is a fixture. All I can see is Dad wiping his face and Tommy disappearing into the tunnel. It's hard to believe. Up until now, it's been just talk.

There's been planning. There was the party. But now it's happening, Tommy is on the plane, and we don't know which face is his in the small windows, if he's on our side or the other side. We can't find him. He's gone.

We watch the plane pull back, then move forward out of view. We stay awhile and watch planes take off, but we're not sure which one is his. I start wheeling Dad away. We find the elevator again, then cross the vast parking lot to our car. I help Dad in, then fold the wheelchair and lift it into the back.

We have two carburetors to deliver back down in Akron, plus a funeral to attend. The place where we're taking them is a used-car dealer. It's a sizable place with some nice cars and some not-so-nice cars. There's a big billboard next to the lot advertising malt liquor. It has ivy growing up one side so you can only see half of the lady in the dress, but you can see most of the guy in the suit and his sports car. The carburetors smell like gasoline. Nick is up front with Dad, but I'm in the back seat with the carburetors, and as soon as we stop I get out and take some deep breaths. Me and Nick, we go into the small building and ask for Paco, and when Paco comes out we tell him we're Mike Beck's sons and we have his carburetors. Paco comes out to see Dad in the station wagon and reaches his hand through the window to shake, and as they're talking we each carry a carburetor inside, and then some lady says we can have a doughnut and some coffee. We tell her thanks anyway for the coffee, but we'll have a doughnut, and she rolls out her arm toward the box and says to help ourselves, have as many as we want. Since we don't hear that phrase too often, except at friends' and relatives' houses, we oblige, not wanting to offend her by refusing her offer. Paco comes back in and looks at us with his hands on his hips and he shakes his head and laughs and says something about *you God damn poor starving kids.*

The funeral is at Anderson's Funeral Home. The Andersons are friends of Mom and Dad. They all go out sometimes to the Brown Derby or Sons of Herman, but they haven't been going out much these days, not since Dad's business tanked. We don't know the deceased. Dad offered us up as pallbearers because the family didn't have enough men to carry the casket. I get out the wheelchair from the back and wedge it between the door and the car, and Dad slides onto it. When we get to the concrete steps Nick takes over. He turns Dad around, I take hold of the foot-rests, and we take him up, one step at a time. Dad grips the wheels and jerks backward each time Nick tugs up one step. There are only half a dozen steps, easy as pie, and then we're in the fancy parlor with the flowers and weeping people and organ music coming from the speakers on the walls. I feel weird because me and Nick aren't wearing our good clothes. Dad's got his pressed white shirt on, and he has the turquoise Indian tie he bought out West the last time, but we're pretty plain-looking. We sit in the last row and it's like church only worse. The last three rows are empty, except for us sitting in the last one.

"Why don't you go up," Dad says to us just as I'm settling into a nice daydream about Teresa Del Rosa singing at the fish fry. In my daydream she's wearing her white bikini and she's singing straight at me.

"Huh?" I say.

He nods with that pained face. "Go on," he says. "It would be a nice gesture."

"You mean up *there*?" I say, pointing a bent finger in the general direction of the casket. I look at Nick, who's as horrified as I am. "But we don't even know her."

"Him," corrects Dad. "It's a man, not a woman." He gives us the furrowed brow, nodding toward the casket again. "It's the right thing to do," he says.

So, slow as molasses we pass by Dad out of the row, and I get behind him to push him up, when I feel resistance.

"I'll stay here," he says. "You two go."

"But—"

"Please, son," he says. "It's the right thing to do."

There's no way out. We jockey for position and I try to push Nick ahead of me, but he's bigger and stronger and it doesn't work. I get in line, hands clasped, trying to look pitiful and sad. The line, like some weary chain gang, curls around and then you can see everyone looking up toward the casket. There aren't too

163

many people, really, but the front few rows are full. I do notice something about them all; they're a hefty-sized bunch, each one about twice Nick's size. I'm a few spots away from the kneeler when it hits me: The guy in the casket is probably the same size as all of them. Jesus, I think to myself, I hope some of those big boys are pallbearers too.

I kneel down and sure enough, the dead guy's a carbon copy of the others. His neck is so thick they unbuttoned his collar and loosened his tie. I've seen my fair share of dead bodies for some-body my age, but I've never seen a corpse like this. And his mouth isn't fully closed. The tip of his white tongue's peeking out from his fat lips like a worm left under water on a hook too long. I picture Teresa Del Rosa, for some reason now wearing Dad's cowboy hat singing at the fish fry in her white bikini, and she starts laughing, just laughing her head off into the micro-phone, and seeing her laugh makes me want to laugh, and pretty soon it's all I can do to keep from laughing for real. I put my fist up under my nose and try and hold my breath, like when you try and hold back a sneeze, and it works mostly but I do make these herky-jerky motions and some sounds seep out. I just hope they all think I'm crying.

Dad must not have been paying attention; in fact, he's almost asleep. After the words are said, me and Nick go up and walk be-side the casket as it's rolled down between the two sides of chairs, and then the two of us and the other four pallbearers lift the casket and start carrying it down the concrete steps. They're all a lot older and scrawnier than either me or Nick. Two guys in the middle barely have their hands on the casket, they're no help at all, and it's all I can do not to lose it—I mean, I'm genuinely afraid we're going to drop this guy and the casket's going to go bouncing down and crash into the hearse. We manage to make it down and slide that sucker in, and all those crying mourners will never know just how sad it really could have been.

We go to the church and carry the casket up the million steps there, then carry it back down and into the hearse, and then final-ly at the cemetery from the hearse to the rectangular hole in the ground. My back is breaking as I stand there, stooped, listening to the preacher go on and on, but I still have Teresa Del Rosa keeping me alive and well and somewhat sane inside my head, singing, and laughing, and swimming until her bikini top pops off. I wonder if Nick is thinking the same thing, more or less, to stave off his own suicidal thoughts. I mean, she is his girl, and I feel guilty for stealing her away for my own personal and selfish daydreams. But, well, they're just thoughts, aren't they, and even though the church treats thoughts and deeds almost the same, I don't believe that. In fact, the difference between doing something and just thinking about doing it is the difference between temptation and sin. Maybe between mortal sin and venial sin, though I'm a bit fuzzy on the difference of those two a good bit of the time.

Mom's at the kitchen table playing backgammon with Anthony when we get home. We stopped at McDonald's so she wouldn't have to cook for us. I got a hamburger and fries and a cup of water, but I'm still hungry and I rummage around the icebox until I find some pickle slices and I make myself a ketchup sandwich with pickles. Mom and Anthony aren't talking any. They're not concentrating extra hard either. They're like Squirt when he sleepwalks and pees on the missals, like they're half awake. I wonder about Tommy and where he is now. He isn't going straight to Vietnam. He has to go to boot camp first, and then he'll go to Vietnam. I looked up Vietnam in the encyclopedia a while ago, and it seems like a pretty nice place if you like the outdoors. They grow a lot of rice there like they do in China. They're having a civil war like we had, where people who know each other and even some relatives fight against each other. Nick told me about Ho Chi Minh, how he's the main leader of the north, and if they got him they could stop the whole thing. Maybe Tommy can be in the group to get him. That would be something. Tommy's a good shooter. He and Dad shot those rats in the garage, and he shot some blackbirds on the telephone wire with the BB gun. He's not real big, but he's strong for his size.

Odd Jobs

Frankie's been making money and helping out with things. He paints rooms of people's houses. He and Sir Henry got the bus running, and so he's driving that now. There's a house over in Fairlawn where he's painting today. He's taking me with him. He's going to give me ten dollars for helping him. I don't think I've ever made ten dollars before. I'm going to buy a big jar of marshmallow crème and eat it all by myself. Anthony ate half a jar once, and he let me have a spoonful and it tasted like heaven. Frankie is saving up to get Aunt Myrtle's car fixed, but he gives most of what he makes to Dad. He keeps a little for his pot cigarettes and his art supplies.

We go across the viaduct and then get on Market toward Fairlawn. Fairlawn is the swanky part of Akron. We don't go there much unless we're going to Swensons or the mall. Frankie's got the bus looking real good with the beads and the carpeting in the back. He painted the outside bright colors with psychedelic images on it, and it draws a lot of attention as we drive along.

It's hot in the bus even with the windows down and I have my arms and legs out wide to try and get some air on them. I notice he's got some rolled up sketches on the floor between our seats, and a couple sketchbooks. I pick up one of the sketchbooks to have a look.

"Go ahead, man," he says to me. His hands are at 10 and 2 with his nose close to the steering wheel, and he's wearing his plain white T-shirt. With his summer tan he looks like one of our uncles, only he's skinny and he doesn't have the baggy eyes. He's not a full-fledged hippie yet, but he's got a peace sign necklace drooping from his neck and it sort of counters the buzz haircut.

The sketchbook is filled mostly with drawings of us, sitting at the kitchen table, or standing outside doing nothing, or Mom or Dad on the couch about to fall asleep, or Gram with her thick glasses staring straight at you with that surprised look. You know, just normal stuff. I set down the sketchbook and pick up the other one, the green one.

"That's not for Mom and Dad to see," he says. "But you can look."

I open it up and there are pictures of this girl sitting in a chair with hanging plants behind her by a window, and then more of her standing, or just her face close up, and then some pages later she's nude sitting on the same chair looking straight ahead, and then more lying down on a couch, some facing you and some turned away.

"That's Maria," Frankie says.

"I thought that looked like her," I say. "Wow."

"Yeah, wow is right."

"How'd you get her to . . ."

"How did I get her to pose? Aw, Puck," he says, "that's not really a problem. She's a model at school."

"Yeah?" I keep flipping through the pages, casual-like, like I'm browsing the Sunday funnies.

"Yeah," he says. "She poses for art classes, for figure drawing classes. They pay her. She does it to make money."

"Jesus," I say. "Where do I sign up?"

"It's groovy, all right," he says. "Those are at her house, not in class. I don't pay her when I sketch her away from class."

"She's your girl, right?"

"Well . . . not exactly. But sort of, yeah, in a way. Not the way you might think of it. She's an artist, too. She does ceramics.

She wants to teach ceramics to disadvantaged kids."

"She seemed pretty nice that day," I tell him.

"She is nice," he says. "She's a real sweet girl with a heart of gold."

There's page after page of nothing but Maria naked, and I can't believe that Frankie gets to see her naked and she'll sit there and have him draw her. I can't believe anybody could be that lucky. In the back pages are regular sketches of Maria, and then some of me and Nick, and one of Gram. I don't like seeing myself. I have these slanty eyes and my head is shaved. I look like an alien. I like posing for Frankie, though, just like I like having Dad give me a haircut the times he doesn't buzz us too bad. It's nice having somebody pay that much attention to you.

I put the green sketchbook on the floor and look out at all the big old houses of Fairlawn. The houses have lawns like small parks with flowers everywhere, and nobody has extra cars on the street that don't run. There aren't any forts made out of cardboard or spare wood piled in the backs of yards, and there's not one single chain-link fence or burning drum of garbage.

"Where are we going?" I ask Frankie.

"It's close, but we have to stop off at Aunt Myrtle's first."

Aunt Myrtle and Bonnie live close to Fairlawn, off on a side street in a compact, normal house. Seems the iron railing along the porch steps is loose. Dad wants us to fix it.

We park in front of the house under these big trees. Frankie's got one of Dad's toolboxes in back, so he grabs that and we head up to the porch, wiggling the railing as we go. Aunt Myrtle opens the door before we get there.

"Boys," she says, and she greets us, holding onto our faces when she kisses us. Bonnie's right there beside her, bent to one side like the Leaning Tower of Pisa, and we each bend to give her a kiss.

They take us into what they call their parlor, which is this small dark room with all the curtains closed, and old furniture and old rugs, but everything is neat and tidy, just ancient. Aunt Myrtle turns on some lights and we sit on one couch and Bonnie sits on the other, and she brings out some milk and cookies.

They're store-bought cookies, kind of hard to bite into, but it's nice to have something to eat.

Aunt Myrtle's a big reader and her built-in oak shelves are full of books. She's active in church, and there are missals on the coffee table, plus a couple *National Geographic*s. She's all for women's lib, and the Equal Rights Amendment, and ending poverty overseas, and urban renewal, and lots of other things. Since she and Uncle Don never had kids, she can spend a great deal of time concerning herself with these varied and sundry causes, whereas Mom barely has time to keep our socks and underwear clean. Aunt Myrtle thinks big, and Mom thinks small, and both ways of thinking are good in their own way, I suppose.

"It's so good of you boys to stop and help us out," Aunt Myrtle says. She wears big bright earrings that look like lollipops hanging from her ears. "I know you must be busy," she winks. "We never get a chance to visit anymore now that you're all grown. Go ahead, help yourselves, eat as many as you want."

Bonnie doesn't say anything. She sits grinning at us the whole time with her happy, appreciative smile, leaning forward on the couch so she's almost on top of the cookies.

"Did you see the railing?" says Aunt Myrtle.

"It's pretty loose," says Frankie. "Aunt Myrtle, you should have told Dad sooner. It's not safe."

"Oh, well, yes, it has gotten worse recently. I do hate to bother you boys, or your Dad. He's busy enough these days."

"Still," says Frankie. "It's no big deal. We're glad to come over."

"You boys are so kind," she says, and Bonnie nods and her grin grows wider.

The bolts holding down the railing to the concrete steps are rusted. Frankie doesn't have any in the toolbox and so Aunt Myrtle tells us where the nearest hardware store is, and we drive there and buy some bolts, and while we're out we pop over to Swensons and get some burgers and fries and scarf them down, and then come back. Frankie drills out the holes some, both deeper and wider, so the new bolts will fit. We forgot to buy washers along with the bolts, but we find some that will work in the toolbox. Once we tighten down the bolts, the railing is solid and doesn't wiggle any.

"All set, Aunt Myrtle," Frankie tells her inside. "Can I use your bathroom before we go?"

Aunt Myrtle and Bonnie act like we just put out their burning house, about jumping up and down.

"How's the wine coming along?" Aunt Myrtle asks me.

Aunt Myrtle and Bonnie make wine in their cellar. They bring it to holidays, Christmas and Thanksgiving mostly, and when we picked those cherries at Mrs. Shiner's house we asked Mom if we could have some to make wine. To our surprise, she agreed.

"I think it's pretty good," I tell her.

"It takes some time," she says. "Give it a couple months and then you can try it."

"Yeah, we have it in the basement next to the sump pump. I think it looks okay, but it's hard to tell."

Frankie comes out and says the toilet is running. "How long's it been that way?" he asks them.

"About a year," says Bonnie, her face now worried and long.

We fiddle with the chain for a while, but then realize it's the rubber stopper. It's cracked and doesn't seal when it sits over the hole. We go back to the hardware store and buy a stopper and come back and swap it out for the bad one, and then it works fine.

"Anything else?" Frankie says to them.

"Would you mind, if it wouldn't take too long, changing a couple light bulbs?" says Aunt Myrtle.

"Aunt Myrtle," says Frankie, "we don't mind at all."

Turns out they have five lights out. They're all too high for them to reach. The last one we change is the one in the parlor, and now with the overhead light on it's a bright and eccentric room instead of being dark and drab.

We finally head out. The house we're painting is only a few miles away, just off Market Street going up this hill. It's a style called *Tudor*, says Frankie. It looks like a gingerbread house to me. The lady of the house, who's got her hair up like whipped potatoes, greets us and shows us in, and we take our shoes off immediately and walk around from now on in our socks. It's hard to describe what it's like inside. I've seen pictures of museums or castles maybe that look similar. I'm afraid to touch anything.

"Are you boys hungry?" the lady says, leading us through some other rooms toward the room we're painting.

"No, thanks," says Frankie. "We just ate."

"You're late," she says, a few steps ahead of us, walking fast on her pointy, tall heels. It's a challenge to keep up.

"Sorry about that," says Frankie.

"Oh, *I* don't mind, it's just that I need to pick up our dog from the groomer. She likes the groomer, so that's not an issue. I don't want to inconvenience the groomer himself, you see. We've been using him over three years now and I don't want him thinking we're undependable clients."

We get to the room—this giant hall with tall windows, mirrors between them, and a table that makes our dining room table look like a toy, even with all the leaves in. There's a statue of a dog on a pedestal and I want to feel it, it looks so smooth, but I figure I better wait until the lady heads out.

"All your paint supplies are still there, right where you left them. I didn't touch a thing. I do hope you can finish the room today, we have guests coming three nights from now." She suddenly twirls around to look at Frankie; it's like she's clutching him with her eyes. "Do what you can do, I know how artists are. You're good, I appreciate that, which is why you're getting more than we've paid painters in the past. You deserve every penny. There *are* chicken dumplings in the refrigerator. Have whatever you want. My husband doesn't eat leftovers. I won't be home for three hours. You're welcome to turn on your music." She blinks, standing pretty close to Frankie, waiting for him to speak up.

"Okay," he says. "We'll have it done by the time you come home. There's just the one wall and some trim."

The lady wastes no time. She flits her fingers on top of his head as she walks past him and, as she's passing me, she cups her hand and blows me a kiss.

We start laying down the tarps along the wall, which is where I'm going to be working, and also below the opening into the next room. Frankie has some trim up above there. We make sure she's gone, peeking out the window, before we start talking.

"Holy mackerel," I say. "What was that?"

"That's who's paying me a pretty penny for this gig," he says.

"Is she for real?"

"As real as that Corvette she drove off in."

Frankie's got some of the trim taped off along my wall. I finish taping, then start painting next to the tape with the brush. The paint is off-white, about the same color the wall currently is. Frankie's on the ladder painting the trim between the rooms a light brown.

"How'd you meet her?" I ask him.

"She put a notice on the bulletin board in the art department," he says. "She said she wanted an artist because her dad was an artist, she knew how artists struggle. She said *she* struggled. She wanted somebody who really knew how to paint. She supports the arts, supposedly. Can't you tell?" His head and eyes roll back toward the marble dog on the pedestal.

"Well, that's nice of her," I say, only a fraction facetious.

"It really is. Without ladies like her, this is the only kind of painting I'd be doing for the rest of my life."

We paint for a while. I watch Frankie. When he's doing what he wants to do, like painting, he's as careful and sincere as they come. He's all business, just like Dad, only he seems to enjoy it more than Dad does his work.

"Frankie," I say. "Are you really going to California?"

"I hope so," he says.

"To San Francisco? To meet up with those hippies we met at the Farm?"

"Maybe, but I've got some other friends out there. One's in the redwoods north of San Fran, and another's outside LA."

"What about art school?" I ask him. "Aren't you going to finish that before you go?"

"Art school's not going anywhere," he says. "Art school can wait. I got my whole life to finish art school."

"But what will you do out there? For a job, I mean?"

"This," he says. "Construction. Picking grapes in vineyards.

172

Hell, I don't know." He stops painting and looks down at me. "Out there, it doesn't matter. Nobody cares what you do for a living. That's how it should be, Puck. Nobody gives a rat's ass about your job. People are more concerned about your spirit, your soul. That's what communes are all about. Community. Family. Loving each other without strings, without the unnecessary burden of religion or politics."

I think about it. I bet California's where Sandy's headed if she does run off. She and Frankie talk the same way. It sounds good, what they say, and I could see myself going with them. But something about it's unsettling. It scares me when Frankie talks that way, like he's somebody else. I really like what they say, but I don't know. It sounds too easy, too good to be true. I try and connect all the dots, and they don't always turn into something you can recognize. It sure would be good to escape, though. Look at this place. The lady who lives here—she escaped something, I bet. She's not down in the mud anymore. I'm not dumb enough to believe she doesn't have some of her own problems, but I doubt if she has oatmeal every morning for breakfast.

I think of her soul, and then Aunt Myrtle's, and Bonnie's. They're all the same silvery globes of goodness, or they were, or could be. Aunt Myrtle got married late, found her happiness, then Uncle Don died of a heart attack. The lady of this house had the looks to marry up, and now she doesn't worry about a thing, materially anyway. Bonnie's mom turned away all her suitors— that's what they called boys who wanted to date you back then, suitors—because she wanted Bonnie to stay home with her and take care of her, and that's what Bonnie did, and by the time her mom died she was too old or too set in her ways to have a husband. Their souls were shaped by their luck, and that's the scary part. But even though each of their souls is good, or was good, or could be good, each one had that thing, that ticking little engine way down deep that helped determine how they'd react to the luck God tossed their way. You put the same circumstances Bonnie had around somebody else and they might have come out a whole lot different. And even that, I guess, is luck, because you don't get to choose that engine, do you.

173

"How soon would you go?" I ask Frankie.

He thinks about it as he's moving the brush along the trim in a horizontal line. "If I do, it'll be before winter," he says. "I don't want to spend another winter in Ohio."

"Maybe you'll change your mind," I suggest, like it might not have occurred to him. "It's a long time before winter."

"Yeah, but I need to decide if I'm going back to school this fall. If I decide not to go, there's no point sticking around here."

"You don't have to live at home. You could get a place over by school. That might not be so bad."

"It's not that it would be bad," he says. "I don't know, Puck. I feel like I have to leave. Dad's not forcing me to. I'm not saying he's making me, exactly. But I get the feeling it'd be better for everybody concerned if I left." He stops brushing again to think. "California's where it's happening. Things are happening here, yeah, but that's where it's all coming from. For me, it's like those astronauts shooting up to the moon. It's the place to go. It's where I belong. It's like I don't have a choice, if that makes sense."

The thing is, it does make sense. I don't understand it all, but I understand enough. I've been born into a time of change. Maybe the biggest changes that have ever hit us. Sometimes I want to be right there with him, like some surfer riding the waves, and other times I wish things were the way they've always been. I don't mean the bad things, I mean the good things. It seems like the waves are crashing down on the bad things, which I'm glad for, but they're sweeping away the good things too, which makes me scared.

The lady comes back and her dog looks just like the marble dog. She pays us and tells us it looks fine, and asks if we want to sit in her Corvette. We take turns sitting in the driver's seat, and she lets Frankie back it out and take it around her neighborhood with her in the passenger seat. Frankie gets out and he seems about ready to explode with excitement. Every time we're about to leave she finds ways to keep us there. Frankie asks her if she wants to check out his bus and she says she sure would. Something tells me to stay put while the two of them go in. They're in

174

the bus about a half hour, more or less, and when they come out they're laughing and hanging on each other like old friends. The lady seems like she wants to cry for joy or for sadness, but I don't know about what.

Finally, we do leave, and as we're driving away she lifts up the dog's paw and makes it wave at us. She seemed like a nice lady, but about as lonely as a body can be.

If Not for Nick . . .

Sir Henry took a couple evenings and showed me and Nick some carburetors and how to fix them. We pull a bench from the basement and set it up in the garage, and we start working on carburetors along with doing the tire business. Since carburetors are smaller and you can make more money for the work you do, we shift pretty quickly to doing more of them than the tires. That's fine by me, since taking the tires off their rims and putting them back on is pretty tough.

Dad and Sir Henry are at the real garage most of the day, but when Dad comes home he usually goes into the basement and works on things down there. Sometimes we'll take a carburetor down to him, if we're having trouble with it, and he'll fix it or find a part for it or make a part, and then we'll bring it back up. He started paying us real money. Not much, but something to show us he appreciates the work we're doing. He says he doesn't know what he'd do without us right now. That's exactly what he said. I couldn't believe I heard him right. But today as we're in the garage working, Nick tells me some bad news.

"Sir Henry's thinking of switching to another garage," he says.

"What?"

"That's why Dad's got us working on carburetors. Sir Henry's thinking it over."

"He going over to Mr. Gordon's?"

"I don't think it's with him," says Nick. "Anthony told me. I don't know all the details."

"Jesus," I say. "I didn't think Sir Henry would do a thing like that."

Nick shrugs. "He's got to eat too."

"But he's getting work. Dad gives him work."

"Anthony said Dad hasn't paid him in two weeks."

"Why not?"

"Why not?" He looks at me like I'm daft. "Are you kidding me?"

"But Sir Henry's single," I say. "He doesn't need much money. Can't he wait? I thought he and Dad were best friends."

"They're best business friends," says Nick.

"They're best friends."

"*Business* friends," he says. "You better learn the difference."

"But Dad gave Sir Henry a job. He taught him how to fix cars. Doesn't he care about that?"

"Look, I'm sure he does, man. You know Sir Henry. He's a good guy. I'm sure it's tearing him up. I'm sure it's the last thing he wants to do. And that's why he hasn't left yet. But he can't work for somebody who can't pay him, Puck."

I'm having trouble accepting what Nick just told me. My hands go sort of numb and I can't think straight. I get up and stand at the edge of the garage, still in the shade, staring out onto the street. It's hot. God, it's hot. I have to sit down. I burst into tears.

Nick keeps working, but then comes over. He sits down on an upside-down bucket and puts an arm around me.

"Crying's not going to do anything about it," he says. "But it's okay. Go ahead if you want."

"What's the matter with us, Nick?" I say, looking at him. I can barely make him out because my eyes are filled with tears. "What'd we do? Why are we cursed?"

"I don't know," he says.

"Nothing good ever happens to this family. Why? We're not

177

bad. Why?"

"I don't know. I don't know."

"What are we going to do? Mom's going to have another baby—what are we going to do, Nick?"

"I don't know. I just don't know."

"Are we going to be split up? Are they going to send Squirt off to live somewhere else? Is Mom going to leave for good?"

"Puck, I don't *know*," he says, and for the first time ever I know that Nick himself is crying. I can feel his own body lurch as he tries not to.

Soon after, Father MacGregor walks up the drive. We're back at the bench, stooped over our carburetors, but barely working. I lift my head. He's in his cassock, standing at the edge of the garage.

"Boys, is your father home?" he says.

I raise my arm and point unsteadily to the side door of the house. "In there," I say. "Right through that door. He's in the basement."

Father MacGregor's head twitches back in surprise, and then he heads over and steps inside.

Father MacGregor's down talking to Dad for a while. Anthony pulls up on his Honda. He stands over our bench like Dad would, inspecting our work.

"Father MacGregor's here," says Nick.

"Oh yeah?" says Anthony.

We both nod.

"What's he doing here?"

"How would we know?" says Nick. "He's inside talking to Dad in the basement."

Anthony walks a few steps, takes off his helmet, and holds it at his side, just staring at the side door.

"Maybe he's here to see you," says Nick.

Anthony doesn't answer him. He stands awhile longer, then puts his helmet on the seat of his motorcycle like he always does.

"You should go see," says Nick.

Anthony twists his body back around at us. "How long has he been here?"

I shrug. "Probably twenty minutes."

He twists forward again and stands there. He just stands there. Then, like he's in some kind of hurry, he puts his helmet back on, starts up his motorcycle, and goes down the drive and onto Tallmadge Avenue heading toward Main Street.

Britt comes out and gives us each a glass of water. She's wearing her bathing suit. Squirt comes out the back door by the family room and in no time flat he's in the pool. Britt gets in with him, keeping her head above water.

Father MacGregor emerges from the basement. He gives us that nod. Even from a distance I can see it, and then he walks over. Father MacGregor is an older priest. Quick to smile, and just as quick to put you in your place. White swirling hair, wire-rim glasses surprisingly like John Lennon's, and that Scottish accent. We always try to lay low around him. You never know what you're going to get.

"Have you boys seen Anthony?" he says.

"No," I answer him quick before Nick can.

"Well, can you tell him I'd like to talk to him when he gets home? He can call me at the rectory."

"Sure, Father," I say.

He's looking around the garage, vaguely, not specifically, with an air of confusion. "You boys haven't been to confession in a while," he says. "I expect I'll be seeing you tomorrow."

I don't say anything, but Nick answers, "We'll try, Father."

He cocks his head. "You'll *try*," he says. Nick freezes up as Father MacGregor approaches. "You'll *try—that's* your answer?"

"We'll try," I say to him, afraid for Nick. "We've been sort of busy working. But we'll try."

"Are you being impudent with me?"

"No, sir," I say.

"When your pastor tells you that you need to be at confession in the morning, your only answer is in the affirmative." He raises his head away as if he's been offended. "You're just like your father."

"What?" I blurt out, not a question, but a challenge.

"I said, you boys are the spitting image of your father. He

179

gave me the same excuse when I reminded him that *he* hadn't been to confession in quite some time. *And* his contributions to the church have dwindled to mere pennies, mere pennies. He came back with a similar excuse about things being tough. Ha! You don't know what tough is! Does he think he's the only one with challenges? Why, any troubles—financial or otherwise—are trifles compared to the suffering our Lord endured. More instruction and less—whatever this is you're doing, whatever *he's* doing in the basement—that's what all of you need." His thick, white forefinger is aimed right at us.

Now, dear reader, what you don't know is that while Father MacGregor has been going on about the moral shortcomings of me, Nick, Dad, and our entire family, my hand has found a hammer resting on the bench between me and Nick. My fingers, like the slow tentacles of an octopus, slither around the hammer and grip it tight. Father MacGregor, from where he stands, can't see.

I feel my heart pounding in my chest. My throat tightens, making it hard to breathe. I feel the most intense urge to jump up from my chair, raise the hammer in the air, and bring it down on Father MacGregor's head, but Nick takes hold of my wrist. I struggle to lift the hammer, but Nick keeps my hand down.

"He, he works hard," I utter, barely knowing what I'm saying, as I begin to rise to my feet. "We have no money. We're trying."

Father MacGregor moves toward me. Nick stands up so fast the bench falls back behind us. He moves between Father Mac-Gregor and me.

"I think you better leave," he says to him, and takes a step forward.

Father MacGregor coils back in real fear, something he's probably never felt since he first became a priest, maybe ever, but what we have to fend off just about every day. He turns, and then hurries down the driveway.

I start walking toward the side door. Nick takes my arm, but I yank it free. I open the door quietly, and start down the basement steps. I keep going, past the washer and dryer and shelves where Dad keeps the machine parts, through the partition between that half of the basement and Dad's home workshop, the lathe and

180

drill press on the left, the table saw and joiner and band saw on the right, toward the far wall where he has his bench. There's only a single light bulb hanging on a string above him. He's wheeled up to the bench, hunched over so I can barely see the top of his head. I can hear him using a file, working on some part to a carburetor, making a pass and bringing back the file, over and over, shaving off bits at a time, but I stop before I get to him. He doesn't know I'm there. I watch him, the external limitations of his body never defeating the throbbing orange glow of a soul that knows no quit. I don't care what's going to happen to me when Father MacGregor talks to him—which he will—because Father MacGregor doesn't count. He's like a bag blowing across the street, not worth the time it takes to look at. He doesn't represent humanity or even the church. He represents his own bitter soul, a soul that *has* been defeated, maybe always was, but I vow this: if he ever comes to our house again and tries to lay it on this family, I will take a hammer to him and even Nick won't be able to stop me.

Stogies on the Lawn

Mom found Brigitte. I don't know how, since we always keep her squirreled away behind the door of the crawl space, but she did. She must have been suspicious and started snooping around. I sort of figured she knew about her, you know, but left us alone with her so we'd at least learn the basics of the female anatomy. Worse than finding Brigitte, she found some cigarettes and matches, and the burnt insulation by Squirt's mattress. Squirt, more than any of us, has a thing for matches and fire. He's fascinated by it. He'll lie there near the corner on his bed and light the paper attached to the insulation and watch it travel up slow like a sizzling fuse, and then blow it out before it gets to the wood of the rafters. Almost all the insulation paper in his corner is burnt. Maybe Mom smelled it, or maybe somebody squealed. By somebody I mean Anthony, of course. Nick's told Squirt to cut it out, saying he's going to burn the house down, and Squirt will listen to him, but then he goes ahead and does it anyway. He's like a dog, and just can't control his urges.

"Wait, just wait till your father gets home," Mom tells us, carrying Brigitte under her arm. Brigitte's arms fall off onto the wooden steps, and I rush over and pick them up and slide them back under Mom's arm, but she doesn't seem to appreciate the help like she normally would. Toss in the fact that Father Mac-

Gregor called this morning, and the thought of Dad coming home isn't something I'm looking forward to.

Dad paid Sir Henry, and so he's still working for him. That's the good news. The bad news is the bank turned down the loan Dad applied for. Without the loan, it doesn't necessarily mean the garage has to close, but Dad can't ramp it up nearly as fast. It's going to be like starting over. Mom offered to sell her car, but Dad wouldn't hear of it. He said he'd sell his wheelchair before he'd sell her car, and that's not happening anytime soon.

Dad comes home, along with Sir Henry, who sits at his left for dinner. With Tommy gone, there's an extra spot. We're having chipped beef on toast, which is pretty good except for the peas. I'm allowed to flick the peas off to the side. Anthony likes peas and scarfs them up for me. Dad's not in too bad a mood, all things considered. Maybe it's having Sir Henry in our midst. Mom's smoking up a storm. Her ashtray is on the counter, but she blows smoke right over the table, giving everything a nice tobaccoy smell. Maybe she's doing it because she found the cigarettes.

"Did you see what's in the trash can?" she says, blowing a big cloud of smoke over the table. She's speaking to Dad.

"Hey," Gram says without giving him time to swallow, "you hear? She ask you a question."

"In the trash?" Dad says without his usual scowl.

"Did you? Did you see?" She's watching him. Staring right into him.

"I saw!" says Squirt, shooting his hand into the air. "The pretty lady!"

Sir Henry grins and blinks big through his thick glasses.

"Oh," says Dad. "Yeah."

"Yeah? Did you say *yeah*?"

"Yes." It's almost like Dad's in trouble. He doesn't want to look Mom in the eyes. "You called me at work, remember?"

"What do you think of *that*? They had it hidden in the crawl space, where we keep our Christmas tree. What do you think of *that*?"

Dad sniffles and Anthony, Nick, and me keep our heads low

and try not to make any sudden movements to draw attention to ourselves. At least I'm the youngest. Anthony's really in for it.

"Well," he says. "It's in the garbage now."

"That, that thing," Mom points to the living room, but she's really pointing to the trash can at the curb, "has been upstairs for I don't know how long. Your sons have been using it as, as—"

"She's pretty, Mom," says Squirt. "She looks like you!"

Mom chokes, and starts hacking like she does sometimes from all her smoking.

"It's hideous," Mom says finally. "What ideas about women are they going to get from playing with a sex doll!"

When Mom says *sex doll*, it's like ripping the room in half. Wow, I think to myself, she's pretty mad.

"But, honey," says Gram, "they boys. Boys do boy things." She shrugs. "My brothers, they play with melons. So what? They play with melons. It doesn't mean anything. Boys are like dogs or monkeys. Don't worry."

I don't know whether to thank Gram or not. I try and imagine her brothers with melons and what they might have done with them.

Mom scoffs and turns her head.

Britt clears her throat. She's got her fake eyelashes on, and her hair is done up. "So, Sir Henry, we're glad you're staying on at the garage. Dad says you're training another mechanic."

"Yeah," says Sir Henry with his wide, smooth smile. He turns to look at Britt. I always thought she had a crush on him. She likes clean-cut Buddy Holly types. "I'm glad, too." He pauses, hesitates, and then swings his fork across the table, but means it for me and Nick. "These guys have caught on real fast," he says. "It sure helps having them fix carburetors here."

"Good job, boys," Dad says, and I about cough up what's in my mouth. He adds, "We'll talk after dinner about the . . . mannequin."

"Oh, I saw you jogging the other day," says Britt, and she touches Sir Henry's arm. "I was on my way to work. Do you jog most mornings?"

Sir Henry bobs his head like he's embarrassed and says,

"Yup. I like to jog. I go with my neighbor, Tim, who leads me."

"You were going so fast," she goes on. "I was going to honk, but I didn't want to scare you—I figured you wouldn't know it was me."

He keeps with the bobbing and smiling. "You should have."

"Can I have some more, please?" I turn around and hold up my plate to Mom. I figure any night Dad says *good job* to any of us for anything is a night to push my luck and ask for seconds. She narrows her eyes like she's sizing me up, but then this slight little smirk comes to her mouth and she takes my plate. She returns it with *two* pieces of toast smothered in chipped beef.

Mom made her chocolate cake with chocolate icing to celebrate Sir Henry staying on. When she makes cake she doubles the recipe and uses this really long pan she has for lasagna. She sets it on the table and hands Squirt the knife. There's a special knife we use for cakes that cuts it smooth and doesn't make it crumble any. Whoever cuts has to pick their piece last, so they always make the pieces as even as possible. It takes Squirt ten minutes. Frankie comes in and sits down, late from painting at a house across town. His arms are smeared with dried light-blue paint.

"Sorry," he says, and Mom hands him a full plate.

The rest of us dig into our cake. It's moist and sweet with this minerally taste that isn't a bad minerally taste, it's a good one. Dad has Anthony, Frankie, Nick, and me stay at the table as the others leave. He and Mom chat together all secretive and low, and then Dad leans over to Sir Henry and whispers something to him. Sir Henry listens, and then leaves in somewhat of a hurry. I hear him go down the basement steps, and then come back up and go out the side door.

"Boys," Dad says, "I'd like to talk to you."

"Dad, I'm sorry about the, uhm, mannequin," says Anthony. The rest of us nod.

"Oh, I understand," he answers, like Mom found a Hershey's bar under his pillow. *"And,"* he goes on, "telling Father Mac-Gregor to get lost, and possibly, just possibly getting us booted out of St. Christopher's . . ." He waves his hand in super slow-mo. "That's okay, too." Uh-oh, I think to myself. This isn't going so good. "*And* smoking on the third floor, allowing Squirt to light the insulation on fire, and putting the entire household in danger of being burned alive," he turns up his hands, lifting them, "well, who could possibly be upset about a thing like that?"

Anthony and Nick take Dad down the steps to the side door and wheel him to the front yard. Mom's out there with Sir Henry, but nobody else. Sir Henry has Dad's movie camera on a tripod facing the house. Sir Henry seems awful fidgety and he fiddles with the camera like he wants to keep himself occupied.

"Did you enjoy dinner?" Mom says.

"*I* sure did," I say.

The others mumble with their heads kind of low.

"Henry, is the camera ready?" says Dad. Sir Henry waves his hand but keeps his eye on the viewfinder of the movie camera.

"I'm so glad you had a nice dinner," says Mom. "Puck, you come with me. We're going to enjoy this from the porch." She takes my hand like I'm five and we head around them and go up to the porch swing.

There's a cigar box in the yard. Dad wheels to it, which is tough going in grass, and leans over to pick it up. Everybody holds their breath that he doesn't fall out of his wheelchair and Anthony helps him get it, then goes back to his position in the row.

"You boys seem to enjoy smoking, don't you," he says. "Mom and I have decided not to fight it anymore. You're young men now, you can make your own choices about things like that. Here you go," he says, and opens up the box. Even at my age I know they're about the cheapest, stinkiest brand of cigars you can buy, at least at Carmelo's. "We *would* appreciate it if you wouldn't smoke on the third floor as we've asked; other than that, go ahead and light up." Here Dad waits. "I mean it, come on, have one." He offers the box up to them like Bonnie Bonnell does her chocolates on Christmas Eve.

They go over and take a cigar from the box and bend over as Dad himself lights them. They stand there like miniature, skinny uncles puffing and joking. Mom's lit a cigarette beside me on the porch swing, sending a stream of smog into my face. I keep us going back and forth with my feet, just enough to make her calm and content and happy with me. From where I'm sitting I can see the legs of Brigitte sticking up from the trash can, along with her arms stuffed beside them. Sure is a bad way to end up, I think to myself. Even though she was just a mannequin she seemed like part of our gang, kind of like the girl who likes hanging with all the guys.

After they're done smoking the first cigar Dad offers them another. They don't really want another, but it's not a matter of choice and they light up again. By now we all get the gist of what's going on. By the end of the second cigar, Nick starts breathing heavy, then he throws his head toward the bushes and brings up a good bit of his dinner. Dad lights up a third one for them and Frankie doesn't seem phased by it any, but Nick and Anthony are heaving off to the side in between puffs. I'm not sure why I'm spared from being out there with them, other than I'm the youngest, but I feel pretty guilty watching. Mom blows another cloud my way and I try to find the right expression that shows I'm appreciative of her pleasure, yet indicates I won't touch another cigarette as long as I live.

"How are you feeling?" I ask her.

"Oh," she says, "I feel fine. You mean with the baby."

"Yeah."

"I feel good. It's early still." She takes a long drag from her cigarette. I like the smell of it when there's not a cloud, but just the invisible smell of it.

"Do you have any names yet?"

"Not yet," she says. She looks at me. "What do you think, Puck? Do you have any good names we should think about?"

"It's not my kid," I say.

"But it'll be your brother or sister."

"Still."

"Now's your chance," says Mom. "Give me a good name and I'll sign it on the birth certificate."

"How about . . . I don't know. I can't think of anything."

"No?"

"I like different names, I guess."

"Do you know how we came up with your name?"

"Nick said it was after watching a hockey game."

Mom laughs. "Oh," she says. "You know that's not true."

"I know," I say.

"Most people think it's a nickname. The nurse at the hospital thought it was the drugs and she had Dad make sure I knew what I was doing. He could have changed it. But, he didn't."

"So how'd you come up with it?"

"Oh," she says suddenly, taking a long, slow drag from the cig. "Dad and I went to Cleveland for a weekend. I don't know who was watching the kids, probably Aunt Myrtle. It was our anniversary," she says lighting up. "It was around Christmas and we stayed downtown. We went to dinner. And then we walked around. The lights were out. It was snowing. It was cold, but I don't remember feeling cold because it was so beautiful. You know how our downtown is at Christmas? How O'Neil's and Polsky's have those wonderful window displays? It was like that only bigger, with more lights. I can't imagine New York at Christmas, can you, Puck? While we were there we saw a play."

"*Dad?* How'd you manage that?"

"I hadn't seen a play before," says Mom, "not a real production. He was fine. He was so handsome in his suit. Everyone says he looks like Humphrey Bogart, but I don't think he does, I think he's better-looking than him. I never saw a better-looking man in my life. We were a beautiful couple. It was like our prom, I suppose."

"You didn't go to your prom?"

"I'm sure we did," she says trying to recall. "We must have." She shrugs. "That's how we were dressed, and that's how I felt. I was pregnant with *you*. But I wasn't showing yet. The playhouse, gosh, Puck, what a place! I'd never been to a theater like that before. I wouldn't have cared if we watched anything; it was amazing just to look around . . . But we *did* see a play, a Shakespeare play."

"Lucky you," I say, as facetious as I can be.

"Shakespeare, Puck," she lights up. "I didn't know how wonderful he was. *A Midsummer Night's Dream*, that was the play.

Boy, it was something else. I can't begin to tell you what it was about, but it was something. So, do you know who one of the characters in the play was?"

"Puck."

"Puck," she says, "that's right. And not just any character. That Puck," she says. "He made me laugh, oh my. I don't think I ever laughed so hard. He was smart, and witty, and . . . a lot like your father." Mom pauses. She watches Dad. "It's hard for you to imagine what he was like when he was your age. But your father, Puck." She breathes deep. I wait. "Sometimes who you are, who you really are, gets hidden over the years. It's not that you want it to, it just does." She smiles and pats me on the knee. "When you were born, I knew I had my Puck."

The guys have the dry heaves. I can hear them, but try not to look. It's better looking straight ahead at the hedges along the drive.

"It'll probably be my last, you know," says Mom. Her free hand is on her stomach. She rubs it slow, like she rubbed my head when I was little and had the croup.

"Well, you've had a good run," I say. She elbows me and chuckles.

"I suppose so."

"I guess we'll have room with Tommy gone now, and maybe Frankie too."

When I bring up Tommy Mom suddenly twists her head around, and right away I'm sorry I said it. Her face takes on a completely different expression. She's breathing in big breaths now but then, after a while, she calms down. The boys are through. They walk with Dad and Sir Henry from the front yard, but me and Mom remain on the swing.

"Where do you suppose he is," she says.

"Probably boot camp," I say in a low voice, not really wanting her to hear me.

"Yes, probably. He'll be there for a while. They don't go over right away. They have to be taught many things, don't they, before going away to fight. He's so slim. I wonder how he'll manage to carry his pack."

I say nothing. I know, as Mom knows, that carrying his pack will be the least of his worries. Tommy will be a David being led into a whole arena full of Goliaths. Beating one is possible. Beating them all, well, he'll have to do that to come home alive.

Heaven in the Bus

We stopped going to church. Gram still goes by herself, and sometimes one of the girls will go with her, but nobody else does. Mom and Dad didn't say anything, of course, so we're left wondering if it was an order from Father MacGregor or if it was Dad's decision. I'm glad. I miss Father Nigh, and sometimes I miss being an altar boy, when it's with him, and I even miss sitting in church in the front pew, staring up at Jesus on the cross, letting my mind wander without anyone bothering me. Sunday mornings are strange, and nobody has it figured out yet. It's exciting, though, seeing Gram walk out of the house while we stay put in the kitchen finishing up breakfast. I saw her talking to the picture of Mussolini yesterday. She was talking, and then praying to him, and she was crying about the woes of our family. She asked if he could do something for us. Hell, Gram, I thought, if Jesus isn't doing anything, I doubt if some dead dictator will.

"Gram," I said to her, "he was a bad guy, get it? A bad guy. Don't you know that?"

"Ah," she waved me off. "He did a lot of good for Italy. He wasn't so bad. He did a lot of good."

"I mean, I'm all about forgive and forget, but it's not like he had a couple minor character flaws."

"Ah," she waved again. "What do you know? Were you

191

there? I was there. I know. I know he did more good than bad. You have to smash some eggs to do good sometimes."

You have to smash some eggs. Yeah, that's a good one. I'll have to remember that when *I* want to go on a rampage of suppression and persecution.

It's our last full week working in the garage. School starts next week. I don't want to go to school, but it'll be a nice break from being stooped over the bench in the garage. Sir Henry's been bringing the new guy along, but from what I've seen he's not going to cut it. He doesn't catch on too fast, but worse than that he acts like he's not listening half the time, like he doesn't want to be a mechanic. It's hard to be good at something you don't like.

"Nick," I say to him. We're in the garage back at a few tires for a change. "Aren't you going to play football?"

"It's too late," he says. "They started practice a month ago. The first game is next week."

"Yeah, but I bet they'd want to have you. You're the best tight end they have."

"They have other tight ends," he says.

We do two more tires, then sit down for a breather. It's hot, but it doesn't feel too bad. Maybe we're just used to it.

"Where's Teresa been? I haven't seen you with her."

"Why, do you want to see her?" he says.

"Me? No, not me," I say.

"Go ahead," he says. "I don't care."

"I don't want to see her."

"We broke up a couple weeks ago."

"Oh yeah?" I turn over my lip in surprise. "How come?"

"I don't know," he says.

"Is it the pills?"

"She's not doing the pills anymore," he says. "At least that's what she says. She smokes pot with Frankie, but that doesn't bother me."

"Then, what?"

"She's like Mom," he says.

"She's like *Mom*? What do you mean?"

192

"I don't want a bunch of kids, man," he says. "I don't know if I want any. She wants a boatload of them."

"Yeah, I kind of get that impression."

"Hey, that's cool. More power to her. But I have a feeling she wants to start popping them out pretty quick. It scares the shit out of me. I'm going to college. And after college I'm moving away from here." He looks at me like he seldom does, right at me, not through me. His eyes get big with excitement. "I want to move to Wyoming and live on a ranch a hundred miles from the nearest city. I couldn't do that married to somebody like Teresa. She'd go bonkers out there."

"You don't have to get *married*," I tell him.

"That's what you think. Listen," he says in his low voice. "Don't tell anybody."

"I won't. I promise."

"We had a close call a while back. I mean, really close."

"Damn," I say.

"I didn't know what I was going to do. Can you imagine—me with a kid and still in high school? Can you imagine Mom and Dad?"

I try—I try and conjure it, dear reader, but it's too over-whelming. Too far beyond my worst nightmares.

"But everything's okay?" I ask him.

He nods. "Thank God."

Later on, after dinner and working a couple hours in the garage, me and Nick pay Frankie a visit in the bus. He's been keeping it parked on the other side of the pool since the fish fry. It keeps it out of the way, but more importantly for him it affords a lot more privacy.

Frankie's got a joint, along with some warm beer. Frankie goes for the joint, while me and Nick sip on beers. It's not too bad, if you wince as you drink it. We're playing Monopoly. Our hair's out of the totally sheared phase; we now look like three GI Joes, though somehow Frankie's hair has grown faster, or maybe it's the way he wears it down in front, but it seems almost normal. He says he's never getting another haircut in his life. Not from Dad, not from anybody. He's got a small turntable in the bus and he's playing *In Search of the Lost Chord*.

"Teresa's coming over," Frankie says.

"Yeah?" I say, trying to act all casual.

"Yeah," he says. "She's been singing with us, you know."

"I thought I heard that," I say. "That's cool."

"Not all the time. Just whenever she wants to."

"Are . . . you seeing her now?" I ask him kind of low, afraid to hear his answer.

"Me?" He laughs his big jolly laugh. "I don't mix business with pleasure, not if I can help it. We're, you know, sort of on our farewell tour. She's along for the ride, when she has time." He stops and thinks. "Yeah, we might've gone somewhere if we had her all along. But, oh well. Thems the breaks."

I drink my beer faster than I want to. It expands in my stomach and makes me feel full. Before too long there's a soft knock on the door and Frankie gets up and leans over and opens the door for her.

Since Nick and Frankie are sitting on the same side, Teresa sits next to me. Frankie cracks her a beer before she asks for it and hands it over the Monopoly board. She looks better than I've ever seen her, and she's perfumed up so sweet and strong, I don't know how I'm going to sit next to her. She's wearing a pair of striped shorts and I'm wearing shorts too, and our bare thighs are pressed against each other.

The Monopoly game fizzles, and Frankie breaks out the cards and we play euchre. He puts on the *White Album*. Teresa's face doesn't have one single blemish, not the hint of a pimple on it. It's amazing. Frankie keeps lifting his eyebrows at me, and I sure wish I knew what he was trying to tell me. Whenever Teresa gets animated from making a play, or laughs, or does pretty much anything, her body moves against mine, not just her legs, but her arms and her side.

"You go back to the scene of the crime?" she says to Frankie.

"The who, what?" he answers her, not exactly sure what she means.

"The other night. After the big getaway. Have you been back for more?"

"Oh, that," he says, then grins. "I'm going to let things stew for a while."

"What?" I look between them.

"Your brother met a friend last Saturday," says Teresa. "Like a lost puppy, she followed him out the door after we were done playing. And then he followed her back home."

Frankie chuckles and slaps down a card. "She told me her dad worked the night shift," he says. "He wasn't supposed to be home until six o'clock in the morning."

"Sounds like *that* didn't happen," says Nick, who trumps Frankie's card.

"No, it sure didn't," he says.

"So what happened?" I ask him.

"What happened? We're, you know, in her bedroom getting cozy comfy with each other, when I hear the front door open. She runs to *her* door and locks it, while I'm trying to jump into my skivvies. The old man hears the rustling, puts two and two together, and next thing I hear is the *cha-ching* of a shotgun."

"Holy shit!" says Nick.

"No shit, holy shit."

"What'd you do?" I ask him.

"What'd I do? I grabbed all my clothes and jumped out the window, man. Had to put them on around the corner behind a tree. Hoofed it three miles before I got a ride the rest of the way home."

Teresa Del Rosa, during Frankie's story, puts her hand on my leg and leaves it there, lifting it only when she has to play a card. I'm smiling and chuckling and feeling pretty damn good. The best part is, Nick and Frankie are just as smiley and happy about it. It's not very late, but Nick says he's going to head in, which leaves just the three of us. Then, about fifteen minutes later, Frankie says he's too hot and he's going to sleep inside, and he leaves. Which leaves me alone with Teresa Del Rosa in the bus.

"So," she says, turning toward me some.

"So, hey there," I say.

"You don't like beer?" she says.

"Sure, why wouldn't I?"

195

"You make a face every time you take a drink. It's all right. I'm not crazy about it either. My mom and dad like wine. I do too."

"We're making wine," I tell her.

"Is that so."

"It should be ready soon. We're making cherry wine from the cherries we picked at Mrs. Shiner's house."

"I've never heard of cherry wine."

"I think you can make wine out of just about anything," I say.

She scratches her nose using the hand that's on my leg, then puts it back down. "I'll have to try it. Will you let me have some?"

I nod, then look into the beer in my hands on the table. I don't know what to do. I want to, I really do, but there's Sandy to think about. I've thought about Teresa for so long, now I have my chance, even if she is just coming off breaking up with Nick. Sandy and I don't really have anything. We kissed at the lake. That's all. Well, and we kissed over the chain-link fence. But I haven't seen her in a while. She'll be off to prison soon, or running away. I know what Nick said about Teresa, but she seems normal to me. I'm sure she doesn't want to marry me, or have a baby with me, or do anything but what we're about to do.

The bigger thing is the deal. I'm probably going to hell for what I wanted to do to Father MacGregor, even though he would've deserved it. And I already did kiss Sandy, and have thoughts about her just like I've had thoughts about Teresa for some time. But all I've done, up till now, is kiss her. There's the brief time with Karen in the barn, but that was more or less her doing—I was pretty much a victim in that episode. What's about to happen, if I do it, is going to break the deal any way you look at it. The question is, do I believe, I mean really believe, the deal is genuine? I pray every night, granted, not on my knees like when I was younger, but I do in bed, and I suppose talking to Jesus in my mind is a form of praying. I pray to Him every day for Dad's legs to get better. I'm not stupid. I know polio is a permanent affliction, even if Mom doesn't think so. But I do believe in miracles. That's what I'm holding out for. I believe in

Jesus and the miracles He can perform. If I go ahead, there's no chance, however slim a chance there is, that Jesus will come through for Dad.

Her hand raises up and rubs against my arm, nervous-like, the way you might sand something.

"You and Nick aren't together anymore?" I say. "What happened?"

"I don't know," she says softly, thinking it over. "We seem to be better off as friends. Boys and girls, they can be friends, you know. We're friends. But I don't just want to be your friend. I've thought of you as more than my friend for some time, Puck."

"But you were with Nick," I say.

"But not now."

"I know, but he's my brother. It's kind of strange. Don't you feel strange about it?"

"I don't know why it's any different than if I'd dated someone who wasn't your brother. Does it bother you?"

"Sort of," I say.

"I'm sure he doesn't mind. He didn't appear to mind when he was here. Don't you think they both left so we could be alone?"

"Maybe," I say.

"I think so. You know something?"

I shake my head.

"It was always you, Puck. I'm not saying I didn't like Nick. Of course I did. But, it's always been you."

"I don't believe it," I say, stunned, to say the least.

"It's true," she says. "I think Nick knew it. I don't think he ever really had it bad for me. Not the way a girl wants a guy to. I don't know what he's told you, but we didn't do much together. It wouldn't matter anyway, not to me, but it might matter to you."

"But Nick said—" I stop myself.

"Nick said what?"

"He said . . . He said . . ."

"He said what?"

"He said . . . you guys had a close call."

"A close call?"

197

I don't think she understands my meaning, so I wait.

"Oh," she says. "That's what he said?"

"Yeah."

"I don't know why he would say that," she says. "It's not true."

"It's not?"

"No, it's not."

"But," I say, rolling it around in my mind, "why would he say something like that?"

"I don't know," she says. "Maybe to protect himself."

"From what?"

"Nick may not have loved me, but that doesn't mean he wasn't hurt when we broke up. I think he knew how I felt about you. He couldn't accept that I wanted to be with you instead of him."

"You mean he made it up? Nick's never lied to me," I say. "Not about anything big. Not about something like that."

She smiles pleasantly, dropping her head. "Don't be too hard on him," she says. "We all have to protect our personal flame. Without that, well, there's nothing stopping the darkness from taking over."

My mind is buzzing and my body's pounding with desire.

She leans toward me, her face dropped so it's covered by her dark, wavy hair, keeping it there below my chin. She looks up, then, and I kiss her. Her lips are soft, but she doesn't dart her tongue out like she did with Nick, or do it like Sandy did. She uses her lips without any of that. My hand moves over her softness. She moans. Her moan is like the opening hymns at church when everybody stands and it's all powerful and beautiful and pure and it's electric in your blood.

The Seventh Step

We slither out the door of the bus, arms around each other, and I walk her to the gate on the chain-link fence. I'm afraid her parents will see us, but part of me doesn't care. I kiss her, and then kiss her again. I don't want her to go. I don't ever want her to leave. We return back to the corner by the bus where we can't be seen and stand there for a while. She's just sweet and soft and perfect. She's nice and lovely and dreamy. She pulls herself away, then comes back for another ten minutes. She makes sure all her clothes are where they should be. I laugh, low, and so does she. Her hair's a mess and mine would be if I had any. I'm never going to wash my shirt. I'm going to keep her perfumed smell on it till the day I die. I kiss her more and more and then, finally, she pushes the gate open, lifting it so it doesn't squeak, and passes through. I watch her walk the short distance to her house. She turns and waves and then steps inside. I bring the gate back and latch it without making a sound.

I sneak inside, Frankie having left the door unlocked for me, and go into the kitchen and put a slice of bologna between two pieces of Mom's bread. I'm starved. It's like I just ran ten miles. Or dug a row of ditches. Or plowed a field by hand. The bologna sandwich tastes terrific! I drink a glass of milk, wonderful powdered milk—no facetiousness here, dear reader! I turn my head

199

and smell my shirt. She's on my shirt, on my face, on my arms, and my hands. I can't believe it. I keep thinking about it. I can't believe it.

I stare into the toaster. It's like I'm floating. It's a strange and unusual feeling. I wonder if this is how it always feels. It feels wonderful because of what we did, and because of what we didn't do. Maybe more because of what we didn't do. But she did plenty. She did everything I could have imagined a girl could do. I think about her and Nick and wonder what she did with him, but of course she did some of the same things. That's all right. It's all right as long as you desire the other person, or love them, or think some day you might love them. I wonder if what she said was true, that she's been thinking of me all this time. It blows my mind—Teresa Del Rosa, thinking of *me*, when she was with Nick.

I take a bite of the bologna sandwich. Wow. I never knew how good bologna was! I'm going to have it every day. Thank God somebody invented it. I really can't believe how good it is—

"Puck?"

I turn my head. My ears are buzzing. I listen.

"Son?"

I rise, and slowly turn toward the steps leading to the basement. The linoleum cracks under my feet. I feel myself move down the steps to the landing by the side door, then turn, hesitantly, down to the basement.

"Can you take me up, son?"

"Hi, Dad," I say casually. "I didn't know you were still working."

"Yes," he says. He's leaned against the wall, holding himself up, waiting. "Frankie and Nick are already up. I think everyone is asleep except you."

"Sure," I say in a low and mellow voice. "Are you ready now?"

He nods several times. He looks incredibly weary, waiting for me.

All right, I tell myself. All right, Puck.

I go down and without delay take my position under his arm,

turning slightly, making it easier for him to curl onto my back. His weight falls onto me, heavier than usual. I'm drunk. Not plastered, but drunk. I'm afraid he'll smell it. I ease my face away to the side opposite his. He wraps his forearms around my neck and locks them, one holding the other. I lift myself, keeping bent, and take hold of the railing. I've not carried him from the basement all the way up. I blink my eyes, trying to focus. I block out everything else.

I take him up the first few steps to the landing by the side door, make the turn, and then start up those few to the kitchen. He feels heavy, much heavier than usual. His forearms strangle my throat. His belt buckle digs into my back.

There are the few dozen blind shuffles from there to the bottom of the steps to the second floor. All the lights are off. Everyone in the house is asleep. For a second I consider setting him down and telling him. I'll tell him I'm drunk, I say to myself. I'll look him in the eye and I'll tell him I found some beer and got drunk behind the garage by myself. I won't mention Frankie, or Nick, or the pot, or Teresa, or what we did, or how dizzy I am, or anything else. But I'll tell him. I'll get Nick and he'll take him the rest of the way. I think all this in an instant, and reject it just as fast.

I feel okay as I start up. I know I'm strong. I've been carrying him some weeks now. I know how to do it. I know the steps and the railing. It's not that far, not like going all the way to the third floor. I've already come up from the basement, I just have to make it to the second floor. I start going. His feet bump the backs of my calves randomly like light weights tied to the ends of ropes. I try not to think. Thinking makes it harder and focuses the effort and pain.

I get to the landing and make the turn. I think I'm all right. There's only one more flight to go. I've done most of it. Then, my vision starts going black at the edges. Soon there's just a circle where I can see, directly below me. It must be his arms. They're choking me. I have no air. I attempt to say something, to tell him to loosen them, but I can't speak. Nothing comes out. It affects my legs. They feel rubbery and start wobbling. It's the

201

lack of air, and the alcohol, and the lightheadedness from being with Teresa. It's everything. My legs are burning. I never have problems with my legs carrying him, but they're rubber and on fire.

On the seventh step from the landing, just a few away from the second floor, I stagger and fall to one knee. His arms tighten around my neck. I hear him trying to say something, but it comes out as just a squeak. Instinctively, I lean forward to keep our center of gravity under me. If we drift backward, I won't have the strength to keep us up, we'll both fall down the stairs and for him it will probably mean the end. It will surely be the end of me after they find out what I've been doing and that I'm drunk. The guilt I already have will be nothing like the guilt of killing him.

I start to say a prayer in my mind, but stop. Jesus isn't going to help me. Nick, or Anthony, or Frankie aren't going to help me. No one is going to help me. My fate, Dad's fate, rests on whether I can gather myself, fight the alcohol and the choking, and move up those last few steps. I use the anger of a lifetime to rouse myself. I crack the invisible whip on my thighs, telling them to move. I command my heart to pump. I refuse to submit to this fate. Then, slowly, I begin to rise. He moans as his back is stretched. I take one step and then another. I discard any worry or outside thoughts. I am moving, a machine, a passenger in my own body. Fate pushes down on my face, I turn aside, grit my teeth, and keep going. Then, I'm on the second floor. We've made it up. I let him down, abruptly, and he makes another frantic sound as we sway to the left. But I widen my stance, I steady us, and soon he releases his choke hold on my neck. He grabs the top of the railing, and I ease out from under him. I gasp for air, and so does he. His face is pink. His eyes are puffy from working late and from the strain. The weariness of a lifetime is there. His weariness of the pain. His weariness of me. There's nothing to say. I notice but don't look at the Fab Four on the door of the girls' lounge, and the luck or bad luck of fate couldn't be starker. There's nothing to say. There's silence. The girls in their room with Sally, and Mom in their bedroom, and Anthony and Squirt and Frankie and Nick upstairs—none of them will ever know what happened, how close I was to losing him, how our family would have been smashed, finally, to bits.

I get his crutches, which are leaned against the wall outside the bathroom. I give him one, and he puts his hand through the loop and takes hold of the grip, and then I give him the other one. He doesn't look at me. I wonder if he knows about the beer and about Teresa. I want to rewind the past few hours. He begins the short journey to his bedroom. I trot ahead and make sure the door is open and there is nothing on the floor he might trip over. He reaches the doorway just as I slide past him. I don't say good night. I don't kiss him. I walk past the picture of the Four and give them the finger, and then go into the bathroom and close the door quietly and turn on the light. I look at myself in the mirror. Tears flow down my cheeks, I can't stop them, and I cry silently. I cup my hand to my mouth as it really starts to come out and then grab a towel and shove it in my face. It's all exploding in my mind. It's too much. It's just too much.

The Knife's Edge

We receive two letters about the same time. The first is from Italy. Gram's sister, Rosina, isn't doing well and wants her to come visit. She says her health is failing and their last brother is old, but healthy, but who knows for how long, and they should see each other before it's too late. Gram carries the letter in the front pocket of her dress and reads from it throughout the day. She reads it to me too, but it's in Italian and she has to translate it, and each time she translates it differently.

"You think you'll go?" I ask her at the kitchen table, eating some peanut butter toast.

"I have no money," she says. "I would go in heartbeat if I had money."

"But doesn't she say she'll pay for your airplane ticket?"

"She have no money," says Gram. "How can she pay? I would go in heartbeat, but we're too poor. I guess I'll die here without seeing my sister ever again."

Gram gets to feeling sorry for herself now and then. Sometimes I can take it but other times, like now, it's hard to listen to her. Still, it has to be tough. She hasn't been back to Italy since she came over all those years ago.

"Did she say anything about that guy?" I ask her.

"Who?" She looks at me a bit startled.

"That guy. What was his name?"

"What guy? Who you talking about? You crazy." She has her plump arms folded over one another and looks worried, like I caught her doing something.

"Carmelo. That's it. Carmelo. Don't you want to see Carmelo?"

"How you know about him?" she says.

"I heard you one night," I say. "You were talking to him and to your sister."

She starts wagging her finger at me. "Oh, you spying on me, eh? You spying on your old grandmother. That bad. You bad boy for spying on me. You know nothing. Can't nobody have privacy in this house? I tell your mama what bad boy you are for . . ."

Her voice fades as I take my peanut butter toast and head outside.

The other letter is from Tommy. It's not to the whole family, but to Mom and Dad. Mom reads it to me one evening after dinner on the porch. It's just the two of us on the swing. She reads it instead of handing it to me to read for myself.

He's in Vietnam now. I can't tell if he's done any fighting yet, or if this was before he saw any combat. He sounds cheery and optimistic, but he says he misses everyone and didn't realize what a nice family he had. He tells them not to worry, that it's hot and steamy in Vietnam, but nothing he can't handle.

Mom puts the letter back in the envelope and slides it underneath her.

"Do you want to feel the baby?" she says to me.

I place my hand on her stomach. She holds her own hands on mine and we wait. Nothing happens. I don't know much about babies, but it seems early to be feeling a baby kick. Mom waits, all hopeful, but finally I move my hand away. She fights the tears, but then cries some. I take her hand in mine.

"I hope he's all right," she says. "He's so skinny. He knows how to shoot a gun, but so do they. He's not built for being a soldier."

I tell her that Tommy isn't big, but he's smart, and I mean the important kind of smart, not the kind you get from books. He'll be all right, I tell her. She nods and gives me a quick smile, but I don't think she believes it.

She keeps the letter on the buffet in the dining room with Tommy's senior picture and a small framed newspaper clipping showing a map of Vietnam. Both Mom and Gram pass it several times a day and say a prayer each time they do.

I'm on the side of the garage. Most of the tires are gone, except the ones on the side. Now that school's going, me and Nick don't have near the time, and we either work on carburetors or do other small things for Dad. I'm sitting on a Firestone. Steel-belted radial. I'm sitting there when Sandy comes around on her side of the chain-link fence. She has a folding chair and sits down facing me.

"If it isn't the wonder boy of North Hill," she says.

I haven't talked to her in a while, and it's different now that I've been with Teresa.

"How's it going?"

"It's going," she says.

I give her a nod and a weak smile. "I didn't know you were still here."

"Oh, I'm still here," she says.

"What happened?"

"What happened? Nothing happened."

"But you're not in jail, and you haven't run away."

"It takes time," she says. "Apparently there are more dangerous delinquents than me out there."

"I thought you were dead set on leaving," I say.

"Oh, I'm leaving," she says.

"You and Frankie."

"Him too?"

"Yeah," I say. "It's not exactly the same thing. But he's heading out soon, I'm pretty sure. He's going to San Francisco."

Sandy considers it and says, "I can see him out there. Sure."

"Can you? I can't."

"You can't because you don't want him to leave," she says.

"He's in art school," I say. "What about that?"

"He can go to art school in San Fran," says Sandy. "But he's bound to learn more on the streets than he will in any classroom."

"Yeah, but what does he know about California? It's crazy out there."

"Which is why he's going, Puck."

"I know," I say sort of quiet-like, dropping my head.

"Frankie's a real artist. The only kind of artists that want to stand still aren't artists at all. They're people who think they want to do art. They want to do it, they don't have to do it. And that's cool. But if you're really an artist, by definition you can't sit still. You can't remain the same as you were yesterday. To everybody around you, you look unstable or indecisive. Or worse—*stupid*. And the way they look at things, I guess you are. But it's just who you are. And it's who *you* are."

I slowly shake my head. "Why do you keep saying that?"

Sandy sits back in her chair and folds her fingers together. She watches me, like she's waiting for me to say something, but I don't want to say anything.

"Why?"

"Yeah," I say. "You have a way of making me uncomfortable, you know."

"Remember when we drove to the lake? I was taking pictures in the car, remember?"

"Sure," I say.

"I wasn't taking pictures, not right then exactly. I was pretending to."

"But why?"

"For one, I was scared. I didn't know you at all. I didn't want to be there, but I was curious about you guys. I had to push through that if I was going to find out. But the other reason was, I was watching you."

"Me? What for?"

"To see what *you* were looking at. You were looking at everybody else, but nobody was paying much attention to you."

"I was the youngest one in the car," I say. "That's natural."

"Sure, you were the youngest, but look at Squirt. Being young doesn't stop him from speaking up." She drops her hands and leans forward. "Puck, I've seen you behind your dad your whole life. Pushing his wheelchair. Doing this. Doing that."

"Look, Sandy, I don't want to go over that—"

"No," she says, "that's not what I mean. I'm not criticizing your dad. This isn't *about* your dad. But, I saw that you were checking me out. The other girls too, sure, but you were curious about me. Maybe Frankie was, maybe Nick was, but their curiosity was nothing like yours. I peered through that camera lens and saw you in the passenger side mirror doing all you could to figure me out."

"That would have been hard," I say, somewhat facetiously.

"Of course. But you tried. You couldn't *not* do it. You've been a shadow behind your dad, behind your brothers, to your sisters; invisible is more like it. That's a recipe for pain, but also for a mind with gears that never stop turning. Your life has been nothing but one big training session to become an acute observer. I envy you, Puck."

I laugh. "No, no you don't," I say.

"Like hell I don't. I envy you because you're like me, but your cynicism hasn't undermined your sensitivity. Somehow, you're still whole, whereas I . . ."

"Yes, *you*," I say, getting her to finish her thoughts.

"You barely know me, Puck, but you know me enough to see that I'm a collection of fragments, I'm not whole. I can be for periods, like right now with you. Something about you makes me calm and want to be, well, normal. But I'm not like you, not in that way. You're on the knife's edge, you can go either way."

"What do you mean?"

"There's not much middle ground with artists, Puck," she says. "It all depends on how much kindness has been tossed in with that pain. There's no glory in falling onto the wrong side. I might act like there is, but that's my jealousy talking. You can't remain where you are much longer—it's impossible. I pray every night for you that you end up on the other side. Some of us have to make it out."

I can't stay any longer. I understand some of what she's saying, but some parts I intentionally don't think about. It's the only way I've found I can keep my head above water.

"I have to go," I say and I stand up.

"Sure," she says, and she stands up with me. "I heard about Tommy shipping off to Vietnam. That's got to really suck. Nobody wants to go *there*, so you see, some have it worse than us. I took some more pictures. I'll show them to you when you have time."

"Hey," I say, remembering, my head still in a cloud. "Have you seen or heard anything? Somebody stole one of the motorcycles out of our garage."

"I don't know," she says. "I heard Lennie's been riding around on a new bike. It's red, though."

"Is it a Honda?"

"I don't know, I haven't seen it."

"And he just got it?"

"That's what I heard."

"All right," I say. I put my hand on the chain-link fence and wiggle my fingers. She takes them in her hand, just for an instant. "Nice seeing you."

I go inside up to the third floor and start on my homework. Anthony's there, but nobody else. Me and Nick noticed the Honda missing yesterday. Nick's been riding it some, but he knows he put it in the garage after he rode it, though he's not sure if he pulled down the door. Nobody else knows it's missing. We thought about telling Anthony, but Anthony's nowhere near as big as Lennie's dad and I don't think Anthony would go over there. Dad's not going to do anything. He'll just chew us out for leaving the garage door up, which is a good point, but still, what's he going to do—wheel over and throw rocks at their window till Lennie's dad comes storming out? Drive up in the station wagon and honk his horn? The girls don't have any idea what it's like having a dad who can't back you up. People like Lennie and his dad don't go easy on you for it, they see it as a vulnerability, like lions do a wounded animal. And it would be one thing if Dad wouldn't expect us to go get the bike back, but he does. How are me and Nick supposed to get a bike back from some ex-con and his bully son?

I try and work on homework, but it's hard to concentrate. I

want to think about Teresa, but every time I do I remember nearly killing Dad on the stairs. I can't picture her without thinking about how I broke the deal, and how it might actually have been the cause of it. Then I wonder if it's going to affect Tommy over in Vietnam, if Jesus is going to be mad at me and take it out on him and not give him any protection. Maybe that's why the Honda was stolen. Maybe that's why we're struggling so bad. I wanted to tell Sandy about Teresa, and I wanted to tell her about what happened on the stairs. I don't know who else to talk to. I don't want to go to bed. I'm afraid of what's waiting for me.

Two Worlds Apart

We're having corn on the cob. Again. The kitchen's a sweltering sweatbox, but nobody seems to care. We're all hunched over our plates, buzzing corncobs like a bunch of typewriters chewing through paper. I sprinkle salt and pepper on mine, along with butter, of course. Mom has two plates of butter on the table and we're allowed to roll the cobs on it instead of having to take some with our knives. It's a lot faster, plus we don't dirty up nearly so many knives. All we're having is corn. Mom made two big pots of it, which took us fifteen minutes to shuck. She's standing between the kitchen and the dining room, staring at the dining room walls. Dad had Sir Henry and Anthony and Frankie put up some wallpaper over the weekend. It's a real fancy design, purplish, and it's made Mom just bursting with happiness.

"I never hear it so quiet," says Gram, her plump forearms folded over her chest. "It like nobody ever eat around here."

Squirt's eating his corn piecemeal, leaving big gaps all over. I make eye contact with him, you know, encouraging him to eat everything on the cob. Nick doesn't wait. Once Squirt puts down his cob and starts on another, he picks it up. Squirt acts surprised, but Nick doesn't flinch, doesn't even look at him.

"I bet I can eat more corn than you," Anthony says to Nick.

"Okay, sure," says Nick.

"How much?"

"What?"

"How much you want to bet?"

"Ha! Here we go," says Gram. She taps Dad with the back of her hand. "See? Your starving boys are going to do it again."

Dad, who I don't think has been listening, looks up from his plate. I expect him to put the kibosh on things, but he doesn't. He sits there chewing the cud, waiting to see what happens next.

"Okay," says Nick. "How about this. Whoever loses has to go get Tommy's Honda back."

"What are you talking about?"

"Lennie stole Tommy's Honda. Whoever loses has to go over and get it back."

"That Lennie," Gram says, wagging a plump finger. "I told you he was bad boy. He end up in jail, for sure. He bad, bad boy. He shoot you! Don't go over there, I telling you."

Anthony's thinking. He never met Lennie's dad, but we told Anthony about him. The thought of going over to his house and somehow retrieving the Honda seems pretty remote, and even knocking on the door without getting a black eye or worse seems near impossible.

"How'd he steal it?" says Anthony. "Didn't you lock the garage?"

"What do you say, slick," says Nick. "I can sit here and eat corn all day. Think you can do that?"

Here's where most dads step in and tell them to cut it out and finish their dinner. But Dad merely fumbles around for the pepper shaker as he turns his corn over. I guess this falls under the fighting-your-own-fight umbrella, and there's no bigger advocate of *that* than dear old Dad.

The corn competition ends up being a repeat of the meatball competition. Nick chomps through eight more cobs before Anthony can get to his seventh, and he gives up with buttery kernels all over his face and more dejection than bitterness. Nick sits back, happy he's not going to have to pay a visit to Lennie's house. I feel bad for Anthony. He'd have trouble taking on Lennie, let alone his dad. I wait for Dad to say something, to yell at

212

us for allowing Lennie to steal the bike, anything instead of letting Anthony go over there. But he doesn't say a word. Mom's been in the dining room the whole time, admiring the wallpaper.

After dinner I go up to the third floor, where Anthony's at his desk. I'm just at the top of the stairs and stop there. He doesn't notice me. He's got his light on, and I'm not sure what he's reading, but he seems to be concentrating awful hard. Me and Anthony never had that connection. We're too far apart in age, and we're too different. He's like Dad: obedient, dependable, a doer, and doesn't go for stepping outside the lines—by him or anybody. He's more Dad than he is one of us, and that's hard to take. He held me and Frankie down while Dad sheared us to the bone, and no brother should ever do that to another, not willingly, no matter what kind of trouble he'll get in. Sure, Nick did too, but he didn't want to. There's a big difference between doing something because you have to and doing it because you enjoy it. I always thought Anthony had it easier than the rest of us. He tells us what to do all the time and we have to listen. He's Dad's voice when Dad's not around. He has a privilege none of us has. But seeing him there at his desk . . . I don't know. He does seem like Dad, which means he's got a lot of responsibility.

I lie down on my bed and look up at the cracks. It's not right that he has to go get pummeled by Lennie's dad just because he lost the bet. He'll either get beat up, or if he chickens out he'll have to live with that. It doesn't seem right. There's no way out.

I wonder what Tommy's doing in Vietnam. I don't like watching the news. Mom watches, but Gram won't and Dad never did like it. He'll read the paper, but he won't watch the news. They show gruesome things on the news about Vietnam. They don't have to show what they do, and it must hurt something bad for the families of the guys who die. Maybe that'll be us one of these days. It's hard to imagine Tommy fighting anybody over there. We're all pretty scrawny, really, except Nick. Nick would do all right. He could carry his pack, and shoot better than average. He's tough. He's a man of action. He'd get through it okay, I bet. I don't know if I would or if Frankie would. Tommy was all gung-ho, but enthusiasm only gets you through the first part, like in a football game. Then it comes down to toughness, grit, skill, and intelligence. Vietnam seems like a card game. You can be the best card player, but if you get bad hands you're going to lose.

It occurs to me that I should try and get Tommy's Honda back instead of Anthony. If I get beat up, nobody will think anything of it. They'll expect it. I don't think I'd get anything worse than a broken nose, and those heal up pretty quick. I'm not going to tell him, I'm just going to go get the bike and bring it back. Somebody's going to be in for it if we want to get it back. It might as well be me, and maybe it should be me.

I get up and go down to the second floor. I wince when I see the mustaches I put on all The Beatles outside the girls' lounge. Britt's still trying to investigate who did it, but she's not going to get too far down that road. I put on a cheery face and knock.

Britt opens the door and right away the music and incense hit me.

"Puck," she says sort of surprised.

"Hey," I say to her.

"You want to come in?"

"Yeah, I guess," I say, and step inside.

It's weird, but I've only been in their lounge a few times since they converted it from a bedroom. I walk past it every day, but it's like some other world. It sure is strange sitting on their couch staring at the wall full of Beatles posters. God, the guilt—the guilt, dear reader.

Britt sits on her big beanbag chair in the corner, lifting her toes to look at them. She's just finished painting her toenails.

"You don't need money, do you?" she asks, suddenly giving me a look.

I shake my head. "Naw, I don't need any money," I say to her.

"I can loan you some next week after I get paid," she says. "But I'm pretty broke until then."

"No, I was just passing by and figured I hadn't stopped in for a while. Nice pad you got here," I say, looking around. She has the lava lamp going on a small table, and a strobe light flashing,

214

even though it's not dark yet.

"You need me to write a note for you?" she says, the thought suddenly dawning on her.

"No, no—I haven't missed school yet. Thanks—I'll take a rain check on that, though."

She shrugs. "I can write you a few ahead of time. Then, you'd have them whenever you needed one."

"I'm okay," I tell her.

It really does feel weird sitting in their lounge. She takes the bottle of nail polish and touches up a couple of her toes. It's nice to sit and relax and not be changing tires or fixing carburetors. It's like I'm on the set of some talk show.

Pretty soon Sissy comes in and sits beside me. She reaches out and scratches the top of my head.

"You look normal again," she says.

"Been out to the bus?" I ask her.

"What makes you say that?"

"Your red eyes." I give her a wink.

She rubs the end of my nose playful-like. She starts gathering her long hair and brushes it.

"Some chocolates?" she says, suddenly lifting a box of Bonnie Bonnell's finest.

"You've mashed them all," I say, taking a gander, flicking through the assorted slim pickings.

"They're still edible," she says, popping one in her mouth.

"How's Teresa?" says Britt.

"Oh, you know," I smile.

"Frankie says you two did it in the bus," says Sissy. She's chewing gum real hard. She blows a bubble and then sucks it back in her mouth.

"I thought Frankie was my friend," I say.

"So, did you?"

"I don't know," I say. "What's it to you?"

"Nothing really," she says. "Just looking out for my little brother."

"I don't need anybody's help when it comes to *that*," I say. They look at each other and laugh just a little, which is worse

215

than laughing big.

"I don't care what you two do," Sissy says, letting the brush come to rest in her lap. "But the *bus*?"

"Dad's always telling us to be resourceful," I say.

"So you did do it," says Sissy. "Tsk-tsk."

"I don't kiss and tell," I say. "That would be dishonorable."

"Did you do the mustaches?" Britt asks.

"Say what?"

"You heard me."

"Well, now," I say, "I wouldn't want to rat on a brother."

"Unless it's you, then you wouldn't be ratting. You'd be confessing," says Sissy.

"I don't see what the big deal is," I tell them. "I mean, they *have* mustaches now. That's an old picture."

"We were pretty sure it was you," says Britt.

"I told you," Sissy says to her. Then to me, "You owe us a picture."

"I'll get you one," I say. "Just, you know, keep it under Dad's radar."

"You're such a goof," says Sissy.

I shrug, not knowing what to say.

As I'm sitting there I realize that I don't know why I knocked on the door. I know there were some things I wanted to talk to them about, but I can't remember what they are. Big, important things. The fog in my head is there and I can't bring up the details, I don't have the questions. I want to push through, to bust out, but of what? The time in the lounge ends up being a trip, as crazy as a few hours in Frankie's bus. Britt and Sissy—they're in another world, all right. As far away from my reality as Akron is from San Francisco. I'm glad I didn't bring up the big things. It would've made facing them at the kitchen table unbearable.

A Universe Apart

Dad closed the automotive garage for good last week. The new guy Sir Henry was training didn't pan out. Plus, without the loan it was going to take too long to build things up again. Dad decided to turn part of the garage at our house into an official workshop where he and Sir Henry can work on engine repairs. We got rid of the garage door and built a wall there instead with two doors. One door goes to the left side, where we'll store things like the Hondas, and the lawn mower, and tools, and things like that, and the other side goes to the shop. There's a wall in between the two sides. He wants to open an automotive garage again once business builds, but for now he's going to run things out of the home garage. Dad says things might be tight for a while, and I think to myself, *how much tighter could they be?*

We're at the kitchen table eating dinner one Friday night, having hash, which everybody except Sissy loves. Mom makes toast from her homemade bread, and when you slather that fried hash on it, it's about the best thing on this earth, let me tell you. Mom's cut down on the smoking now that the baby's growing. She says cigarettes probably aren't the best thing for a baby and she doesn't want it to come out hooked like she is. Frankie and Nick and the girls are heading out after playing euchre with some of their friends, but me and Dad are going on deliveries to

Strongsville. He usually goes with Sir Henry, but Sir Henry has a date tonight, much to Britt's chagrin. I'm sort of looking forward to going and sort of not. I'll miss Friday night euchre. Plus, Nick's having his new girl come over. He says she's not Catholic, but he's not telling Mom and Dad yet. He's not going to tell them unless they get serious.

Everything's going just fine when Dad says, "We're going back to church." A man of few words, Dad is, and so I have to chime in and ask the obvious.

"What do you mean?"

"I mean, we're going to start attending church again." He looks up at us with those Humphrey Bogart eyes and dark hair, and it's hard not to find him a pleasant man to look at even when he's telling you bad news.

"Aw," says Squirt. "I hate church." He flings his hash toast onto his plate.

"That'll be enough," Dad tells him.

"But why do we have to go to church? It stinks in there and I hate it."

"Go stand in the corner," says Dad, and off goes Squirt to stick his nose in the dusty corner.

Now, I say it's bad news only because facing Father Mac-Gregor after all this time isn't something I'd like to think about. He'll probably have me say a thousand Hail Marys the first time I go to confession. I do miss Father Nigh, and Father Mann too. And I'll admit, there's been something not quite right come Sundays. It's like a rotten tooth was pulled, but nothing was put in its place, like there's this empty hole in my mouth I can't quite get used to.

"I hope Jesus forgive you," Gram wags that fat finger. It's pointed right at Dad. "You have a lot of sinning to make up for. All of you. You all need to apologize. You hurt Jesus's feelings—I know. It about time you go back to church."

"You been keeping our pew warm for us?" I kid her.

"It not funny," she says. "You'll see. Yeah, you think it's funny, Puck, but it's not."

Dad frowns at me and shakes his head.

"Aw, I didn't mean it, Gram. I'm actually glad we're going back. See?" I give her a wide Alfred E. Neuman smile.

She tries keeping the scowl, but she doesn't have the will-power and she laughs and wags that finger at me again for good measure. "Funny boy, you." She hits Dad with the back of her hand. "You old frowny face."

Nick and Frankie help carry things to the station wagon and put them in the back. Two carburetors, two radiators, and a full-sized engine. I never get to sit in the front seat with Dad. As soon as I sit down I close the ashtray, which is overflowing with butts and ashes and stinks to high heaven. Frankie puts Dad's wheel-chair in the middle seat since the back is packed with the repairs. He comes up to my side and taps my forearm, which is hanging out the window. Dad backs onto Tallmadge Avenue and we get on Route 8 heading north.

Dad turns on the radio. We listen to the station that plays old guys like Glenn Miller, and Tony Dorsey, and all those other big bands, and mixed in are some Gordon Lightfoot, and Glen Campbell, and Sandra Dee, and Petula Clark, and maybe some covers of The Beatles or The Monkees. Britt made some popcorn and we keep it between us in a rolled-down brown paper bag. We get out of Akron and into the countryside and I let my hand dan-gle out the window, and I move it up and down against the wind, just looking at the fields and trees go by. It's hard to believe there's so much green away from the city. I wonder what people do. I wonder how many trees there are in the world. I wish we'd see a deer. Frankie saw one once. I'd like to see a deer just once.

Dad asks about school, and I tell him it's okay.

"What's your favorite subject?"

"History, I guess," I tell him.

He nods. "I like history, too. What kind?"

"Greek or Roman."

"Math was my favorite subject," he says. "I was always good at math."

"Math's okay," I say.

"Math and some science."

"Yeah."

"It was always easy for me, I don't know why. English, you can have that. Shakespeare." He makes a bitter face. "The girls liked that, but I didn't understand it. It seemed like fluff."

I move my hand against the wind. My hand feels escaped from my body. It's like a bird flying with us beside the car. It makes me smile.

We get to the motel just off the highway near Strongsville. The motel is halfway between Akron and Cleveland. The guy from Cleveland who runs the garage is a normal guy, but the other one has one arm smaller than the other. It's about half the size of a regular arm and it dangles at his side like a kid's arm, only he can't move it. It's just a small arm without any strength. Me and him move everything. We move the things from our car to the back of their pickup, including the engine, and then move the things from their truck to our car. They give us broken things, and we give them fixed things. The guy who owns the garage is in the front seat beside Dad. I get in the back seat after we've moved everything, and the guy with the bum arm gets in back with me. We both stay by our door. He's grown up, and I don't know how to talk to him because of his age and his funny arm.

"How's business?" I ask him.

"Pretty good," he says. I'm sure he doesn't want to make conversation with somebody my age.

"I've only been to Cleveland a few times. It's a nice town."

He clears his throat. "Yeah," he says. "I guess."

Dad and his boss talk for a while, and then he gets out and the guy next to me gets out, and I get back in the front seat.

The sun is going down on the way back. It shines bright orange in the mirror on my side when we're going directly away from it.

Dad tells me about last week when he and Anthony and Frankie went fishing at Mogadore. Then he tells me when he and Tommy went before he left when they caught fish for the fish fry. He said it was some of the best fishing he's ever done. They weren't fishing for bass, they were fishing for bluegill, but they hooked a couple bass. That's how good it was. It was the prettiest he's seen the lake. I've never been with him to Mogadore. You can only fit three people in the boat safely. Whenever he starts getting the itch to fish, I hope he'll ask me to come along, but my time will come, he says. I guess so.

I've been having dreams. They mix with my thoughts and sometimes I can't tell what's a dream and what's a thought, or even what really happened and what's just made up in my head. The other night I was awake for a few hours thinking. In the middle of thinking I went up with Dad to the lake. Jesus wasn't there. It was just me and Dad. We weren't in lawn chairs. We were standing some distance apart tossing the football. The only time I've ever tossed a football with him for real was last year in the backyard, and I was trying so hard with every throw not to hurt him that my throwing was off and I hit him in the shin, but there at the lake he was standing and he was strong, like he would be without polio. We're tossing the football and nobody else is there. It's just me and him. There aren't any brothers, or Father MacGregor, or Lennie, or school, or church, or Vietnam. There's no partner to run off with all our money, or bank to turn us down, or arrow above my head following me around wherever I go, pointing me out, laughing at me. He throws a beautiful spiral. I could toss the ball with him all day. But the boat's there waiting for us. It's a different boat. A new boat without a past filled with the ache of being left out. A boat for just the two of us. The sun is setting as we get in. I don't have to hold the boat for him, or put his wheelchair in, or worry about him. He's strong and capable. He holds the boat for *me* as I get in. I push us off and he starts the motor, and he brings us in a nice pretty arc close to shore and then back out to open waters. The lake's immense. It's so big, you can't see the other shore. It's shimmering and massive. We're moving toward the center, but there's no end, no other shore at all, we keep going, using the orange sunset as our guide. Then I see, just below the surface of the lake, the face of Jesus. His face, and then His body. His body encompasses the whole lake. I realize He is the lake. We're riding on holy waters where there can be no pain from want, or abandonment, or physical pain for either of us.

I gaze at him looking tired but satisfied after getting a new batch of carburetors to fix. He doesn't really know who I am. He doesn't know the thoughts in my head. He sees a wise guy, a misfit, a set of hands who's helped him through the summer. I could reach out and touch his cheek. But we're a universe apart.

"What do you want to be?" he asks me. It takes me a second for it to register.

"You mean after high school?"

"Yes," he says. "Have you thought about it?"

"A little."

"Uncle Dobbs could probably get you on at Firestone. I know some people at some other places. Or, there's college."

"Yeah," I say.

"I can help you with your first two years of college, if that's what you want to do. After that, you're on your own. That's what I offered the older boys. I want to be fair to you all."

"I . . . don't know what it's called," I say.

"What you want to be?"

I nod slowly. "I don't think there's a name for it, but it's what I want to do."

"What's that, son?"

"I . . . want to help people," I say.

"You want to help people?"

"I think so."

"How?"

"I . . . don't know. That's why it's hard to say."

"Why do you want to help people?" he asks me. "You'll have a hard enough time helping yourself. I mean, look what happened with Lennie. If Nick hadn't come along . . ." His face looks pained.

"I don't know."

"That's nice of you," he says. "Sure, it is. But . . . Do you have an actual vocation you're interested in?"

"What do you mean?"

"A job," he says. "Is there a specific job you want to have where you could help people? Like a doctor or something?"

"I don't know," I say.

"A doctor's going to be tough. We don't have the kind of

money for you to become a doctor. I wish we did. Plus, I doubt if your grades are good enough to get into med school. It's a tough thing to accept, but you probably aren't doctor material."

"Yeah."

"I can talk to Mr. Del Rosa," he says. "You could work for him next summer, I bet."

"No, I can talk to him," I say.

"You work for him and after a few years you'll have some good experience. He's a good man."

"Yeah. Maybe I'll talk to him."

"You mean like the Peace Corps? Is that what you mean?" He suddenly becomes alert. "I don't think that's something you'd like very much. I think it's a total waste of time, to be honest. It might be a good idea, but good ideas on paper aren't always good ideas in practice. From what I've read, the Peace Corps doesn't accomplish much. Don't get me wrong, it's a nice thought, a nice gesture, but you wouldn't be happy in the Peace Corps. You're too smart. You're a hard worker."

"I was thinking, you know, I might become a writer," I say to him.

There's silence. I don't look over. I fiddle with the knob of the door lock.

"A writer?"

"Yeah, I think so."

"But . . . how's that going to help people?"

I pause, pulling the knob up, then down, then back up. "I don't know exactly."

"I'm not sure how being a writer helps people," says Dad. "You mean you want to be a newspaper writer, a reporter, or do you mean a novelist?"

"I guess a novelist," I tell him. "I started writing awhile back."

"You have? What do you write about?"

"Just stories. Well, not even stories yet. I'm writing down my thoughts."

I reach for some popcorn and look at him, briefly. He's not scowling, but he looks deeply pained.

"Son," he says, like he's trying to catch his breath in desperation, "people don't want to read your journal. And they're sure not going to read a whole book about your thoughts." He pauses, I can still see him peripherally as I get more popcorn, as he tries to clutch at a response. "You think too much," he says. "That's the problem. I've always said that. You, Frankie, you two spend too much time thinking when all it does is make you anxious. Look at Frankie. He's like you. He says he wants to be an artist. Okay. How's he going to make money doing that? How's he going to feed a family? Nobody buys paintings anymore. He's good, don't get me wrong, but you have to be really great to make any money being an artist. I'm afraid he's going to spend his whole life thinking it's one thing, when it's another." I see him now looking at me in between looking at the road. "Son, you're no better than anyone else. I don't mean to be harsh. I'm not trying to squash your dreams. But—"

"I don't think I'm better than anyone else," I say somewhat defensively.

"I'm trying to help you," he says.

I nod, quickly. I feel nauseous. Maybe it's all the popcorn, maybe it's him. I don't know. I feel like I have to get out of the car, but I can't.

"Yeah," I say.

"Like I tried to tell Frankie, do your art on the side. Everybody needs a hobby. I have hobbies. Fishing. The ham radio. I'm not telling you to stop doing your hobbies, but you need a vocation or at least a decent job that'll bring in steady income. I don't think being an artist or a writer is too practical. Do you understand what I'm trying to tell you?"

I nod, but don't answer him. My face feels hot along with the nausea. I feel foolish for bringing it up. He's right—how the hell do I think I'm going to help anybody when my own life is a wreck? But what I couldn't tell him, what I can't tell anyone, is that I don't think I have a choice. I lie awake for hours every night, thinking. I think when I'm at school. I think at the kitchen table eating. I think when I'm doing chores. I can't turn it off. Writing helps organize my thoughts. It's a kind of purge. It frees

224

my thoughts and it frees my guilt, and afterward I'm lighter and less burdened. I suppose that's what I meant. It's narcissistic, but if I can purge my thoughts, if other people read them, maybe they can purge their own.

Rubber Love

Me and Nick are up on the third floor. Nick's doing push-ups. He has me put books on his back to make it harder on him. He's training so when Anthony makes him hold books out, it'll be easier. When we don't make our beds just right, or we make too much noise while he's trying to study, he punishes us by having us stand with our hands out parallel to the floor and then he gives us books to hold. I only have to hold small books normally, and I'll even get away with a paperback now and then when he's feeling particularly kind. But Nick has to hold hardbacks, and sometimes an encyclopedia volume. It's a real bitch for him when Anthony hands him the B or the S.

"You're doing real good, Nick," I say to him. He can do fifty push-ups without stopping with a book on his back, and sixty without.

Nick does a set, then rolls onto his side. He's breathing hard and his arms are puffed out and veiny.

"Hey," I say to him. "I want to show you something."

"What is it?" he says.

"Hold on."

I go over to the door of the crawl space and move his weight bench aside, then pull out the middle part of Brigitte. He lights up when he sees her. Well, just the middle, crucial part, like I said.

226

"How'd you get her back?" he says, sitting up on the side of his bed now.

"I snuck out that night and got what I could," I tell him. "I wanted to get all of her, but her arms and legs and head kept falling, and I thought I was going to wake up the dogs. But I got her, uh, good parts."

"I see that. Nice work, slick," he says.

I set Brigitte down on the floor. Surprisingly, she doesn't fall over.

"I took some alcohol and rubbed out the marks Anthony drew. They were kind of crude."

"Yeah," Nick winces, "I never did like them either. Couldn't save her boobs?"

"I tried," I say, "but it was raining and her chest was too big and slippery to hold with one hand. At least I saved this."

We look at her, or what's left of her. I turn her after a while so we can see her other side.

"I have a couple questions," I say to him.

"After your big date in the bus? I thought you'd have it all figured out by now."

"We didn't do as much as you think," I tell him.

"No? What did you do?"

"We just fooled around a little."

"That's it?" Nick cocks his head and gives me his skeptical, high-eyebrow look.

"Sure," I say. "You think I'd lie to you?"

"All right, don't get huffy."

"So, I was wondering. I mean, I don't really understand it."

"What's there to understand?" he says.

"Well," I say, sort of scratching the old head, "I mean, look at it."

He lifts his eyebrows even farther. "Okay."

"I don't understand what's what. It looks so simple, but I don't think it is."

Nick clears his throat and turns Brigitte toward him, then tilts her back like you would some piece of pottery at an antique store you're thinking about buying.

"It's not that hard," he says. "You'll figure it out when you get there."

"But what if I don't?" I tell him. "That's what I'm afraid of. What if I get there, and I still don't know what to do? She's going to think I'm a real idiot."

"Puck," he says. "Don't take this the wrong way, but she'll know what to do."

Nick's raised eyes are accompanied by a forced smile.

"I guess so," I say to him, surely disappointed that he couldn't offer more details into the quandary sitting before me.

"What are you going to do about her anyway?" he says to me. "She calls, you know. Why don't you want to talk to her?"

"I don't know," I say. "You've been with her, Nick. You've been with lots of girls, and she knew you knew what you were doing. I'm going to look like a real amateur."

"Ah, don't worry about it. Girls don't care. You like her, right?"

"Sure," I say.

"That's all they care about. Most guys just want to bang them and move on."

"Seems like a lot of girls go for guys like that," I say.

"Some do. But sincerity will take you a long way, and you've got that going for you."

"I guess so."

"She's a nice girl," he says. "You should talk to her."

"Yeah," I say. "Maybe I will. But what about the pills?"

"You'd have to ask her," he says.

"You think she's still doing them?"

"I don't think so."

"Was she doing them that night in the bus?"

"I don't think so," he says. "She was smoking some pot, but mostly she was drinking."

"Maybe it was just a phase," I say. "Maybe she's not like that. You know?"

"Yeah, maybe," he says. "You better put that thing away before Squirt comes up. Mom will hear about it in two seconds flat."

228

A couple days later I call up Teresa and she sounds happy on the phone. I tell her I'm sorry it took so long, and I ask if she wants to come over. She says okay, but it's hard to tell how she feels about it.

She wants to go swimming and so she comes over in her bare feet with a towel wrapped around her like girls do after a shower. It'll be one of the last times before we pull the cover over the pool and shut it down for the year. I dive in first. The water's not freezing, but it's lost the heat of summer. I tread water to keep warm, then stand there squatted down some moving my arms underwater. She's still sitting on the deck, skimming the water with her toes. She looks just as pretty as she always does and I feel bad about not calling her.

"Why wouldn't you talk to me?" she says in this quiet voice. Not mad, not overly sad either. Just low and thoughtful. "I called and called."

"I'm sorry," I tell her. "I . . . don't have a good answer. I could tell you some things, but I don't think you'd understand."

"I probably would," she says.

"Yeah, you probably would," I say. "I know."

"Is it something about me? Something I did or said?"

I shake my head. "Teresa, you're just as fine as can be. It's not you."

"Then what is it, Puck?"

She's waiting with the look of patience and acceptance I usually only see on Frankie's face. What I told Nick was true, I did feel like a chump compared to him, but that's not why I haven't called her.

"You go to church, right?" I say.

"Yes," she says, "of course. I see you most Sundays. I'm glad you're going again."

"Do you believe what they tell you?" I ask her. "I mean, do you really, truly believe what you hear in church?"

"I believe most of it," she says.

"Do you?"

"Sure," she says. "But if you're asking, do I believe every single thing they tell us, or everything in the Bible, I believe

229

some of those stories are to make a point. But I believe the ideas they're trying to teach us."

I think over what she says. I think long and hard before I go on.

"Ever since I was little, Mom would have us get on our knees and say our prayers. You probably did too. We prayed for our aunts and uncles, and our friends, and for Squirt when he was a baby, and now Sally. We prayed for special things, like keeping our soldiers safe in Vietnam, and for the war to stop. But we also prayed for Dad. We prayed for his legs to get better. It was the last and the biggest thing we prayed for. I remember squeezing my eyes shut and praying as hard as I could. Me, Nick, and Frankie, at the side of the bed, praying as hard as we could.

"Well, nothing happened. His legs didn't get better. We prayed each night, but nothing came of it. This went on for years. We prayed and prayed, and yet Dad's legs didn't heal. I thought about it. I obsessed over why our prayers weren't being answered, and I could only think of two possibilities: either God wasn't listening because He doesn't exist, or we were doing something wrong. *I* was doing something wrong.

"You're going to say that it's not for us to say how or why God decides to answer our prayers. I considered that. But, come on. You could rationalize anything you want, then, based on the indiscernibility of God." I shake my head. "That's beyond belief. If there is a God, then there must be a reasonable and discernable way for us to understand Him. We may not know the full breadth of His plans, but our minds must be able to comprehend basic cause and effect, sacrifice and reward.

"I settled on reaffirming my belief that God does exist, but that we or *I* haven't satisfied His requirements for answering our prayers. This seemed plausible. The Bible is full of situations where someone had to perform some act to appease God. I fully realize these may be stories, fables, but there are scores of them. I had to ask myself, are all these stories completely made up? I looked at history, at fables outside Christianity, and nearly all were based on some truth, or kernel of facts. Again, I had to ask myself, do I fundamentally believe what I hear each Sunday at church or don't I? If I don't, then why am I, why are any of us, sitting there? And if I do, then the things I hear, the lessons, the stories, the miracles, have to be a living, breathing realm just as much as they were two thousand years ago.

"I came to the conclusion that I needed to demonstrate my faith, or better yet think of some sacrifice I could offer in return for God healing Dad's legs. I had nothing like Abraham offering his son. I thought about it for months, unable to come up with anything. Then it hit me. It was so obvious: I'd resist temptation. I'd deny myself the pleasures of youth, and in return God, *Jesus*, would answer my prayers."

"I don't think I understand," she says. "Puck, what are you trying to say?"

"I'm saying that I've made a promise, Teresa. A promise to Jesus. I won't be with a girl and if I do that for a long enough time, my dad's legs will get better. That's why I didn't want to talk to you. It's not because I didn't like what we did that night. I liked it too much. I'm afraid we'll go even further. I'm afraid of myself."

"Do you think I'm a bad influence, Puck?" she says. "Is that what you think?"

"No," I tell her. "Of course not."

"It sure sounds like it."

"It's not that," I say. "It's nothing you've done. I think you're as nice and sweet as you are pretty. But . . . I can't help feeling like I'm responsible for my Dad's condition."

"But that's silly."

I don't say anything.

"What I mean is," she says, "when your dad got polio, you weren't even born, like you said. And even if you were, how on earth could you have been responsible for giving him polio?"

"I know," I say to her. "I understand that. But, what if I'm not necessarily responsible for his condition, but maybe I'm the one who can reverse it? Don't I have a responsibility to do that?" I look up at her.

"Do you really think you can?" she asks.

"If I can't, then what good is praying? About anything?"

231

"Prayers don't always come true, Puck. It's not up to us to decide when they do, or why, or why they don't. What if you wait and wait, and it doesn't happen? What then?"

"It will," I say.

"But what if it doesn't?"

"It *will*. I know it will."

"Puck," she says, "I hate to see you—" She stops herself. "I just can't help thinking about what it could mean for you if nothing happens. I know you believe it will, and it might. I'm not saying it won't. But if it doesn't . . ."

"But isn't that the whole point? It has to be difficult. It's a test of faith."

She lowers her head, slowly running her hand along the edge of the towel over her legs.

"Where does that leave us?" she asks.

"It shouldn't change anything," I say. "It doesn't for me."

"It sounds like it changes everything."

"It doesn't have to."

"But don't you want to be free to love me without anything else, including the church, getting in our way?"

I start nodding my head, slowly, then I shake it, not sure.

"I don't know," I tell her. "I feel like I'm being pulled apart. I know what I want to do, but that may not be what I should do. I just don't know."

I stare into the water between us. Small, undulating ripples fan out from her feet, which move slowly, absently as we both try and think.

"Will you come here?" she says finally. I walk toward her until I'm close enough so she can place her hands on my shoulders. "I'm sorry about your dad. I can't imagine what that must be like for him or for you. You must love him very much."

I can't look at her directly. It's too torturous.

"I'm the one that should be telling you I have to wait. What kind of girl am I?"

I smile and look up. "Normal," I say.

"I wouldn't want you to do anything you think you shouldn't. You believe me, don't you?"

"Yeah," I say.

"I was going to wear my white bikini for you," she says. "I know how you like it. A girl can always tell. But, I couldn't find it. I don't know where it went. My mom probably hid it; she thinks it's scandalous. I don't think it is, do you, Puck?"

"No, I think it's just right," I say.

"I looked for my purple bathing suit, but I couldn't find that either. It's crazy. I don't know where they went. So," she says, "I decided I wouldn't wear either one."

"Aw," I say, "don't tell me that."

She loosens the towel and opens it up like a book, revealing her naked body.

"Aw . . ." I look away. I have to look away, but then do look.

"I don't want you to do anything you don't want to do. I'm not trying to get in the middle of anything. I know you love your father, and I believe what you said. I believe *you* believe it. But I believe you can find salvation in other ways. I can't say I love you yet, and I'm sure you don't love me, not yet. But we're young—we're young, Puck, and that's not going to last forever. You're different. All the boys want one thing from me. You're not like them. You're the first boy I've met who doesn't want to take it. You don't want to possess me. I don't know what will happen if you let me take off this towel and I come down into the water with you. I mean, I know what I *hope* will happen. But, well . . ."

I take a long, *long* look at what seems to be the closest thing to perfection I've ever set eyes on. She isn't demure but sits erect, legs out, as if daring me to refuse. I feel a fool standing there. I feel a fool and phony. I *do* want to possess her the same as all the other boys. I've dreamed about it day and night, and now here she is presenting herself to me like some throbbing angel. I hate that she thinks I'm better than anyone else, because I'm not. If it weren't for what I've promised, holding me back like some rope around my neck, I'd lift her into the pool and take her right now.

But I can't. As much as I want her, I cling to the fluttering hope seemingly just beyond reach. I take either side of the towel

233

and bring them together. I expect her to be mad and run off, but she remains where she is smiling at me pleasantly, believing I'm somebody I'm not.

I let my hands drop to her knees and it's like poking her with a live wire. She lets out a gasp and her body arches backward. The skin just above her knees is so soft, I can't help it and I begin moving my hands up and down her thighs, reaching beneath the bottom of the towel. She looks at me, her eyes half-closed, now with her hands on my forearms, guiding me along her glass-like skin. I realize in that instant I can't stop myself. And, more importantly, I don't want to.

"Come on," I say to her and I climb up the ladder out of the pool.

I guide her down off the deck, but there's nowhere to go. We can't go in the house, and there's no place in the yard that's secluded enough. I lead her to the far side of the garage where the stumpy tree will hide us from her house. Sandy's house is right there, but it's dark the way it always is. There's only the dirt and the stacked tires. I look at her, in despair, apologetic.

"I don't care," she says.

She drops the towel and lies back on the rubber where the tires are butted next to each other. I peel down my wet bathing suit and, just as Nick said it would be, I know instinctively what to do. I lie with the beautiful Teresa Del Rosa. I kiss her wide, soft lips. I clutch her draping hair. She clings to me like a babe and I attend to every whim she demands of me, my mind exploding in a thousand brittle pieces.

At the Gorge

She comes over Fridays for euchre, and Frankie is her partner sometimes, and Nick is too, and it isn't like I have to hoard her all to myself. She's bright and cheery and the girls like her, and so do Mom and Dad. Gram will sit with us and watch instead of being with Mom and Dad in the living room. She stares into Frankie's head like she does Dad's at dinner. Gram tells me I should marry her. I just shake my head and pinch her cheek and wiggle it like she did to me when I was little. Whenever I look at Teresa I have a hard time looking away. I'm usually thinking of how soon it'll be before we can be alone. Sometimes we go get a bite to eat, or maybe go bowling, or see a movie. We like to go to the Loew's Theatre downtown. The Loew's is some magical place. When the lights go down, these stars come out on the ceiling. Clouds move across the night sky in front of them. I'll hold her hand as she leans into me, and she'll put her head on my shoulder. I didn't know something could feel as good as having your girl's hand in yours with her head on your shoulder. After the movie we'll park somewhere and make out and do other stuff, and it's like some new miracle every time we do it, but holding her hand in the Loew's Theatre is as good as anything.

We go to the gorge when we have time and I'm not helping Dad. We take a blanket and hike into the woods where we can see the reservoir and the water flowing over the small dam. She brings a picnic lunch like she did that day at Cutter Lake, and sometimes Frankie will give me a couple beers to take.

One day we're there and it's sunny and dry and the cicadas are still singing up above. She's wearing a dress, lying sideways on the blanket, facing me. We just finished some salami and cheese and crackers we bought at DeVitis's. Our hands are together above the food. Her eyes are lemon green.

"Puck?" she says in her low, dreamy voice.

"Yes?"

"What did you think of me before we met? We've been neighbors for so long. Isn't it strange how we've been neighbors, and now we're like this?"

"I thought you were like some Greek statue in our history books," I say.

"Italian," she says.

"Yeah, all right. Italian. But really, I did. When you were young, you were just some girl I hardly noticed. But as we grew up, I could barely look at you."

"But why?"

"You know why."

"I don't, I really don't."

"Because you're too beautiful, too beautiful to look at. Too beautiful to imagine we could ever be together."

She brings our hands up and kisses my fingers.

"You are sweet," she says. "But that's silly."

"You asked me," I say. "I'm telling you the truth."

She puts her hands under her head like a pillow, and I stroke her shoulder and arm. She closes her eyes, then opens them.

"One time I talked to your father through the fence," she says as though she's almost asleep.

"Yeah?"

"He was nice. I could tell even then he was a really nice man. He pushed a sucker through the fence."

"I've never known him to have a sucker on him," I say. "I'm jealous."

"A purple one," she says. "It tasted like grape jelly. I was us-

236

ing my jump rope and he asked if I could do ten in a row. He held my sucker while I did thirty. He gave me the sucker back and wheeled away. My dad thinks your dad is something else," she says.

"He is," I say.

"No, you don't understand, Puck. My dad doesn't think that about anybody. He's a macho guy. He doesn't look up to anyone, but he looks up to your dad."

I pull my hand away from her arm and move it to her hip. "You don't mind, do you?" She shakes her head, barely, and closes her eyes.

"Your writing is wonderful," she says. "I want to read more."

"It's not much of anything right now," I say.

"It is. Who said that?"

"I'm saying that."

"Well, you're a fool, then. It's wonderful."

"It's amateurish," I tell her, "but it helps me."

"I understand that," she says. "I write in a journal. Nothing like what you write. I don't mean that. But it helps me too."

"Can I read some of it?"

"Not on your life," she smiles, barely, her eyes mostly closed.

"All right," I say.

"I never considered it," she says.

"What's that?"

"When you talked about how two people can be in the same situation, yet they're not at all. From the outside, they appear as if they should feel the same, be the same, but that's never how it is."

"Not in my experience," I say. Her dress has ridden up from stroking her hip. I flatten the hem and push it back down, then continue rubbing.

"Like George Harrison."

"Yes."

"That's how you described it; just like George Harrison, who's stood in the shadows for years behind John and Paul. We expect him to remain there because it suits our desire, our desire to have these four boys playing together the way they always have. George probably wants to scream."

"I know I do."

"And you have every right to," she says. "You should. Poor, poor George."

"My dad thinks I'm a fool for wanting to be a writer," I say. "I can't blame him, really."

"He says that because he's not a writer," she says. "He's like my dad. They're men of action, and of duty. They lived through tough times. Of course they don't understand why someone would want to be a writer. But it's not 1945 anymore. What you have to say is important."

"He thinks I should work for your dad next summer. I wouldn't mind."

"I'm sure he'd love to have you," she says. "You're a hard worker. All you boys are. But it doesn't change who you are, Puck."

"I wouldn't mind masonry work," I say.

"I'll pack your lunch every morning and give you a kiss before you leave. Would you want me to?"

"I want a kiss on each cheek," I tell her.

"And on your big wide lips," she says.

"And anywhere else I might want one that day, to keep me going."

"I'd never get tired of kissing you. Or of having your hands on my hip. Or anywhere else."

She rolls onto her side away from me. I move the salami and cheese and crackers and lie around her. My face is lost in her dark hair. My lips press the back of her neck, I kiss her there and keep my lips on her skin until I remember nothing and drift to sleep.

When I wake the light has shifted, the shadows are longer, but it's nowhere near dusk. I smell the leaves now along with her. I hear an airplane up above, alongside the sound of water gushing over the dam.

When she wakes we gather the basket and walk to the reservoir. There's another couple along the far edge, swimming. The girl waves, and then the guy waves, but they're far enough away

238

that we can't see them clearly.

"Should we?" she says.

"Why not?" I tell her, and we remove our clothes down to our underwear.

The water's cold and it makes us laugh and jump around. The ground is muddy with sticks and it's hard to walk. She's exotic wet. She comes to me and wants me to put my arms around her, and I do. We walk to shore and sit down facing the sun, and lean back on our hands. Small minnows jump near shore and there are small, dirty snails on the algae-covered pebbles near our feet. She's too beautiful and I have to lean over and kiss her, and feel the weight of her breasts, and then her hip, and her thighs. I can't keep from touching her. I don't think I'll ever tire of wanting to have her in my arms. I lean back again, gazing at the water.

"I've been thinking," she says.

"Yeah?"

"I don't feel bad about what we're doing, but I have thought about it."

"What have you thought?"

"I wonder if what we're doing is right," she says. "I wonder if I've ruined anything for you. I didn't mean to."

"You haven't ruined anything," I tell her. "You've made it all better."

"Have I? Have I, really?"

"You sure have," I say.

"Because, well, I believe everything you told me, Puck. I always believed you, and I still believe you. I just wanted to be close to you. If you broke the agreement you had, then I feel just awful. Is there anything that can be done?"

I sit forward with my knees up, my hands clasped around them. "I don't see any difference since we've been doing things," I say. "Nothing's better, but nothing's worse. It's the same as it's always been."

"But," she says, "I don't see how you could ever mend what's been broken, not with what we've been doing. I feel awful, Puck."

"I wonder if it's all been in my head," I say to her.

"You mean your conversations?"

"I've wanted to help my dad for so long," I tell her. "It's burned inside me since I can remember. I'm bound to see what I want to see, to hear what I want to hear. Maybe all this time it's just been hope."

"Hope is necessary in a difficult world," she says.

"It is," I say. "But where does hope end and delusion begin?"

"If what you hope for comes true, then that's not delusion."

"It could just be luck."

"It could be."

"I don't know what I think anymore," I say.

"I hope you don't turn away from the church, if that's what you mean," she says.

"I don't know what I mean. I don't know what I believe now. I ask for answers, and receive nothing. I beg for a sign that my faith is justified, and hear only silence. I see you, and receive more than I could have imagined. For now, that's what I believe. It's tangible. It's real. If anything is miraculous, being here with you is."

I turn toward her and kiss her. My head is alive and unburdened. We're free. We're young and filled with the energy of our time, and nothing can stop us.

And Then This . . .

It's bright and warm, and across the city I can see the leaves going to yellow and rust, and there are big clouds of birds in the sky shifting into different shapes as they get ready to fly south. I'm hoofing it across the bridge that passes over Route 8 just after school when I pause to look down to the cars below. The traffic's heavy going both ways. It never stops, just like a river.

I pass St. Martha's with its statues of saints, and topiary all nice and neat, and the old brick exterior standing strong, like it's been there a thousand years and will be there a thousand more. Some high school kids are sitting in a circle playing music, clapping their hands, swaying to the guitars and tambourines. A couple of them look up and give me the peace sign and I give it back. They're out there once or twice a week playing music, being happy. I see Mrs. Shiner on her small front porch swing. She waves and I wave back, and then I think how I should stop and thank her for the piece of pie she gave me two days ago. I was on my way to school and there she was, waiting at the end of her driveway with a piece of apple pie. She said she made two pies and had lots left over and knew how much I liked pie. She had it wrapped nice and neat for me, all ready to go.

I walk up to her porch.

"Hi, Puck," she says, her kind old face coming to life.

"Hi, Mrs. Shiner," I say to her.

"How was school?"

"It was all right," I say. "Nothing I can't handle, I guess."

"Did you like the pie?"

"That's why I stopped. I wanted to thank you. It was the best apple pie I've had in a long time."

"Oh, I'm so glad you liked it," she says.

"I mean it, it really was."

"Would you like another piece?" Her eyes lift up all bright and hopeful.

"Oh, I couldn't, Mrs. Shiner," I say.

"But I still have a whole pie left," she says. "I'd hate to see it go to waste."

She has a good point, that Mrs. Shiner, and so I figure, why not? We head inside and she cuts me a piece bigger than the one I had for lunch two days ago. She insists on bringing out some vanilla ice cream with it, and I have to help dig it out of the carton because it's hard as a rock and probably a year old. Still, once it starts melting it goes just right with the pie. I've only been inside her house a few times. She has pictures all over of her and Mr. Shiner and her kids and grandkids.

"How many grandchildren do you have, Mrs. Shiner?" I ask her.

"Seven," she says. "That's a lucky number, but I wouldn't mind having more."

"I've seen a couple of them," I say. "Climbing the cherry tree."

"Oh, I know. I get nervous every time they do. But I suppose I did the same thing when I was their age."

I nod and when I'm about finished she asks if I want just a bit more, maybe half a slice, and I tell her sure. I give myself a small scoop of ice cream to go with it.

She has a big jade plant sitting by the window. The thing looks like a small tree, and the way the light shines through the window it seems like it's glowing silver. It's almost perfectly shaped. She sees me looking at it.

"Do you want to start one?" she says.

"What's that, Mrs. Shiner?"

"Do you want to start your own? My grandmother gave me a cutting shortly after I was married. They're easy to grow."

"Sure," I tell her.

Mrs. Shiner pulls out a steak knife from her drawer, and hands it to me telling me I should do it. She puts her finger where, and I cut off a piece and she runs it under water, then wets a paper towel and wraps it around the cut part.

"Put the end in water for two days, then plant it in some good dirt. If you don't have any, come back and I'll give you some. They like light," she says. "Put it on a windowsill. When you're as old as me, yours will be just like this one."

"Thanks, Mrs. Shiner," I say, lifting up the cutting in appreciation.

"You and that girl can watch it grow your whole lives," she says. She puts her old hands around mine and squeezes them a little.

She walks me out and I say so long, and she stands there waving goodbye.

When I get home Dad's sitting outside the garage, which is sort of unusual. Nick's standing beside him. They're waiting for me.

"Where have you been?" Nick says.

"Nowhere," I tell him.

"You're supposed to come straight home," he says. "You know that. You're supposed to come right home."

"I'm *sorry*," I say, more than a little mystified. I look at him, then Dad, then back at him. I shrug. "I stopped and had a piece of pie at Mrs. Shiner's. She invited me in." They both look like they've been punched in the face. "What's going on?"

"Your mother," Dad starts to say, then stops himself.

"What about Mom?"

"Your mother had a miscarriage."

"A miscarriage?"

"Yes, son," Dad says. He's trying to keep it together and swallows hard.

"A . . . *miscarriage*?"

He nods. "It happened this morning."

"But . . . how?"

"Puck," says Nick, shaking his head.

"She's inside," Dad tells me.

"Have . . . you seen her?" I'm speaking to Nick.

"Yeah," he says, staring into the ground.

"Go on in, Puck," Dad says. "She's been waiting to see you. I've been with her all day. Aunt Myrtle was here. She just left. Go on, son."

I go to say something, I don't know what, but nothing comes out. I go inside to the kitchen, where Britt, Anthony, and Sissy are sitting at the table. Nobody's eating or drinking or talking, they're just sitting there.

Anthony stands up, walks over, and puts his arms around me.

"She's upstairs, Puck."

"Is she all right?"

"Yeah," he says. "She's still weak and—"

"But she's *all right*?"

"She's going to be all right," he says.

I squeeze his shoulders, hard, because there's nothing I can crush. Anthony gives me another embrace before I go upstairs.

The door to the bedroom is open. Gram is sitting in a chair on the opposite side of the bed, stroking Mom's arm. I feel myself wilting, but I know I can't. I knock lightly on the outside of the door.

"Hello?" I say.

They look over and Gram goes to get up, but I tell her to stay. I sit down gently on the near side of the bed and take Mom's hand and bring my face next to hers. She doesn't cry, but I do, and then she does. She looks tired. Her eyes are dark and her grip is weak. I don't let go of her hand.

"I'm sorry," I tell her. "I'm sorry, Mom."

"I'm glad you're here."

"I just heard," I tell her. "I didn't know."

"Oh, Puck," she says in a low, dreamy voice, "I'm so glad you're here."

I sit upright on the bed against the wall and she puts her head on my shoulder. I stroke her forehead.

"I suppose it wasn't meant to be," she says.

"It's all right, Mom," I say.

"There was nothing any of us could have done. It's just the way of life. Do you understand, Puck?"

"I know," I say, but I don't, I only say it.

"I have you, I have a wonderful family. This is the exact number that was meant to be."

"I know. I know."

"I think . . . I've had enough children now."

"Yes," I say.

"I probably shouldn't have had any more."

I don't know what to say. I want to say the right thing, but I don't have the words.

"I love children, Puck," she says. "I love babies and children."

"I know."

"I'm sorry you won't get to name the baby."

"It's all right, Mom. It's all right."

"But you'll get married. Maybe you and Teresa. Oh, she's a nice girl, Puck. I hope you know that."

"I do," I tell her.

"You'll get to name all your own children. It's a wonderful thing. There's nothing better than naming your children."

"I know," I say.

She gives a sigh and I think she's drifting to sleep.

"And how was your day?" she says in her dreamy, distant voice.

"It was pretty good," I say. "Mom, if you're tired, you don't have to talk. You can go to sleep."

"Oh, honey, I'm not tired. I've been lying here all day. I'm not tired . . . What special thing happened today? Every day has something special in it, doesn't it, Puck."

"I don't know," I say. "Nothing much."

"Nothing?"

"Not really."

"Do you know what I realized today?" she says. "I thought of

245

it just a while ago. I was sitting here talking to Gram, and it occurred to me that by having so many of you, I've given each of you less." She lifts her head from my chest.

"Mom," I say, "it's all right."

"I didn't mean to, but that's what happened. I didn't mean to."

"It's okay," I tell her. "You've given us plenty."

"I love children, Puck. But by wanting more, I've given each of you less. Think of how much love I could have given you if you were an only child, or one of just a few. It's not fair."

"Mom," I say, "you have nothing to be sorry for. My God."

"You're a good son," she says, patting me without looking, weakly. "You're all good."

"You should sleep now," I tell her. "You're tired."

"I suppose I am. I hadn't noticed until now. I'm sure glad you came. I wanted to see you."

"Sleep as long as you want," I say. "Sleep until morning. You need to sleep."

"I'm glad you're here, Puck," she says, barely awake. "I wish Tommy was here. I don't want to think about where he is right now. I miss him. He's gone away, hasn't he. To that war. I'm glad I don't know every detail about the war. It's better not knowing too much. Remember that, Puck, when you have children. Sometimes you can know too much. He's out there, in a dangerous part of the world. But that's what children do. They're supposed to go out into the world, aren't they. But it doesn't make it easy. It's a hard thing to accept, if you love your children. All children should be loved. Every single one."

She closes her eyes and soon falls asleep.

Downstairs Anthony, Nick, Britt, and Sissy are playing euchre at the kitchen table. It's not like Friday nights. They're just killing time, not having fun. They make room, but I don't play. I watch, but even watching them is torturous. I look over and see Dad sitting at the dining room table by himself. He has his back to us, but I can see his hand on his temple, his head dropped lower than usual. Nobody's talking to him because they don't know what to say, just like I don't know what to say. But Jesus, Mom's

246

up there in bed and he can't see her because he's in his wheel-chair, and yeah, she needs rest, but I'm sure she'd like to have him there beside her the way I was, her husband for Christ's sake, saying things that I can't say.

Anthony's made popcorn, so I put some in a bowl and walk into the dining room and sit down in the chair next to him. He doesn't notice me at first, but then he does and he gives me a tired smile.

"I brought you some popcorn," I say to him. I raise it up for him to see, then set it down.

He's not really a popcorn fan, but he acts interested and takes some.

"Did Anthony make it?"

"Yeah," I say.

"He makes the best popcorn."

"He makes better fudge," I say.

"That hard stuff?" He chuckles.

"I like it."

"It's like rocks."

"Yeah, I guess. But that's why I like it. I like to suck on it."

"I guess that's one way to look at it," he says.

"Hey," I say to him, "do you really like tongue?" I wince.

"Sure," he says. "Don't you?"

I make a face. "Haven't you noticed?"

"I like tongue sandwiches the best," he says.

"It's not so bad in hash," I say. "Especially with Mom's toast."

He smiles, but it's forced. He puts his hand to his temple and rubs it, gazing straight ahead.

"I'll take you up," I say. "Let me take you up."

He lifts his head away from his fingers. He's surprised, but grateful, I can tell. I nod, and he knows I'm right—this time, I'm right. I wheel him over to the bottom of the steps. He locks the wheels, and locks his brace, and turns in the chair, and I hook my fingers in his belt loops and help him swing up, still bent over with his hands on the seat, and I crouch low beside him, and he puts his hands on my back and curls around, and then lets himself fall onto my back, his forearms wrapped around my neck. I carry him up to their room where Gram is in her chair, asleep, and Mom is on her back on the bed, asleep. I help him onto the bed, lift his legs slowly and carefully up, and roll him onto his side so he's facing Mom. He won't be able to move, but I know that he wouldn't want to. Not tonight. I know if I were in his place, I wouldn't want to.

Night Longings

Mom and Dad get another letter from Tommy. Mom doesn't read it to me, and she doesn't set it on the buffet next to the others. She cries that night during dinner, and she goes outside and Squirt thinks she's leaving again, and he starts crying and runs for the door, and then Britt carries Sally on her hip and takes them outside so they can see Mom. I watch them sitting at the picnic table through the family room windows. After some time, Britt comes back in with Squirt and Sally, and then she brings up the laundry basket from the basement. I tell her I'll do it. I take the basket out, and me and Mom pull off the wooden clothespins from the dry clothes and fold them and set them in the basket.

"Doesn't it smell good?" she says, holding up a shirt to her nose before taking it down.

I smell a towel. "It sure does."

"It doesn't matter that we're in the city. It smells as good as it did down at the Farm."

We fold the sheets together, which seems to make her happy. I like helping Mom with chores. She slows down time with her observations, and the care that she takes. I learn something every time I help her, even if it's a small thing like taking down the laundry.

That night I lie in bed thinking about that letter, and it's killing me to see what made Mom cry. It couldn't be too bad, but it had to be bad enough. It's close to midnight and I go downstairs slow and quiet and look around for the letter. I figure it's in the living room, but it's not. I check the buffet in the dining room, just in case she did put it with the other one, but it's not there. I go into the kitchen and Gram's up, sitting at the table. She's got her fingers around a cup of tea and has a half-eaten cannoli on a plate.

"What you doing up?" she says.

"I thought I heard a rat," I say, and sit down across from her.

She waves me off and grins. "A rat. You," she says.

"Is there any more?" I point to her cup.

"Plenty more," she says. "It's on the stove."

I pour some of the hot water into a cup and sit back down. She starts opening the tin containing the tea bags and I frown at her and take her tea bag and slip it into my cup of hot water.

"You trying to send us to the poor house?" I say to her.

"Ha. You funny boy."

I dump two spoons of sugar and a little milk in and stir it up. I slurp it a long time on purpose. She chuckles.

"Thinking of Carmelo, were you?"

"Thinking of Teresa Del Rosa?" she mocks me.

"You know it," I say, slurping the tea.

"You be careful," she says.

"Oh, I am."

"She nice girl. Don't get me wrong. But I know how it is with you two."

"Do you, now?"

"I know."

"Spying on us?"

"Don't talk to me like that. It disrespectful. I see. I know. You going to end up in trouble if you don't be careful."

The clock on the wall above the pew clicks every second. It's the only sound in the kitchen. I don't slurp the tea anymore and I put my hand on hers and rub it and shake it some.

"Gram," I say. "Did you read Tommy's letter?"

"I read it," she says. "I don't want to, but your mama want me

250

to."

"What did he say? She seemed pretty upset."

She gives a big, heavy sigh. "I worried about him," she says.

"Sure, sure you are. But what did the letter say?"

She sighs again, not as big. "They all getting killed. Everyone over there getting killed."

"You mean the guy's in his unit?"

"That's right. They dropping like flies. Tommy says one die yesterday, and four die before that. He say he don't want to worry them, but he want them to know in case they don't get any more letters."

"Fuck."

"Yeah, I know, fuck. Fuck is right."

"Is that all he said?"

"No, he say but don't worry about me. Ha! After he say all the boys are dying, he say don't worry about me. Of course a mother is going to worry. When you say a thing like that?" She taps her thumb to her chest. "I worried too. I worried sick."

I put both hands on hers. I shake my head, then shake it harder like I'm trying to sling out the thoughts.

"I tired of seeing young boys die. I see it when I was young, and I see it again now. What for?" She makes a raspberry sound. "You carry a baby for nine months, then love it to death for it whole life, then have some general come and take him away for his stupid war." She makes another raspberry sound.

I'm about to say something about her hero Mussolini, but for once I keep my mouth shut. I stand up and give her a kiss on the cheek. She holds me there and pats the side of my face.

"I'm going out to the bus," I say.

"Now?"

"Frankie's probably up."

"Don't make the dogs bark," she says. "You wake up the whole neighborhood."

I sneak out and when I get to the bus I put my face to the side window and call Frankie's name low and secretive, and he opens the door for me and I step in.

He's got the small lamp on and some incense burning.

251

"What are you up to?" I ask him.

He holds up a book.

"*Lord of the Flies*? What's that?"

"You never heard of *Lord of the Flies*? Just reading about the family," he says.

I sit down and he hands me a warm beer. I crack it open and taste the salty bitterness. I pick up the book and flip through it, stopping to read a couple paragraphs. When I put it down Frankie's getting his sketchbook out.

"Go ahead, man," he says.

"I don't feel like reading," I tell him.

"You don't have to. Pretend."

I do what he wants and hold the book open and try and keep still.

"You're the one who was reading," I say. "How about if you read and I'll sketch you."

"Sure, man," he says. "Right after I'm done."

"Hey, Frankie, have you gotten any letters from Tommy?"

"A couple."

"Yeah? How's he doing?"

"He's doing all right," he says. His eyes flicker up and down as he sketches; I try and move only my mouth.

"Did you read his last letter to Mom and Dad?"

"They got another one?"

"Yeah. He doesn't sound too good."

"Ah, he'll be all right," he says.

"I don't know," I say. "Sounds like his outfit is getting hit hard."

"Well, that's Vietnam."

I lift up the beer and ask him if I can have some and he says go ahead, he's working on my shoulders.

"When are you leaving?" I ask him.

"Not soon enough," he says.

"How soon is that?"

"Could be next week. Or the week after."

"Are you still going to San Fran?"

"That's the plan," he says.

"I still don't understand what you're going to do there. Are you going to try and get in a band? Or do painting?"

"Man, I don't know that until I get there. But I'll be away from this place. That's enough for me."

"Heck, you should go to Kent like you wanted. Me and Nick could come out and visit all the time."

"I don't want to go to Kent," he says. "Look, don't you understand? I can't take this shit anymore."

"But Kent would be far enough away from Dad. You could still see us. You'd still be away."

He stops drawing and looks at me. He seems mad.

"Dude, don't you get it? I want as far away from this place as I can get. Kent? Are you kidding me? Man, I'd go to China if I could get there. I'd go to *Vietnam*," he says, leaning in toward me. "I wish I was in Tommy's place. Anything beats this nuthouse. I'm going to *California*. Where there's no Dad, no good ol' Saturdays, no sharing a room with a hundred brothers, no belt or having my head skinned, no getting beat up on the way to school, nobody filling me with old-fashioned notions of how this broken-down world should stay how it's always been. *California,* where there's freedom and new ways of thinking, man. Where I don't have to deal with Sgt. Carter as I'm shoveling in my morning gruel. I want to go where there are other people like me. Don't you understand? How can you live here, man? Aren't you going crazy?"

My throat's tight. My face feels hot.

"Yeah, sure," I say. "I mean, I don't know."

"Look, Puck," he says and he gives me his smile, that same smile he'd give me whenever I wanted to crawl behind the couch after being yelled at, or ignored, or crushed to powder, and he'd let me know he was right there with me and everything was going to be okay, "it's going to suck leaving you and Nick, hell, and most everybody. Even the old man himself. It's not him. It's not me. It's the two of us rowing in opposite directions. It's time I go. I need to get out there, spread my wings, see if I can fly after being cooped up all these years. It's *the* time for this here generation. We got to see if we can do something. We got to see if we can take the empire and shape it into paradise. And maybe have some fun along the way. You dig, man? Do you know what I'm talking about?"

"Sure, Frankie," I tell him. "I just don't want you to go."

"I know, I know you don't, man," he says. "But things don't stand still. You might want them to, and you might think they are, but they never are. The world's not a pond, it's a river. You got to ready yourself for the next storm, when that quiet creek explodes and sends you downstream whether you want it to or not. I'll miss you, man. But I have to go. I just have to."

I let him finish his sketch. I finish my beer, and I tell him I'm heading in, I'm tired. In bed I think about what it's going to be like without the bus sitting in the back. Part of me wants to go with Frankie, and part of me wants to stay here forever. I think about how he said things are always changing, and he's right. But just because he's right doesn't mean I have to like it.

Frankie's Send-Off

The night before Frankie leaves Mom asks him what he wants for his last dinner here and he says he wants chipped beef on toast. He's a pseudo-vegetarian, that's true, but he says he deserves one carnivorous meal before heading to California, the land of milk, honey, and tofu, whatever that is. Teresa comes over, and Sir Henry, and Mr. Capp stops by, and Aunt Myrtle and Bonnie Bonnell, and even Jack from the filling station.

Dad loves chipped beef on toast almost as much as tongue sandwiches or hash. He peppers it and salts it and nudges the creamy sauce to the edge of Mom's homemade toast, but he doesn't push the peas off to the side like I do. He has Sir Henry on one side of him and Jack on the other side, and Mr. Capp, who's always trying to flirt with Mom, is on the bench beside Gram holding a plate in his lap, staring at Mom's legs.

"California, eh?" says Jack. He's got his garage cap on at the table but Mom doesn't care, because it's Jack. "How many days you figure it'll take you?"

"I don't know," says Frankie. "I'm not going straight out. I'm going to see some sights first."

"Oh yeah? Where you headed?" Then Jack remembers he's wearing his cap and removes it and places it on his knee. "I'm sorry, ma'am," he says to Mom, who just pats his shoulders.

255

"I want to see America," says Frankie. "From sea to shinin' sea. This land is your land, and all that jazz. I wanna hop in Kerouac's footprints and see where they take me. I want to lie in the grass where Lewis and Clark slept. Maybe dance on a volcano or an Indian mound. I may not even get to California, Jack."

Me and Nick look at each other, because it's pretty obvious Frankie's had a few hits.

"I went out West once," says Jack. "Back when I was about your age."

"Oh yeah?" Frankie sits up all of a sudden like somebody says we're having pumpkin pie for dessert.

Jack nods. "I went all over. I read that book by Kerouac. I did all that stuff before he was in diapers. I guess I should have wrote a book."

"Jesus, Jack," says Frankie. "Woops, yeah, sorry. I mean, *groovy*. And you came back to Akron?"

He cuts a corner of toast with the creamy chipped beef and eats it. We all wait while he chews and then swallows it. "I was out there a couple years," he says. "I ain't from Akron. I'm from Cleveland. I left from Cleveland and then came back to Cleveland, then came down here to Akron." He stops and thinks about it, looking right through the wall over Gram's head. "I could've stayed. Maybe I should've stayed. I worked some tough jobs. But good, interesting jobs. I worked in a slaughterhouse some. Then in an ore mine. Then in a factory that made iron pipes. Then on a ranch. I liked working on the ranch." He looks around the table. "I don't know that there's a better job than working on a ranch."

"But why'd you come back?" says Frankie. He's about as desperate as I've seen him. It's like Jack's holding the secret to the pyramids behind those dark bloodshot eyes.

"Why'd I come back?" He's chewing, thinking about it. "The same reason I left, I guess. It's where I had to be at the time."

"Holy mackerel," says Frankie. "I know *I'm* not coming back."

"You'll be back," says Nick.

"No way, man. I'm heading out, moving on, and never even *looking* back."

"Yeah, okay," says Nick. "We'll see."

"The things is," says Jack, "it's exactly as it had to be."

"What do you mean?" I ask him.

"I mean that I had to go see the country like Frankie here's about to do, like a lot of young men have the urge to do. No, I'd say it's more than an urge, it's a need for some. My folks weren't too happy about it. My dad wanted me to follow him into the steel mill. I respected him for the work he did, but I didn't want to do that. He told me I was wasting my life. It was difficult leaving. But a young man's gotta do what's in his blood. It can't be stopped. I came back and I didn't feel like I had my tail between my legs. Not at all. Once away, home isn't the same place, and that's good and as it should be. The old city has a different face. Your old neighborhood. Your old friends. Your family. The hardest part isn't leaving, it's deciding to leave. It's knowing whether that's the right path for *you*." He looks at me for some reason, not at Frankie. "Some guys read Jack Kerouac, but others have to *be* him."

After dinner we pour into the living room and dining room, and it's like Friday nights with the adults plus Anthony in the living room and us kids at the dining room table. Hoss and Ollie are over, and they're talking about the band and how it could've gone somewhere.

"Yeah, but you can't keep a beat, man," Frankie says to Ollie, draping his arm around him. He says it affectionately, not meaning to hurt him.

"I don't think anybody can tell," says Ollie, pinching his eyes together as he considers it.

Frankie pretends to strangle him, shaking his hands back and forth on Ollie's neck. "We need Ringo. Where's Ringo?"

"Teresa, you should have joined us sooner," says Hoss. "That was the problem. With that sweet voice. Man." It looks like Hoss is going to break down and cry on the spot.

We bring out the cards and play euchre. We put three more leaves in the table and have two games going since there are so many of us. We even let Squirt sit in, which thrills him to no end.

Over in the living room Mom's sitting on Dad's lap in his

wheelchair. She's sideways with her arms around his neck, and he has his arms around her waist. Mom doesn't seem sad exactly, but preoccupied. It feels different from when Tommy was leaving. Mom keeps looking at Frankie with Dad's face buried in her neck. Dad's not paying much attention to anything but Mom. The thing is, she always liked Frankie a whole lot. Frankie was more trouble, like me and Squirt, but the same thing that makes him trouble makes him special. Mom knows it, even if Dad has a hard time seeing it. I watch Mom watching Frankie, and then I watch Frankie myself. I wonder how much Frankie wants to leave, and how much is because he feels like he's being nudged out. There's a lump in my throat, for real, and it's hard to breathe. Nick's glum just like me and he's making mistakes and playing the wrong cards. He never plays the wrong cards.

"Hey, man, the wine!" Frankie suddenly says.

"What are you talking about?" Ollie, who's still bruised, says.

"The wine—the cherry wine we made. Let's bring it out."

I look over to Mom and Dad. "Can we?" I ask them. They didn't hear Frankie, so I ask them, "Can we try the wine now?"

"Sure," says Mom. "I forgot all about it. I'm sure it's ready."

Nick carries up the carboy, which is this big glass container with a small hole on top. We have it plugged up good so nothing bad gets in. It had a cork stopper, but it kept falling off from the pressure. We got a rubber one that fit so tight we had to tap it in place. Nick carries it nice and slow so he doesn't slosh it around and make it cloudy and sets it in the middle of the table.

Sissy gets some Dixie cups as we examine the rubber stopper. Frankie tries twisting it off, then Nick, but it won't budge. Aunt Myrtle and Bonnie come over, and Jack too. Jack tries using his big, muscled hands on it, but no dice.

"You got any vise grips?" he says.

I get some from the garage and hand them to Jack, but he defers, telling Frankie it's his send-off, his wine, and he should do the honors.

Nick holds the carboy on one side and Jack holds it on the other side as Frankie takes the vise grips, squeezes them around the rubber stopper, and gives it a quick twist.

What ensues is difficult to describe, at least the first part, because I'm blinded for a couple seconds. The wine comes shooting out of the carboy like Mt. Vesuvius on those poor Romans, spraying onto the ceiling, the walls, and all of us. In no time at all we're dripping in red-purplish wine. Bonnie shrieks in shock. Jack stands there sad-looking and at a loss for words. Nick, and Ollie, and Hoss, and the girls yell at Frankie to make it stop, like he's spraying them with a hose. Squirt jumps up and down, giddy, like he just got off a roller coaster and he wants to do it again. Ollie tries putting his hand over the hole, but it just makes the wine spray sideways on the new wallpaper.

Mom drifts over from the living room once the wine volcano goes dormant, looking at the scene like somebody stumbling on a car crash. She goes up to one of the walls and lays her palm against it. She reminds me of Squirt when he's sleepwalking. She turns to Frankie.

"I guess you'll have to delay your trip," she says, smirking, about to bust out with a laugh or a cry, I can't tell which.

And Frankie does delay his trip a week as we strip off the stained wallpaper and put up new. It gives him a chance to finally get Aunt Myrtle's car fixed, which he forgot to do with all the excitement and planning surrounding his adventure. Sir Henry banged it out in a flash and said he wouldn't tell a soul.

Frankie leaves the following Saturday morning. Me and Nick sit with him on the cement steps by the sidewalk. Tallmadge Avenue is sluggish, not with its usual craziness like during the week. Johnny Eyelids and his two little brothers walk past and Frankie sticks his leg out as a joke, but they walk around it.

"Nice try," says Johnny.

"Have a good life," says Frankie.

Frankie lights a cigarette and passes it around.

"Well, boys," he says. "It's been a trip."

"Got her gassed up?" says Nick.

"Naw," says Frankie. "I'll stop at Jack's on the way out of Dodge."

My stomach hurts. It hurts to think of Frankie leaving.

"Do you know the way?" I ask him. I ask without looking at

him. We all stare straight ahead.

"Sure," he says. "Take a left at Hibbing, Minnesota, hang a right at Hannibal, Missouri, and don't stop until I see the flowers pushing through the clouds of good ol' San Fran."

Nick takes a drag from the cigarette and hands it to Frankie.

"Well," he says deadpan, the way only he can, "you have a good life, too."

We finish the cig then get up, dust ourselves off, and walk to the bus, which is parked in the drive facing the street, ready to go. They're all waiting. Mom and Dad are by the passenger-side door. Britt and Sissy are each holding small brown bags of food to give him. Anthony is bouncing Sally in his arms, and Gram's standing small and weepy-eyed next to Dad. I have no idea where Squirt is.

Frankie goes down the line, giving everybody a hug, and then trots to the far side of the bus and hops in. There's not the heaviness like there was when Tommy left. I'm sure Mom and Dad are somewhat glad to see him go, but not nearly as glad as he is. He starts up the bus and eases it forward when Squirt runs in front of it and makes like Batman. Frankie slams on the breaks. I just shake my head. The last image Frankie sees in his rear-view mirror is Dad wailing on Squirt's bare butt.

Pain and Secrets

It's early morning but I'm still in bed when I hear this *tink . . . tink . . . tink-tink*. I raise my head and wait. It comes again, *tink . . . tink . . . tink*. I look out the window and see Sandy down below waving at me. I creep downstairs to the side door to see what's up.

"Hey," I say to her. It's cold and I put my arms around myself.

"Sorry to wake you up," she says.

"What's going on?"

"Can you meet me at the gorge?" She's agitated and anxious.

I'm still waking up. "What for? Sandy, we have school."

"Puck, please," she says, and she grips my arm for a second, then let's go.

"Okay," I tell her. "Give me a few minutes."

She nods and then leaves.

I put on my school clothes, get my books together, and head out the door. It's one of those crisp early mornings where your fingers hurt from the shock of it and your lungs work overtime, like you're running a fast mile. I head straight for the dam and find Sandy there standing by the railing.

"What's the matter?" I ask her.

"Gary's back," she says. She's got on an oversized coat and

her hair's a mess. She has bags under her eyes.

"Who's Gary?"

"Gary—don't you know who Gary is?" she about yells at me.

I shake my head. "Who is he?"

"He's Gary, just Gary. He's back and I can't stay—I can't stay another minute. I don't know what I'm going to do."

I approach her, but she steps back like she's afraid of me. "But I don't understand," I say. "Did he hurt you?"

She winces and cocks her head. "What do you think?"

"Sandy, I don't know—I don't have any idea what you're talking about."

"Sometimes, Puck," she says, just seething like she wants to scratch my eyes out, and I don't know why. But then I think more on it, fast, and though I don't understand it all, I think I understand the gist of it.

"You want me and Nick to come over?" I say.

"And do what?" She crosses her arms, sneering at me.

"Get him out."

"You have a shotgun on you? Because that's what it'll take. He's got real guns, Puck, not those little BB guns you guys have."

"Did you call the cops?"

She laughs a single laugh. "Oh, God," she says, turning her head, then back again. "Sometimes."

"What? *What?*"

"The cops; really? You think I want the cops running around our house?"

"If you want him out, yeah," I say.

"Me—on probation, waiting to be sent away as it is? Are you flipping out of your mind?"

"Then how are you going to get him out?" I say. "I don't know what other choice you have."

"I don't know, Puck," she about screams. "If I knew that, I wouldn't be standing here talking to you."

"But, is this guy your mom's boyfriend?"

"What do you think?"

"I don't know," I say, getting pissed myself, about yelling at

262

her.

"Yes, he's my mom's boyfriend. He's why I hid the key to our house that day. Don't you *get it*?"

"Okay, then. Why does she want him around if . . ."

"Oh, God, *Puck*," she really does scream now. I rush over, go to cover her mouth, but put my arms around her instead. She fights to get away, but I don't let go. She thrashes, but I don't let go. I hold her a good long while until she stops fighting and then loses all her energy and starts falling to the ground, and then I really hold her, tight. She lets loose and cries a river as I'm holding her.

I lead her to a bench and we sit down. I still have my arms around her. She holds onto me with her head on my chest.

"I have to do something," she says. "What am I going to do, Puck?"

"I don't know."

"I'll shoot him myself. I don't care. That'll take care of it."

"No," I say. "Don't do that."

"But why not? Doesn't he deserve it?"

"If any kind of person does, he does. But you can't."

"I'll kill them both."

"Sandy," I say.

"Come run away with me," she says, and she lifts her head to look into my eyes. They're the saddest, most desperate eyes I've ever seen.

"Maybe you should, but I can't."

"I'll kill them if I stay."

"Is there anywhere you can go? Do you have any relatives?"

"I have an aunt and uncle in Michigan," she says. "They're the only ones who'd take me."

"You should go," I tell her.

"Come with me."

"I can't."

"But why? Puck, we need to get out of here."

"Look," I say, "I'll help you. I have some money. You can take a bus."

"I want you to come," she says. "Puck, I need you to come."

"I can't."

"Because of Teresa? Is that it?"

"Sandy," I say.

"I thought it was you and me, Puck," she says. "I thought we were together on this. Why do you like her anyway? She's just some dumb girl who's going to drag you down. Can't you see that? Can't you look around the corner to see what's coming?"

"I don't want to go," I tell her. "I'm not you, Sandy. As much as I like you, I'm not you."

"She's been with every guy on North Hill. She was with your own *brother,* for Christ's sake. She doesn't love you, Puck. Do you think she loves you? She's just desperate—more desperate than I am—only she's going to use you the way your dad has all this time. She knows exactly what she's doing. She sees your weaknesses. She's a vampire, Puck, and she's going to suck out your soul before she's through."

I don't say anything. Suddenly, I feel a fool. I tell her it's getting late and I gently ease her off me and stand up.

"Come on," I say to her. "We need to get going."

She shakes her head with her feet on the bench seat, holding her knees.

"Sandy, you can't stay here. That's not going to do any good. At least come to school."

She keeps shaking her head.

"Look—if you need anything, I'll be working in the garage after school," I tell her. "Me and Nick are in there until dinner. Call me anytime, I don't care how late it is. Sandy."

She stares straight ahead like she doesn't hear me.

I start hoofing it. It hurts to think of her sitting alone, afraid, not knowing where to go, but what can I do? I just don't know what I can do.

For a couple nights I see Sandy's light on in her room. It's on until I figure she goes to bed, then it goes out. She has thick blinds that cover her window, so I can't see in. Then the light doesn't turn on anymore. After her light stops coming on, I don't see her in the hall at school and it's pretty clear she must have finally left like she always wanted to. That, or she's in jail. Both possibilities make me sad, but for different reasons.

A few days later me and Nick take Gram to the doctor's. It's over near Highland Square and we check her in, but we don't go in with her. She comes out smiling, holding her purse with both hands like a bag of chocolates.

"Want to go anywhere?" I ask her. "Since we're out?"

"I need some pantyhose," she says.

"Okay," I tell her. "But I mean, is there any place you'd like to go, anything you'd like to do? You don't get out of the house that often."

She thinks about it, she really does.

"The zoo," she says.

"The zoo?"

"I want to go to the zoo."

"You're kidding," I say.

"You ask me," she says. "I never been to the zoo."

"Aw," I say.

"There wasn't any zoo where I lived, and since I come here I never go."

"You never took Mom when she was little?"

"She went in school," says Gram, "so I never take her. You think you telling you a lie? Is that what you think?"

"We'll take you to the zoo, Gram," says Nick. "Come on."

It's not too far and when we park, Gram gets out and shuffles along as fast as she can. We run up beside her and each take an arm so she doesn't trip.

She gets a kick out of the flamingoes, the rhinos, the elephants, and the monkeys. She likes the monkeys more than anything. She says they remind her of Squirt.

"Look at them," she says. "Aren't they cute?"

We go past the zebras and then sit under some trees for a breather. She swings her feet under the bench as we eat some peanuts. The air's dry and clear and the sun's not too hot anymore. A squirrel comes up and I toss him a peanut. He takes off with it and hops on a rock.

"I still can't believe you never went to a zoo," I tell her.

"No, never," she says.

265

"Well, what do you think?"

"I want to go back to the monkeys," she says.

"We can go wherever you want," says Nick. "We can sit and watch them all day."

I hand her a peanut and she tosses it to a squirrel. She watches it go all the way up a tree. She tosses them more peanuts.

"Who was Carmelo, really?" I ask her.

She's surprised by the question.

"You sure are nosy," she says.

"I'm just curious."

"Curious, nosy. Same thing."

"You don't have to say," I tell her.

"Sure, I don't have to say. I know I don't have to say—what, you think I'm your prisoner?"

"If you were our prisoner, we'd ask you to make some spaghetti for us when we get home, not tell us about Carmelo," says Nick.

She swings left and right to look at us through those thick glasses, then shrugs. "Looks like I don't have choice. Okay, I tell you." She wipes her hands together and the salt from the peanuts falls away. "I tell you, so listen, both of you. Nobody listens anymore. You listen now . . . Okay. You think you know things, but you don't. I tell you. I tell you now, you nosy little monkeys. When I was a young lady, not too old, I met Carmelo. He was young man in my village. He like me, see? That's what this is all about. He liked me and I like him, too. We begin seeing each other. Like boyfriend and girlfriend. In the olive grove. It was all secret, see? You know *Romeo and Juliet*? This was *Romeo and Juliet* for real. It happens to people; it happened to me. My parents, his parents, they no get along. They hate each other. Why?" She shrugs. "Who knows? They not want us seeing each other. They forbid me to see that boy. But I know in my heart that he was the one for me."

"How?" I ask her.

"What you mean, how?"

"How did you know?"

"Because," she says, "I just know. When you know, you

266

know. I know he was right for me, and he know I was right for him. I try talking to my parents. Papa would listen, but not mama. She no like that family for before she was born. So, we meet in the olive grove." She makes the sign of the cross. "I know it not right, going against my mama and papa, but I couldn't help it. We were in love. What else could we do? But then we get caught. My mama figure out where we were and she come with my uncle and he nearly shoot Carmelo. I beg and cry, but it make no difference. She tells me I am forbidden to see him again." She looks at us and cups our cheeks, one at a time, lovingly. "That why I come here. My mama send me here when I was eighteen to keep me away from Carmelo, so I could never see him again. All those years, I never write him, I never get letter from him. I don't know what he doing. My sister swore to my mama not to tell me about him. I know nothing."

She begins to tear up. I take her hand as Nick rubs her back.

"I'm sorry, Gram," says Nick.

"How long I not see my family. My mama, my papa, my sister, my aunts and uncles. I all alone here. Sure, I loved your grandpa. Sure, I had good life here. I have wonderful family with you, and you, and everyone. But I miss my family back in Italy. If I could just see them one more time, I could die and be happy. But," she shrugs, "I don't think so."

On the way home we ask if she wants to stop anywhere else, anywhere at all.

"McDonald's," she says. "I want one of those hamburgers."

We stop at McDonald's and eat in the car. The air is cool and soothing. She tells us more of Carmelo, and of the Farm and grandpa.

"I not right when I first get married," she says. "I was in bad way. I think I go crazy. I loved your grandpa very much. He was so kind and good, how couldn't I love him? But I also miss Italy and my family. That's when I get pregnant with your mama. I was sick the whole time. I mean sick in the head, here," she says, tapping her finger to her head. "I barely make it. Your grandpa stay with me all the time, even though he work all day in the field. He good to me. He very good to me. Then I have the baby, your mama. What a beautiful baby she was. All babies are beautiful, but she especially beautiful. Look at her. She even beautiful now. So, some say we should give up the baby."

"For adoption?" I ask.

"Yes, for adoption. They say since I almost crazy all during the pregnancy, I should not keep this baby. How can I take care of her when I nearly crazy? This baby would be better with someone else. They try to make me sign papers. They try to take this beautiful baby away from me. But I tell them, you not touch one hair on this baby. She's mine. I going to raise her, and love her, and give her a wonderful life. And that's it. You see?"

"What, Gram?" I ask her. "See what?"

"That why your mama want so many beautiful babies. She was almost sent away. But I love her, and tell her she's the most beautiful thing in the world. She would have a hundred babies if she could. After your mama, we have your aunts and uncles. We have more babies. Each baby is precious. Each baby in the world is a gift. She know that. Your mama want to give life to you the way we gave life to her. You see? You see?"

Across the Viaduct

We get our first snow of the year, an early wet snow that sticks to the ground and makes everything look like it's been covered in frosting. The driveway doesn't need shoveling, but I go out anyway and scrape it as the snow falls. I like being out in the snow. Flakes fall onto my eyelashes and melt and blind me until I blink them away, and they fall onto my cheeks and nose making them cold in a good way. My old corduroy coat gets covered, and so do the tops of my rubber boots. I glance up at Sandy's window when I go to toss my shovel on her side, but there's no light.

Everything is bright and good with the snow falling. When I'm done shoveling, I lean the shovel against the garage and pass through the gate into the Del Rosa's yard, and knock on the back door. Mrs. Del Rosa greets me and invites me in.

"I was wondering if Teresa was home?" I ask her.

Mrs. Del Rosa's happy to see me and she calls upstairs, but Teresa's heard our voices and she comes running down and puts on her coat and boots and we head outside. We walk to the corner of Crestwood and Tallmadge and decide to head toward Main Street. We hold bare hands and slide together across the uneven sidewalk. I try and get her with snowballs, and make sure to only hit her on the back or on the legs and not in the face like I would if I were aiming at Nick or Frankie. I pick her up and twirl her around and pretend I'm going to toss her, but I don't. It's just fun to see her so afraid.

"You want to go across the viaduct?" she says.

"Really?" I say.

"Why not? I've never walked across it in the snow. We could walk around downtown."

"It's a long walk," I say. "Think you can handle it?"

She slugs me in the side. I grab her by the wrists and pull her against me and kiss her. Her nose is cold, just like mine, but her lips are warm. We get a couple honks and laugh it off and start moving again.

It's Sunday afternoon and kids are outside trying to scrape up enough snow to make snowmen or forts. Cars fishtail, especially around corners, and some people are out walking like us, enjoying the first snowfall. We turn south on Main. The snow comes and goes and it's pretty serious at times for being so early in the season. It hits us in waves and we lean forward with our heads down as we come to the viaduct.

You can see everything from here—the wide-open space and downtown lit up through the gray of the snow, and down below once we get part of the way across to the scant river and industrial buildings and old houses. We stop and lean over the railing and look. There's nothing to see really, but it's high and dizzying and mysterious. Teresa hooks her hand around my arm. I can feel her shivering.

"Cold?" I say to her.

"I should've worn a winter coat."

"Wear mine."

"Don't be silly," she says. "Just put your arms around me."

I do, rubbing my hands up and down her body. "Let's get off this thing."

"Wait."

"But you're freezing," I say. "It won't be as bad once we're off."

"Not just yet." She's looking down below. It's gray and bleak. The viaduct is more than a bridge connecting the two parts of the city; it seems to be an elevated path between the hard, unsympathetic sidewalks of reality and the throbbing spires of possibility.

We get across and it's like entering another time. Some stores are closed because it's Sunday, but most are open. I have money from the carburetor work and we stop in O'Neil's and sit at the counter and order hamburgers and fries. We move from side to side on the swivel seats waiting for them, sipping on the straws of our Cokes, watching the cook. It's warm by the grill and she's happy and smiling and prettier than ever.

Our burgers and fries arrive and we dig right in.

"You want to see what's playing at the Loew's?" I ask her.

"Not really."

"No?"

"Not really, Puck."'

"We could sit in the balcony and, you know."

"Sure, we could," she says.

"But no?"

She shakes her head as she takes a bite of her burger.

When she's done with her bite she says, "I like it right here. This is the best thing I can think of doing. It's wonderful."

I nod and look around. The cook is scraping the crud into the hole in the grill. A guy down the counter, smoking, his movements in slow motion, doesn't take his eyes of Teresa. He's not leering, he doesn't seem too creepy. He's just some middle-aged guy who recognizes how I'm the luckiest guy in the world. I gaze at the side of Teresa's face when she doesn't notice. There's pain in her face, beneath her beauty, but there's joy too. I'd do anything to make her happy, I think to myself. And I will too.

We ride the escalator to the second floor and listen to records for almost an hour in the listening booths. Then we go to the women's clothing section and she tries on some dresses and a couple blouses and even a wig, but she says she'd never be caught dead in a wig. We end up walking through the jewelry section. It's not something we plan on doing, we just end up there.

"Well, well," I say to her. "Pretty tricky."

"Me?" she says. *"I* didn't lead us here."

"Right," I say, as facetious as can be. "We might as well take a look."

"Sure," she says. "What could it *possibly* hurt?"

"I mean, we're here."

"We're here."

We lean over the counter and peer through the glass at the rings. There are all sorts of sizes and shapes of diamonds, rubies, emeralds, and stones I've never heard of. Most of the rings don't have prices on them, and I know what that means. I can't imagine how I could ever afford one. It must take years to save up enough money. Teresa isn't giddy about the whole thing like you might think she'd be. She knows how expensive they are and understands that buying one is something way beyond my means, at least right now. But who says she's even thinking about *me* buying her a ring? It's unsettling to think that there are guys out there who'd give their right arm to be with her, older guys, who do have the means for a ring right this very second. I mean, dating a super-hot, super-sweet girl is tough. Guys are always chiseling away at their contentment. But then I don't believe Teresa is the kind of girl I need to worry about. She doesn't flirt with other guys. She doesn't give two bats of the eye when guys stare at her or make passes right in front of me. In fact, she gets annoyed. She could have any guy she wanted, and here she is with me. It's a humbling thought, dear reader. It makes me want to be as good to her as I can.

We leave O'Neil's and walk around some. We end up behind the buildings along the canal, and we stop and kiss over the small bridge there. She smells like a dream from all the sample perfumes she has on. We stop in this little peanut store and buy a bag of warm cashews. The snow had let up, but now it's returned as we start across the viaduct toward home. At least the wind is at our backs.

From this direction you can see the hospital across the valley sitting over to the left. It's where we were both born. It's where everyone on North Hill is born.

We stop halfway across. *She* stops and I stop with her. It's dimmer than before. The early-fading light of autumn can't push

272

through the waves of snow, and it seems much later than it is.

"You know," she says, "people jump off here. They do. Every year, it happens. Some poor soul without a speck of hope walks out here and jumps. There's no turning back when you jump. It's not like taking pills or even cutting yourself. If you jump off this viaduct, you're certain you don't want to go on any longer. There's no doubt."

She turns around to face me. I rub the sides of her arms.

"What's the matter?" I ask her.

"I understand them," she says. "I don't think I could ever jump, but I understand what could make someone want to."

"Teresa."

"No, it's all right."

"Let's go," I say to her, trying to pull her along. She stands firm.

"It's amazing that more people don't jump. There's got to be something, some reason, *someone*, to take hold of. To give you time so you can work things out in your head and see all the happiness that's out there just waiting for you. It's there, Puck, but much of the time it's hidden. Buried beneath a mountain of pain. You know what I mean. You don't talk about it, but I see it in your writing. You, more than anyone, understand. Meanwhile, the clock ticks. There's only so much time to run across the viaduct. If you linger too long, if your sadness is unbearable, you'll do it. You have to race across or you'll surely jump."

She leans up and kisses me, then. She wraps her arms around my neck, clutching me hard, and I hold her tight. I take her hand and we start walking the second half of the viaduct. It's cold, the wind gusts move us along, and suddenly I start to run, pulling her beside me. I keep her on the inside away from the railing as we race across to the other side.

273

Time Stops

I get a phone call about a week later. I'm on the third floor doing homework when Sissy calls up the stairs. I yell back down:

"Is it Teresa!"

"What!" she calls back.

"Is it Teresa!"

"No!"

"You sure?"

"It's not her!"

I pause, debating on whether I should go down. I figure anybody else can wait. I'll be done with my homework in half an hour.

"Tell them I'll call back!"

"You're not going to get it!"

"No—I'll call them back! Can you find out who it is and I'll call them back!"

"Okay!"

I go back to the books. It's been a busy week. Two tests already, one tomorrow, and a paper due on Friday. Anthony is at his desk studying, and Nick is on his bed with his books on the floor, studying too. Nick's got a candle on the floor to give him more light, even though it's not dark outside yet. He's been doing that lately, studying with a candle. He says it's how knights would've studied.

I have a little more to do, but when I'm at a breaking point I go downstairs for some bread and jam. Sissy and Britt are at the kitchen table. Sissy's showing Britt how to macramé.

I sit down with my bread and jelly.

"Impressive," I say. "How about making me one of those?"

"You want one?" says Sissy.

"Sure. It's a plant holder, right?"

"Yeah."

"I wouldn't mind having one upstairs," I tell her.

"Hey, that was Sandy that called," she says.

"You mean a while back?"

She nods. "She wanted you to go to the gorge." She looks up at me. "I think."

I take a bite of the jelly bread. "The gorge?"

"That's what she said."

I take another bite. "That's all she said?"

"Well, I didn't want to stay on too long," says Sissy. "I didn't want to get in the middle of you and her and Teresa. But, she seemed pretty upset. She must have seen you two."

"Why do you say that?"

"Look, Puck, I really don't want to—"

"Sissy—what did she say?"

"I mean, I wasn't really listening, and part of the time I had my hand over the phone when I was yelling up at you, and she kept on talking."

"What did she say?"

"She asked me if I knew you used the tires as your own personal waterbed. And she said she should have pushed you and Teresa off the viaduct when she had the chance." Sissy shakes her head. "That's one kooky chick you have for a friend. You should really stay away from that one, Puck."

I jump up from the table, grab the keys to Anthony's Honda hanging from the hook by the sink, and run out the door.

I start it up and head toward the gorge.

Traffic's heavy and I have to dodge between cars. I pull back on the throttle all the way, but the bike won't go fast enough. I go

275

through a red light and nearly another and almost spill it going around the entrance to the park. I give it all the gas I can as I head down toward the dam. I hop off the bike, letting it fall to the grass, and run to the place we went before. Sandy's not there. I look around but don't see her. Then, over to the left at the edge of the water, I see her. She's standing there waving at me.

"What the hell?" I say as I walk toward her. "What are you doing?"

"What's it look like I'm doing, Puck?" she says all normal-like. "Enjoying a beautiful fall day."

"Why did you follow us?" I say. If she was a guy I'd hit her.

"Follow you? Looks like you followed me."

"You know what I mean. Me and Teresa. You followed us downtown."

"I actually never made it across the viaduct," she says. "A terribly cold evening, wasn't it?"

"Why?" I demand.

"Why not? You're not the only ones who enjoy a good romp through snow squalls."

"You . . . spied on us," I say. I can barely control myself.

"Have camera, will spy," she says, lifting the Leica from her chest.

"You watched us at the side of the garage. Why? Why would you do that?"

"Now, now," she says. "The real question is, why would you rather spend time with the neighborhood slut than with me, and not more than a beanbag toss from my bedroom window?"

"You have no right," I say.

"Puck, you two were making so much noise—I thought those cats were duking it out again. First rule of having sex outdoors—keep her mouth covered and find a leafy shrub to hide behind."

"But . . ." I'm looking at her, just beyond any sort of possible understanding. "Why? I thought you were leaving, or were on your way to jail. I thought that's what you wanted."

"Who the hell wants to go to jail when the boy of their dreams is living just across the hedges?"

She cocks her head and gives me a sarcastic smile. I don't

know what to say. She's waiting, but I just can't speak.

She walks toward me, then stops. Her hand strums the leather strap of the camera.

"The thing is, Puck, the day you and the bimbo took to the tires, well, the fire sort of went out inside of me. When Gary came back—ha! Talk about a kick to the groin."

"Where've you been?"

"Not in *that* nuthouse, which is all that matters. Once I skipped out, I didn't know what to do with myself, so I started following you two." She makes a point to sigh big. "It's perverse, I know. A form of self-torture. But I'm pretty sure I'm not the only one who's ever done it."

I shake my head. "You should have called."

"I did—not an hour ago."

"Before."

"I wanted to," she says. "It's not always so easy."

She walks away from me and leans her head against a tree, staring at the ground near my feet.

"Sandy," I say, and I reach out my hand.

"I'm not completely delusional," she says more softly now. "But I did think we had something special going on. You're the first one who listened. You're the only one who didn't think I was some freak."

"You're not a freak," I tell her.

"Well, I *am*. I guess I should say you're the first person who accepted that. You looked at me like I was all right."

"I should have made it clear about Teresa and me," I say. "It seemed like you already knew."

She doesn't answer. She bites the side of her lip and kicks at the ground. I can see the pain pouring out of her.

"When I followed you that night, I really thought about pushing you two off. It would've been epic, classic. The snow and dark skies would have made it memorable. You sure deserved it. But, I couldn't do it. As much as you broke me in half, I just couldn't. Her, maybe, but not you. After you went ahead, I walked to where you stopped. Yours were the only footprints in the snow. I took some photographs of them. I took some nice ones where your feet are touching toes. That's when you were kissing. You'll have to see them. She'll think they're romantic."

She starts walking slowly along the edge of the water, moving in between tree trunks like lampposts. I follow her.

"It's not the fact that at some point I'm going to have to spend time in jail," she says, talking to the ground. "It's that I can see it all laid out—my life—a stream of pain with nothing significant to balance it. *You've* been a real joy, but that's just it. You're now with her. And, the next boy I meet like you, who I've got some sort of understanding with, he'll do the same. I can't compete with the Teresa Del Rosas of the world, can I." She furrows her forehead, concentrating, thinking it through. "This is a long-term problem I've got, you see. It's not a phase or a passing storm I've got to weather. It's who I am. It's my life."

She leans into the metal railing where you can look out over the reservoir. The waterfall over the dam isn't far behind.

"I don't particularly wish to experience it, Puck," she says, turning her head away like she's trying to avoid her thoughts. "It's just not a ride I'm going to get on."

I don't expect it. She ducks under the railing and jumps into the reservoir. She splashes water high and I think she's just making a scene, but she moves toward the waterfall.

"Sandy!"

I go to jump in, but she's already too far away from me to reach her before the falls.

"Sandy!"

She flaps at the water, frantic, swimming away from me. Then, just before she reaches the falls, she becomes still. She treads water briefly before leaning onto her back, arms out, as she lets the slow current take her. I grip the railing, squeezing the metal rod, but can do nothing. I see her lift the camera above her head, aiming it to the sky.

I run along the water's edge past the dam and look to see Sandy falling down the vertical drop to the concrete spillway. She hits it, slides forward, then somersaults as the whitewater tosses her into the shallow, rocky river. I run alongside her as she's beaten by the violent turbulence. I want to scream, but

nothing comes out. I watch as her body floats limply away, beyond my sight and out of my realm of sanity.

The Flaming Cross

One night during dinner Sandy's mom's boyfriend comes to the house and tells Dad to keep me away, that I can't go to the funeral. He says that I'm the reason Sandy killed herself, and if I show up at the funeral or on their property he'll shoot me. I don't go to school for a while. I lie in bed mostly, staring at the cracks in the ceiling.

I do a lot of thinking. Everything seems to come together. I don't necessarily mean in a good way, or in a productive way. The anger that's been building inside of me, which has been kept down by being with Teresa, swirls into a force that I can't control. Outwardly I'm calm. I eat dinner like normal, though I don't say much. I talk to Squirt or Nick when they're up with me, though I'm a bit morose. I talk to Teresa on the phone, and she comes over sometimes and we sit in the living room. She doesn't push, doesn't pry, and gives me space. But beneath it, just under my skin, I'm ready to explode.

I keep thinking about Sandy. I think of a hundred different things. Her sarcasm. The way she dressed. The way she always happened to pop up at just the right or wrong time. Her honesty. She didn't always put things the best way, but she gave them to you straight. She was like Frankie, but without any filter whatsoever. It's what I loved about her, and what needled me too. She made me see things I'd never have had the courage to see for myself. It's what made her unlikeable to everyone else. If Sandy's taught me anything, it's that most people don't want to see the truth, especially when that truth's unsavory and is at the core of your world. This is what I think about as, finally, I get up and go sit in church.

It's during the morning, after the schoolkids have been to mass. No one else is there except a couple sisters, and Father MacGregor and Father Nigh up at the altar. They see me but don't say or do anything. They know, vaguely and probably inaccurately, what happened.

I'm there a while, when Father Nigh sits down beside me. It's odd having him beside me. I turn to look at him. He's got his ever-smiling expression, optimistic, quietly confident, as he looks at the cross.

"I'm sorry," he says to me in his deep, soothing voice. "I know you and Sandy were close. I know you weren't allowed to attend the service. I'm sorry, Puck."

"She . . ."

"I didn't know Sandy well," he says. "But if you were her friend, she must have been something."

"She . . . was."

"Let me know if you want to talk. I don't mean in confession. We can just talk like this. It doesn't have to be in church. We can take a walk or have a cup of coffee somewhere. Whatever you want." He turns his head to look at me. "It's easy to lose faith when things like this happen," he says. "Especially for young people."

"Yeah," I say.

"I can't tell you what to think or what to do," he says. "I can only try and guide you so you can find the way for yourself. Do you understand?"

I nod, automatically. We both look at the cross, silently.

"Father?" I say.

"Yes?"

"I haven't told anyone what I'm about to tell you."

"What is it, Puck?"

"No, I've told Teresa, but only some of it."

"Teresa Del Rosa?"

"Yes."

"I see."

"She's my girlfriend."

"You can tell me," he says. "Or not. Whatever you want."

"Well," I begin, "I made this . . . deal with God, you see. With Jesus."

"All right," he says.

"You might not understand," I say to him. "What I'm about to tell you."

"Go on," he says without any hesitation. "I'm listening."

"I believe in miracles . . . Do you, Father?"

"Of course," he says.

"All the miracles can't have been used up in the time of Jesus."

"God is ever present," he says. "Our time is no different from any other."

"That's right," I say. "That's what I think too. That's right. So, I made this pact. With Jesus."

"Go on," he says. His voice cracks, slightly.

"Do you still believe me? I haven't lost you, have I, Father?"

"I believe in the power of our Lord," he says. "I believe He can perform miracles today just as He did years ago."

"But . . . Do you believe *me*?" I ask him.

"I don't know what this pact is," he says. "Tell me."

"I will, Father," I say. "But do you believe it's possible, whatever I tell you, that I've conversed with Jesus for real? Not symbolically. Not in my head, but for real."

"I'd need to hear more," he says. "Tell me about this pact."

"Because I have. I've talked to Him. Maybe you haven't, but I have."

Father Nigh seems visibly uncomfortable. He swings his feet forward a couple times, then lets them come to rest beneath our pew.

"I'm not doubting you, Puck," he says.

"But, *you* do, don't you, Father?"

282

"What, son?"

"You communicate with Jesus."

"That's what a priest does," he says. His voice is deep and solid again.

"You do for real, Father? I mean, for real, you talk to Jesus?"

He nods, slowly, smiling. "Yes."

"Because if you can, there's no reason that I can't, is there?"

"If God wishes it so, then of course. But that's not up to you or me, but to the Lord."

I go to say something next, to start telling him about my dialogues with Jesus, and the deal we made, and how I broke it by being with Teresa, and how I don't know what to think anymore about God and my faith and what I should do with the anger inside me, but I stop myself.

Father Nigh is a good priest. He's a good guy. If he weren't a priest, he'd be doing something else to help people. But he doesn't believe me. It hurts now sitting beside him. I wish anyone but him were sitting beside me.

I say nothing more. There's no reason to. Eventually, he pats my knee, puts his thumb on my forehead making the sign of the cross, says a prayer, and leaves the pew.

I gaze at Jesus up on the cross. He never moves. He's always in the same defeated posture with His drooped head, the gash in His chest, and His limp hands at the ends of the crossbeam. The three spikes in Jesus—one through each palm and one through his overlapped feet—aren't the same size. I've often thought about this. Whoever made those spikes wasn't too concerned about it. He didn't measure twice and cut once. He couldn't have been a Beck. We Becks would have made them exactly, and I mean exactly, the same size no matter who they were for. Whether we thought Jesus was a somebody or a nobody. It's a matter of pride, of caring about the job at hand. Nobody needs to tell you something like that. You just do it, you make them exactly equal. Also, the vertical beam doesn't rise to the top of Jesus's head. I guess it doesn't have to, but if we were cutting the beam we'd make sure it went up high enough. Those are details, see. Details that matter. Then there's the railing around the altar. It isn't horizontal, not precisely. On the left side, for about two feet, it dips an inch. It might have warped over the years, but doubtful. There's no humidity to speak of in church. The carpenter probably noticed the dip when he was constructing it, but thought it was good enough. No, I think to myself, it's not good enough. It's the first thing you notice right after the spikes being different sizes. The third stained glass window on the left side is ever so slightly crooked. It's . . .

I begin shaking my head and then lower it. I stare at the floor and then raise my head again to look at Jesus.

What the hell, man? I mean, what the hell?

I stare at the wooden cross until it fades into the wall and it's all a black-brown blur.

"You should be on your knees," I hear someone say.

My eyes are closed. I open them.

"What?"

"You should not be sitting. You should be on your knees." It's Father MacGregor, leaned down close to my face.

Without thinking, as natural as breathing, I do as he says. I reach with my hand and pull down the kneeler and slide onto it. Father MacGregor continues walking to the back of the church, his heels clacking the floor.

I look up at the cross. It's flaming now, glowing orange-red. I think of Tommy in Vietnam. The flames flap brilliantly, gracefully. I think of Dad, almost losing him on the steps. They throb like a thousand eyes of mystery. I think of Mom losing the baby, and Gram apart from her family all these years, and Sandy. The whole apse is a fireball of white-hot heat. And, finally, I think of Teresa. The one truly good thing in my life. The person who has entered my soul and settled like a warm fire there. I pray then. It doesn't make sense, but I need it. I can't lose Teresa. I pray like I've never prayed before.

I feel my anger slowly being released. There's too much. It's got to go somewhere. I have to do something before it explodes in my face. If I don't do something, it's going to destroy me.

One for All

I'm on the corner by Jack's Filling Station after school. From there I can look down Blake Street, where Lennie lives. I stand there a few days. I don't see him the first or second day, but on the third day he comes out on the Honda toward Tallmadge Avenue. I step behind the wooden fence there and let him go by. He comes back a while later and putters down Blake back home, carrying a paper bag under one arm.

Jack comes out and gives me a nod.

"What are you looking for, Puck?" he asks me, wiping his hands with an oily rag.

"Oh," I say, "can I not tell you?"

Jack pulls back in surprise. "Sure," he says. "I don't need to know. You want a drink?"

"I'm okay," I say.

"You sure? It's on me."

"Yeah, okay. You have a Coke?"

"We have plenty," he says, and he walks inside the station. He comes back out and hands me the Coke. "You want me to go with you?"

"Go where?"

"Down there. I can talk to Lennie's dad."

"Aw, I don't want to get you into it," I say.

285

"I noticed him riding that thing," he says. "It was black before, wasn't it?"

"Yeah, it was black," I say, "just like the other one."

"Well, what's your plan?"

"I don't have a plan," I say. "I'm just going to go down to his house and get our bike back."

Jack pauses as he thinks it over. "I don't know," he says. "You can try that, but I don't think that's going to get you too far."

"Well, it's what I'm going to do."

"Sure," he says. "I understand."

"I'm going to give him a chance to give it back. To make things right. That's what I'm going to do, and then if he still doesn't give it back I'm going to take it. Isn't that how you have to do things?"

Jack nods, then twists his head some like he's thinking. "Sometimes," he says. "And sometimes not. It depends on the situation."

I know what he's getting at. It does seem pretty dumb to walk up to Lennie's house, knock on the door, and ask for the Honda back. Yeah, I know that. But what other choice do I have? I could try and sneak it out, but he'd probably steal it right back. Lennie's got to know *I* know he took it, and he can't have it.

"Give a holler if you need me," says Jack, and he walks toward a customer who just pulled in.

I get this bad feeling and my legs don't want to move, but I know I have to. If I wait any longer I might not go, so I start walking toward Lennie's house. It's not far, just five or six houses down. His house is this dirty white place with some trash cans in front, some stacks of bricks and some lumber lying around, and a lawn with grass so tall it's going to seed. It's got a side door on the right, like our house, and I decide that's a better place to knock than going up to the front door. It's really strange how much it feels like our house—there's even a row of hedges on the right side of the drive about the same as ours, and a small garage with a peaked roof.

I knock on the door, not real hard, and when nobody answers

I knock louder. I wait, then walk slowly to the back. Lennie's back there standing by a tree. He's got some rope and he's flinging it against the tree. It's a big tree with a big trunk, and he lashes the rope against it about as hard as he can. I stay behind the corner of the house so he doesn't see me. I don't understand what he's doing or why; he just keeps hitting that tree like it did something to him. I hear a door open, some rumbling down some steps, and Lennie turns and gets this scared look. It's Lennie's dad. He walks out toward Lennie. He looks bigger than I remember. He's not wearing a shirt and he doesn't walk in a straight line, and I know he's drunk. Lennie clutches the tree like he wants to hide behind it, but stands there frozen waiting to see what his dad's going to do.

"You got me warm beer," he says.

Lennie doesn't seem to be able to talk. He tosses the rope toward his dad and when it lands on the ground I realize it's not a rope, but a thin chain wrapped in a long sock.

"Why'd you get me warm beer?" he says to Lennie. "Are you that stupid?"

"I'm sorry, Dad," says Lennie. He's about crying. "I'm *sorry.*"

"Explain yourself," his dad says. "What kind of stupid-ass kid gets his dad warm beer? I'd like to know."

He leans over and picks up the chain covered by the sock. He starts lifting it and letting it fall on the ground, and when it does dust rises from the dirt and Lennie cowers back, like he's been hit.

"I, I went to Taylor's like you said, but they wouldn't sell me any. I was going to steal some, but there were too many people in the store. And if Mr. Taylor caught me, we wouldn't be able to go back. So I went to The Star Café and talked to Louie, who usually sells me some, but he couldn't on account of he said the cops had been around lately. He said come back later tonight and he'd sell me some. I ran into Taco and he said he'd buy me some, but he bought me warm beer—he bought me warm beer, Dad! I told him I couldn't have warm beer, but he told me to get lost, and so I figured I'd bring it home and put it in the icebox and it'd

287

be cold by the time you woke up. I didn't know you'd wake up so soon. I'm sorry, Dad. I'm *sorry*."

Lennie's dad lifts up the chain and moves his wobbly arm toward this beat-up doghouse in the corner of the lot. I don't see any dog.

"That damn dog's got more sense than you," he says. "Come here."

Lennie shakes his head, just as petrified as can be, but he starts moving toward his dad. Lennie's dad waits, wobbling so much he has to catch himself a couple times so he won't fall over. Lennie starts crying for real and he holds out his arms.

"Get them out here," his dad says.

Lennie pushes his arms closer. His arms are shaking. He turns his head and closes his eyes, and then his dad hits his arms with the chain and Lennie lets out a howl you could probably hear a block away. His dad only hits him once, but it's enough to send Lennie to his knees.

"Oh, Dad," Lennie cries, "I—I—I'm sorry . . . I—I—I'm sorry." He shakes violently.

"Yeah," his dad says. "Sure, you are."

"Dad . . ." Lennie cries. "Dad . . ."

His dad tosses the chain on the ground and turns to go back in the house. He catches sight of me.

"Hey, you," he says and heads my way.

I want to run, but I don't. I can't. I stay where I am, reach into my back pocket and bring out Nick's slingshot. I fumble in my front pocket for a rock and wrap the leather pouch around it.

"Get the fuck off my property," he says, tossing his big hand at me.

"I want our motorcycle back," I say.

"What're you talking about?" he slurs.

"Our motorcycle. You, or Lennie, took it. It's ours. I want it back."

His eyes narrow. He wipes his face with his hand as his eyes travel up and down my body.

"You're the kid who killed the girl," he says. He makes a gurgling, chuckling sound.

"Is it in the garage? I'll get it myself." I go to walk past him, when he shoves me.

"Like hell you will." His eyes get mean, as mean as can be. He walks backward a few paces, leans down, and picks up the chain. "Yeah," he says, "I thought it was you. Your brother shot poor Lennie with that slingshot. You're from that cripple family. I should've beat you and your brother to a pulp. I should've come to your house and pushed your cripple dad down your drive." He lowers his head into his neck and starts swinging the chain.

My whole body's shaking. I can barely stand. I raise the slingshot, pull back on the rubber band, and aim it at his head.

"If my dad could walk, he'd be here instead of me," I tell him. "He'd make things right. He'd put you in your place. He would. But since he can't be here, I am. Now, give me our motorcycle."

He makes the grotesque chuckling sound.

"Oh, boy," he says. "You think that's going to stop me?"

"Give it back," I tell him again.

"You know what, kid? I think I'm going to beat you to death, then walk over to your house and beat your old man. What do you think about that? Eh? You fucking punk kid murderer."

He starts coming toward me, staggering, but moving fast.

I let go of the rubber band. The rock misses, passing just to the side of his head.

I turn and run across their front yard, but I step in a hole and fall hard to the ground. I try and get up, but my knee's hurt bad. I flip onto my back and watch Lennie's dad get bigger and bigger as he barrels toward me, that chain dangling from his right hand like a whip. He comes up and stands over top of me, so big he blocks out the sun entirely. I lift up my arms, quivering, and know enough to turn onto my side so I won't get it in the face. I cover my head as much as I can and wait for it, and sure enough it comes. He lands that chain right in my ribs—the pain's like nothing I ever felt—all the air pushes out of my lungs, and then I gasp. It feels like my whole insides have been pulverized into mush, and in the corner of my eye I see him get ready for another blow, that mean, dirty face seething with anger.

But it doesn't happen. I see this white flash coming from the side, and it hits Lennie's dad in his big fat belly. It's a two-by-four, and the person wielding it is Jack from the filling station. I see him swing back the two-by-four again, and this time he hits Lennie's dad on the shoulder—I'm sure he was aiming for his head. Lennie's dad staggers, dropping the chain, but Jack doesn't wait. He lands a final blow on his right knee, which sends him crumbling to the ground like a shot buffalo.

Jack pulls on my arm, dragging me away from Lennie's dad, helps me to my feet, and we rush on out of there. One of Jack's workers, Bobby, runs past us toward Lennie's house—he's got a piece of pipe in his hand—but Jack stops him.

"No!" he says. "Go back—*now*!"

Bobby turns around and gets on the other side of me, and the two of them carry me back to the station.

They call home, but don't wait and take me straight to the hospital. I can hardly breathe and when I do it hurts something fierce. Bobby doesn't let go of my arm the whole way and says, "We got him good, kid. We really got him."

I don't remember entering the hospital. The rest of the day's a blank.

I'm lucky. I have two cracked ribs with nothing mashed up too bad on the inside. My knee's screwed up and they say they could do surgery, but I'll probably be okay without it. Dad opts for the wait-and-see approach, which is fine by me. I don't want to go through that when I can just hobble around for a while and let it get better on its own.

I'm laid up for a couple weeks. They set me up in the living room on the pull-out couch so I don't have to go up and down the stairs. Father Nigh stops by a couple times, and so does Father Mann, and it's good to see them. Teresa's over all the time and we do homework together. Sometimes Squirt sits on the bed and eats dinner with us while everybody else is in the kitchen. She really likes him. He makes her laugh. She never makes him get off the bed and acts like a big sister to him.

Nick sits on the bed with me when he can. We stay up late and watch movies. One night we're both tired and sort of drifting off, but neither one of us wants to go to sleep.

"You hear about Lennie's dad?" he says, slow and tired-like.

"Not much," I say.

"The bastard."

"Is he going to jail?"

"Dad's not pressing charges," says Nick.

"Yeah, well, I figured."

"But Jack and the guys at the station went over. They had a talk with him."

"Oh yeah?"

"They said if he or Lennie so much as looks at us, the whole garage is going to take turns with that chain on him. They mean it," Nick says, giving me his look.

"Good," I say.

"I wasn't going to tell you yet," he says. "Something else."

"Tell me what?"

"You know what Jack did?" I shake my head. "He got the Honda back."

"You're kidding."

"I watched. I was standing on the other side of the street with Anthony. Jack and his guys stood there with pipes in their hands as Lennie walked it out to the curb. His dad couldn't do it because he's laid up like you, only worse."

"Good old Jack," I say.

"He painted it black again. It looks just like it did before Lennie stole it. Jack's bringing it over tomorrow."

"Man," I say. "He's some guy."

We've been staring at the TV, our eyes drooping, when Nick brings his head around. "Hey," he says. "What the hell were you thinking?"

"What do you mean?"

"You know what I mean."

"Why'd I go over there?"

"That wasn't too bright," he says. "You could have been killed."

"I guess I didn't think about it," I say.

"Well, you should have. That was pretty dumb."

"Thanks. I appreciate it."

"I just don't know why you'd do it," he says.

"I couldn't let Anthony go over there," I say. "*He* would've been killed."

"Anthony wasn't going over there. Nobody was. It was just some stupid bet. Nobody took it seriously."

I give it some thought. "That's not why I went," I say to him. "It wasn't the bet."

"Then why?"

"That Honda," I say, "that's Tommy's bike. I couldn't let them get away with taking the one thing he loved while he's fighting over in Vietnam. He's fighting for his life every day while we're sitting here on Lucky Street. Dad couldn't go over. That's the least I could do as his brother."

"You mean getting *yourself* killed?"

"It's not like that's what I had in mind."

"No, but that's what could've happened."

"Nick," I say, looking at him, "think of Tommy over there. Every day he's dodging bullets. Every minute some guy might blow his head off. And over here people are protesting against the war, calling all those guys baby killers." I shake my head. "That's not right."

Nick shrugs. "It's a fucked-up war, man. Some of them are baby killers. That's pretty messed up."

I don't answer him. I know what he's saying, and I agree with a lot of it, but I'm tired and don't want to argue about the war. It's not only about Tommy. It's about Dad and this family. Dad bought Anthony and Tommy those bikes. When Lennie stole the bike, he stole Dad's sweat, his daily pain. He stole Mom's hours of cooking, and feeding Sally, and sewing. He stole the hours me and Nick spent changing tires and fixing carburetors. That's what he took. He stuck a middle finger right in our faces. A long time ago polio turned us into a family of victims. Well, I've pretty much had enough of that.

292

Strapped In

It's raining and cold. Not a hard rain, but coming down steady and light like it does in fall, just enough to smack the leaves and make them drop one at a time like parachutes. Me and Nick are out back planting grass seed on the rectangular bare spot where Frankie's VW bus sat. I'm tossing, while Nick's raking it in. Dad says fall's the best time to plant grass. It's cool and wet and the grass likes it. It sure is strange tossing grass seed on that bare patch, though. Seems like we're tending to a grave.

"Uh-oh," Nicks says.

"What?"

"Look," and he points to a spot with the corner of his rake.

"What is it?"

"Oil," he says. "Or maybe radiator fluid."

"Uh-oh is right," I say. "I wonder how far he'll get."

"Could have been there for a while," he says. "Maybe Sir Henry already took care of it. If not, he'll be having issues right about now."

"Alongside the Missouri, maybe," I say.

"The Missouri? Is that the route he's taking?"

"Aw, who knows? I figure that's the way anybody who wants to see America would go."

Nick uses the tines of the rake to work the seeds into the dirt.

"You need to get some over there."

"I see it," I say.

"Put a little more on. It's not enough."

"I know, I see it."

"There," he points. "Right there."

"All right, *Dad*," I say.

"Well, you're not doing it right."

I do what he says, laughing to myself.

"You know something," I say. "After the grass fills in, no-body will ever know Frankie's bus was here. Ten, twenty years from now, maybe after Mom and Dad have moved, nobody will ever know. Think of that bus. Think of all that happened in the short time it sat here."

"Frankie's lucky he didn't burn it down—the whole backyard and even the house—with all the incense he burned."

"Everything's changed," I say.

Nick makes a frown, all irritated-like. "You think too much, man. Come on—you're spilling the seed now."

"It was just some dumb old bus that he painted psychedelic and turned into his own personal mystery tour. But for a while, it seemed like the center of the universe."

"Slick, you're not paying attention to what you're doing," Nick tells me.

I stop tossing the grass seed and look at him.

"Don't you think we've been changed?" I ask him. "You real-ly don't think a lot's happened over the summer?"

"Hell, I don't know," he says.

"I think we've all changed. I think *I* have."

"Maybe you have."

"I think everybody in the family has changed," I say. "Even the girls."

Nick shakes his head and finally stops moving the rake.

"Hey," he says. "Did Frankie really say he was going to fol-low the Missouri?"

"Not in so many words. But why wouldn't he?"

"I sure do envy him," he says.

"I envy him, and I'm happy as hell for him."

"Because he got out?"

"No, man," I say. "Because he finally strapped in."

I sprinkle more grass seed onto Frankie's patch, and Nick, just like Dad showed us, works the tines into the dirt to mix it with the seeds, then turns the rake over and tamps it down. I drag the hose out and water the patch, using my thumb to make the water spray since the nozzle broke a while back. I wet it down good, let the water soak in, then water it again.

The rain lightens up to almost nothing and the sun tries to finger its way between the gray-bottomed clouds moving at a steady pace across the sky. I give Nick a look and toss my head to the garage.

"Come on, man," I tell him. "Let's go."

We go into the house and change into our riding jackets. Squirt's at the kitchen table glued to the small TV. Sissy's doing up some dishes and I can see Gram's feet on the couch as she takes a nap. I lean over the sink to look at the jade plant on the sill. It's small, with only a few thick leaves, but it's alive.

"Where are you guys headed?" Sissy asks us.

"I don't know," I tell her.

"You don't know?"

"Nope."

"We need bread."

"Can't you run across to Romano's?"

"It's just as easy for you to get it while you're out," she says.

"No room on the bikes," says Nick. He flicks her nose playfully as we walk past.

"Bread, eggs . . . and coffee."

"Yeah, sure," says Nick.

Squirt lifts his head from his balled-up fist. "You guys going for a ride?"

"That's right," I tell him.

"I want to see!"

The twin Hondas are sitting there like shiny black horses in the left side of the garage. We push them out and strap on our helmets and start them up. It feels strange being the one to rev up Tommy's bike, but it also feels good.

"Where to?" Nick asks me.

"I don't know, man," I say. "Where do you want to go?"

"No, you decide." He revs Anthony's bike, which makes Squirt dance. We rev the bikes more and more until Squirt's a writhing octopus of unbridled energy.

"I always wanted to go over the viaduct on one of these," I say to him. "Yeah."

"Let's do it then, slick," he says.

Nick backs up his bike to get around the trash cans, then pulls forward to the middle of the drive. I follow him, then pull alongside him. We're revving them up, getting ready to ease down the drive when I happen to look back to see Dad wheeled partially out his door. I expect something not good and prepare to turn off the bike, when he lifts his hand and waves me off. I keep the bike running.

"You two be careful," he says.

We tell him we will.

"I used to ride a motorcycle in Italy," he says. "I rode that thing in the mountains just behind enemy lines. I had a priest friend. He had me over for dinner sometimes, and he had a motorcycle. I went to see him and rode it every chance I could. It was the best time I ever had."

He wheels backward, pulling the door behind him. Just before the door closes he gives us the peace sign. In his day, the very same gesture meant V for Victory. I give him the sign back and, though he doesn't know it, I mean it as the victory sign. But hell, maybe he does know. He's a smart old guy.

Somewhere over in Vietnam Tommy hears our engines revving, and somewhere up in the heavens God lets go of the tether around my neck. I pull down my goggles, coast down the drive, then turn left onto Tallmadge Avenue toward the viaduct with Nick close behind.

Books by William Zink:

The Hole
Isle of Man
Torrid Blue
Ballad of the Confessor
Riffs from New Id
Homage: Sonnets from the Husband
Ohio River Dialogues
Pieta
Wild Grapes
In Despair
Eddy and Julia

Made in the USA
Monee, IL
26 December 2022